after the death of the ice cream man

Also by
Todd Michael Cox

Dizzlemuck
love in the time of wee folk

For more information visit
toddmichaelcox.com

after the death of the ice cream man

todd michael cox

Sybil ❦ Press
Wisconsin

The characters in this book are fictitious, and any resemblance to real people, living or dead, is purely coincidental. Likewise the situations, which, though perhaps recognizable to anyone who grew up in a setting similar to that described herein, are not meant to reflect actual incidences from my life or the lives of anyone I know. In some cases I also took liberties with the several real locations in this work, altering physical details and highway names as I saw fit.

Only the emotions are real.

Also, this novel contains references to the following works: "America" (Allen Ginsberg); "Song of Myself" (Walt Whitman); "I am Trying to Break Your Heart" (Wilco); "How to Disappear Completely" (Radiohead); "Shelter from the Storm" (Bob Dylan); "A Whiter Shade of Pale" (Procol Harum); and "The Ice Cream Song" (Billy Moll, Howard Johnson, Robert King).

--TmC

ISBN 978-0-9843661-6-3

In memory of
Patricia Jayne Keefe-Cox
(1940-2003)

Mother

Mom

after the death of the ice cream man

1. Skull Island

Mom died, Tina said into the phone, and it was strange the thing he first thinks of, the time his mind slips away to:

1976. He was in a Marcus Cinema on the North side of Green Bay, Wisconsin watching his first movie unfold before him like a dream. Someone had dared to remake *King Kong* and Jonah Swain was loving every second of it: the darkness, the screen before him like an immense idol, the feel of his mom's shoulder against his own, the heavy sweet smell of over-buttered popcorn, the sound of ice in soda cups like plastic rain through glass gutters.

At some point he had fallen asleep, waking just when the giant snake attacked, opening his eyes in awe as the great ape ripped the serpent in two, sending tongue and guts into the air, then tossing the snake aside and raging after his stolen love. The boy sat up from where he'd been curled fetal-like in the seat, and pressed to his mom as he stared with gaped mouth at the images before him, wonder and awe and fear racing through him in one joyful, triumphant stew. If he had been dreaming there in his seat he had opened his eyes to find himself in another dream, from one set of marvelous scenes to another. Years later he might think back and wonder if he had ever awakened at all, or which was dream and which was reality. Everything that came afterwards had been unreal, after all. But back then he had been too young, too virgin of mind, to even contemplate such things. Philosophy classes were still a good fifteen years away. He was only six.

You all right? his mom had whispered, leaning down to him. She was smiling, her eyes bright in the darkness.

He nodded. He was more than all right. He was a child, he was at his first movie, he was watching King Kong roar and stomp through the jungles of Skull Island. Everything was good and fine in his world, that world six years old and full of tomorrows. He'd seen the posters for the movie weeks ago and now his mom had taken him, and he knew his parents would always be there to give him what he needed, what he wanted. He was safe. Loved. The tale of King Kong might have been an old one, forty-three years, but he didn't know it, to him it was as fresh as a daydream.

Why did they have to remake *that*? his mom had asked those weeks ago, sounding disappointed, crestfallen, damn close to disgusted. The first is a classic.

He paid her no mind. That poster had pulled him in, the great barrel-chested ape standing on the twin towers of the World Trade Center, a foot on each, holding the pinched and pathetic wreckage of a train in one hand, the shapely figure of a blonde in the other, while below and beyond him spread the terrified and terrible city. And now here it was, the real thing, in the celluloid-flesh, larger than life... or life-sized, perhaps. He stared up to the great shambling monster and lost himself in that world.

The boy cried at the end, of course, the destruction of innocence was just too much. Kong's heart beat slows and slows to one final *thump* and falls silent. The camera pulls back to show the crowd gathering around the great dead hulk of the beast, and the image would stay with the boy, all those people staring at death, at the dying of a mystery, the dying of not only innocence but of spirit, tradition, idolatry. Something had been taken from an island and destroyed for no reason. This couldn't be the way it was in real life, it just couldn't be, what was the point? The words the boy would search for were pointless, senseless, ridiculous, but of course he would not find them and would sniffle back his tears when the lights came up because he didn't want to look stupid and his brother might make fun of him and he held his mom's hand and let her lead him out into the night, feeling the senselessness of it all washing over him, like a baptism into something dark, Christianity's black twin. A sensitive child, they would call him later. He felt that loss of innocence, loss of *meaning*, as deeply as he would feel anything. The blood dripping from Kong's lifeless lips was the first wound in the boy's heart.

2

They went to McDonald's afterwards, which is what they always did when they came to Green Bay. They lived thirty miles north, the small bay community of Oakton, a place which had yet to see anything even resembling a fast food restaurant, so McDonalds was always a treat. The boy ordered what he always ordered: a cheeseburger, fries, chocolate shake. He was a thin child, though later he would turn soft, just as he began to turn inward. He had the bowl-cut hairdo that was standard in his family, and which his mom would administer herself at the kitchen table. She had a little kit with scissors, combs, electrical razor, and picks, and she would set her children in a chair and go to work, working with the concentration and confidence of a master even though she lacked skill. Oh, she was good at those bowl-cuts, but for anything more complicated she grew frustrated and impatient. Many times she would snip too close and nick an ear. Dammit, she would say. Sit still!

What do you want? she asked him, her youngest, that night after *King Kong*. The movie was still playing like an echo on the screen of his mind but he perked up when they pulled into the drive-in lane and shouted out his order:

Cheeseburger, fries, shake!

His mom smiled. Of course. Same old, same old.

Of course! He flopped back in the seat and stared smugly at his older brother, who was sitting opposite him. Their sister was spending the night at a friend's house this evening, otherwise she would have been where he was, and he, the youngest, would have been forced to sit in the middle, his feet resting on the hump in the old Buick's floor. With her gone he was able to rest his head against the cool glass of the window and stare out at whatever caught his interest.

I suppose a chocolate shake, his mom said.

Of course!

Of courth, his brother said, mocking his lisp.

Shut up!

Both of you be quiet, their mom said. She pulled up to the window and placed their orders. Fifteen minutes later they were headed north, down the darkness of Highway 41, back to home, with the radio playing James Taylor, the Neils (Young and Diamond), the Beatles (just five years defunct), Gordon Lightfoot, Billy Joel, Elvis Presley (just one year yet to live), Willie Nelson, those days before everything was categorized and labeled and you could lay your full and tired head next to the speakers of a giant old Buick and listen to the bass lines and cymbals of "Blue Eyes Crying in the Rain" and "Heart of Gold" and "Seasons in the Sun" and "You Never Give Me Your Money," all back to back, like the different parts of some strange and glorious suite that never seemed to end, that just swept you up and took you off past the darkness of the highway, the speckled stars above, the weak sweep of headlights over asphalt, out past the farm fields, the woods, the lakes, the arc of the bay like a void under the moon, all the way to your peaceful and silent home.

He closed his eyes, dozed off, kicked at empty hamburger wrappers with his feet, felt his brother's finger in his ribs, shrugged it away, felt the darkness over him like a blanket, dreamt of great apes falling in love, then falling to their death.

*

The Swains were members of a small family, an anomaly in what was otherwise, elsewhere, a collection of large, noisy Catholic units. The Oakton Swains remained Catholic, but ones of a much more pragmatic sort, having decided early in their marriage to settle on three kids: Tina, the eldest, Thomas the middle, and Jonah, the youngest, the baby. Technically:

Tina Marie Swain.

Thomas Michael Swain.

Jonah Paul Swain.

Three years, roughly, separating each of them, one after the other. There was a dark and whispered rumor of a first child, stillborn, that each of them would pretend never to have heard and which they never mentioned to each other and never asked their parents to confirm. They were smart children, the Swains. Bright.

There was a voice in the stillness: We're here, wake up.

He opened his eyes a sliver to see the front yard light glowing like a beacon... an unwanted beacon. He closed them again and hoped it was just a dream.

Get up, get up, his mom said, her voice gentler than the first.

Tom helped by shoving him, fairly hard, against the door.

Knock it off! their mom said, slapping at him.

4

Jonah finally sat up, groggy, worn out from food and film and unfinished sleep.

Can Dad carry me...? he mumbled.

Your dad's not here, silly.

Right. Dad was gone for the weekend, off to some convention in Illinois. He missed him. Sometimes his Dad would carry him in from the car and he wouldn't even wake up, not until he was set down with a kiss on the forehead and an order to brush his teeth.

He climbed out of the old car and stood for a moment in the coolness of the summer night. Moths hovered around the yard light, crickets purred from the backyard. Their little home sat there, permanent and strong, a fortress, solid against the amorphous and transitory haze of night's shadow. A lone June bug knocked against the great bay window, the sound of its repeated collisions mimicking the ticking of the car's engine. Nothing could get in, though, only the Swains. This house would always be there for them, a place where the runaway slaves could rest, eat, drink, sleep. A place that would always take them in, wrap itself around them, hold them tight, safe, secure. Home, of course. Simply home.

He took his mom's hand and followed her inside.

*

It was later that night when he woke from a terrible dream, opening his eyes to see a deathly glow, like a living thing surrounding him, infesting the air. He was aware he may have called out, but that light was suffocating him now, pressing to his throat and chest, a death hug, constricting not only his breathing but his movement. He tried to push it away, fight it off, flailed his arms out violently to hit whatever might be there, but he felt weak, his blows falling without effect on nothing at all. He was aware, more so than he should have been at that age (not having anything to relate it to, after all), of life being stripped from him, slowly. Life being drained. This ghostly stillness, once his room and now some strange evil landscape of haze and death, was the last thing he would know of this earth. The ceiling he knew intimately, with its water-stained tiles in the shapes of snakes and crows, could not be seen now: there was nothing but that amorphous and sickly glow. It wanted him. He felt it squeezing him, wrapping itself around him, holding him tight, making his lungs useless. He

5

opened his mouth, not to take in a breath but to call out, to scream....

"Wake up, honey, it's all right." A soft voice, like the feel of velvet on his ears.

He opened his eyes, came out of the dream within-a-dream to find his mom holding him, rocking him. His mom. Of course. That was the only voice that mattered in his young life. She was sitting on his bed holding him, preparing him for the journey from nightmare to reality. The weak light around them was not so heavy, not so still, her face nearly haloed from the moon glow through the window across the room, the faint but powerful pinpoints of the stars, surgical, silver, golden.

He was hot, sweaty, struggling for a moment or two with breathing. He looked around his room, saw all the familiar dark silhouettes, then looked at his mom. She was smiling down at him and he felt suddenly safer than he ever had before. He was in his home, being held by his mom. Nothing bad could happen here.

"You were dreaming," she said. "Must have been some dream."

He just nodded.

"What was it about?" she whispered.

He told her all he remembered, and speaking it now it didn't seem as bad as it had felt: "I lived on Skull Island, and someone took me away, and I looked back and there was you and Dad and Tom and Tina on the shore. I wanted to get back because that was our home, but they kept taking me away. I just wanted to get back to you...."

She half-frowned, half-smiled down at him. "Why would you want to go back *there*, to that island? All those monsters, giant snakes...."

"Because that was my *home*. And you were all there."

She pushed the hair back from his forehead. "Well, you're back now. Sleeping in tree houses, like on *Swiss Family Robinson*—"

"But—"

She nodded. "But only on Skull Island. If there really was a place like that, would you want to go there?"

"Yeah. I would *love* it!"

"Shh... don't wake your brother." Tom was sleeping across the room, lightly snoring.

6

"I would *love* it," he whispered dramatically. "And there'd be another King Kong and no one would ever come to take him away."

"Or you."

"Or me."

She smiled again, massaged his temples for a bit, tucked him under the covers, kissed his forehead.

"Well, you're back here, safe again on Skull Island. And don't forget your guardian angel." She gestured to the wall behind his headboard. "Watching over you all the time, so nothing bad can happen."

He lifted his head, studied the wall.

"He's there," she said softly. "Watching, protecting you. We all have a guardian angel. I know for a fact that yours is one of the best around."

He smiled.

"Now, sleep good, and pleasant dreams."

"Say it like Gramma does...."

"How's that?"

"Sleep tight and don't let the bed bugs bite."

She smiled again, half her face like a beautiful painting brushed by moonlight. "All right. Good night, sleep tight, don't let the bed bugs bite."

She kissed him again and left the room, and he slipped off to a dreamless sleep.

2

Hearing the news was one thing, seeing the casket that contained his mother was something else. When he finally ends up at the little Oakton Funeral Home and sees that box lying clean and gleaming at the front of the viewing room he realizes that goddamnit, there's a person in there, a human being, someone who once loved and hated and hurt and laughed. A real person, a woman. Not just his mother, not just a symbol, but someone who trailed her own history, her own long line of memories and emotions. You don't always realize this, you know. You look at that hunk of over-priced wood and think of what it meant for you, and how you yourself felt, and not about who lay within, and what they had, and what they lost, and what they had once been way back before you were even born.

A real person, full of blood and passion, dreams and desires. Full of everything, full of life.

3

Linda Conner met Harold Swain, ironically enough, because she used to go out with his cousin, and later, when she thought about this fact, she wondered why he had agreed to even talk to her at all, let alone swap spit in the back of a dying '49 Ford one god-awful hot July night in 1963. His cousin was largely considered scum of the earth, even by his own family, though perhaps that was too harsh. Certainly he was not a very bright man, and certainly he had no decent prospects (or even any foreseeable prospects) for the future... and certainly, and most importantly, he had a small but impressive criminal record. Nothing serious: some battery, a drunk-driving thing that he claimed was a set-up. Probably not the sort of record to garner even a raised eyebrow in, say, Chicago, but definitely one that was frowned upon up in little old Crandon, Wisconsin, land of snowmobiles, fishing, campfires, lodge-pole pines, a thousand streams and lakes. Why she had gone out with *him* in the first place could best be summed up by these few words: she wanted to piss off her mother. And it worked, too, Loretta Connor was indeed pissed off by the whole incident. But what could she do? Nothing. And so she did nothing... other than give frequent and vitriolic voice to her dissatisfaction. Loretta Connor was a small, slight woman physically, but the power of her voice, when she wished it to be so, was legendary. Flash forward twenty or so years and her grandchildren would find this fact impossible to believe. Their grandmother would be a soft-spoken, warm-hearted woman with a voice so low it was fragile.

Linda Conner, faced with the fact that she had chosen as a means to piss off her mother *this* small-time crook, and knowing everything he ever did *would* be small-time, finally, unceremoniously, told him they'd just be friends. He seemed not to care. Within a week he'd been seen vandalizing some county trucks that were parked on the side of Highway A, and a week after *that* he was engaged to some bimbo from Goodman. A month later and Linda herself had forgotten the whole incident. Then she met his cousin.

8

She would never be able to say how they met, and she would tell her kids it was because she was old and her memory was shot, even if she was just thirty at the time. Come on, tell us, tell us, they would insist, usually on those nights just before Christmas, when they'd all be huddled together in the livingroom, a fire going, perhaps something sweet and doughy in the oven.

Oh God! she would say, putting a hand on her forehead in mock exasperation and looking at her husband for help.

Tell us Dad, tell us!

It was an arranged marriage, he would say, smiling.

No! they'd scream, teased like they teased each other. No!

And finally their mom would relent and say simply: We met through my friend Sally. No big story there, sorry.

The truth was, neither of them could remember meeting because they'd been drunk as sin when they had. This is what people did up there in the North woods of Wisconsin… it's what they do all over: teenagers go out and drink beer while driving around in cars and listening to whatever music happens to be cool at the moment. There was little else to do in the deep woods of the Dairy State. The nearest town of any decent size was Iron Mountain, Michigan, an hour and a half away, and there was little to do there, too.

The official, true meeting most likely happened in someone else's car, a group of teens meeting in the dark of a youthful night, saying hey, what are you up to, come and join us, he probably sliding in next to her, crushing her pleasantly against the door, introducing himself on Pabst Blue Ribbon-breath:

Harold Swain, holding out his hand.

Linda Connor.

Yeah I know. You dated my cousin.

How he could know that and still be interested in her she would never know. Others would have seen her as tainted and stained by her association with that known criminal, but not Harold Swain. A few days later, having shaken off the fog of that night's malt and hops-induced daze, he had called her. The very next night he picked her up and they drove to the Keefe Theatre in Crandon to catch a movie.

That was summer, 1963. It often seemed to them that they had never had a first meeting at all, that they had always known each other, that they always would. Their dating had

9

been effortless, comfortable. If it wasn't a movie it was burgers, some roller-skating, maybe some pool with their friends at Bunny's Pool and Darts in beautiful downtown Crandon, perhaps some fishing in the Laona millpond. Harold Swain lived just East of Crandon in Laona, a very small rustic community based around the lumber industry, like many towns surrounded by forests, and though that industry would putter on for decades to come it was even then in the waning days of whatever passed for its glory years. Harold Swain's father had worked at the mill, as had his grandfather. Harold himself had grander ideas.

I'm going to college next year, he told Linda Connor one night, when they were parked in that '49 Ford of his. Crickets pulsed and rhymed around them, and the heat was like the breath of the sleeping sun.

She asked him what he hoped to do.

I'm going to be a teacher, he said. Then he asked her what her plans were.

I want to go to the city, was the answer.

It hadn't been a lifelong goal, but had nonetheless been there in the back of her mind for some time. Linda Connor was a smart girl, she could look around and see that there was nothing to gain from the forest and these little towns that lay speckled throughout it. Why not hit the city? Her friend Debra was planning on going to Milwaukee the following summer, after graduation. Linda figured she'd tag along, get work as a secretary perhaps, maybe even take a few classes at the university. The idea excited her to no end.

Harold Swain had nodded. The city, he said, his voice dreamy, far off, as if he were invoking some sacred incantation. Wow. Think a small town girl like you can handle the city?

She smiled at him, her face half-lit by moon and starshine, her makeup smudged, her hair disheveled, her clothes (if we're to be honest) wrinkled and askew. She smiled at him, a girl not yet eighteen, her face a moon itself, beautiful, porcelain-perfect, soft as rising dough, her eyes taking in that minuscule bit of cosmic light and sending it back as effervescent sparkles.

I believe I can handle anything, she said.

There was a wavering trill, eerie, ghost-like, echoing over the treetops, spooking everything within earshot, disturbing the thick silence of the October night.

"What was that?" she asked.

He pulled away from her, sat up, listened. The sound never came again. He smiled and said:

"Owl."

"Owl?"

"Owl." He leaned in to her, careful of the steering wheel. "Kiss me…."

"Are you sure? An owl?"

"Of course I'm sure. I know what an owl sounds like."

She pushed him away, gently. "I've never heard anything like that."

"Trust me." He leaned in again, and was this time able to get her cheek… she offered him that much, a quick and nearly coquettish upturn of her head so that his lips just barely brushed her skin, and then she pulled away again, squinted out at the black night. The radio was on low. Johnny Mathis.

"What kind of owl?" she asked.

He sat up again and laughed. "You're funny when you're drunk."

"I'm not drunk. And I'm not funny."

"Trust me, you're drunk."

She glared at him. "Trust *me*, old man, you'll know when I'm drunk." This *old man* was a private joke, he being six months older than she. The oldest man, she liked to say, that she had ever dated.

"You're right," he said, quietly. Then: "Screech owl." He waited for a reply to this, then, when none came, he looked out his own window. The forest, though feet away, was not visible, just that blackness, omnipresent and impenetrable. And beneath it, faint, the silvery sketch of his own face.

"How long have we been going out?" he asked her.

Johnny Mathis finished singing. A voice came on, selling something. He flipped the channel and found country music. Lonely pedal steel, as ghostly as that owl, and a haunted voice, hollow, skeletal.

"Three months," she said, and placed a hand on his knee. "Why?"

11

He said nothing for a long moment, then: "No reason."

She looked at him, as much of him as she could see. Her man, so smart, so bright, so rugged. He was like no one else she had ever met. He actually seemed like he might go somewhere, whatever that meant. Everyone wanted someone who was going somewhere. She too, of course, but more than that she just wanted *him*. Her man.

Is it possible to feel the first stirrings of destiny and fate? It was love at first site, some girls said, and everyone laughed. And yet you can know, can't you? There must be a way.

"They've been a good three months," she said, and leaned over to press her face against his arm. He was warm. Solid and warm. His bicep was sturdy and dependable against her cheek, and he smelled of pine needles.

"They have been," he agreed, touching her head tenderly, stroking her hair, rubbing her temples, soothing her into a light sleep.

There was nothing but quiet, all around them.

*

Her mother was up waiting for her that night, when she finally came ambling in at nearly two. But Loretta Connor said nothing, just gave a look and then went right to her bedroom. It was the next day when she said:

"You had me worried last night. Where were you?"

"You know where I was. I was with Harold."

"Harold." Pause. "You live in this house, you come home at a decent time. Do you think you need a curfew?"

"No, Ma, I don't think I need a curfew."

"If this had been a school night you—"

"If this had been a school night I wouldn't have been out."

"Don't get smart with me."

"I'm not getting smart. But I *do* have a head on my shoulders, you know."

"Really?"

She sighed. "Listen, Ma, do you like Harold?"

Loretta turned away, pursing her lips as she washed potatoes over the sink. She did like him, it was a well-known fact. There wasn't much not to like, he was a boy who was going places.

12

"You know you do," Linda said. She was smiling, knowing her mother was not really mad. Annoyed that her daughter had come home so late, yes, but not angry. "You know you do. I'm sorry I came in so late, but we were talking."

"Talking."

"Yes, talking."

"And what do two kids your age have to talk about?"

"The future."

"The future?"

"Yes. The future. Listen, Ma… what if I told you we were going to get married?"

Loretta Connor was not the sort of woman to spin around at such news… she simply pursed her lips tighter, grabbed another potato and went to work with her knife. She was an expert with a paring knife, peeling carrots and potatoes with effortless grace and ease, never cutting herself though the blade would always come to rest against her thumb after sliding under the skin of the vegetable. Her own skin was calloused from such work, forty-something years of peeling and sewing. Loretta Connor had worked hard all her life.

"Did he propose?"

"Well… no."

"But you think you're getting married," she said simply, without emotion.

"Well… not anytime soon. But maybe. And… yeah, I think we might. It feels right."

"You're still in school."

"This is my last year."

"And isn't he going to college?"

"Yeah."

"Where?"

"Birnbaum."

"Birnbaum. Isn't that far away?"

"Yeah."

"So when would you get married, if your husband-to-be is away at school?"

"I don't know. Before. During. After. I don't know."

Loretta Connor turned now, finished with the last potato, and smirked at her daughter. "Don't do anything like run off and elope," she said.

"We can't exactly elope *here*, Ma. You sort of have to run off to do it."

"Don't be smart. Here, quarter these."

13

Linda took the bowl of potatoes from her mother and smiled at her. "You're so funny, Ma."

"Why is that?"

"Because you know damn well you'd be happy for me if I got married. You like Harold, you know you do."

"Maybe I do." She had turned to fetch milk from the fridge. "And don't swear in my house."

Linda smiled at her mother as she bent to the open refrigerator, looking so familiar and so different, as if she were standing in a new sort of light or being seen with new eyes. Maybe that was it, being seen with new eyes by a daughter in love. "Ma?"

"What now?"

Pause. Then, still smiling: "Damn shit hell."

She had to duck to miss a flying carrot.

*

The first snow of the year fell in early November and stuck around long enough to see the second, which came three weeks later. Up there in the far north of Wisconsin the snows came on with attitude, fat storms dumping forceful, dominant, aggressive mounds of the stuff, layering the meshed worlds of small towns and deep pines with clean white drifts, a billion or so crystals working in tandem to form smoothly arcing hills of soft snow over sidewalks and yards and streets and forests. Linda Connor's stepfather worked for the County, and he was out that early-November evening, driving a plow mounted on the front of a giant dump-truck, pushing the white stuff around, forming it into compact mounds against the Courthouse parking lot and the curbs of sidestreets; it was just one of the many jobs the County required him to do, and just one of the reasons he was rarely around. Loretta Connor liked to say she hadn't married a man, she'd married a check-stub. It was, indeed, his stub from the County that was most often seen around the house, lying on the dining room table. A good man, was Charles Donlevy. He'd been married to Loretta for most of Linda's life, and she loved him as much as she had loved her real father. She liked to believe, perversely perhaps, that if Ray Connor had not succumbed to cancer he would have been a man just like Charles Donlevy, attentive to his wife, playful and loving with Linda, warm of hands and heart. But she would

14

never know. Fathers die, and daughters grow up without them, that was just how it happened.

Technically, of course, her marriage to Charles Donlevy made Linda's mother Loretta Donlevy, and though this was true on legal and tax forms Loretta continued to consider herself a Connor, if only for what she saw as the sake of her daughter. And Linda believed that her mother may have harbored some guilt over remarrying... not guilt in the actual act, for she loved Charles, but guilt that she had to do so at all, and guilt that she might be giving her daughter the wrong message. Many times, when Linda was much younger, her mother would set her down and tell her that she still loved her father but that he was gone and people had to go on with their lives. That was how it was done, she said. You go on with your life. You never forget those who pass, but you go on with your life. It was what they would have wanted. So she married this nice man Charles Donlevy and there were pictures of the wedding on the wall in the hallway, as well as photos of his family, but there was also a photograph of Ray Connor, his head turned a bit to the left, his eyes kind, wise, his mouth set tight with determination to face the future and whatever it might bring.

On the night of the first snowstorm of 1963, Linda Connor stood for a moment before this photograph. Just a moment, significant only as a moment and not in the general run of Time, but long enough for her to miss him, her father, her daddy, her hero. She had been just five when he went but she remembered he went quickly, within weeks of the diagnosis. He died at St. Mary's Hospital. She had been brought in to touch his hand and look at him one more time. That was it. He was gone.

"Bad one," her mother said, entering the hallway.

"What?"

"This storm. Bad one. They're saying maybe up to six inches. Reminds me of the storm of...." She'd been watching the tortoise-shell cat that was winding its way around her feet but now looked up and saw where her daughter was looking.

Linda turned away and smiled at her mother, whose return smile was odd, sad, hesitant.

"You miss him?" Loretta asked.

"Daddy? Of course."

Loretta walked to the picture and studied it for a while before pronouncing: "See that suit he's got on? I made him buy that, just for that picture. That was when he finished his Associate's degree, and his old suit was just nasty, all worn and old. I made him buy that suit and he swore I was trying to make him look like a banker. He doesn't look like a banker, does he?"

"Ma?"

"A lawyer, maybe, a *doctor*...."

"Ma?"

Loretta turned to her daughter.

"You know I love you, right?" Linda asked.

Her mother laughed. "What a silly question. Of course I know that."

"You know I love Charles, too, right?"

Her mother's smile was lovely, pleased. "Yes, dear."

"Then...." Cautiously, yet playfully, with a bite of her bottom lip and a girlish look sideways, she said: "Then, do you know I love Harold, too...?"

Loretta half-smiled, half-frowned, and shook her head. "I could have guessed it, the way you carry on these days...."

Linda's turn to laugh. "Carry on? What do you mean?"

And Loretta started prancing around, dancing stupidly, playing with her hair, her face, patting imaginary blush, blotting imaginary lipstick, mocking the way a girl in love acts, all the giddiness, the crazed joy, the silliness. "I'm in love!" she sang. "I'm so in love! Oh Harold I love you...." She looked into the hall mirror and admired herself, spun circles, pretended to straighten a gown, made kissy-faces at the air.

Her daughter stood behind her, embarrassed, laughing, while outside the world turned quiet and white, as hushed as a whisper.

*

Talk of the future came quickly to them, as if it were just one of those things, an inevitability, just one among many specters hanging over them, patiently waiting, just another part in what was becoming, for them, an increasingly longer and more complicated beast. That beast was even given a name, and this too had occurred quite early in their relationship, barely a week into it in fact: it was called Harold and Linda, a two-headed beast once able to separate its heads but growing ever more dependent on the two of them together. To separate

16

one from the other felt somehow wrong, the whole thing off kilter, out of balance, not alive. When someone saw Harold they asked him where Linda was, and vice versa. People were always wondering what Harold and Linda were doing, were Harold and Linda coming along, was there room for Harold and Linda, had anyone seen Harold and Linda. They had become that most mysterious and yet most common of animals: a couple. It was only a matter of time, not long at all, that there began to hover over them that even greater inevitability, that even more common and yet mysterious of beasts: the future.

He brokered the topic first, not really meaning to, it just sort of came effortlessly to one of their normal conversations. He was talking about college one night, a few days before that first snowfall of 1963. College was a topic of deep concern for him, bordering on the obsessive, and she loved that about him. Her man dreamt of college, dreamt of a life far away, dreamt of better things somewhere out there, in the world....

Once I get my degree, he was saying, and get certified, I'd like to end up teaching down around Green Bay.

Why Green Bay? she asked. They were eating at a small café on the very outskirts of Crandon, soup, salad and sandwiches on a crisp October Saturday. She posed her three-word question as absently as he'd been speaking, not so much out of interest but just to keep the natural flow of conversation going.

Because, he said, sounding like he was practicing for a job interview, I think I'd like the challenge of working in a more urban environment. I don't know if I want to teach *in* the city... but around there. What do you think?

She shrugged.

Think you'd like it down there? he asked.

And there it was. Simple, easy, arising out of one little breath. She looked at him and frowned. It was a forced frown: what she really wanted to do was give a sassy smirk.

Why should that matter? she asked.

He tried to shrug, but it came off awkwardly as he realized what he'd given voice to, what it suggested.

What are you saying, Mr. Swain? And now the smirk came out and she watched his face, waiting to see it flush red.

It did not. He lifted his head and looked her deep in the eyes, as serious as he'd ever looked at her before. He was a baby-faced young man, but it was possible to look at him at

17

certain moments and see age hidden there, veiled by his youth like the secrets of a magician's trick veiled by a kerchief. Every so often that age revealed itself, you caught glimpses of it, brief little smidgens of the man he would some day be: a wrinkle at the corner of his mouth, a strange sparkle in his eye, deeper than normal lines across his wide forehead, a spattering of furtive grey in his temples, speckled through his dark curls like a trick of light. From now until the day of his death his head would be the same shape, square of jaw, wide of forehead, strong of features... though not chiseled, unless it were at the hands of a hesitant sculptor who had not wished to risk damaging the whole simply for the sake of more profound lines, more definite etches of masculinity. It was an adult's head, signifying dignity and authority. His students would respect him even though he would start off only four years older than them, it would be his presence, the weight he'd been given at birth, the gravitas. Such it was now, as she looked into his eyes and face. She saw an insight into the man he would some day be and it made her tingle, acted like a mirror and made *her* flush.

He said, quite simply: I'm not playing here, Linda. I want you to be part of my life.

It wasn't an engagement, or that more vile of things, a *promise*. Yet she didn't know exactly what it was, despite all that tingling, despite the sudden warmth that coursed through her, despite that deep part of her brain that knew what he meant and understood its significance to her future. She looked back into his eyes and was not at all sure what had just happened, only knowing it was good, only knowing it was right.

She told no one about it. As far as she knew, neither did he.

Those were good days. It seemed they would never draw to a close.

4

Jonah Swain sits up front at his mother's funeral in the St. Michael's Catholic Church in Oakton, Wisconsin, flanked by his brother and sister. He hears nothing that is being said by the various people who walk up to the podium and give readings from the Bible, their voices are just a steady monotonous hum he finds easy to tune out.

Linda Swain was killed three days earlier when she pulled out in front of a Peterbilt semi that was going just a tad too fast to brake or swerve. She'd been visiting a friend who lived seven miles outside of Oakton and her last words had been: *Take care, give me a call next Tuesday.* Jonah had gotten the call from Tina that evening:

What's going on? he asked her.

Nothing good, she said. It's nothing good…

And that was it, it was that simple. She pulled out in front of a semi and here they were at her funeral. Amazing how easy it is to tell that particular story. One minute you're alive, the next you are not. Life is a fatal disease.

"Let us pray," says the priest. Heads are bowed, a few throats are cleared. Jonah doesn't glance around, not even at the casket. Nor does he pray. He closes his eyes, imagines the young woman his mother had once been, the person he himself had once been, the life that was and the life to come, all of it mixed together, thrown tossed splattered strewn wild across his mind. Around him all is quiet as a hundred prayers of forgiveness and acceptance are sent out to the black nothingness of space to float forever or simply fade. "Amen," says the priest at last, but Jonah keeps his eyes closed, staring deep into the formless darkness behind his lids.

Float forever or simply fade.

2. Slowly coming apart

1

It was a beautiful September day, that one, a final fling for summer, and the quad was full of gorgeous girls wearing very little clothes. Some looked earnest in their studies but most were absorbed in the presentation of their hair, their tans, their playful breasts, their muscular legs, their reserved horniness, balanced as they were on a precipice they couldn't even notice: innocence to knowledge, a yawning darkness below them they couldn't sense. Future mothers, most of them, but such concerns were eons away, their lives now were all play and fun, that precipice would hold them until the last moment when they were forced to face the other side, to see over the chasm to maturity and responsibility, the grand canyon of growing up. September on the campus was like spring all over, a parade of strut and display.

Jonah gave them little notice, even as he passed within feet of their orbits, even as he could smell the lingering trace of fresh perfume, clean soap, sweet shampoo, honeyed tanning lotion. To his right there were three girls in neon-colored bikinis lounging on blankets, legs bent deliciously, the sun playing where playful shadows had once hid in delicate nooks and crannies, but he gave them only an absent glance. It was four in the afternoon and that sun was burning like it was noon, blazing on his neck and forehead, blinding him. He walked quickly past all the girls, and the boys that hovered there as well, playing Frisbee or football, also balanced on a precipice, their horniness not so reserved. Future fathers, bankers, captains of industry, trophy husbands. Proud goddamn peacocks. A football bounced past his feet and Jonah didn't glance at it. He continued his steady march for his dorm, eyes on the door, barely feeling his feet and legs at all. Birnbaum

University had seven dorms and this was his. Abbey Hall. Named for Maurice Abbey, a 1945 graduate who went on to some prominence in state government, a man mostly forgotten now save for the gloomy cream-colored box of brick that bore his name and where, at least once a year, some undergraduate was found dead of suicide or overdose.

Jonah slipped in the back of Abbey Hall and took the stairs sullenly, all the way to fourth floor. He hoped his roommate wouldn't be in, and when he found the door locked he sighed. Good. At least there was that. He pulled out his key and unlocked the door, stepping in to a dark and dusty space that smelled of stale breath and beer, the same place he had left just an hour before. He took off his shoes and jumped into his bed, stared at the closed curtains and wondered if he should open them and let in that sun, maybe a bit of the breeze. He could hear laughing, giggly voices through the window and in the hall. It seemed nobody had classes on a day like this.

After a few moments he did indeed roll out of bed and pull the cord that slid the curtains open. They hissed like a serpent. His room looked out on Buffeck Street and he could see just a few people walking on the sidewalk below, a couple hand in hand and a group of five. Tanned skin, all of them. They had all worked outside the previous summer, camp counselors and lifeguards and god knew what else. Jonah had worked in a factory, Webster Services, mindlessly pulling the levers on an ancient and dangerous machine that molded hot plastic around groups of wires. Or something. He never quite knew what the machine did, was always too intent on watching his fingers. Someone had once gotten their fingers in the machine's maw and lost them all. They found a mush of flesh and bone when they went to clean it out later. His supervisor told him this story on his first day. She's safe, otherwise, he said. Just keep your fucking fingers out of her.

All day long, eight to four-thirty, he sat there, occasionally standing to stretch or run to the bathroom. At ten-fifteen he took his first fifteen minute break. The first time he'd done so his immediate supervisor, the son of the owner, asked him what he thought he was doing, sitting there in the lunchroom like that. Taking my break, he said.

You don't get breaks, the prick said. You see anyone else taking a break?

The law says I get a break.

What law?

The same law that says I can kick your ass if you keep me from taking my break. He said this with a smile, not being physically imposing at all, and the prick took it as a joke.

All right, he said, smiling back, a smug smile, like he was relenting and being nice. All right. Jesus, Swain, you're gonna be an instigator.

An agitator, Jonah corrected, thinking of the line from *The Graduate*. An outside agitator.

The prick frowned and moved on.

All day long he'd sit there, while outside the summer blazed. He had friends who worked second and third-shifts, and while he was in the factory they were out hiking, biking, swimming, inner-tubing on the bay. He went home at four-thirty, ate supper, maybe headed out with someone, and while he did a lot of things outside, even caught some basketball in the St. Michael's schoolyard, he never had been able to get a tan. He was as white as flour, his mother always said. You could see blue veins through his skin. And this life was sedentary, and he was getting a gut. He had never been a muscular boy, never had any sort of definition, but it was catching up to him only now: he was softer than he ever had been, with a belly just starting to jiggle and arms without tone. He even detected a second chin under his first. He wanted to chalk it up to genes, but his father had been sharp of features and so too his mother, and Tina as well, and Tom... well, Tom was the athlete, wasn't he? Chiseled features, damn near classically handsome, the proverbial chick magnet, off at college in Arizona, most likely tan as leather, breathing all day the thin desert air. You're not like your brother at all, someone had once said to him. He's so good-looking.

He's also a fucking idiot, he'd said... and he'd been just twelve then, building up those defenses.

The truth was, Tom was not a fucking idiot, though he was also not in any way a bookish sort. He was majoring in business out there in Arizona, and school was school but that didn't match up to English, philosophy, biology...just three of the subjects Jonah was pursuing with dedication but, he would admit, not much purpose and not much brilliance. Another of the problems, he believed: this lack of focus he'd been cursed with. He would graduate at some point and then what? The future was a strange blackness, either a wall or a tunnel.

He stepped away from the window and all those tan healthy souls down there, and looked around his room. His roommate Mike's bed was lifted up as a loft by a primitive design of four-by fours and bolts, and underneath was a ratty old couch they had gotten from a graduating senior. An ugly couch, all brown and red plaid, which they called Mr. Furley. He'd been sitting there when the call came.

It's me, Becky said. She sounded like she was miles away.

Hey. He was instantly on guard, something in that voice sounding bad, full of news, and all news in such a long-term relationship is bad. When two people who had previously talked with the ease of lifelong friends, all jokes and laughs and allusions, start talking *this* way, with *that* sort of tone, you know the news is bad. She sounded like she'd been crying, like talking to him now was taking all of her strength.

We have to talk, she said.

And then he knew: nothing good had ever come from those words. She hadn't even said those four words when she'd had the pregnancy scare last year, she'd just come out and said what she had to say. So this was bad.

What's wrong? he asked, instantly on edge.

Come over.

Becky, what's wrong?

Just… come over. Just come over.

So he had gone over to her dorm, Harrington, and now he was back. He had gone over there with a girlfriend and had returned single, it was as easy as that. Simple. Like pushing the buttons on that machine and pressing melted compound down around wires. Easy.

Except it hadn't been easy, he'd cried in her arms, like a baby, feeling crushed, defeated, torn apart. She wasn't physically attracted to him anymore, she said, and she'd been seeing another guy during the summer. While he was wasting away inside that factory *she'd* been seeing some other guy. Not physically attracted anymore… he thought of his pale skin, flabby gut, useless muscles. And he had given her so much, his whole heart, his soul. They'd been together three years and everything had been wonderful and he'd actually begun to start thinking of the future, marriage, jobs, whatever. He had never suspected a thing, had called her whenever he could (maybe too often), wrote her long, loving letters, and she'd been cheating on him, breaking the rules, breaking his heart. She'd been breaking his heart for three months and it was just now catching up to him.

23

I'm sorry, she said. I'm sorry. She said it over and over while he cried like a baby, unable to control himself, sobbing and heaving in ragged breaths.

This is worse than my dad dying, he'd thought at some point, and it was: there was here the very real sense of a trust breached, a cruel act by a previously kind heart. Dropping dead of a stroke had not been his father's fault, but this was all Becky.

At last he'd managed to get control of himself and make that long march back to Abbey, and now he was standing in his room, nothing around but college-life clutter, a few warm cans of beer, full garbage, a plate of food moldering on Mike's desk, some books tossed here and there, crumpled bits of paper, a few magazines, CDs and tapes.

He stood there for a very long time, not sure what to do with himself. There was homework to do, books to read, papers to write, but none of that seemed important, it was all somehow superfluous now. His heart was broken, and his mind could not focus on anything else. After a while the only thing that seemed right to do was pick up the phone and call home, his real home, that tiny river-bound town of Oakton, where Webster Services sat, yes, but where also sat the yard he once played in, the garden now gone to grass, the endless gray waves of the bay, the surrounding forest and fields, the sidewalks he'd haunt at night, the streets he would bike, the secret places he'd sneak off to when he needed to hide, the house he grew up in and the mother who wandered it now, alone.

"Hey, Ma," he said when she picked up.

"Hey, what's up?"

"Umm...."

He couldn't speak, the words just wouldn't come. He hoped nobody walked in.

"Jonah?" his mother said, instantly alert, worried.

He tried to speak again, could not.

"Jonah, what's wrong?"

He had time to wonder, during these few seconds when he couldn't talk, when he was barely able to breathe, shaking with sobs and nerves, what she might be thinking: was her son in trouble? On drugs? Drunk? Hurt? Expelled? Flunking out already, barely two weeks into the semester? With her youngest, anything was possible. And he felt bad, not being able to tell her, keeping her in suspense, worried, confused.

"Honey, what is it?" she asked.

24

And he finally told her, spilled it all. Becky, this mysterious other guy, the whole scene in her room... sparing her, of course, that thought about his father. And his mother's response to all this?

"Things will work out," she said. "Everything comes out in the wash. You know that, right? You can always come here if you need to get away, too. You can come back any weekend you want. There's always room on Skull Island, okay honey?"

He smiled. An ancient reference, that. Ancient. Hilarious.

"Okay?"

"Okay," sniffling, laughing.

"I love you," she said.

"Love you, too."

*

The thought of going home on the weekend to be comforted by his mother was distasteful and made him feel childish. He had been dumped, that was all. Unceremoniously, yes, but it happened all the time, to everyone, and if he was going to be realistic he had to admit that it was probably going to happen again at some point. He wanted to be a cynic and see in this situation some sort of universal truth about the nature of love, its transparency, its destructive tendencies, its inherent malice, its inborn viciousness... but all he could see now was its fragility. He supposed a much more natural cynic could make of that fragility a statement about love's instability, the habit it had of coming on strong and then, like *that*, making for brighter ports, leaving what had appeared to be a strong and sensitive heart like his and heading for elusive, unstable, perhaps even harsher shores. He was not that natural a cynic. It was possible Becky fell in love with this other guy, no one could control what their heart was going to do, least of all the young, but there was something about her little affair with this guy that spoke of a summer-fling, a momentary infatuation conceived by circumstance and chance. Sure, it was entirely possible she had met her *man*, the one she would marry and spend the rest of her life with... but Jonah was at least enough of a cynic to know that they too would likely break up once the first snows fell. Summer love dies come winter. This was a maxim.

It would have been easier for him to acknowledge the new reality of his life if he had not had so much invested in her: she might have seen what they had as nothing special, she might have had no problem with treating it frivolously, but he had given his heart away... perhaps too much, yes, but what was done was done. He had loved her. Late at night he imagined them married, growing old, being together forever. Now it was quite clear to him that he had given too much to the relationship, had much too freely given away his love, his concern, his feeling of solidarity with her. Perhaps he should have known better, perhaps he should have been able to see what it really was. And what was it? In the end nothing. Nothing at all.

Well, never again would he give anything away so easily, so readily. Never.

"Jesus, that sucks," Mike said when he finally came into the room and Jonah had explained everything.

Jonah shrugged. He was lying on Mr. Furley and staring at the underside of Mike's bed. Life was weird: he had woken up this morning in love, and now....

"We should go out this weekend," Mike said. "Hit the town, get her out of your system."

Jonah shrugged again, trying to play cool. "Maybe."

"Get you all drunk, like a baptism... get drunk and get on with your life. Maybe get you laid."

Jonah nodded, his mind elsewhere.

"You hungry?" Mike asked.

"Nah...."

"You sure?"

"Yeah."

"Well, I'm gonna head over, get a bite. If you want company you can tag along."

"No, I'm good, Mike. Thanks." He turned his head and offered what he thought was a pleasant smile.

"All right, then. I'll be back." He gave a little wave and went out the door.

Jonah looked back at the underside of the bed above him, the various mysterious stains in the mattress, ancient remnants of a still-thriving culture. He could feel the springs in the couch, like the ribs of an underfed dog. Out in the hallway he could hear Mike greeting some other guys, the rowdy, ritualistic offerings of scatological wit and wisdom, his own name mentioned then followed by a hushed whisper, the

26

whisper followed by a respectable quiet. Through the window came the sound of car horns, music, laughter. University life was going on around him and at that moment he did not feel like part of it. He did not feel like part of anything. He stared at that mattress above him and let entropy have its way. If it was possible to sit still long enough to fade into the world at large, to cease to exist on any level, then he wished it would happen now, right here. He wanted to be nowhere, wanted to feel nothing, wanted to think nothing. He wanted to close his eyes and simply cease to *be*.

I think, therefore I am. Well....

He closed his eyes and tried not to think.

*

They did not, in fact, go out that weekend. Jonah did not get either drunk or laid, yet nor did he go up north to see his mother. Instead, he and Mike and a few other guys stayed up late on Friday playing cards and drinking contraband beer snuck into the dorm via a large duffel bag and further camouflaged with gym clothes. Jonah was a virgin poker player yet he had a run of good luck, making thirty-five bucks by evening's end. Mid morning Saturday they went for breakfast at the commons, made fun of the arty goth freaks and the even freakier muscle-heads, slobbered at the pretty coeds. It was apparently National Short-shorts day, and they were exposed to much delicious flesh. Jonah enjoyed looking as much as any of them, yet it also made him sad. One of the unspoken curses of the newly single male: that uncertainty about future fucking possibilities. You wonder if you'll ever hold someone again. He also felt a little like a nervous squirrel constantly on the lookout for a cat: he kept glancing around to see if Becky was in the room. She was not. He figured she had gone to visit her new man. Good for her. Life goes on. He *did*, however, see a few girls who looked like her, either in their facial features or their choice of clothes. A few times a tangle of black hair over a forest-green sweatshirt caught his eye and he would do a double-take, not realizing before how much her look had owed to the rigorous demands of conformity, the rules of coed compliance. They had not talked since their breakup and he wondered what he would say if he should happen to run into her: Hey, what's up, how are you doing? That sort of thing, most likely. Inanities. Cushions. Pleasantries. Well,

27

that was how the game was played. They would be nice to each other and then move on with meaningless smiles, perhaps never to speak again.

Saturday night he and Mike stayed in to watch a movie, something stupid with car chases and things getting blown up. When the movie was over Mike ran down the hall to look into a possible card game and Jonah laid on his bed and opened his copy of Plato's *Republic*. He had three philosophy courses this semester, and two biology classes, but he hadn't particularly devoted himself to any of them. In fact, they were starting to seem trivial, not worthy of his time or attention. He was beginning to feel closed in by university life, and perhaps this had something to do with the breakup and perhaps not. Either way, he was feeling called to somewhere else, some place distant, wild, secluded, where he could be alone. At the same time he felt entirely without ambition to go forward. If a fork in the road was presented to him would he have the energy to choose? Would he even recognize the fork for what it was? He closed Plato and rolled over to press his face into his pillow. He felt cut off from reality, from life, a castaway from the world at large, his ambition drained, his energy spent, his mind no longer functioning. Lost, was the word. Lost, discarded, alone. Alone? Yes, alone and lonely. Never mind the people around him, the thousands of faces he saw all day and night. Never mind the roommate he slept five feet from, the roommate whose face was the first and last thing he saw every day. He was alone. Lonely. A meaningless one among a meaningless many. Sadness slipped over him like a shadow. He felt useless, depressed. Vestigial.

Mike came in and saw him lying like that, face in the pillow, like a weak-minded suicide trying vainly to suffocate himself.

"Dude," he said, "you're letting that girl get to you. She's just a girl, there's a million of 'em out there."

It was more than that, he knew, much more. But some things you can't say to a roommate, some things you can't tell. Roommates were transitory, like most anything in life. Like life itself.

Apparently there was a flaw in Harold Swain's aorta, and apparently this flaw had been there since his birth, biding its time, waiting for the right mixture of circumstance and incident with which to make its presence known. Apparently this mixture could have taken place anytime, anywhere, when he was five or thirteen or twenty or thirty, yet none of this mattered, really, when it came down to it. What mattered was that the mixture of circumstance and fate came when he was thirty-four, father to three, the oldest 16, the youngest ten. The obituary would call him a loving husband and father, yet what did that really mean in the larger context of a life, a hundred memories and emotions? Absolutely nothing. He dropped dead in his own yard and the lives of his family went to hell. Everything changed.

The ten-year old, Jonah, left Washington Elementary School that day and stood for a moment in the bright sunshine of early winter. It was early-November and there was no snow yet, just a deep cold, temps only slightly above freezing. He stood there for a moment, looking at this day, and felt a strange sensation, as if something was hovering above him. He thought of guardian angels and those balloons they put over people's heads in comic books. He felt foolish, but he looked up anyway, saw nothing but a faded blue sky haunted by wispy clouds. Then he looked around to see if anyone had noticed him, but there were few kids out now, just he and the five other Catholics in his class, and they were all headed down the walkway, headed to the school behind St. Michael's church. It was Wednesday, CCD day. Religious class. You sit in a tiny little classroom on the second floor of the Catholic school and draw pictures of Jesus. Nothing to it.

The other kids were far ahead of him by the time he ran down the walkway to catch up. They hadn't even noticed him lagging behind and he slipped back in step with them easily. St. Michael's Catholic Church sat just two blocks away, an easy walk down a quiet residential street, and while there had once been a teacher who led them they were alone now. They were big kids, maturing every day. So far none of them had skipped out or run off or been kidnapped so it was all fine. The world was a clean and pure place, lit brilliantly under that cloud-striped sky. There were no shadows, no dark alleys, nothing rank or evil in Oakton, Wisconsin.

I hope it snows, one of the other kids said as they walked. I want snow.

A snow day tomorrow!

Yeah!

It sure felt like snow, the air thin and dry, with a wind that smelled of old leaves, frozen mud. In a few weeks it would be too cold for them to walk to St. Michael's and a small bus would be employed to pick them up.

You ever notice how everyone looks at us when we get up to leave? a boy asked.

They're *jealous*, a girl answered.

The boy scoffed at this: If they want to sit and talk about God all the time, they can do it. It's a waste of time.

Shut up, Bobby.

No, Bobby said, kicking a stone.

It was true, as the only Catholics in their class they were allowed to leave Washington early, around two-thirty, and head over for CCD, but Jonah had never noticed anyone who looked jealous... in fact, he felt strange, weird, like an outcast, as if everyone was looking at him, like he was ugly or had peed his pants. He wondered what religion they were, the ones who stayed behind. He knew nothing about religion, but he could draw a great picture of Jesus.

What does CCD stand for? another kid asked.

Crazy cuckoo doggy.

Crappy crap doo-doo.

They all laughed.

Jonah couldn't shake the feeling of something hovering over him, following along with him as he walked. The only thing he could liken it to was when you'd done something wrong and were waiting for your punishment, like when he had gotten that D on his report card last year. It was a sense of something about to happen, an energy rising, a heaviness on your heart.

Their CCD teacher was Miss Carlson, and she was a nice woman. She told them all about God and Jesus and the Apostles and they recited the Our Father and took little quizzes and did fun play-acting things she called Prayer-plays. Jonah had been Jesus in one of the Prayer-plays, leading a long prayer with a lisp and a booger hanging out of his nose. Miss Carlson always made them stand when Father Healy came in the room, but Father Healy would laugh and tell them to sit, sit, he wasn't the Pope or the President. Miss Carlson, he would say, why do you always do that? And they would laugh together, as if it was a private joke. Father Healy was a nice man but he was intimidating in his black clothes and white collar. He smelled like incense and candy and cigarettes, and before he left the room he would always single out one kid and ask him a question: Cindy, what did Jesus say on the cross? or something. Or he might ask the whole class if they loved God. Do you love God? he would ask, looking them all in the eye. It felt like a quiz, too, this question, only if you got the answer wrong you went to hell. Yes, they would say. When they had been getting ready for First Communion they had gone to a little chapel in the rectory for a "run-through," as Father Healy called it, and he gave them candy instead of wafers. Go in peace, he said. They had gone (not really in peace) back to their little classroom and drew pictures of what Communion was, what it meant to them, what that day would be like when it really came.

On this day, this cold November 3rd, Miss Carlson had the little wooden chairs all arranged in a half-circle, facing her old chipped desk. The classroom had probably been a broom closet at one point in its past, judging by its size. One single window, barely two feet wide, sat on the wall opposite the door, giving a view of a giant leafless elm.

Sit down, Miss Carlson said when they all came tromping in. Sit down. I'm going to read a story.

Yeah! someone said. Bobby promptly hit him on the shoulder.

They all sat and gave their attention to her. The room was beastly hot, the air difficult to breathe. In the hall a nun went swishing past, her habit trailing like a vampire's cape. Nuns were mysterious, moving about busily, saying little. Classes were in session in the rest of the school but Jonah knew the bell would ring in a few minutes and all the kids would file out. He wondered why he and these other five did not go to the Catholic school but he was secretly pleased that he didn't. This school was old and dark. It smelled like ancient smoke and candles and the hallways were narrow and claustrophobic. It was a strange, mysterious, vaguely scary place. And he had friends in the public school, not many but a few. He knew no one here but these five. And Father Healy. And Miss Carlson, who was reading now.

31

The story was about a fish swimming in the sea. It didn't seem to have a point, this story, and wasn't even funny. The fish just swam around, meeting other fish, doing nothing. There didn't even seem to be any religious references in it, nothing about Jesus or God or Mary or Joseph. Still, Jonah listened intently, never taking his eyes off Miss Carlson except to glance at the cover of the little book: the fish there was purple with white and orange eyes. It looked neither happy nor sad. Just a fish. He could have drawn a better one. Jonah listened to the fish's story, waiting for something to happen, even smiling a bit, knowing *something* had to happen, it couldn't just go on like this. This is the last thing Miss Carlson read:

"...then he swam up onto the beach, out of the water, and died in the sun."

Jonah couldn't help himself: he burst out laughing, just a quick laugh, some part of him recognizing the absurdity, the pointlessness of the whole story. Miss Carlson had wasted fifteen minutes reading it and nothing happened except the stupid fish swam up out of the water and died.

And then, almost as quickly, he stopped laughing. Sadness swept over him in a wave, strong, unnerving. He felt bad for laughing. He felt sad for the fish. He was almost sad enough to cry, suddenly depressed, heartbroken, a feeling he couldn't name weighing him down. He didn't look at anyone, not even Miss Carlson. The bell for the school rang, loud and brash, echoing down the halls, and the rest of the classrooms filed out in a mad rush of kids, all ages moving down the halls and looking in at the five of them there in that hot room, faces full of curious looks, some smiles, a few laughs. Jonah tried not to look at any of them. He stared down at his feet.

Does anyone know what that story was about? Miss Carlson asked, ignoring the kids in the hall.

A dead fish, Bobby offered.

A girl raised her arm, sword-like, into the air. He wasn't dead for the whole thing, she said, he was living, swimming.

He still died, Bobby said.

Does everything die? Miss Carlson asked. Some of the kids nodded, some looked confused, their mouths open, their eyes blank.

Not rocks, said Bobby.

Jonah? Does everything die?

He looked at her.

And nodded.

*

He didn't live far from St. Michael's church, and was able to walk home after CCD class. When it was too cold his mom would pick him up. On this November day he left the Catholic school and started home immediately, not bothering to play on the swings like he often did. He was feeling weird, there was no other way to put it. The sky above him was full of clouds now, still wispy yet binding together, making a ceiling of white, turning the previous brightness into a motionless gray that made the leafless branches of all the trees look bony, a creepy reunion of skeleton fingers and arms. He walked home accompanied by the sound of his tennis shoes on the sidewalk and the dry scraping of crinkled, dead leaves in driveways. It felt like Halloween, though Halloween was ancient history and Thanksgiving wasn't too far away. A newly risen wind was cold on his cheeks and ears. Cars passed him. A school bus rumbled by, trailing fumes. The town felt larger than normal, as if he could get lost there. The homes he walked past were empty and quiet, their windows black as a deep sea.

His brother Tom was home when he arrived, but Tina was not.

Where's Mom and Dad? Jonah asked. The house seemed too quiet.

It was then that he saw his Mom's friend, Sandra Conley, in the kitchen. She was holding a towel in one hand and a plate in the other. Doing dishes? Strange.

Where's my Mom? Jonah asked.

We're meeting her at my house, she said. You can put your stuff away and we'll head over. Your sister's there already.

He didn't know why, but this seemed perfectly natural to him. They went over to the Conley's house quite often, but never at three-thirty on a Wednesday... yet even so, this felt normal, perfectly fine. He put his books in his room, then followed her and Tom out of the house and out to her car. He hadn't noticed that car before, it was parked up the street a ways, against the curb. Neither he nor Tom spoke, they just climbed into the car with Tom shotgun and let Mrs. Conley drive off. None of them said anything for the whole trip.

33

It was at the Conley's that he was told his dad had died. Just like that: Your dad died. No attempt to be subtle, to cushion the blow, just a simple, absurd statement, and perhaps that was what made it sound so terrible, what made it sink in like a chill. Your dad died.

He started to cry immediately and didn't stop for what seemed like hours. By that time the entire Swain family was together.

Slowly coming apart.

*

Those were dark days. The wake was unbearable: he had to wear dress clothes, talk to strangers, see his dad in a coffin. It didn't look like his dad, the man there looked fake, something from a movie, the most lifeless thing Jonah had ever seen. An absolutely inhuman object, lying cushioned on an ugly, repellent pearl-pink satin interior. Even the hair looked phony, plastic. Who had made this replica and why? The skin was hideous in its lifelessness, the stillness of the hands and eyelids frightening. No muscles jumped under that skin, no eyes twitched, no bones shifted. Those hands, so neatly folded on the chest, would never hold or touch anything ever again, not a tool, not a wife, not a son, not a daughter. The reek of death, of something no longer living, of flesh no longer vital, was palpable on every soul that witnessed this scene. At the funeral Jonah sat next to his mom in St. Michael's church and thought nothing, felt nothing. He was numb, exhausted. Many people came to the funeral, kind words were said about his father, Father Healy spoke of life and death and re-birth through Jesus, and then the coffin was wheeled out, taken away, as if it were that simple to be rid of someone, as if it were that easy to move on.

His dad was cremated. And then, the following Spring, they buried the box of ashes up north, under the spreading shade of an old oak that grew proud and strong in one corner of the Laona Cemetery. Tina and Tom and their mother said a silent prayer, but Jonah did not.

He was watching the crows that were sitting in that oak, black silhouettes on newly-budded branches. He wondered what they were thinking.

34

If he remembered anything about the night that followed his father's death, it was that his mother did not come to comfort him. The four Swains sat in the Conley's house, crying and numb, but it wasn't his mom who came to ask him if he was hungry, it was Sandra Conley. All he remembered about his mother was her sitting at the Conley's kitchen table and crying into her hands while those around her tried to comfort her. His dad's brother, his Uncle Andy, came to town a few hours after hearing the news and made all the phone calls to the immediate family. Jonah's mom spoke to no one on the phone; she waived her hand dismissively whenever Uncle Andy asked if she wanted to speak to someone. Jonah saw all this from the Conley's rec room: his mother a hunched shape at the kitchen table, broken down and exhausted, while the others hovered over her, touching her, giving her water, whispering soothing words into her burning ears. It was not the way a child should see his mom, but there were worse ways.

3

He called home two months after his breakup with Becky, just to talk. His mother asked him how he was doing, how school was, and he said fine, good.

"You're coming up for Thanksgiving, right?" she asked.

"Yeah."

"Tom and Tina will be here. It won't be anything big, I'm not doing any of that again, but we'll have a big turkey breast, some potatoes, just the box stuff, I don't have time for the whole shebang."

"Sure, I'm coming."

"Well that's good, that's good. So... what's up?" Her voice was suddenly perky, sunny. He imagined her there on the sofa, the television muted, a cigarette burning in an ashtray, the omnipresent Diet Coke by her side. The Coke with a touch of brandy, the cigarette ringed with lipstick.

"Nothing," he said, "I just had some time, thought I'd call. What's going on there?"

"Oh... nothing much. Finally got my Halloween decorations down, was thinking about starting on the Thanksgiving stuff, but I have to dig those boxes down from the attic and I really don't want to do that. Maybe I can get Biff to do it."

"Biff is there?"

"No... but he's coming for the weekend. Is that all right?"

"I don't care."

"Well," she said in mock annoyance, like he had insulted Biff. Truth was, he didn't mind Biff at all, Biff was an okay guy. A man entirely different from his father but not from the other men she had dated in the past eight or so years: not a teacher among them, only welders, managers of auto-shops, over-the-road truckers, all successful but coming from a different place, Jonah believed, than Harold Swain. There had been maybe five of them, some just brief flings, some lasting a year or so, off and on, before... well, Jonah understood quite clearly that some of them had been turned off by *his* presence, especially when he had been younger, a thirteen year old boy without a father and here *they* were trying to make moves on his mother. He had spent time with most of those guys and had sensed the tension. They tried to be nice, friendly, gracious, but there was a wall there that was impossible not to detect, and they had carried on as long as possible before they couldn't take it any longer and told his mother goodbye. He didn't care for at least three of them, they were not worthy of his mother, simple rugged handsome roughneck uneducated guys he was glad to see go, but the other two might actually have been nice men who had his mother's (and perhaps his own) best interests at heart, believing that their presence might be interrupting a family, that it might have the potential to cause a permanent rupture in the fabric of that vital mother-child bond. Maybe. He hated to think of this as a possibility because it made him sad to think of his mother being denied happiness because *he* just happened to be a fatherless child. Those had been hard times for her, right after her husband had died, trying to raise three kids. Yet when first Tina, then Tom, had gone off to college it hadn't changed much. In fact....

His mother now, softly into the phone: "You know... we were thinking of heading off somewhere together, he and I."

"Yeah?"

"A trip somewhere. Would that be all right?"

"Of course, what do I care?"

A pause, then: "Do you like Biff?"

"Sure. Why?"

Perkier again, an attempt to diffuse something: "Oh, no reason, I just... listen, you're coming for Thanksgiving?"

"Yeah, I said."

"Cause Tom and Tina are coming. It might be the last time Tina can travel before the baby comes. She'll be getting *big*...."

"Ma?"

"Yes?"

"What's going on with you and Biff?"

"Oh..." in that sing-song way, as if nothing was going on, everything was normal, nothing was strange. Then, immediately, a long sigh, loud in his ear. And:

"It's not easy being here, you know."

He frowned.

"In this stupid house all alone. It's not easy...." She sounded like she was crying.

He wanted to say something comforting. "What's wrong with you?"

Another sigh, deep, loud, and when her voice came it was obviously through tears: "It's not easy being in this stupid fucking house," *fucking* spat out wetly, violently. "Do you know that? Do you understand that?"

"Yes...."

"*Do* you?" She was outright crying now, almost hysterical. "It's not easy... why can't any of my kids ever be happy for me?"

"Mother, for Christ's sake...."

"Why can't anyone just be happy for me...." This last was barely intelligible, the crying taking over now. She fell into sobs and he just listened to them.

"Ma... stop it, everyone's happy for you...."

And then, like that, nearly violent in its suddenness, the perky voice was back, overriding the tears and sobs, and she said:

"I know. I know." Sing-song again: "So, when will you be here?"

His head hurt from the change in moods, though he should have been used to it, it had been a constant since he was eleven, omnipresent, the steadiest thing he'd ever known. He sighed.

37

"Probably that Wednesday, afternoon or night."

"Good. Good. Like I said, I'm not doing anything big, unless someone wants to help me."

"Tina can help you."

"Oh, she won't want to stand on her feet all that time, she's pregnant, remember."

"True." Pregnant, right. Life goes on. "Listen, I have to get going, okay?"

"Study hard, keep those grades up."

"Right. Bye."

"Bye. Love you."

"Bye."

Hanging up the phone was sweet relief, bringing him back to this hot, dirty, messed up little dorm room that stank, today, of pizza and cologne. Both his and Mike's beds were unmade, left as-is from that morning... from *every* morning. A magazine full of naked women lay curled on the couch, purloined from a nerdy freshman. Someone had put out a cigarette on his desk, years ago maybe. There was a garbage can someone had once puked in, full today of napkins stained blood-red by grease and pizza-sauce. His schoolbooks lay on the floor by the couch, poor sad fraying Mr. Furley. His closet was a tightly-packed mess of dirty laundry, jeans and t-shirts and underwear and towels.

Home, he thought. The word was meaningless to him, like everything.

*

It was a crisp afternoon when he pulled into his mother's driveway, the wind sharp but the sun bright. A clichéd Autumn day, the sort that served Oakton best, that made it shine, that made it seem like a good place to live, to raise your kids, to spend the rest of your life. Jonah turned off his car and sat for a moment looking at the house before him. His house. His childhood home. The trees and bushes that surrounded it were fat and healthy, blocking most of the house from view, giving the little ranch a mysterious, exotic quality, as if it were located in the center of some lovely wilderness. A single streetlight sprouted in the front yard, like a sentry, or a scout for future invaders. He had never liked that light, its unearthly glow had infiltrated his nights in this house since he'd been ten, creeping around the blinds, oozing through the

38

cracks in the window frame, casting his bedroom in a death-yellow haze.

His mother met him at the door.

"Oh," she said, as if surprised to see him there. "Oh, I was just going out to look at that bird feeder."

Jonah looked at the feeder next to the driveway. "What's wrong with it?"

"Well, nothing. I just wanted to see if it needed seed."

"Oh. Doesn't look like it."

"No. Come in, then." She opened her arms and he went into them, gave her a small hug, pulled away, followed her into the house.

Hard to be noncommittal, coming home, that word carries so much weight: *Home.* You ought to feel comforted there, secure. *Ought,* of course, is another word of big weight, carrying everything from guilt to frustration, from insecurity to shame. One ought to feel this way, yes, but....

Well, it wasn't really *coming home,* though. Hard to consider it coming home when he'd never quite left. This coming summer would be the first he wouldn't spend in this house since starting college, if he got the newspaper job he wanted. Editor of obituaries. Exciting.

So, not being a homecoming, he saw this as just a run of the mill home for the holidays sort of thing, that most classic of American traditions in the most classic of American settings: the small town. Oakton was certainly nothing if not American, not only in its physicality and surface-essentials (the flag on the courthouse and its miniature brethren hanging from the sides of garages, the typically American hallmarks of close-cropped grass and clean-cut bushes....), but in some other more elemental way. Certain symbolism was inherent here, if one took the time to notice and observe. Jonah, coming into the town via Highway 41, could not help but apply various segments of his segmented education to this task. By the time he came to his mother's street he felt he had assimilated his observations down to one basic theorem: Oakton symbolized America because it was getting bigger and yet most likely not better. The jury was still out, of course, but it seemed likely to Jonah that another truth would hold sway in the end: this country cannot be made better by the blight of McDonalds and Taco Bells and Citgo stations, all three of which he saw as he drove through town.

So, then, here he was, home for the holidays. An objective observer would have thought how lovely the scene was, the mother greeting her college son at the door, with a day so bright and clear it was more than cliché, it was definitive. A more observant soul would have seen the truth, that current of unease running between them both.

The house looked as it had the last time he'd been in it, just a little more than two months earlier, though decorated now with various Thanksgiving-themed knick-knacks and adornments, from fake gourds on the kitchen table to grass baskets filled with plastic vegetables, cardboard cut-outs of turkeys dressed as Pilgrims on the windows, at least three real pumpkins (quite large ones) on the floor in front of the livingroom's bay window.

She loved holiday decorations, his mother. Too much, really, and it got worse every year, most every available surface, vertical or horizontal, carefully high-lighted with a well-placed bit of season-themed color. He was glad he hadn't come home around Halloween, which was her favorite time of all and for which she pulled out all the stops, plastering the place in vampires and witches and broomsticks and black cats. He was glad he'd missed it because of the memory it conjured.

And yet, it made her happy, what was the harm? He looked around the house now, nodded at the decorations, and told her he thought it looked good.

"I couldn't do as much as I wanted to," she said. He didn't press her on why, detecting something in her tone that he felt he'd be better off not knowing. He thought about hauling in his stuff but instead went down to the bathroom. When he came out he casually glanced into his old bedroom across the hall.

"Hey," he called out playfully, "what did you do to my room?"

She came up to his side, then maneuvered past him into what had once been his bedroom but was now something else altogether. There was still a bed, dresser, end-table, but the room had been emptied of any style, either contemporary or classical or Linda Swain's own trademark neo-clutter. It looked damn near like a hotel room.

"Well," she said, standing there in the middle of it. "I'm in the process of making a guest room."

"Looks like you're making a bed and breakfast."

"No, silly, it's supposed to be calming, all neutral colors and such. What's wrong with it?"

"Nothing. It's just...." He stuck out his bottom lip, pouting. "It doesn't look like *my* room anymore...."

She laughed. "It's not your room...."

"Right. But...." He frowned, looked at her. "If I have to come back next summer, are you planning on charging me rent?"

"Now there's a thought...."

She laughed, then started into another elaborate explanation of her decorating plans, telling him about the beige walls, the simple monotone colors and geometric pattern of the bedspread, the desk and light she wanted to buy, the future of the floor.

"I want to get rid of this ugly carpet. Put in something nicer."

She was about to say more when there was a sudden loud ringing. Jonah tensed, almost instinctually, thinking of fire drills, like the one his dorm had had just the night before. His mother rushed past him, making a point to touch his arm as she did, and ran to the kitchen.

"My lasagna," she said.

He turned and followed, thinking: *Lasagna?*

"I thought, if you were all hungry you could have this," she said as she pulled the tinfoil-covered pan from the oven.

"They're all coming tonight?"

"Well, Tom and Kathy are, Tina and Mark are coming tomorrow."

"Oh." He watched as she lifted the tinfoil carefully, sending steam rising fog-like to the ceiling. He could smell the hot, wet smell of spices and tomato and beef, a husky odor of garlic. He wasn't hungry until that moment, not in the least, but when she offered to fix him a plate he said sure and went to the fridge to fetch something to drink.

She cut herself a small slice too and they sat together at the kitchen table while they ate, her doing most of the talking, occasionally asking him how school was, if he was talking to Becky, if he'd maybe found someone else.

Found someone else. He and Becky had been together for three years, he didn't think it was time to find someone else. Or was it? Two months had passed since she'd fucked him over, perhaps it was time after all... but he hadn't the heart for such things, that looking for someone new. Not yet, if ever.

41

And that wasn't how things worked for him, he didn't go out looking for someone, they either sort of fell together, matched by mutual friends, or, as in the case with Becky, he hemmed and hawed and ignored the signals (or missed them altogether) until she grew frustrated enough to literally jump him... with Becky this had happened after he and some friends had watched a movie in her room; the others left, perhaps too conveniently, leaving she and him alone together, and she had rolled over to where he was lying against the couch and started kissing his neck. Just like that. Subtle. Her lips on his skin, her breath deep and urgent, and he frozen in shock, hesitating a near full minute before turning his head to reciprocate. No, not too bright was Jonah Swain. Not too quick... and most certainly not any sort of ladies man. A girl pretty much had to have him naked before he realized she liked him.

"No, I haven't found anyone," he said to his mother. He bit into an uncooked noodle and listened to it crack like plastic under his teeth.

"Well... you should," she said.

It was at this moment that he came to a realization that bothered him terribly:

He was avoiding looking his mother in the eyes.

It wasn't a conscious avoidance, either, and that was somehow worse. He realized right at that moment that for some reason his mind would not let him keep and hold the gaze of his mother, as if there was something behind her eyes that was repelling his own. As he realized it now, he tried to look deeply into her eyes as she explained something or other, and could not. He had to look away, down to his plate, where he was pushing around a tiny mound of spilled sauce. Why this should be, he had no clue. It was enough to be aware of it, though. He felt suddenly ill. This was not how a son should be with his mother. And worse: this is not how they had once been. Mother and son. Jonah and his mom... they had been inseparable once upon a time, he'd been called her shadow, visible as a small little head behind her left shoulder in every photograph, hanging by her at parties, a wallflower growing comfortably in her shade. Insecure, they called him, a momma's boy, but it was just that he knew a safe place when he found it.

Warmth, sickening and heavy, coursed through him. He pushed his plate away and leaned back in his chair, looking not to her, no, but to the window behind the table, where three

42

squirrels could be seen crossing the backyard, in front of the now-bare garden.

"Do you have baffles on your feeders?" he asked.

"Baffles?"

"To keep the squirrels out."

"Oh. Nope, no baffles." She sighed, looking where he was. "I should, though..."

He nodded.

What did this mean, this new revelation? he wondered. Why can't I look my mother in the eye?

He thought of guns. Alcohol. Locked doors. Bizarre statements made to a frightened child. Dark nights. Dark souls. Guardian angels on furlough.

"Hey," he said perkily, trying to shake free of such things. "Hey, this was good," meaning the lasagna. Then he gestured to the decorations everywhere. "Everything looks good here, I think. You've got an eye for decorating." It sounded like something to say, a suitably empty sentiment, a buffer.

"Ah," she said dismissively. "It's not what I had in mind."

*

The smell of cheap brandy and Diet Coke, vile as a rebuke, a wiping away of childhood.

Brown pools of vicious liquid on the lip of an aluminum can. And the taste, when not expected, when a boy takes a sip from his mother's soda, is like all the shrewdness of the world suddenly raining down on an innocent head.

You know you've got a problem when you hide it, that's what everyone always says. Conventional wisdom.

Jonah snuck a look into his mother's cupboards this weekend: two plastic bottles of cheap Kessler's brandy.

Half empty, both.

4

"Can I do it?" he asked.

His mother thought a moment, briefly, and then handed him the cigarette. He stuck it in his mouth, picked up her seasick-green lighter, flicked it into life and touched the flame

43

to the end of the cigarette until it flared. Once the tip was orange he handed it back to her. She took it without a word.

"Let me know when you want another," he said. The faintest swirl of smoke parted his eleven-year-old lips.

"Why don't you go outside?" She sounded annoyed, staring over to the TV blabbering across the room. Bob Barker was talking to a Beauty.

"And do what?"

"I don't know," she said, eyes on the TV, cigarette jutting out from between her fingers. The smoke rose straight to the ceiling before breaking apart.

He sat watching her until she turned to look at him.

"You're just like your father."

He cocked his head, puppyish, curious. "In what way?"

She studied him for a time, no emotion on her face, her chin on the palm of the hand that held the cigarette, the end of which was dangerously close to her hair, recently-permed and perhaps highly flammable. She studied him absently, they held each others' eyes for a long time. He could not tell what she was thinking or feeling. It was a Monday morning, early summer, a day warm and benign.

"Just go outside," she said again, turning back to the TV.

"And do what?"

Her voice was soft but husky:

"And leave me alone."

He started to laugh. This was how they played, in those first few years following his father's death. His siblings had slipped into lives outside of the house, Tom focused on various sports and Tina developing that moody isolation that comes with entering high-school and which seems to find its supreme outlet in teenaged girls. This was perhaps a subconscious attempt to avoid spending too much time among all the memories the house conjured. After all, it was in the kitchen where their Dad had dropped dead, you had to think about that every time you opened the fridge or poured a glass of water or sat at the table and tried to eat. There was also, of course, the very real possibility that they were just normal American kids, doing normal American kid things, moving away from dependency on their home and starting to enter the wider world that lay beyond their yard and neighborhood. There was the very real possibility that they were doing what was good and healthy for them: moving on. If this was the case, what did that say about their younger brother, the baby, Jonah? Well, he too had moved on, though in a rather different sense: he had moved on but not away... he had moved *inward.*

Shy, some would call him. Others would say sensitive. None of those labels meant anything, however. He was, in the end, just a boy. Just Jonah.

And what did it mean to be this boy, Jonah Swain?

*

His world back then was his bedroom, his books, his yard, and his mind. Not that he was overly smart, or even inclined toward intellectual pursuits of the sort that sharp but not brilliant kids fall into, like chess, or stamp collecting, but he was instinctually inward-looking, a daydreamer, blessed with a poet's heart but not his wit or ear for language. Had he been given heightened language skills perhaps he would have been a writer, even a teacher like his father, someone possessed of intelligence and wit. As it stood, he was little more than a daydreamer. Yet it wasn't that he could not think but that he lacked, in the words of nearly all his elementary teachers, *focus.* Jonah could make something of himself, they all said, but he has no focus. His mind wanders. He grows bored. He daydreams.

What these people missed was that Jonah Swain possessed the sort of mind that, if properly nourished, could lead him into that oldest of traditions, that once-venerated but now slighted of professions: philosopher. Years later, of course, he would pursue philosophy in college, but only half-heartedly, feeling the pull of the old instincts but no longer the spark. He would see it as a natural offshoot of literature. And the reading of literature, of course, is just another form of daydreaming.

So, his world, this little corner of Wisconsin, was insular. He spent it mostly alone, having only one real true friend who lived across town and was therefore not available for play every single day of the week. When he was alone he watched clouds. He watched birds. He doodled in notebooks, made up stories, thought about nothing at all... which is the natural philosophy of a boy. He lacked focus, yes, and therefore tended to daydream about everything and anything. There were no subjects that did not cross his young mind, if only fleetingly. When you lie on the ground and stare at clouds moving hypnotically in front of a blue sky you had no say in what shapes were presented to you, you simply took them in. He saw elephants in the clouds, of course, and lions, and old men... but he also saw great castles and dragons and spaceships and all sorts of strange, surreal shapes, and he would spend hours watching them, laughing as this grand bit of theatre played only for him.

That more than anything might sum up what it meant to be this boy, Jonah Swain: he found joy in almost everything around him. Later this gift would be threatened by varying degrees of cynicism, sarcasm, even depression at the whole sorry state of the world, but back then he was simply entertained by what appeared to be the absurdity of life. He was only eleven the summer after his dad died, and eleven years is nothing. And yet, of course, being without a dad (a half-orphan, some wise ass somewhere had called him) he felt somehow older than that. He felt dirtied, beaten, more experienced than most of his peers. He felt as if he had been given an insight into the darker corners of life, and it colored who he was now and how he saw things. Losing his Dad had been a blow to him, no matter how much he'd like to claim otherwise. With each month he grew to remember the man less and less, but also to feel whatever had replaced him more and more. He no longer had a dad, but he had something else now: this unnamable *thing* that would haunt him forever, this feeling that everything is transitory and illusory and destined to end. This thing would come to distort his view of life and love, giving him an impression of existence as a fatalistic enterprise. LIFE IS A FATAL DISEASE, he would one day idly etch on a desk in a college classroom. Indeed, and though there's an unfinished part of that thought it would take him many more years before he would realize what it was. Before that happened he would take this view with him like a shield, like armor, into what he saw as the battlegrounds of life, where the smog that hovered over the hills was depression and the enemy was everyone.

He was not, though, a depressed child in the first few years after his father died. Gradually it came to seem natural, this father-less life. Gradually he came to forget the sound of his Dad's voice, the things he said, the way he acted. He would always remember sitting on his lap in the big recliner, hugging him and feeling his father's rough whiskers against his own smooth baby-fat cheeks, but not anything the man might have whispered to him. If Harold Swain had imparted to his youngest child any words of wisdom to live his life by, Jonah could not recall them. Within a year of the funeral he was able to tell people who asked that his father was dead and not feel any stirrings in his own heart, not once hesitate with the words. Is this moving on? Or was his young mind developing its own form of denial, a denial that both embraced and rejected the fact of the man's death? Perhaps it was just the act of growing itself, his young mind developing new brain cells every second, these new brain cells coming into existence without the details of Harold Swain imprinted on them, just the feel of the rough beard but not the weight of his presence, not the truth of the man. Jonah Swain was a growing young boy, and perhaps he was just growing away from his dead father. Perhaps in a few years he himself would be an entirely new person, with all new cells and blood and bone, and not have any memory of his dad whatsoever. Perhaps by the time he was thirty he would not remember he had had a dad at all.

It was in that summer he was eleven, just eight months after his father's death, that Jonah first realized he could not remember the sound of the man's voice. This terrified and fascinated him. That voice had been an important part of his life, announcing departures and arrivals ("I'm home!"), giving mini-lectures on natural history, telling his kids about birds and deer and insects, but it was gone now, as unknown to him as the plains of Africa, the surface of the moon.

He was walking to the very far ends of his yard, ambling mindlessly along a mowed path that ran through the wildflower field, when it occurred to him. He saw a butterfly skim past, a flittering streak of black and yellow four-inches across. He stopped to watch it, amazed by a sudden beauty that seemed to come from nowhere to whiz past his nose. He watched it until it was gone and wondered what his dad would have said about it. Harold Swain was always pointing out such things and telling his kids what they were and what they meant. Jonah remembered watching turtles lay eggs on the sides of gravel roads while his father told him what kind of turtle it was and how many eggs it would lay and when they would hatch. He thought about the butterfly and wished he could give it a name. His Dad would have named it instantly. But….

Just like that, it hit him. He couldn't remember what his father had sounded like, not even what sort of voice it had

47

been, smooth or gravelly. He stood there a long time, considering this thought and what it meant. Was he the only one this had happened to? Certainly his mother could not have forgotten that voice, she'd known it for so many more years than he, but what about Tom and Tina? He wanted to ask them but knew he could not. He was afraid he was the only one who had forgotten, and what did that say about him? Had he loved his Dad less than they did? He didn't want to be looked at as a kid who had forgotten his father.

He turned from that backyard field, full now with summer's fat bloom, all subtle colors and the buzzing excitement of insect and bird life, and looked at the little home sitting three acres away. Two huge maples sat on opposite ends of the house, like sentries, obscuring most of it, their leaves so dark and green they looked like jungle trees. He could see the kitchen window, mirroring the blue clarity of the sky. He could see the picnic table. The Webber grill. The lawnmower sitting silent in the shade by the garage. A basketball at rest on the grass. The whole house quiet and dark even in this daylight. Was anyone home? You wouldn't think so, looking at it. You would think it was a house emptied of life, as if everyone had suddenly abandoned it, taking nothing with them… leaving this little boy out in the field.

For a few minutes he heard nothing except insects and birds. No cars passed on the street out front. No airplanes cut through the sky. No dogs barked. No chainsaws stirred, no mowers roared. No one laughed, screamed, called children in for lunch. There was just him, left behind to face whatever was coming. They'd forgotten him. Maybe they didn't even exist anymore, maybe he was the last person alive. Maybe he was alone from now to the end of time.

He listened to the songs of birds, the chittering and chattering of insects, looked back at the house and this little quiet sliver of the world. How long would it take for me to forget what *they* sounded like, Mom and Tom and Tina? How long before any of this life here just faded away? He was alone. The last living person on Earth.

In the sky he watched an old jet contrail slowly break apart and dissolve into tiny puffs of clouds, watched until even those puffs were gone, faded into the blue. This world, he thought. This world, could it all just change…?

He stood there until he heard a car approaching from the east, the sound rising and rising until it passed by, trailing the thump and crash of a cranked radio. With that it seemed all noise returned, like a door was opened to the aural world. He heard car horns. Dogs. Kids laughing in distant yards. The sound of a skateboard on a sidewalk.

Overhead there was another jet making its way North, piercing that icy blue like a needle. Moments later he heard the sound of its engine, like thunder rumbling across the sky.

The world came back. Jonah sighed.

*

He finally worked up the courage to ask his mom if she remembered Dad's voice.

"Do I what?" she asked, not turning her eyes from the television. The show now was *Match Game*. He didn't know exactly how it was played but he liked the music.

"Remember what Dad sounded like?"

Now she turned to him, considered him for a long time, this look of confused worry on her face. He wished he hadn't said anything at all, what he was asking was wrong, it was wrong and he was bad.

"Yes," she said finally, her voice husky. A cigarette burned in an ash tray. The smoke seemed to rise up and darken her eyes, and she turned away from him and gazed blandly back at the TV screen. "Yes," she said, "I hear him every night."

*

When he dreamed about his father the man had no face and never spoke. He just stood there looking at his youngest son in a way that could have been judgment or simply silent observation, like a naturalist watching wildlife.

Jonah had such dreams once a week that first year.

*

"Mom?" he called. The house gave no voice in return, but it was not silent. As he stood there in the kitchen, having just come in from smashing caps with a hammer in the driveway, he heard the familiar rustle and thud of the drier in the basement, the zipper of a hooded sweatshirt clanking and clanging, the ragged sound of the old drier itself, just six

49

months from its death. So she was doing laundry. He thought about going down there too but instead walked over to peer into the livingroom. The television was off, but there were records out near the stereo, Andy Williams looking back at him, ditto Barbra Streisand, Elvis (of course), the Statler Brothers, the Carpenters. The Williams (*Andy Williams Sings Movie Love Songs*) was leaning against the stereo stand, boldly smiling out at the world, a handsome man who looked like he hadn't done a lick of real work his whole life. Jonah stood looking at the scene for a moment, then walked into the livingroom to stare out the bay window. He could see the burn marks the caps had made out on the driveway, and he realized he'd forgotten the hammer there. If he didn't pick it up Tom would yell at him, tell him he was a baby and if he couldn't put stuff back where he found it then he had no business touching anything at all. He'd have to remember to get it.

He looked down at the records, thought briefly about how many times he'd heard them (the Elvis, in particular, had been familiar since he was a baby), then turned and started out of the room, thinking he'd go grab a book or break out the clay and see what he could make.

He stopped at the end table by the couch. His mom had a favorite end of the couch, the one closest to the kitchen. That was her spot, she always sat there. His dad had of course taken the recliner in the opposite corner, unless he'd been in the mood to throw down a pillow and stretch out on the floor.

Jonah glanced at the recliner, empty now and seemingly darkened by shadow. He realized that no one had sat in it since Dad had died.

He looked back at his mother's spot, saw the corpse of a cigarette butt lying in the ashtray on the table, and a can of Tab. He could use a quick sip of Tab, it might be refreshing, even though he favored root beer or grape. He picked up the can and took a swallow.

The brandy didn't burn his throat so much as numb his tongue. He made a face of distaste and set the can back down.

"What are you doing?"

His mom was standing in the kitchen, watching him.

"I wanted a drink," he said. "What's in there?"

"Do I drink from your cans?"

"No...."

"That's right. And I don't expect my children to grab mine. For crying out loud, can't I have *anything*?" She turned and went to the sink, started slamming plates together, banging silverware.

"I just wanted a drink..." he said, following her, feeling an incredible wave of tension rising from her back.

"Just go play," she said, not looking at him. "Just go play."

He left her there, putting dishes away. She did it like it was a violent act. Murder. Battery. He could hear her from his bedroom, with the door shut, with his nose in a book, with his mind trying to escape.

*

The first real book he remembered reading was called *Rigby*, about the adventures a dog finds after it escapes from its leash. After that, and the ones they gave him in school, he raided his mom's old books. For a time she had been a member of the Book of the Month Club, and so there was an odd assortment of books in the house, none having much to do with each other, just a haphazard collection of genres and styles. He didn't know how many she might have actually read, or how many might have been his dad's, but he loved to go through them every now and then, see if things he'd passed up before might catch his eye now. There were four boxes of books in the basement and he would spend hours going through them, opening every other one, reading paragraphs until he got bored, smelling the glue and starch, looking at the author photos. To say that the collection was eclectic is an understatement: by the time he was fourteen Jonah had read *The Odyssey, The Godfather, The Complete Short Stories of Ernest Hemingway, Our Town*, the poems of Edgar Allan Poe and Emily Dickinson, *Catcher in the Rye*, Bradbury's *Martian Chronicles, The Lord of the Flies*, something by Jackie Collins, two Sidney Sheldon works (one he liked because it was about gangsters, and he was in his gangster period at the time), three Danielle Steele masterpieces, the nearly complete (at the time) works of Stephen King, various extremely violent Westerns (most part of the same series), collections ranging from tales of haunted houses to portraits of true crime, at least one slim little volume of terrible poetry, and what proved to be his favorite (and which he'd still consider *the* American novel decades later), *To Kill a Mockingbird*. He absolutely loved *To Kill a Mockingbird*. He spent two months of his thirteenth summer absorbed in that world, reading slowly, savoring the details. He fell in love with Harper Lee. He wondered how old she was, where she lived, what else she wrote. When it came time to read the book in school he was sixteen and had read it three times. By then he knew she had never written or published anything else.

During the time he was eating through those books he never passed judgment, unless it was to label something boring. That was his only criteria: did it hold his attention? For him a novel was a success if it created a world and brought you into it, if it kept you there while beautiful summer afternoons came and went around you. He didn't care if it said something important or not, or if it was regarded as "serious" or "low-brow" by critics, the only thing that mattered was how it made him feel to read it, how each page affected him, how every sentence sent a ripple of emotion through him like the tolling of a bell. If it did that, then it was good.

These books formed an early core of thinking for him. They were the books he cut his teeth on, so to speak, and they made up what was for him the life he lived at the time. When he needed to escape his little corner of Oakton, it was to the world of these books that he went.

Got your nose in a book again? Tom would say with a look of distaste when he'd come in and find Jonah sprawled on his bed. Go out and get some sun.

Shut up. Leave me alone.

And Tom would, most of the time, but quite often he'd shut off the light and shut the door and leave his young brother in darkness.

I'm gonna tell Mom! Jonah might yell.

Moments later the door would open a sliver, a hand would come in, the light would be flicked back on, and Tom would whisper:

Baby.

And Jonah would turn his eyes back to the book, to the world it contained, to the peace it offered. He didn't want to go out in the sun, didn't want to play basketball or baseball or football, didn't want to go swimming, didn't want to ride his bike… not when he was caught in one of these worlds, not when he had business there. Sure, he'd slip into the little wildflower prairie in the backyard when he wanted to get away, lose himself in the yarrow and thistles and coneflowers, but mostly he went to books for escape. As a result, he was beginning to feel different from Tom and Tina and the other kids in the neighborhood. Even his mother would sometimes tell him to go outside when she found him reading on the couch. She was a big believer in the sun. The sun is good for you, she said. You need it. It keeps you healthy. Go out and do something.

So he did.

He read books in the backyard, and made his own stories from the passage of clouds.

5

Tom and his girlfriend, Kathy, pulled in around five, and with their arrival there was a palpable shift in the energy of the house. Not that it was previously heavy, but there had been a withdrawn, introverted, *hesitant* mood with just Jonah and his mother, the conversation stifled, monotonous, the same topics left and returned to minutes later. Jonah couldn't explain what he was thinking and feeling as he sat there with her: that old familiar mix of guilt and regret and unease and insecurity. After finding the bottles of brandy he had tried not to think too much at all, and in reality he had entered a form of denial, blacking out the truth that had been presented to him, the reality that was lying right there in front of his eyes. They say it's hard to watch a person kill themselves, much easier to look away. Jonah sat on the opposite end of the couch from her and watched her flip through the TV.

At the sound of Tom's car in the driveway Jonah stood and felt relief wash over him. The more the merrier. Family was a buffer. He stretched out his back and said:

"They're here. Let the fun begin."

His mother smiled at him as if he'd said the strangest thing in the world. "Why do you say that...?"

He shrugged.

When Tom and Kathy entered the house they did so smiling grandly, skin tanned by the Arizona sun, eyes bright and yet tired from the drive. Tom had met her just the previous August, but she was essentially part of the family now. She was his girl, he said. Things were getting serious.

"Little bro," Tom said, holding out his hand for Jonah to take. Tom Swain shook hands like a car salesman, and all car salesmen, of course, shake hands like assholes.

"How's it going?" Jonah said. An inanity. A wasting of breath. He hated small talk, but that's all Family is, gatherings of small talk. The weather. Sports. Movies. Family gossip. And, of course, he was glad to have it now.

Kathy smiled at Jonah and looked for a moment to be on the verge of giving him a hug; it wouldn't have been out of character for her, she was a friendly, warm person who probably came from a family that gave each other hugs all the time. Instead, though, she reached out and touched him on the shoulder. Her touch was firm yet gentle, suggesting strength withheld. She was a pretty woman, glowing with health and youth, all bright eyes and quick smile. Jonah had liked her the first time they met.

"How's school?" she asked. Another inanity, yet he couldn't blame her. Small talk was reserved for in-laws and co-workers.

"Fine," he answered.

"Passing?"

"As far as I know."

Further inanities followed: Tom asking Jonah if he'd gotten there yesterday or today, Jonah asking how their drive had been, Kathy and her future mother-in-law discussing the holiday decorations and dinner plans, Tom saying Jonah's little Escort looked like it was leaking oil, Kathy asking about Tina, and so forth. Jonah took it all in as best he could, then faded away from the conversation, a talent for which he was uniquely skilled. A master wallflower. He made his way into the kitchen where he poured himself a glass of water and stared out at the backyard. He thought about his mother and this house and memories and other families and gardens gone to grass and this town here whose name he'd always hated but whose presence he'd never been able to shake from the back of his mind. Oakton. It was as if the whole town was a ghost that haunted the lonely halls of his mind. Good god, he knew that image was full of self-pity but it was accurate. He couldn't shake this place. This town, this house... they were there, imprinted on his subconscious like water-marks. There were good memories here, yes, but even they seemed haunted, or perhaps shadowed by the presence of something waiting in the wings, a shape dark and troubling. He remembered playing with Matchbox cars on a bare patch of ground at the side of the house, making roads and intersections for the little hot rods and trucks. He remembered banging on caps with a hammer in the driveway, or climbing trees, or watching the stars come out over the backyard, but the images were darkened by that shape in the background, just out of eyesight, hiding, waiting. He'd been a mostly happy child, yes, but there was something ominous hovering in the future. Obvious what it was, of course: the death of his father. But even later there was this other shape, the slow wasting away of his mother. It was she who haunted him the most, she who had once been so happy, so full of life, his best friend, the place he went to for comfort.

"Not the same, huh?" Tom said behind him.

"What?"

"The garden." Tom stared out the window to the odd rectangle of lawn where the garden had once been, the grass there many shades darker than the rest. "It used to be something," he said. "I'd like to have a garden like that again."

"Yeah," Jonah said. "Yeah."

They fell into more small talk. Tom asked deeper questions about Jonah's schoolwork, what courses he was enjoying, what steps he was taking towards future employment, what it was like being on campus during the mid-nineties. The grunge faze was blazing then, everyone was struggling to look poor and despondent. Jonah said there was indeed a feeling of community in the air, a sense of excitement, and yet at the same time this new community lacked focus and direction, was turning more to fashion than to revolution, was more about the music than anything resembling an issue or a Movement... exactly what the Sixties revolution became once the Seventies arrived. Was a kid with dirty long hair deeper than a kid without? Jonah didn't believe so, but he knew most Movements (if this indeed had the makings of one) were changing beasts, and that this grunge thing here might blossom into something resembling true political unrest. It was certainly possible. The following year was an election year and anything could happen. Bush wasn't fucking things up as bad as Reagan, but he was still fucking them up, in his own wimpy way. The right wing was still the right wing. You can poison my air and water, hobble my union, and send my jobs overseas, but I'll be goddamned if you'll take my gun.

Jonah didn't say any of this latter to his brother. He didn't know what the political leanings of Thomas Swain were but it was best to tread safely on this ground. Certainly he looked like a Republican: deep as a mirror.

It was when Tom started talking about his own experience on campus (a term Jonah liked, and which reminded him of *in country*) that Jonah started to tune him out. Tom was just three years older than Jonah but he'd graduated from college in less than four years, so that now, at nearly twenty-four, he'd been out long enough to start both a career and a family. In a way Jonah envied him, and in a way he feared his brother's sort of life. There was quicksand on that path, and he had to be careful.

He only listened to Tom talk with half an ear, choosing instead to ponder quietly the course of his own life in comparison with his brother's. Tom Swain, businessman. Jonah Swain... what? He didn't know. He would likely graduate with a double degree in Literature and Philosophy and what the fuck good were they? Even Biology would have been a more practical choice, but he'd flipped that coin and Lit and Philosophy came up heads... less math, you know.

He tried to keep good eye contact with his brother as he talked, nodding at all the right moments, keeping a look on his face at once concerned and goofy. Tom was indeed only three years older but he already looked fully mature, thirty-four instead of twenty-four. He was possessed of the same square-faced preternaturally aged features of their father, and a look in the eyes that spoke of responsibility and intelligence... if you didn't already know his age you would have had a hard time pinning it down. You'd look at Thomas Swain and decide he was anywhere from twenty-eight to thirty-seven. He was even dressed older than his years: crisp khaki shorts in which a buttoned white shirt had been tucked. He wore tennis shoes with white socks, and his hair was sharply cut, short and serious. A man who would not be out of place schmoozing on a golf course. To look at him was to think of golf balls and martinis and cigars.

Jonah himself was wearing a ratty, scuffed leather vest over a dark green t-shirt, with faded jeans and brown boots. The boots, too, were scuffed and scarred. He wore them everywhere. His hair was not long but it was trending shaggy, little wild ragged curls lifting off on their own around his ears.

"Any girl?" Tom asked.

Jonah shrugged. "Nothing serious."

"Wasn't there one? Betty? Brenda?"

"Becky. We're not together anymore."

Tom clapped his younger brother on the shoulder, car-salesman-style. "Nothing wrong with that, that's all right. No need to get serious. You're young. This is your time to play and have fun."

He flashed a salesman smile which Jonah mirrored half-heartedly. "Right."

"Is anyone hungry?" their mother said behind them.

"No," Tom said.

"No, I'm good for now," Kathy answered.

"Well... why did I make all that lasagna, then?"

"Maybe in a little while, after we get settled here," Kathy said.

"Or maybe I'll just throw it out!" snapped Linda Swain. She turned and left the room.

Kathy and Tom exchanged looks, Kathy raising her eyebrows in confusion, Tom just shrugging.

"So," he said, turning back to Jonah. "Did you come in yesterday?"

*

The conversation drifted in and out of simple topics the rest of the day, moving effortlessly from matters of catch-up to brief comments on what happened to be on the television at any given moment. Their mother was an obsessive flipper, holding the remote like a sword, guarding against something only she could see, alighting on any given channel for no more than four seconds before moving on. Jonah was sitting on the opposite end of the couch from her, with Kathy in the recliner and Tom on the floor at her feet, massaging her calves. The brothers gave each other a look when their mother started on another cycle, hitting channel two for the tenth time. Channel two just happened to be showing the news, some square-jawed, quasi-pompadoured exercise in dullness reading from cue cards, telling a story about a Green Bay man who had had a deer stolen from the bed of his pickup.

"No hunting for you this year?" Jonah asked Tom, who shook his head.

"No money," Tom said. "Actually, I *do* have the money, I just need to spend it on other things. Which is too bad, I really wanted to get up North."

Jonah nodded. The images they had chosen to illustrate this story were, perversely, a static shot of an empty

57

truck bed alternating with scenes of whitetails running across open fields. Jonah contemplated the message this was relating and its relevance to the story being told. A deer was shot, placed in a pickup, said pickup parked at a bar (while the hunter had a shot or two himself), then the deer stolen by unknown thieves. The hunter seemed upset. Not as much as the deer had probably felt, thought Jonah, but he kept this to himself. He wasn't necessarily against hunting but he had never met an actual honest-to-goodness hunter, either. The folks he knew were vandals with permits, sadists in blaze orange, disrespectful of the creature they took from the wild; he knew of dead deer having celebratory shots poured down their throats. You do not have a right to hunt, you have an obligation to that which is hunted. You can't have a connection with the world around you if you only go into the woods one week out of the year. And you can't be part of the cycle of natural life if you only take and give nothing in return. Sure, go ahead, hunt, take an animal, but be prepared to leave the earth your own corpse. Be prepared to—

Jesus, he thought, such bitterness. Take a deep breath....

His mother stayed on the news longer than any other thing she had come across but she still finally flipped again. The next few channels had sitcoms, commercials, more sitcoms, and Lawrence Welk. She hesitated on Welk and Jonah made an audible sound of disgust.

"What?" his mother said, her mouth in a half-smile, her eyes dark and tired. "It's Lawrence Welk. You used to watch him all the time."

"I did not. When?"

"When you were younger. All the time."

Jonah shrugged. "I don't remember that."

"I remember everything."

The woman singing on the television looked way too clean and virginal to be real, and as they listened to her Jonah thought about the disparity between the people on this show and the private lives they must have had back there in the mid to late sixties. Jesus Christ, so much was going on in the world and there they were in their pastel clothes, singing songs that were fifty, sixty years old already, the music *their* parents had dug. He watched the pretty little woman twirling her umbrella and tried to imagine her in a protest line, throwing epithets and rocks at the pigs, shouting death to capitalism, down with

Nixon, save the whales, whatever. It was impossible, there was no life in that face, those eyes. A meaningless woman. A prop. A human widget in an endless assembly line. He wondered what she was doing now, nearly thirty-years later. No longer singing, probably. Looking back on her life and trying to remember anything of consequence....

After the song was finished Linda Swain flipped again, instantly falling into the same rhythm of click, watch for a few seconds, click again, sit-coms and commercials and old dramas on an endless loop, until the loop itself became the entertainment, a show all its own, perhaps more fascinating than anything else, a mindless run of events and actions out of sync and order, making no logical sense whatsoever, a form of ultra-modern art. Jonah realized he was watching this with fascination and he glanced at Kathy and Tom: they too were staring at the constantly changing images, eyes focused intently on the television, mouths open just slightly, just enough to take in air and keep themselves alive. If they weren't careful they'd all get caught like that, get stuck in the loop forever.

He shook himself loose from the temptation to just sit and watch those images and looked at his mother. "Tina's coming tomorrow?" he asked.

"Yes."

"Is Biff coming?"

She looked at him, that same half-smile on her mouth. "Why....?"

"Just wondered."

"Yes he is. Is that all right?" She said this playfully, but he was very aware of the ground he was treading on. There were dangers here, he had to be cautious.

"Of course," he said. "The more the merrier."

"Biff's joining us?" Tom asked. Jonah tensed, hoped the topic would change quickly, remembering as he did how his mother's mood had switched violently over the phone when Biff's name had come up.

"Yes," she said, turning what was now just a quarter-smile (quite dangerous) to her older son. "Biff is coming to dinner tomorrow, I invited him."

Tom shrugged, looked back at the television.

"Cool," he said.

Kathy, quite the mediator, smiled perkily at her boyfriend's mom and said: "How are things with you two?"

Oh god, thought Jonah.

59

"Pretty good," his mother answered flatly, looking back at the television with the remote at the ready. She sighed, and though Jonah detected something meaningful in that sigh he found it ultimately impossible to read. He looked at her out of the corner of his eye but could tell nothing from her tired face, either. If anything, she just looked like she needed a good night's sleep. He wondered if that was it. Just a good night's sleep.

The next day she told her kids she was getting married. And life goes on.

*

Jonah would always remember the look on Biff Oldenberg's face when the woman he loved told her children she was getting married. It was during the Thanksgiving dinner, everyone at the table, Jonah, his mom, Biff, Tina and Mark, and Tom and Kathy. The food had been excellent, the wine cheap but pleasant. Conversation had been equally pleasant, all surface topics of the sort that are best for table talk. And then, a little more than halfway through the meal, Linda Swain had leaned back, sighed, looked at her kids and their significant others, and said she had something to announce. She looked at Biff and asked if he wanted to tell them. You go ahead, he said, smiling in a way that could only be called sheepish. In the two years Jonah had known the man he had never seen him smile any other way. All right, she answered, looking down to her plate, then back at her children. Biff and I... we've decided to get married.

Jonah would never be able to recall how he and Tina and Tom took this (he supposed they had smiled and said congratulations and all that sort of crap) but he would never, ever forget the look on Biff's face. It was a look of both anxiety and happiness, mixed equally into something that closely resembled pain.

It was the look of someone who was preparing to be hated.

*

Jonah heard Tina and Mark whispering in the hall. It was early afternoon the day after Thanksgiving, and Tom and Kathy had gone with Mom and Biff (as they would from then

60

on be known) to Green Bay for shopping. Jonah had been napping, dozing away into a troubled dreamscape where strangers had familiar faces and everyone expected him to do something. We're waiting for you, these strangers said to him. We're waiting.

What am I supposed to do? he asked, but they would not say.

He came out of this light sleep slowly, at first not aware that he had done so, opening his eyes to see above him the old familiar ceiling of his bedroom. Through the window flowed the slanted, diffused light of afternoon, lazy and golden. It was another beautiful Autumn day outside, bright and fresh.

It was after a few minutes of just lying there that he heard his sister's voice. The door to his room was shut but it was a thin door, just as the walls were thin walls. This was not a house for secrets.

"I know she did," his sister was saying. "She tries but you can't hide that."

Mark, sounding calmer, said: "What do you want to do about it? You can't say anything."

"Well why not? Why the hell not?"

Tina was speaking quietly, just slightly above a whisper, but the emotion was clear in her voice. She didn't sound angry, just determined. "Why not?" she asked again. "Someone should say something."

"How?" Mark asked. "How would you bring that up?"

"I don't know."

"Do Tom and Jonah know?"

"I don't know. Tom might. Jonah…."

She let that trail off, as if there was a meaning implicit in it, and Jonah frowned. He lay there listening a moment longer, but he realized they had moved out of the hall and into the kitchen, where they continued to speak softly. He supposed they had just been walking down the hall when they'd had that conversation, but it struck him as strangely theatrical: like in a play when characters have a whispered conversation within the convenient earshot of another. They didn't need to be whispering though, he knew what they were talking about almost immediately, just from their tone. The strange Dark Secret, more dark and shameful than even the drinking... and yet understood by her children almost instinctively, without its name ever being spoken. It was as if they understood what was going on intuitively, perhaps feeling it as a disturbing hole in

61

their hearts and souls. It was in many ways simply part of who their mother was now. Linda Swain was slowly killing herself.

She was bulimic.

*

It was like seeing something terrible, a strange nightmare shape in the shadows, but being unable to acknowledge it… if you looked too closely, if you really *saw* it, you might go insane.

You'd hear the retching in the bathroom. There was a radio in there, but you could hear her, hacking away. You'd ask her if something was wrong and she'd say she wasn't feeling good. Sometimes she didn't clean up too well and you'd see trace evidence and when you asked her if she was sick she'd grow defensive, angry, snapping at you as if you had no business asking her anything, as if you were being nosy. After that you'd just ignore it. You'd hear those sounds in the bathroom and you'd shut them out, put your hands over your ears, your pillow over your head. You'd notice the smell when she came out, and the yellowing of her teeth. Then, later, you'd notice how thin she was. Skeletal. But still, even noticing, what could you do? You'd long since shut down, sent this aspect of her life to a land which you never ever visited. It was like an instant shutting down of concern or care, as if your senses immediately closed off whenever any evidence of her slow suicide was presented to you.

This was a recipe for future guilt, of course. Some day she might succeed in finally killing herself and you would have to look in the mirror and ask yourself why you never confronted her, why you never tried to help her. You'd have to look at her tiny little body as it lay fragile and pathetic in her casket and ask yourself how things might have been different if you'd just had the ability to intervene in some way, if you'd just been able to talk to her.

Perhaps even then you'd still be in denial. There was nothing you could do. She hid it so well. She seemed to be getting better. Didn't she know what she was doing? Didn't she see the damage she was doing to herself?

Jonah would never remember the first time he knew his mother was bulimic. He would come to believe there had never been a first time, that it had always been part of his childhood landscape.

62

My name is Jonah Swain. My mother is an alcoholic and a bulimic. My father died when I was ten. I have a brother, Tom, and a sister, Tina. We grew up in Oakton, Wisconsin. I will never amount to anything. I lack focus. I keep people at a distance. I am part of a broken family. I....

That Thanksgiving weekend when his mother announced she was going to marry Biff, Jonah Swain thought that maybe, just maybe, this was the fresh start she needed, that remarrying would reinvigorate her, get her happy again, get her healthy again.

It was 1991. What could anyone say? Another decade was over, a new one had begun.

6

Here's a scene from the previous decade: a depressed Linda Swain running down the hall to lock herself in her bedroom, shouting back to her youngest child that she was going to shoot herself with one of her dead husband's rifles. And Jonah, aged twelve, crying in his own bedroom, listening to the quiet, waiting for it to be broken by the violent blast of a gunshot. Which never came....

*

Or: his mother taking off in the car, saying she was going to "wrap it around a tree," and not returning for more than two hours.

*

Or: out of nowhere would come tears, cryptic, crazy statements, the brutal pushing away of loved ones. Violent shifts in mood. Drunken stumbling. Midnight rants. Falling asleep on the kitchen floor. Smell of beer omnipresent, ominous. Sitting on the couch one Halloween evening, dressed all in black, Elvira-style, with her deeply black mascara running for its life down her cheeks, tracing the tears that had flowed there just minutes before. Half-empty can of Tab, on the top of which rested a pool of amber. Ash tray full of rejected cigarettes, all lit at the wrong end. I can't get one of these fuckers lit, she was saying. I can't get one of these fuckers lit.

Tom, seventeen at the time, was nowhere to be seen. Jonah, fourteen, had to stand there in the livingroom, his mother a sunken shape before him, tossed haphazardly on the couch, thrown gracelessly to the world. Ma, you all right? he asked. Don't call me Ma, she said, it makes me feel old. I can't get one of these fuckers lit, her fingers fumbling with the lighter, getting nothing but a spark and then, once a flame appeared, once more touching the filtered end of her Light 100s. Shit! she hissed, and threw the useless cig in the ashtray.

Should I do it? Jonah asked. Cautious. Nervous.

Her eyes were cadaverous pools of black, reflecting no light. She looked at her youngest and then told him to go away. No, wait! she called. Wait, watch this with me.

On the television was a Halloween special about old horror movies. Jonah looked there and saw Lon Chaney Junior becoming the Wolf Man.

All right, Jonah said, and he sat on the floor in front of the TV.

Have some of this, his mother said, handing a large plastic bowl of candy to him. Bite-sized Snickers and Kit-Kats and small bags of Jolly Ranchers were heaped inside of it temptingly.

What about the trick or treaters? he asked.

No one's coming, she said.

He selected a Snickers. She took the bowl back.

No one ever comes, she said, finally getting a cigarette lit. He didn't look at her, couldn't bear to, instead watched a half-man half-alligator thing chase a woman down a dark alley.

This reminds me of when I was a kid in Crandon, she said. God I miss that. To be a teenager....

Jonah didn't have to turn around to know she was crying again.

*

Or: late at night, long after the news was over, long after the Johnny Carson theme, long past the canned laughter of *MASH*, Jonah would lie in bed, unable to sleep, tossing and turning, with the glow of the streetlight leaking in to what should have been his dark room, spilling around the shade, like a living thing seeking and gaining entry, brushing over Tom's oblivious and sleeping face, perhaps keeping him asleep so it could continue its assault on Jonah's own slumber. Eventually he would sleep, finally slipping away around one in the morning, waking strangely refreshed and alert anywhere between six-thirty and seven, greeting each day with a simple yawn and a momentarily happy mind. But for those first few hours he was miserable, wanting to fade into dreamland but unable to, wishing he could shut out the desire for sleep because it seemed the more he desired it the more it stayed away. He would press his face to his pillow, not caring if it suffocated him so long as he could sleep forever, and then, that failing, he would put the covers over his head, which failed also. Tom across the room would be snoring lightly, the sound like a frog calling for a mate, and Jonah would listen to his brother's breathing, try to hypnotize himself with each breath he took in and released. There was always something comforting in the sound of his brother's breathing, but it wasn't enough to lull him to sleep. So Jonah just laid there, contemplating the odd shadows the terrible streetlight threw on the ceiling. Why can't I get another type of shade? he'd asked his mom, but she said there was no other kind, and anything else would be ugly. He had really only asked this once, and then Tom had gotten into him about being a spoiled baby and he'd never brought it up again. What the window needed, he knew, was to be painted over, some thick tar-like paint blacker than black, but he knew it would never happen... he was doomed. He watched the ragged and bony shadows of the trees and bushes that sat between the house and the light creep slowly across the ceiling. There was nothing else to do but watch. And listen. And every once in a while he heard....

He heard everything, of course, because it was that sort of house. He heard it all but tried not to take in too deeply the words and sounds.

The crying. The talking. The moans.

The walls of the house were so thin they let everything through. He listened to the life his mother was living and sometimes found himself crying as well. How could he not?

He heard everything.

*

There was the smell of coffee and cigarettes, with a hint of Endust or something, that lemony-chemical scent. The house was quiet save for a faint rustling noise, like papers being shuffled, and occasionally a soft whispering voice. Jonah

65

awoke from a nap he'd not meant to take, a Spiderman comic book spilled on his chest. He lay there on his bed, feeling something strange in the air, like humidity, heavy and vaguely threatening. He didn't care for the feeling at all, it reminded him too much of the one he'd had the day his dad died, that premonition hanging over him like a ghost. When he heard the soft rustling sound and the whispering voice a ripple of shivers raced up his spine. The water stains above him were shapeless, amoebas, not like clouds: in clouds you could make out elephants, hawks, turtles... in those water stains was only formlessness, a dull yellow-brown Nothing.

He lay there thinking about his mom. When he'd gone to his room to read she'd been outside, lying in the sun. The sun was good for you, she said. She'd had wet cotton balls on her closed eyes, and a radio playing early Eighties country music by her head. The smell of sickly-sweet Coppertone tanning lotion was thick as a fog around her, and Jonah could hear Kenny Rogers singing about cowards and card games as he went into the house. He poured himself a glass of Kool-Aid and then went to his room, where he sat down to read.

He turned his head now and looked at the window across the room, where the light was gray and dusty. The day was dark. Perhaps rain had come in. He sat up and rubbed at his eyes, waiting as long as he could before he had to rise and see what that sound was. The way things had been going he knew it could be anything. He felt frightened and sick. Just last week there'd been the thing with the gun. He was sick of the crying and the fear.

When he finally left his bedroom and walked down the short hall to the rest of the house he found his mother sitting on the livingroom floor. She had a stack of records next to her and was going through each of them, opening their jackets, removing the records from their sleeves. There was nothing on the stereo and the TV was off. The house was quiet and dark.

She heard him as his weight made the floor creak.

Hey, she said. It lives.

Yeah. What are you doing?

She seemed fine, all smiles and teeth. She still trailed that Coppertone stink, he could smell it across the room, but the tan looked good on her, made her look like an Indian. She had once told him she had an Indian grandmother or something and he didn't know if that was true but it was possible to believe it looking at her there, all dark-skinned and tough as a native.

66

Going through all these old records.

Why aren't you outside?

Rain.

Jonah saw then that the sky through the bay window was thick with swirling clouds.

Oh, he said. He waited a moment and then walked over to her. Her skin was shining in the pale light and there was a ladybug on her shoulder.

You've got a bug on you, he said. Before she could answer him he reached down and picked the insect up, let it crawl over his fingertip.

That's good luck, she said. Put it outside.

Jonah went out on the front steps, held his finger to the air, and flicked the ladybug off into the gray. It wasn't raining yet but the air was heavy and dull, as if someone had smudged off what had been a brilliant blue just a few hours earlier.

He went back by his mother.

Why are you going through them? he asked.

She sighed. Oh, some are old, some I never listen to anymore... I just thought I'd see what I have.

He saw the usual Elvis, Carpenters, Peter Paul and Mary, as well as strange collections of honky-tonk classics and polka favorites. She kept the records in the bottom of the stereo-stand, and though he himself had been through them all before he didn't seem to recall half of them now.

Hey, she said, pulling up a white record. Hey, you'd like this. She handed the record to him. He read the title:

GERSWHIN'S GREATEST HITS.

What is it?

It's got "Rhapsody in Blue," she said.

What's that?

She sighed again and looked up at him like he was crazy, like he'd said the strangest thing in the world. What's *that*? she mimicked. What do you mean, what's *that*?

He smiled. What is it?

Here. She stood, took the record from him, and marched down the hall of the quiet house. Jonah followed her into her bedroom, where she had a smaller little stereo. She removed the Gershwin record from its sleeve and placed it on the turntable.

Lay here, she said, indicating the bed. Lay here and listen.

He did as he was told, climbing up onto her big soft bed and lying on his side to watch the record spin under the needle.

When it's done, come out and tell me what you think.

She left just as the song began, that woozy, crazy, slow-starting clarinet struggling to rise like a butterfly caught in the wind. Jonah closed his eyes.

More than eighteen minutes later he finally emerged from the room, looking dazed, awestruck. The rain had started by then, a light sprinkling from the low sky. There was no heaviness, though, no oddness, no presence hovering over him. The world had lightened. Opened.

Linda Swain smiled at her youngest son. He smiled back.

Well? she asked.

I loved it, he said.

I knew you would.

7

"What do you make of that?"

This was Tom speaking. He and Jonah were doing the post-Thanksgiving dinner dishes. The hot soapy water felt like earth and darkness to Jonah's hands, engulfing them, caressing them.

Jonah knew what his brother was talking about but played stupid. "Make of what?"

"*That*. Marriage, Biff, everything."

"Oh." Jonah shrugged. "Whatever. It's cool. Whatever they wanna do."

Tom nodded, but he was staring over the sink and out the window.

Jonah frowned. "You got a problem with it?"

"No, shhh, keep it down!" Tom banged two bowls together in frustration and glanced back to see if anyone was listening to them. Everyone else was in the living room, though, and couldn't hear.

"Whatever," Jonah said, softly now. "It's fine. They're adults. Who cares?"

"It's kind of weird," Tom whispered. He was staring down at the plate in his hand, which he was drying with a kind

68

of mindless back and forth movement, using the towel the way one used an eraser to wipe clean a chalkboard.

"Weird how?" Jonah asked.

But his brother said nothing more, just moved over, opened a cupboard, put the plate away. That was the last Tom Swain would have to say about the impending marriage, that it was weird.

Biff and their mother were married seven months later, in June. They honeymooned at the Swain family cabin in the Nicolet National Forest, surrounded by starshine and woodsmoke, the same starshine and woodsmoke that had lulled the Swain children into beautiful complacency at least four times a summer all those years before.

And life goes on. In the town or the forest, on and on....

8

The call came the way monsters in old horror movies did: in the night, out of nowhere.

Hello? answered Jonah Swain.

Hey Jonah, this is Tina.

What's going on?

Nothing good. It's nothing good....

What is it?

Mom died.

What?

Yeah.

What?

Yeah...

How?

Car accident. She was hit by a truck on 41. I don't know the details.

Shut up.

Yeah....

Oh my god.

I know, Jonah. I'm sorry. I'm so sorry....

I... I don't know what to say.... I don't... it's crazy.

I know. I know. I'm sorry guy, I'm so sorry....

*

And life is a fatal disease.

3. Woodsmoke

1

The facts in the case of Jonah Swain are easily stated: he was thirty years old, single, worked a job he hated, and never did anything that he considered overly important or interesting. In short, perhaps, he was a typical American. It was downright depressing.

"What are you thinking about?" Hawkins asked.

"How depressing my life is."

Hawkins nodded. "That's what I thought."

They were headed north for some much-needed camping in the Nicolet National Forest, Hawkins at the wheel of his old Jeep Cherokee, Jonah sort of half-slumped in the passenger seat. He was excited for the trip but they'd fallen silent for several miles and he'd found his mind wandering to his life and everything he was or wasn't doing with it.

The part about being single perhaps bothered him most of all.

It had been two years since he'd had any sort of relationship, and it was getting harder now, all his friends marrying, having kids (for chrissake, kids!) and some even moving far away. Even the ones who lived nearby never saw him anymore, they either didn't have the time or he just felt awkward calling them up. They were raising their children and he was single, absolutely without responsibility. Anything they had once had in common had gone by the wayside. Hard to call up a new father and ask him if he wanted to hit a bar... or, worse, to sit down and have the sort of marathon conversations they used to have, discussing matters of philosophy or religion or art or sex until the wee hours of the morning.

There was still Hawkins, though, and though Hawkins did indeed have a son the two had been estranged for years.

71

The kid was Jonah's age, which would have added a strange wrinkle to the relationship between Jonah and Hawkins if they'd been the sort to care about such things. Yes, Hawkins was fifty-eight, but he was nevertheless Jonah's closest friend. Friend, mentor, sensei, oracle, debating partner, intellectual foil. It was Hawkins who had introduced Jonah to what was now his favorite joke, about Jonah being swallowed by a whale of an argument.

You're being swallowed by this argument, Hawkins would say when he figured he had the younger man in a logical corner. His eyes would crinkle, the corners of his mouth would lift, spreading out the great white beard. You're going under, young man... under....

And Jonah would flip him the finger and they'd both laugh.

They had met by accident on a bird-watching trip, discovering over the course of a long day that they were both virgin birders, that they both had backgrounds in literature and art, and that they both had irreverent, blasphemous senses of humor. Jonah had mentioned an old Ed Abbey joke about birding: the only birds I know are the rosy-bottomed skinny-dipper and the Kentucky Fried Chicken. The leader of their troupe had glared at him, obviously not seeing the humor in this, and Hawkins and Jonah had shared a delightful and delicious little private laugh, like giddy schoolgirls in study hall. They each pointed to that moment (and the troupe leader's reaction, mostly) as the beginning of their friendship.

I don't want to be around people who aren't irreverent, Hawkins once said. I don't want to be around people who can't joke about the sacred and profane, equally. People who can't say shit piss or fuck and *Jesus* in the same sentence.

I know a joke that uses all four, Jonah said.

Let's hear it.

Yes, no chance of Hawkins obeying conventional rules of etiquette and taste. Thrice divorced, Hawkins had long ago forsaken anything resembling domesticity. When Jonah met him he was working on the local newspaper as a features editor, honest if rather menial work.

Are you doing a story on birding? Jonah had asked him that first day.

No, was the response, wholly dry and serious: No, I just have a thing for tits and boobies.

They were headed now for a favorite campsite that sat along a lake they had found the previous summer, a rather quiet and isolated lake, rarely visited by humans save the deer hunters who flocked to the area in their blaze-orange fright suits. But the gun-deer season was a month away, this was October, an unusually warm late October, and they were each looking forward to silence, solitude, campfires, good beer, some deep (or otherwise) conversation, and the serenity of a primitive and dark forest. Hawkins had brought his canoe and both of them were excited to get out and explore the lake.

They'd be up there for four days, two single men separated by twenty-eight years of meaningless age, escaping reality and merging for a little while their concentric and private circles of solitude. Well... this makes it sound sad, nearly pathetic, but alone is not the same as lonely, and neither man would call himself that. They were, in fact, both used to being solitary, thinking their thoughts, living in worlds of their own creation, answering to no one and having no one answer to them. It was, in many ways, the way they each wanted it. And yet....

Well, there was a new girl at work now. Jess, lovely Jess, the sort of girl you could imagine riding a horse across some wildflower-speckled field, sun on her face, her hair wild around her head, a smile bright and joyful making her face look prettier than any of the coneflowers and tulips and goldenrods she passed. He didn't *want* to picture her this way, didn't want to feel the things he was feeling, but whenever he saw her he imagined her bathed under sun and wind, wild as a forest beast, playing in some fantasy wilderness of peace and beauty. He couldn't stop staring at her whenever she came into the lunchroom or when they happened to pass in the hall... and they happened to pass in the hall quite a bit lately, he apparently having much to do in her end of the building, which was no small feat considering he worked in the printing department and she in human resources, two areas separated by not only a good hundred yards of office space, bathrooms, lunchroom, and storage, but also by a considerable difference in dress code. She was always wearing black pants or khakis or the occasional skirt showing nice legs, and he... well, he was wearing jeans and often ratty flannel shirts over white tees, his brown boots scuffed and scarred and trailing dirt, himself trailing the smell of ink and chemicals. People always looked at him when he passed through those halls, but no one ever said

73

anything to him, no one asked him if he was lost or what he was looking for, because he moved with deliberation, confidence, like he belonged there, like he had every right in the world to be moving through their clean and quiet world of suits and ties and humming air-conditioning and whispering fax machines and blinking computer monitors. He moved through this end of Jetco Printing the way Michael Corleone moved through the restaurant after killing Sollozzo and McCluskey: he didn't make eye contact but he didn't look away, he moved quickly but he didn't run. The truth was, of course, that he had no business whatsoever in that end of Jetco, but he hated the goddamn job enough to wish someone said something to him just so he could say something back, vent a little, unleash some of that smart-ass wit of his. So far, no one had, and he was able to walk those alien corridors, past those freakish cubicles, without trouble, searching for sweet lovely Jess.

It took a few weeks before she started to smile at him when he passed. She made good eye contact, but he never said anything to her, he was not that sort. His wandering over to her section of the building was not part of some deliberate plan, he was simply following his legs. He felt *pulled* to her side of the company, as if drawn by a magnet. Most of the time he had no idea at all what he was doing, would just up and leave his post... maybe, if he was in the mood, give his boss a small smile before heading down the hallway. Everyone thought he had urinary troubles. If anyone asked him he'd tell them he had VD, then they'd never ask him again.

Eventually she'd spoken to him, and her voice was exactly as he had pictured it, if a bit huskier, smokier, sexier:

"How are you doing?" she asked. It was a throwaway question, of course, the sort of thing often said in passing, but combined with her direct, rather unnerving eye contact it seemed to him like flirting... possibly... maybe....

"Good," he answered, turning back to look at her as she passed, in the process giving her what he felt was a nice friendly smile. "And you?"

"Good," she said, with what he thought was a sassy wave of the hair and a perk of khaki-covered butt. She continued down the hall, and though he watched her she never looked back. She slipped around a corner and was gone.

Maybe she was smart and knew what he was up to... even if he himself didn't. And if he thought about it, it seemed

74

she was always in the halls when he went down there. Was it possible she herself was up to the same thing... whatever it was?

He contemplated this possibility as they drove, and the idea actually unnerved him. He didn't need that, he was unnerved enough as it was this year, and this trip was supposed to be an escape, remember?

It was an election year, the wonderful peaceful unexciting year 2000, sure to go down in history as the year when everyone of a certain age realized they'd been lied to since birth: no one was driving hover-craft, vacationing in space, or working twenty-hour weeks. In fact, son of a bitch, the work week was longer than before. Nothing they'd been told about the future had come to pass, and nothing was different. 2000 was 1980 was 1970 was 1940. The only differences were the hairstyles.

They spotted a NADER FOR PRESIDENT sign in a yard on the way up North.

Jonah thought a moment. "Who do you support? In this election, I mean."

Hawkins frowned thoughtfully and shifted himself in his seat. His Cherokee was humming along quite nicely down Highway 41, passing all those monotonous towns that form the backbone of the country. Ah yes, Oshkosh, Appleton, the legendary twins Neenah-Menasha, famed in song and story.

"I don't know," he said. "What's the difference, really? Aren't they all the same?"

Jonah looked out at the unwinding highway. Cars would go past with BUSH/CHENEY stickers, or GORE/LEIBERMAN.

"What about you?" Hawkins asked. "I assume you're not a Bush man." He was smiling, he knew the answer.

"I believe you should always vote for the smartest person," Jonah said. "Barring that, I believe as Aldo Leopold believed: in wilderness is the preservation of the soul. I know what we *don't* need: oil men. When fucks like Bush and Cheney look at a spot of wilderness they get hard thinking about drilling there... maybe there's a phallic-envy sort of thing here I might have to explore later. Small dicks, big oil drills."

Hawkins nodded approvingly. Then, a moment later, after a respectable pause, he said: "The actual quote, though, is 'In wilderness is the preservation of the world.'"

"Oh."

"And it was Thoreau."

75

"Oh Christ, old man, do you always have to know everything?"

"I can't help it, Sonny boy. It's the product of accumulated years of wisdom. Maybe some day you'll get there."

The highway carried them up and up, ever further, ever closer to the primordial forest.

*

The Nicolet National Forest unfolds either gradually or violently, depending on which angle you approach it from and your degree of sensitivity to such things: they approached it from the South, via the Menominee Indian Reservation, where the introduction to the Forest was harsh, abrupt. They had left the cliché cornfields of Wisconsin long ago, but the going had been straight and flat enough until just past Shawano, when they had found themselves in an entirely different landscape; indeed, the route along the Wolf River was curving and, though not hilly, entirely full of jagged corners of earth, these latter visible when the trees pulled back along the river and they were afforded a gorgeous view of what looked, at first glance, to be a virgin landscape, pure river-country, the sort of scene that might have greeted fur trappers, traders, assorted outlaws, a sparkling expanse of water broken here and there by the soft curves of rocks and the crumbling, rough land the river had to wind around. At the first of these openings they had seen the black shape of a large bird flying downriver, briefly glimpsed above the treeline. Hawkins insisted it had been a golden eagle, Jonah maintained it was a red-tail hawk. They were both wrong: it was just a super-sized average American crow, made unnaturally hefty by the readily available garbage of the nearby Indians. This was still civilization here, despite its wild appearance. A month or two earlier and that river would have been burdened by a mass transit of river-running folk, rafts stuffed with screaming idiots, kayaks piloted by drunks. If they had stopped and gone down to the river's edge they would have seen the remnants of these mysterious people: an assortment of soda cans and broken kayak paddles discarded along the way. Poor, sad, majestic Wolf River, abused by those who love her. Well, that season was over, and the only humans in sight were Hawkins and Jonah, neither of whom were interested in dipping one single toe into the river's waters. They loved her, too, the

76

way a peasant should love a royal lady: from a distance, respectably.

On the opposite side of the narrow, winding road sat a forest of tall pines, neither of which the two men could name. Hawkins called them lodge pole pine, Jonah just shrugged.

"I thought you knew all that stuff," Hawkins said.

"I know absolutely nothing about flora. I never took one single botany class."

"Now, that surprises me. I would have thought botany was right up your alley."

Jonah shook his head and made a look of distaste. "Lettuce," he mumbled.

"Lettuce pray," Hawkins added, then: "Have you ever thought of going back for more biology classes?"

"For what?"

"I don't know. Teach?"

"Nah. I don't think I'd be a good teacher. A teacher has to care." He shivered. "All those kids... those lousy insubordinate spoiled-rotten kids."

Hawkins laughed. "You have a point there."

Jonah looked over at him and smiled. He let about a quarter-mile go before he said: "Thank you."

"For what?"

"For not telling me I should go back to school and get my life in order and get a real job and grow up and... you know, all that sort of shit."

Hawkins shifted in his seat and grimaced, made a deep guttural sound of disapproval. "I gave up on advice, taking or giving."

Jonah smiled again. "That's what I like about you."

*

The tent was up and late afternoon was settling peacefully, quietly, around the lake. Their campsite was high on a hill that sloped down to the water and which gave a panoramic view to the south-east, so that the tent would warm up nicely come morning. They had scraped up a fire-pit, ringed it with rocks purloined from the surrounding area, and were sitting on lawn chairs, a celebratory Central Waters Ouisconsing Red Ale in hand. The forest around them was clinging to shadow already, though the western sky was ablaze

77

with orange and red. The silence of the lake was broken only by the sound of scampering chipmunks, and then only rarely.

"Well... what do we do now?" Jonah asked.

Hawkins sighed peacefully, leaning back in his chair. He was the sort of man who belonged in such surroundings: rough, wrinkled, husky in the shoulders, a slight but well-earned gut, a great Hemingway-esque beard, icy blue eyes, all serving to make the sort of handsome American guy men want to be friends with and women want to cuddle. He was, though, the last of a dying breed, a coarse man, strong, adaptable, handy, at home in a nylon tent, comfortable breathing woodsmoke and soot, a man unalloyed and rugged, the sort who would have been a lumberjack once, or a miner, a river-guide... and yet, a man not uncomfortable with the world of literature and art, refined of mind if not body and spirit, a man who could fix your broken back stoop one moment and then discuss the finer points of Voltaire and Degas the next. He had even tried his hands at sculpting once upon a time, though he claimed to have quickly discovered he had no talent for it. Could I see some of your work? Jonah had asked him on many occasions, but the older man shook his head and said he didn't have any, he'd lost it all years ago in a fire. Like an idiot I chose materials that were easy to burn: wood, plaster, whatever. Poof. I'm sorry my young friend, it's no longer of this earth.

Jonah, thinking of this now, looked out over the lake below them and said: "You know what you should do...?"

Hawkins sighed. "I don't give you advice but you can give it to me?"

"Yes. You should take up sculpting again."

"No... no, Jonah, I'll tell you: honestly, no bullshit, I enjoyed the process but I really had no skill. Loving something is one thing, being good at it is quite another." He tipped back his bottle, finished it, and set the empty on the ground. "What do we do now?"

"You wanna hit the lake?"

Hawkins examined the western sky. "We're losing light, aren't we?"

"Well, that's one way to look at it."

"What's the other?"

Jonah finished off his own beer and smiled at his friend.

"We're gaining darkness," he said.

*

The lake had the general shape of the ball pad of a dog's paw, wider at its southern end, tapering to the north, with various little inlets here and there along its other shores. They carried the canoe from the Jeep, down the hill, and set it at last, with relief, into the easy and calm water. There was a tiny beach here, where others had probably set their own boats. It was a secluded and isolated lake, and though neither Hawkins nor Jonah were naïve enough to believe they were the only people who ever visited it, it was still possible to imagine such a thing, with the silence pervasive, the woods around them thick and wild, no car horns in the distance, no hum of a highway, no radios thumping... only the very rare domestic canine barking from some primitive home a few miles off, a house trailer, a shack, maybe even another campsite. It was entirely possible to enter into a fantasy in which you were early woodsmen or trappers, living far from the circles of other men, isolated from civilization, needing nothing but that which could be found in the woods and fields. That is, until the Coleman's glow became too strong, or the beer ran out, or the shining silver dot moving across the sky was revealed to be not a falling star but a 747 headed East. Mankind needs wilderness for such fantasies, both men would agree, and though this was hardly *wilderness* by technical standards it would do for a few days away from work, subdivisions, CNN, crime.

On this day, once the canoe was in the water, Hawkins and Jonah stood before the lake, neither speaking for a long time, each seeking their own lost totems in the scene before them: Hawkins looked hard for an eagle or two in the sky, Jonah searched for turtles basking in the last remnants of October sun. Minutes passed and neither of them saw anything, just a lovely rise and fall of forest on the other side of the lake, the pointed tops of fir trees, the straight, defiant rise of a birch here and there, white as a ghost among their darker brethren. At last Hawkins gestured to the canoe.

"Shall we?" he said, softly.

They climbed in and paddled out, breaking the smooth surface of the lake with a steady and quiet rhythm, leaving a wake that sent dissipating waves into the blue-blackness of the water.

79

*

Evening. The fire roared and spat, the coals below pulsed hypnotically, a gentle line of smoke rose undisturbed to the starry sky.

"How's work?" Hawkins asked. They hadn't spoken for some time, each staring into the flames, dreaming, thinking. He asked this question mindlessly, perhaps not even knowing he spoke at all.

"Same," Jonah said, not taking his eyes from the arcing, dancing flames. They had eaten already, he and Hawkins, and they were slow, satisfied, dreamy. The woods around them were quiet and dark, growing darker with each snap and crackle of the fire.

A moment later: "Sucks, you mean."

"Yeah."

Hawkins reached out with a thumb-thick branch and poked at the fire, turned over a log, sent sparks into the air, then settled back in his chair with a sigh.

"You still looking for another?"

"Always." Sap was boiling out of one log, turning instantly to froth and then steam, sizzling into vapor.

Hawkins nodded. A few minutes later he shifted in his seat and smiled, leaned forward a bit excitedly and looked over at Jonah.

"You know what I'd like to do?" he asked. His face was glowing, shining in the campfire light. "I've always wanted to start my own bookstore. Bookstore slash café, something like that. Not a chain, not anything big, just a little place, my own place, selling my kind of books for my kind of people."

Jonah took the bait: "What kind of books are those?"

"Good kind." His smile broadened. "Books that mean something, books that touch people, books that shake people up, make them feel and think and see. Is that too much to ask?"

"Are you sure other people want those kinds of books?"

"No." Pause. "Fuck 'em if they don't, the store's for me."

"Never took many business classes, did ya Hawkins?"

Hawkins just smiled and continued to stare into the fire. There is perhaps no finer hobby a man can have than to sit and stare into a good fire, no greater expression of one's humanity,

80

no other animal ever sitting to study flames in such a way, not even the domestic dog, which will lie sleepily before such a fire but which shows little inclination or need to sit back and watch the flames devour log after log. Life is full of its assorted pleasures, but none are as complete, as mysterious, as utterly without exterior *meaning*, than staring into the wonders of a campfire. Has to be a campfire, too: fireplaces offer their own pleasures, yes, but they are in the end facsimiles of campfires, civilized cousins twice removed, not mockeries but mimics. And a gas fireplace is pure travesty.

Small wonder that aboriginal peoples all over the world have held fire as sacred, that they dance around them in ceremony and celebration. Fire *is* magic, swirling and growing as if alive, able to transfix the mind of a human, revealing secrets in the eddies and tongues of orange and yellow as they arc and spit. Fire consumes, not only wood but flesh, and by consuming releases the spirit. Jonah thought of his father, cremated and placed in a box, the box then buried. He wondered what the point of that had been. Cremated *then* buried. Pointless.

"What do you think, Hawkins," he said, "do you want to be buried or cremated?"

Hawkins laughed. "Do I look like I need either?"

"More so than me, old man."

Hawkins shifted in his chair, thought long and hard about the question. "I guess cremated, if I have a choice. I guess I should put that in a will or something in case I drop dead and some asshole buries me. Stuffs me first and buries me in some cemetery." He shivered. "Actually, what I'd like is to die somewhere like this, out in the forest, and never be found. The coyotes and raccoons and bobcats can eat me."

Jonah nodded. "We should have little sections of forest set aside just for that, to lay out the dead, send them back to the earth, keep the cycle going."

"The Christians and Jews would never go for it," Hawkins said.

"Fuck 'em."

"Have they ever come up with a way to reconcile cremation with that, what's it called, the *rapture*, or whatever? You know, where the dead rise and the holy go to heaven."

"No clue."

Hawkins nodded. "I used to know more about those sorts of things. I got into studying the religions of the world out of... I guess, more out of historical interest than in actually thinking any of it was true. There are some interesting stories in that stuff, and of course everything either comments on or reflects Judeo-Christian thought and imagery. When I was getting into art fairly seriously I noticed how much that sort of thing influences people. I mean, the symbolism is everywhere: snakes, water, wine, crucifixion, rebirth, all that. I didn't exactly put it in my own works but I wanted to know about it so I could read it in other people's. Not that I ever became an expert or anything... I've forgotten most of it, as you can tell."

"I was raised a Catholic," Jonah said. "Kicking it was like kicking heroin."

"Do you have any religious beliefs?"

Jonah shrugged. "I believe in many things religiously. Does that count?" He gestured for Hawkins to throw him the marshmallows, which Hawkins promptly did, with a daring throw right over the center of the fire, the bag just inches from the highest flames. Jonah took his own stick, which had also been lying at his feet like a patient dog, and speared his mallow. He tried a different tactic from Hawkins: whereas the older man had tried for a subtle attack, slowly browning the marshmallow, Jonah went right for the flames, crisping the damn thing.

"Jonah," Hawkins said, with that tone he took before imparting wisdom, "I don't think that's the way a true mountain man would do it."

Jonah smiled as he blew the marshmallow out and pulled its crisp shell from the stick, leaving the tender, melting viscera behind. "No? And how exactly did mountain men cook their marshmallows?"

Hawkins held up his own. "Like this."

"I see." Jonah returned the stick's end to the flames, frying off the remaining marshmallow afterbirth. "Look around, old man, do you see any goddamn mountain?"

They fell into respectable silence again, for maybe a good fifteen minutes. Hawkins added a few more logs to the fire, then looked skyward, squinting at the stars there.

"Pegasus," he said.

Jonah looked up too. Their campsite was sitting under trees but there was a broad opening in the little canopy, permitting a view of the sky that was lovely and deep.

"And Cygnus."

"Did you study astronomy?"

82

"Not really. If that tree wasn't there we might see Sculptor."

"You made that up. Sculptor...."

"I'm serious. It's a constellation."

Jonah shook his head and started to point out his own favorite constellations: "Look, Old Bastard. Lying Fuck. *Dirty* Lying Fuck. And gee, I think I can just make out Pathologic, the god of truth...."

"Can you see Asshole?"

Jonah laughed. "I certainly don't see *Sculptor*...."

"You look it up in a book sometime," Hawkins said, laughing. "Go to a library sometime, make yourself useful. Get your nose out of whatever it is you read."

"I'll go to Hawkins's New and Used Books That Mean Something. Will I get a discount?"

"No."

"I'll have to steal one, then."

Hawkins sighed. "Pass me the marshmallows, boy, and keep your mouth shut."

"Respect my elders?"

"Yes."

Jonah threw the bag to him, choosing to go around the fire rather than over it, and Hawkins had to reach out to grab it from the air like a football player retrieving a badly-thrown ball.

Jonah smiled. "Hey, do you want a beer?"

"I shouldn't." Another poor marshmallow was sacrificed to the stick. "But sure."

*

Later that night, lying in the tent, each in their respective mummy bags, smelling that familiar and comforting odor of nylon and cotton and down, feeling the cold night on their faces, listening to the dying fire snap and pop its last few breaths, hearing as well the whisper of a rising breeze through the treetops, hearing and feeling everywhere around them the thick and total presence of a forest night, they wished for each other good sleep and pleasant dreams. Minds buzzed and lulled by beer and cold air and the drone of the woods, they each doubted they would dream at all. There was nothing around them for miles but woods and swamp and field. Back in civilization, wherever that was, there were things to worry and

83

think about. Here, deep in the heart of the Nicolet, there was nothing.

*

There was a rising, tremulous, high-pitched, urgent howl, followed by a series of equally urgent yips and yaps, not too far off, perhaps fifty to a hundred yards to their right. Hawkins's hand came out and slapped Jonah's sleeping bag.

"You hear that?" he asked. There was excitement in his voice, genuine and childlike.

Jonah, only half-pulled from a young sleep, said:

"Coyote."

Hawkins whispered: "He's close…."

"He's separated from the pack. Listen, maybe you can hear them…."

They lay listening for a long time but heard nothing. After a while sleep took them over again.

*

Much later, the night wind having died off, nothing but stillness in the forest, the calls of the pack finally came, far to the left now, the other side of the lake. Happy yips and howls, echoing over the water and through the trees, ghostly in their distant hollowness but joyful and jubilant in their rhythm. Their long-lost brother was home.

*

Morning. They could feel it before they saw it, a gently rising warmth shaking off the coolness of night, making their feet hot, their bodies uncomfortable. Hawkins woke first, rising and exiting the tent to start breakfast. Jonah heard him as he lit the Coleman stove, but he decided to lay there a little longer. He listened to the sound of morning birdsong and loved its bright, joyful optimism. He could tell there was a bright sun rising, and by the time he rose from his own mummy bag it was to greet a warm day flush with energy.

"Morning," Hawkins said. The hobo coffee was on the stove, steaming. The other burner held a frying pan in which butter was melting. "Hungry?"

"Absolutely. What'd you kill for us this morning?"

84

Hawkins held up a box. "Pre-made Aunt Jemima pancake mix. It was quite a battle. Epic."

"I bet."

"Coffee's almost done."

"Good." He wandered off into the woods to piss, returning only after he had watched a gray jay fluttering in the trees just a few feet away. When he had been a child his father had called the bird a Whiskey Jack. Others called it a Canada Jay, but whatever the name it was a strange bird for such wild woods: tame, brave, confidently coming to campsites to rob food from tables and plates, as if it felt it was owed something by the invasive humans. Perhaps it was right.

"Pretty nice show last night," Hawkins said when he came back.

"The coyotes?"

"Yeah. I love that sound."

Jonah nodded, poured himself a cup of joe, sat down by the dead fire.

"Lonely, haunting, sad," Hawkins was saying, mostly to himself, as he prepared the first of the pancakes, adding water to the plastic bottle of mix and shaking it, then finally pouring some into the pan, where it sizzled nicely, browning at the edges, sending a teasing smell to Jonah.

"So what's the plan?" Hawkins asked.

"Eat and hit the lake."

And that's what they did.

*

They knifed through the calm water, headed to the far side, taking roughly the same path they had taken the day before, tracing the shore easily. This day was brighter, the new sun shimmering off the tops of the pines that lined the lake, making their tips look emerald, each needle seeming to stand out in sharp relief from the one next to it.

They spoke little as they rowed, Jonah in stern, Hawkins at the bow. A pileated woodpecker tapped at a tree somewhere to their right, not a drumming but loud nonetheless, like someone cutting into a trunk. A few minutes later the bird called out and flew straight over them, making quickly for the far shore. All around them other birds sang, blue-jays and cardinals and chickadees. Fish broke the surface, grabbing morning meals of water-striders and flies. Painted turtles basked on logs that lay half-sunken against the shoreline, and when the canoe glided too close they slipped clumsily down into the water, leaving concentric wakes and scratched-up logs as tell-tale signs of their presence.

They rowed on to the very farthest end of the lake. When they had first come to this place the year before they had both been surprised to stand near such a big body of water and not see a single house or cabin on its shores. They figured they were seeing things. Yesterday, taking the canoe around, they had felt certain that they would spot a domicile of some sort, half-hidden in some bushes, or carefully concealed high on the hills that overlooked it, but there had been nothing. Just forest. Quite unusual in this unfortunate day and age. Nothing lived here but wildlife.

As if on cue a whitetail bolted to their left, along the side of a sparsely-wooded hill, moving quickly, gracefully, jumping deadfall and maneuvering around stumps. Hawkins and Jonah watched it for a time, then looked to see what had spooked it.

"Was it us?" Jonah asked.

"Shhh," Hawkins said, holding up one hand. They listened, watched, heard and saw nothing. Hawkins turned sideways to glance back at Jonah. "We're not wanted here, apparently."

They continued, now about two hundred yards from the far shore. The land that surrounded this lake was a mixture of types, and a good example of that offered by the whole of the Nicolet itself. Where their camp was set up was an open, second-growth deciduous forest, all brush and thin-trunked trees. Further north-west of there the ground sloped to swamp, a place of rotting logs and moss. The other direction was steeper, the beginnings of the hill that deer had run across, this place more open than where the tent was, much less shrubby, the trees slightly larger. The other side of the lake mirrored this, yet with more shrubs and thicker trees, probably impassable to any but the most determined humans. From there the ground on either side of the lake sloped to swamp (and, on the north-side, the little slow-moving stream that fed the lake) before rising again to become a strange, dense, dark forest of solid ground and trees with exposed roots, a sort of primordial place where it was possible to imagine strange creatures living and dying, mythic beasts and forest legends. Both men were subconsciously headed to this place, each possessing an

86

unspoken desire to hike and investigate the shadows there. But first....

"Look," Hawkins said suddenly. He pointed across the lake, where two dark shapes were moving in the water.

"Loons," Jonah said. It was hard to see them, but what else could they be?

They watched for a time, moving the little boat slowly in that direction. A moment later the two shapes dove.

"They're fishing."

They reappeared a good fifty yards to the right. Hawkins and Jonah paddled stronger now, wishing to see the birds.

As they drew closer, though, they could hear an odd sound, like a woman taking quick sharp breaths during labor. The sound echoed over the lake, eerie and disorienting, and though Jonah's imagination was capable of running on overdrive at the drop of a hat, it was nearly impossible to think fantastical thoughts in such a setting: here, under the brilliant blaze of a morning sun, in the crystal clarity of a waking forest, there was only reality, immediate and omnipresent. Still, he'd never heard a sound like that before.

They came closer to the loons, and as they did Hawkins reached into his vest pocket. He was wearing one of those photographer vests, the sort with myriad pockets for film and lenses, and Jonah was pleasantly surprised to see him fish forth a pair of binoculars.

Hawkins glassed the lake for a few minutes, then pronounced:

"Those aren't loons."

"No?"

Hawkins handed the glasses back and Jonah peered through them. The creatures he saw were round of head, beady of eyes, their fur slicked and gleaming with water.

Otters.

Jonah smiled brightly. Not only otters, but the first otters he'd ever seen. A pleasant warm feeling rose through him and he couldn't stop smiling.

"Let's get closer," Hawkins said. They waited until the animals dove before paddling, stopping as soon as the otters broke the surface again. The third time they did this another otter had appeared, all three playing like children. When they dove the humans paddled madly... of course, the animals always surfaced far from them, most likely seeing the bottom of

87

the canoe and hearing the rushed paddling through the murk of the lake. Nevertheless, Hawkins and Jonah continued to paddle in such a way, thinking they had a chance to outwit the critters. They were determined, seeing the situation as a challenge. Unfortunately, the otters were determined as well, seeing the situation as a good opportunity to play... as if they needed one, and as if they even cared about the humans at all. They swam proverbial rings (literally, in this case) around the canoe.

Hawkins and Jonah did not speak for nearly a half-hour, just sat there watching the otters, listening to that odd nasal breathing they did. Jonah assumed they were venting any water they might have inadvertently taken into their noses, but he was unsure. It could have been a defense of some sort, an attempt to scare off the humans. The sound echoed hollowly around the lake, adding to the atmosphere of wildness that permeated the area.

It was Hawkins who spoke at the end of the half-hour. He said one word: "Eagles."

Jonah looked up. Sure enough, two eagles soared directly overhead, in concentric circles, their white heads standing out clearly in the glow of the sun.

Awesome, Jonah thought. Magical. He and Hawkins handed the binoculars back and forth, falling silent for another half-hour, just admiring the beauty of the great birds as they flew and the otters as they swam. Neither group of animals inhabited a realm mankind could ever truly know, and that was the part that was magic.

*

After they lost site of both the eagles and the otters they slowly paddled over to the shore. They made a very clumsy landing: Jonah was ostensibly the one doing the steering but he failed miserably, sending them straight into the half-sunken tree trunk they had been meaning to come up alongside.

"You'd never make it as an Indian scout," Hawkins chided him.

"My name would be Canoes For Shit."

This cracked Hawkins up. He nearly fell into the lake as he climbed out of the canoe. He looked back at Jonah with eyes squinted, face red.

Once Jonah was out of the boat they pulled it up onto dry land, securing it there with nothing more than its own weight, each hoping it didn't somehow find its way back out to the lake. The walk back to their campsite was not an overly long one, but there was all that marsh and upland to bushwhack through.

This shore was dense with trees, their roots exposed from years of erosion. The ground was odd, nearly hollow, with little caves under those roots where animals could hide. Outward, away from the lake, the trees grew thick and the shadows dark, like a primeval forest full of monsters. To look into such a woods was to inhabit a fairy tale. Each man stood for a time to study this area, aware of that ancient feeling, that sense of time caught and held. Then, slowly, carefully, they started down a natural path that ran along the lake. This path was the result of compacted earth, and made its way along a hill that overlooked the water five feet below. Both men tripped now and then and were told to be careful by the other. Occasionally Hawkins would chuckle and say: "Canoes For Shit...."

There was no sound here, save the very soft rush of the lake lapping on the shore. No birds sang. No small mammals rustled the leaves or bushes. The only animals stirring were these two bipeds here, these naked apes, thundering along over this hollow ground. Sacred ground? Not the sort of place for a burial site, but it certainly had an atmosphere of death, an ambience of the dead. Perhaps a place outcasts were sent to live out their lives and die alone. Yes, there was very much that feeling, as if this was indeed a land of pariahs, exiles. They wouldn't have had decent burials, either, not in this ground, swampy away from the lake and hollow alongside it. They would have been left as they had lived, alone and unloved. The forest animals would have come to take final care of them.

Jonah was letting his imagination run wild with this idea, picturing all the various reasons an Indian might have been exiled from his tribe to live in this haunted, dark place: forbidden love, broken protocol, alternative views of life, anti-social behavior. He wondered if he himself would have been cast out from a tribe, and whether in the end such an exiling would have been a good or bad thing. Society offers only so much, after all. Community is one thing, to live free and wild, at liberty to be yourself without the need to conform to the standards of others, well that's quite another. He was about to

89

ask Hawkins what his views on the subject were when something caught his eye.

It was an animal carcass, so thin and desiccated it was nearly impossible to identify... but the fur was unmistakably canine, coarse and heavy and gray with black tips.

"Coyote," Jonah said when Hawkins came up.

Hawkins nodded. They stared down at it for some time, then Jonah knelt and began feeling the corpse.

"What are you doing?" Hawkins asked. He sounded shocked.

Jonah ignored him, concentrating on feeling through the fur to the flesh and bone beneath, moving the legs as much as was possible, then finding the head and neck and studying the vertebrate, the way it moved and felt, and then tracing the coyote's head. When he didn't feel anything he put his face close to the animal and squinted down at it, searching its fur, its teeth.

"What are you doing?" Hawkins asked. "Get your hands off that!"

Jonah said nothing, just shook his head and then carefully flipped the animal. It was nearly mummified, yet not so stiff as he would have assumed. This other side of the animal was flat, deformed by the ground. He examined it as he had the other, then sat back and shook his head.

"What are you looking for?" Hawkins asked.

"Bullet holes."

"You think someone might have shot it? Out here?"

Jonah stood up and looked around. No, not likely: this was too wild, too secluded. There were no farms or homes nearby, certainly none close enough to make the animal a problem. Yet still, there were always assholes, some fucks out in a boat, armed with shotguns and rifles, shooting indiscriminately at trees and birds and whatever else crossed their path. Jonah had seen enough empty shells on forest paths to know this is how some people acted. This was how some people liked to "enjoy" nature.

"No," he said, shaking his head. "No, she died of natural causes, I'd guess. I couldn't feel any trauma."

Hawkins reached one foot out and pushed at the dead animal. "All dried out, hey? Why do you think nothing ate it?"

Jonah looked down. "Oh, something's eating it, all right. Bacteria. Insects."

"Wouldn't other coyotes eat it?"

"You would think...." He looked up at the forest around them, dark and silent, all those captive shadows, like bits of night caught and enslaved. And the trees, lined with moss and dark with moisture. And the dark caves under their roots where anything might hide.

"Let's go," he said.

They walked on.

*

No matter how much Jonah washed his hands, using the bottled water and anti-bacterial soap Hawkins had brought, the old man wouldn't let him touch anything related to that evening's food once they got back to the campsite.

"I'm cooking," he said. "Again. Was that your plan, to cop a feel on some disgusting dead animal so you wouldn't have to do any work?"

"No. But it's a good idea, I'll have to remember it for next time."

He was instead given the job of starting that evening's fire. He first sorted out various sizes of kindling, then laid out a pile of the smallest in the fire-pit, adding progressively larger sizes when the first were lit. Soon he had healthy flames going, and he was able to sit back and relax a moment, proud of this accomplishment.

"Want a beer?" Hawkins asked now as he was hunched over the cooler.

"Sure."

Hawkins handed him one, then went back to prepping supper. The man worked expertly in this environment. It suited him perfectly, he being a rough man, a lover of simple amenities, a man comfortable in the wild. Jonah was able to study him for a few minutes, and he wondered, not for the first time, what the details of the man's life were. Hawkins rarely spoke at length about his past, a fact that made most people even more curious. Jonah had known this man for some time now and yet really knew very little about him at all. He suspected, though, that there was quite a bit to know, if only he could be given the chance. He knew Hawkins came from California, and had lived for a time in Canada and the Southwest, but that was all. There had been wives, but he didn't know how many. And that one son, rarely mentioned.

And at fifty-something, there had to have been an assortment of interesting jobs.

"Tell me about your life," Jonah said, opting for a direct approach as he bent to feed the fire. He did it more as a joke, to annoy the old man, and it worked:

"I'll pass."

"Oh come on, old man...."

"It's not that interesting, it really isn't. I'm boring."

"Well, I know *that*, but I want to hear some details. You're still a mystery to me."

"That's the way I like it."

Jonah smiled and nodded. Once he had set a larger log to flame he sat back again, sipped his beer, examined his friend. Hawkins was, really, his only friend. His only *true* friend, anyway, the only person he could be honest with, the only person with whom he would really have wanted to share such a place as this. He imagined being here, near this glorious lake in the middle of this forest, with any of his coworkers... and he shuddered. Some of those guys would have wanted (claimed they *needed*) a radio, and Jonah would have had to strangle them in their sleep. Fucking radio. Jesus.

For some reason this made him think of Jess, this girl he had a crush on. A crush? Who knows, maybe it was love. He wondered how she would do up here, in the middle of the forest. Because he didn't know her yet he was free to indulge in a perfect fantasy, she not yet being clouded by the disappointments of reality: he imagined her fitting in quite well here, at home with the dirt and trees, comforted by the sound of coyotes in the night, lulled by the pop and snap of a good fire. He imagined her being everything he would have wanted in a camping companion. Hawkins was all right, yes, but with Jess there was the possibility of good wholesome lovemaking, hot bare skin against the coolness of a sleeping bag. He smiled at the thought, debated telling Hawkins about her and decided not to. Not yet. He sat there watching the older man prep that night's supper: chicken sautéed in a sauce of Hawkins's own creation, potatoes, various veggies. When the fire was ready and there were suitable coals he laid a grill across the heat and started cooking, sending a delicious and intoxicating smell out to the trees.

They ate in relative silence. When a Whiskey Jack visited them Hawkins tossed him a few bits of carrot, like the bird was a welcome old friend. And he was, of course.

Gradually, beautifully, peacefully, evening slipped into night.

*

"Jonah, what's your take on life?"

"You mean, in general?"

"Yeah."

"The meaning of life?"

Hawkins shrugged. He was quite visible in the glow of the healthy fire, his skin painted a warm yellow by the flames, clearly standing out against the black forest behind him.

"Huh…" Jonah thought about that as he stared into the fire, watching sap boil out of a fresh log. Finally he said: "I think I'll have to defer to you on that one. You know, all that age must have brought some wisdom."

"Age brings no more wisdom than anything else. What it *does* bring is knowing how to cover your ass."

"That's wisdom."

"I suppose."

Jonah studied Hawkins, thought he detected more than a trace of melancholy in him. He thought about asking him if he was all right but instead looked back at the fire and watched the sap steam and roil over itself, as if in agony, turning to steam just as the wood it came from turned slowly to coal and ash. Nothing ever goes away, the scientists will tell you, it just changes form. The essence of everything is always present, everything that ever was is still here. Some call it the cycle of life, others prefer the more analytical, less spiritual-sounding term recycle, but it means the same in the end. You cannot be rid of something entirely, not even fire can render something nonexistent. The essence remains. The carbon goes back to the earth, where it came from.

He thought about saying some of this to Hawkins, knowing the man was aware of the idea, of course, but thinking perhaps it sounded profound enough to maybe approach something like the meaning of life, but decided against it. He would let the topic fade away. The idea that there was a meaning of life was absurd to him, not a topic he was interested in. Certainly someone might see in the rather simple thought stated above the beginnings of a philosophy of life, but it was, in the end, just a fact that could be made to *sound* profound if spoken in the right way, if the speaker used the right words.

93

Yes, nothing can ever go away, the essence of everything remains right here on the planet, but there was nothing of a Universal Truth to the idea. It was science. Nothing ever goes away, right. Just like every action has a reaction. Just like an object in motion tends to remain in motion unless acted upon by an outside force. Just like what goes up must come down. These were facts, simple and plain. Certainly if there was indeed a meaning of life it would be contained in something more complex, deeper, more poetic. This was a big *if*, though: Jonah doubted there was one statement that could sum everything up.

He looked across the fire to see Hawkins staring back at him.

"You look deep in thought," the older man said.

Jonah thought again of telling Hawkins about the girl, but what was there to tell? Nothing yet. It was just a crush.

Hawkins tossed another log on the fire, pushed it around to situate it properly, then leaned back with a sigh.

"Yes sirree, young Mr. Swain, this here is what life is all about, in my book. A good fire, the taste of meat and beer on the tongue, and good conversation." He paused. "Well, *okay* conversation."

"I thought you didn't have a meaning of life?"

"I never said that. I said age doesn't bring wisdom. And it doesn't, in this case: I learned that camping is what life is all about when I was a teenager. I learned you have to get out and away now and then to clear your head of all the bullshit life brings. This sort of thing cleanses the soul, if there is such a thing. Clear air, a lake nearby, the smell of smoke, the dark and silent forest around you, all of it... a man needs that."

"*Mankind* needs it," Jonah added. "And maybe when people realize that they'll stop bulldozing it under."

"Maybe," agreed Hawkins. "Doubtful, though. People are stupid."

"You're a pessimist."

"Just because everything always turns out bad doesn't mean I'm a pessimist."

Jonah poked at the fire with his own stick, each man having one at their side for such a purpose. The arranging and rearranging of campfires is a ritualistic process, a religion all its own.

"The day they try to develop this area here," he said, "is the day I buy a gun."

94

"You know, I always took you for an eco-terrorist."

Jonah shrugged. "We shouldn't speak about such things. The woods have ears." He paused for suitable mysterious effect. "But we prefer the term eco-warrior. The only people who should be terrorized are the accountants."

Hawkins smiled. "If Bush wins, you'll have plenty of opportunities for sabotage. That fucker will do everything he can to help his oil buddies."

Jonah nodded.

"Some people just don't understand," Hawkins continued. "They think anything that makes more money is inherently good, and damn the consequences."

"Growth for the sake of growth is the ideology of the cancer cell," Jonah said. "Edward Abbey."

Hawkins nodded. "All progress means war with Society. George Bernard Shaw."

"Touch this land and I will fuck you up. George Washington."

"I don't think so."

"Martha Washington?"

Another period of silence followed, each man staring deeply into the roiling swirling flames, the pulsing coals, the hypnotic rise of white smoke that sat angry and magical before them. What is it in this destruction of wood, this creation of fire and heat, that fascinates? Power, possibly. The controller of fire is the controller of life. There are primal things at work here, as Hawkins had said. Mysteries and meanings ancient and wise. It is possible to sit before a fire and communicate without speaking… or, more precisely, to lose the *need* for speaking, to talk via the gentle prodding of coals, the introduction of a fresh log, the tapping of a smoldering branch and the corresponding arc of ashes to the night sky.

"Jonah," Hawkins said after a while. "Where do you see yourself in five years?"

"Right here."

"Ten years."

"Right here."

Hawkins smiled as he stared at the fire, and Jonah risked a glance in his direction, sensing that there was something he wanted to say. There was a definite look on the man's face of something being withheld.

"Out with it," Jonah said.

Hawkins looked up. "Out with what?"

95

"Whatever it is you want to say or ask."

Hawkins shrugged, picked up his stick and prodded the fire. "Nothing."

"Something. Spill it."

Hawkins took in a deep breath, then shrugged and shifted in his little chair. "I was just thinking about what I would do if I was a young man your age."

"And?"

"And I think I'd... well, I don't know. I'd like to say I'd hit the road while I still had no connections, no ties anywhere, but maybe I'd just do the same thing I did."

"Which was?"

"Settle down with a good woman and live in one place for a time, get to know the people, get to know the landscape."

"So that's what you did. And where did this settling phase in Hawkins's life take place?"

"A few places, actually. Most of my life was settling of some sort. California, Arizona..." He shrugged. "This is a boring topic. Let's talk about something manly. Beer. Women." In the red and yellow light of the fire he looked suddenly embarrassed, uncomfortable.

"Sure. How about beer-drinking women?"

Hawkins smiled but fell silent for a long time. After a few minutes he leaned over and placed two new logs in the flames, good fat thick segments of a birch felled not too far from the campsite. Knocking down healthy trees was illegal in the Nicolet, a fact Hawkins countered by saying the tree wasn't healthy, was in fact suffering from depression. He had placed his ear to the trunk, listened, and then nodded. Yep, depressed. And I have just the cure. He placed his saw next to the tree and winked at Jonah, who asked:

You're gonna cut through that thing with that old saw?

This saw has seen me through some times, my boy. Good and bad. Some day when you're old enough I'll tell you about them. He began to draw the teeth back and forth across the trunk. A serious twenty minutes later the tree was down and he was taking a break on a nearby stump. Jonah, having wandered off, returned to see the old man breathing deeply but looking healthy, satisfied.

Better than sex, Hawkins pronounced.

A crotch is a crotch, Jonah said.

Now he watched the flames test and taste the wood and he reflected for a moment on the great forest around him. A

96

lovely forest. Heavily logged, yes, and in dire need of a cleansing fire, but beautiful nonetheless, and more wild than most suspect. It lay around them black and deep at night and deep and green during the day, full of secrets, ghosts, hiding swamps and streams and the bones of lost hunters. There were parts of this forest that looked ancient, with fir trees poking against a blue sky along hidden rivers, eagle nests perched high in white pines, dark old logging paths overgrown with weeds and walked by raccoon and whitetail and bear. Here and there, hidden by the depths of the woods, were the ragged remnants of shacks and cabins, occupied now by fox snakes and skunks. Expanses of lush green carpet speckled with half-buried giant boulders could be seen on the far sides of hills, like places where wee folk might come to sing and dance. A gorgeous forest. A place of dreams and memories. Jonah wondered if it would ever need fighting for, if he'd ever have to come back here and champion it from destruction. He thought about the election a million miles away, thought about the forces lining up to ravage such places. Some people hate the color green. They claim to love their God but not His lovely and precious works. He felt alternately joyful and sad. He was here, in this forest, held by its black and cold arms, sheltered by its lonely trees, a friend to its animals and plants, but he knew, too, how fragile such things are. Forget ecology: he had gone camping here with his family when he was a kid, this place was fat with haunted memories, fragile moments held captive in the twisted arms of dead trees hanging skeletal over lakes, mirrored in the thick green water. Moments lost wandering through canyons of balsam fir, laughter and wonder tied forever to hemlock and spruce and jack pine and sugar maple. Somewhere out here he was still a little kid, paddling with his father in a canoe, following his brother and sister down country roads, sitting by fires just like this one, listening to the snap and crackle of the flames, watching the moon rise yellow and bone-like into the sky.

What is it in a fire that fascinates? Indeed. A good question. An eternal question, worthy of contemplation over just such a blaze, with the birch taking to flame like a lover to a kiss, and the sound of crackling tongues of fire, the smell of smoke like the ancient essence of the forest released to the air, the great and wondrous pagan ritual they were engaged in now, the liberation of not only that forest spirit but their own souls and minds, each finally free to float heavenward on that smoke,

97

to rise towards the stars, to close their eyes and think about times past present and future.

Jonah remembered being a boy, sitting on his father's lap before such a fire, held safe and comfortable in those arms, slowly mesmerized by the flickering flames and pulsating heat that lay before him.

You awake Pumpkin? his father whispered.

Jonah could only nod, the back of his head against his dad's whiskered chin.   Somewhere not too far off a whippoorwill began to call, and a night breeze drew up like a sudden breath.

The Nicolet National Forest, then as now, was full of ghosts.

2

Anyone know any ghost stories?

Someone, inevitably, would ask this question as the fire got going and the darkness fell over stunted conversation. It would become a family joke, mostly because no one ever really had a ghost story and it would be up to their Mom to tell the same one she always told, about a friend's house up in Crandon that had been haunted by a little boy. It seemed this little boy had drowned in a creek that ran past his house and ever since had wandered the property, a mischievous little spirit prone to annoying but harmless acts like stealing cigarettes and matches and pens. It wasn't a scary story, but she tried her best to infuse it with a mood of gloom and creepiness. She failed, of course, since her family was well versed in the tale and found it more humorous than scary, but they would listen intently as they sat before the fire. Out beyond the rim of the firelight's reach, of course, was a darkness thick and impenetrable, and they all decided instead to focus on the bright throbbing orange and yellow of the coals and flames. Easy to smile at ghost stories when surrounded by heat and light and family, not so easy *out there*, in the blackness of a cold forest night.

The Swain family had a cabin on a lake in the Blackwell area of the Nicolet, though *shack* would have been a more fitting term. It had been in Harold Swain's family for two generations, each successive generation keeping it well-tended and comfy. It was basically a concrete box, painted lime-green, with a heavy roof and heavy windows. Inside there were two rooms: a kitchen and the bedroom, the latter stuffed with three massive bunk beds, the former functional if not pretty. The Swains had no need for form over function, they came to the forest for the forest itself, and any talk of luxuries or comfort would have been greeted with disdain and mockery. As it was, the cabin's utilities were powered by propane and the "bathroom" was an outhouse of indeterminate age and stability. The only amenities the place had was a basic stove (new around the time of the Depression), a fridge (rescued from a dump) and the hissing yellow glow of gas lights. It was not a place to come for a cushy vacation. You slept on ancient mattresses, ate with the spiders and mites, pissed in the woods, shit in the rickety outhouse, and bathed in the murky fish waters of Loon Lake.

For the Swains, it was paradise.

Jonah would never remember a time when he had not known the cabin. He'd been six-months old the first time he went there, and had taken his first real steps about three feet from a roaring campfire. Other stories would abound as well: the time when he was four and fell off the dock, only to be scooped out by his father; the time his mother had taken him for a ride on a snowmobile one winter weekend and had driven him into a tree, giving him a fat lip; the evening he and Tom had melted the bottoms of their tennis shoes by resting their feet on the campfire's ring of stones; the night a cougar (perhaps the last in the area) had screamed up the road, rousing the Swains from sleep; the first fish Jonah had ever caught, a bluegill snagged off the end of the dock; the swimming the kids did in summer and the skating they did in winter, their father shoveling off a square from the frozen lake to reveal the smooth clear ice below; blue-berry picking and the pancakes they would make with them; spotting a black bear as it crossed an old county road; Tom chasing Tina with a captured fox snake; the day their dog Muffy had gotten loose and swum across the lake, only to be returned by a man who had been camping over there; the next evening after that, when they'd heard that young man playing his guitar around his own fire; the sound of loons in the twilight; the incessant call of a whippoorwill; the kids following their dad as he hunted partridge on old over-grown logging paths; all the whitetails spooked across meadows and fields; the safe comforting laziness of a family campsite after the brats have been eaten, the Doritos finished, the sodas slurped, the beans tossed to the dog, the crumbs of bread left for the gray jays and ground squirrels.

Each family has its legends and myths, some good, some bad. The good ones for the Swains were centered here, in the heart of the Nicolet, surrounded by lake breezes and woodsmoke.

Paradise indeed.

*

Harold Swain had always said, perhaps half-jokingly, that he wanted his ashes scattered around Loon Lake. It was not to be.

He was cremated, yes, but then his ashes were buried near his mother, in the Laona cemetery. What was the point of that? Jonah always wondered.

It was for the best, though, his not being scattered at Loon Lake.

This paradise was lost.

3

Jonah opened another beer and cocked his head to the night. Away from the snapping of the fire he thought he heard something else, another sort of snapping, steps on the forest floor.

"Hear something?" Hawkins asked.

"I don't know." He kept listening, then gave up.

Hawkins poked at the fire. "You haven't spoken in a while. Want a topic?"

"Sure." He sipped his beer, then set the bottle down. "Hang on, though, I'm gonna take a piss." He rose and walked away from the fire's flickering yellow glow, off into the depths of the night's blackness.

It was measurably colder away from the flames, and there was a strange breeze in the woods... strange because it was not steady, instead rose every half-minute or so, like the exhalations of some giant beast. The Hodag, Jonah thought with a smile. The mythical monster of Wisconsin's north woods.

He walked further into the blackness than he needed to, stopping only after he could no longer hear the popping and snapping of the flames, just a silence broken only by the breathing of the night. He unzipped and pissed, keeping his ears tuned to the forest. Goddamnit, he had too great an imagination. Thoughts of Bigfoot snaked through him and he felt himself shivering, felt as if he were being watched, perhaps hunted. He turned his head this way and that, seeing nothing but a great ebony fog, motionless and impenetrable. When he looked back the way he'd come he could only barely make out the glow of the campfire and the slightest sketch of Hawkins's figure slumped comfortably next to it.

Though feeling oddly creeped out, he zipped up when he was finished and stood there a bit longer. There was something both eerie and soothing in such perfect darkness. It was the sort of darkness he had tried to capture back in college, when he and his roommate would tape over their room's single window to create a womb-like black space, the great Nothingness that would allow them to sleep late on weekends. It was the sort of darkness that had been denied to his childhood bedroom when the city put in a streetlight outside his window, the sort of darkness he'd been trying to get back to ever since. In this way, perhaps it *was* womb-like, a regression back to a pre-natal state.

And yet, if so, it was also the sort of blackness that made his imagination conceive monsters and demons. The sleep of reason breeds monsters, Goya might have said, but for Jonah the darkness was their mother.

What a strange image, he thought as he stood there in the pitch-black forest. And yet, strange or not, it was strong enough to make him feel as if hands might reach out and grab him, as if eyes that glowed red and yellow were on him at that moment, watching his every move, calculating how quickly he could make it back to the safety of Hawkins and the fire.

A twig snapped off to his left. He looked there and of course saw nothing, just the night. And perhaps it was the night itself that was the monster, a living veil of blackness slowly closing in.

He felt suddenly alone, lost. The world was nothing but the night and the night would never let him go. He was a child here, in this forest. Essentially naked, defenseless, without sanctuary. If the night did indeed take him, who would know? He was more than alone, he was lonely, lost in the void of midnight.

101

Then, from back at the fire, Hawkins's voice: "You all right in there?"

"Yeah!" he called back, maybe too loudly. He took in a deep breath of the night's exhalation and returned quickly to camp.

4

Crowds of flittering, fluttering butterflies would gather on the old gravel road that ran past the cabin, rising when the family approached, hitting the air like little slices of energy released to the open sky, to the world, to the Universe. The boy, Jonah, always liked the butterflies, but he went near them with caution: as energy, they seemed out of control, unpredictable. They didn't fly like birds, they took odd, crazy ziz-zag routes through the air, not unlike the way the sparks flew up when his dad stirred the campfire coals. But Jonah knew the sparks would rise and burn out... the butterflies would go on and on, maybe, if he wasn't careful, right down his throat.

Jonah's afraid of butterflies, Tommy said, laughing and pointing at his younger brother.

I am not!

Hush, their father said simply. Up North, in the woods, their dad was a man of few words. *Hush* was all that would be needed to silence his rowdy children. If they continued to fight he would stop and glare at them, threatening them with... well, neither child knew with *what*, since it had never gotten that far. Little did they know that there really was no *what*, since Harold Swain was not a man given to any sort of violence. He liked the power of the Dad Glare because of the vague, ominous threat it contained, but he would have done little more, if challenged, then tell his kids that they had to keep quiet, using perhaps just a few more words than *hush*. As it stood, he was never challenged, and never would be: by the time he dropped dead only Tina would be at that age when she felt the need to challenge her parents, and yet was not that sort of child. Each of the Swain children would some day regret this fact: they had never gotten to have those typical father-teen arguments that everyone else gets to have. Just one of the many things, good and bad, that death steals from us.

When the whole family went for walks like that, down the old gravel road in the Nicolet, Jonah liked to lag behind, lost in his own world. The gravel road had been used extensively for logging once upon a time, and before that, in an even earlier life, it had been the route of train tracks. It was still possible to spot ancient gray chunks of wood rails poking out from the compacted gravel, and even, if you were lucky, the rusted nails that had kept the ties down. The boys would always stop and try to pull those nails free, a job that could go on for nearly a quarter of an hour. Tom had five back at home, sitting on a shelf, but Jonah only had one... and a gnarled, almost unrecognizable one at that. He spent every walk down the old road searching for more of the nails, and as a result, of course, his eyes were always on the ground.

This prompted his dad to once say: Look at that boy, staring at his shoes.

I'm not staring at my—

He's not staring at his shoes, his mother said. He's looking for frogs, aren't you?

He's watching for butterflies, Tom said. So they don't fly in his *mouth*....

Shut up!

All right, hush hush.

And then the Swains had kept going, marching steadily down the old road, ever further into the forest, and Jonah had not been allowed to explain himself. Instead, he searched harder for old nails, hoping that he might vindicate himself by finding one. He was not, after all, looking for frogs, or staring at his shoes, or watching for butterflies. The butterflies he was most concerned with were the ones in the air, and those tended to hover a few feet off anyway, awaiting their return to whatever it was they found of interest on the gravel.

On walks like this, down the road and then up a grassier path into a thick pine forest, it was possible to feel as if that other world, the world of televisions and radios and highways and movies and school, no longer existed. This was a pleasant feeling to Jonah. He would not have minded staying up at the cabin permanently, and yet, even so, he always loved going back. After three days he missed his toys, his room, his bed. He missed Spiderman and Sigmund the Sea Monster and Tarzan. He missed his home.

Things they saw on these walks: lonely trilliums blooming at the edge of the road; a thousand partridges thundering out of undergrowth; great horned owls floating away ghost-like through the trees; a great blue heron rising like

103

a pterodactyl over the lake; the distant blur of a black bear racing across a meadow; a million butterflies; a million dragonflies like sparkling gems on cellophane wings; garter snakes caught in the act of basking in a pool of sun; thousands of wood frogs lying half-hidden in vernal ponds; countless white-tail asses scattering over fields; turtles laying eggs; any number of strange deep-forest birds that Jonah would not learn the names of for more than a decade, among them the pileated woodpecker, that giant of the old forests, a bird so shy and mysterious Jonah would grow to believe his memories of it had been a dream.

Thousand of plants, animals... a million sights to behold on any given walk. And yet, too, there was a simple, casual rhythm to those family excursions, an effortless rhythm, just a family out walking in the woods, with much to see but no need to see any of it, just that grand old ancient need to be out there, in the wilderness, away from civilization, breathing cool clear air, watching lake waters ripple in the early morning sun, smelling the rich odor of swamp and prairie, feeling sphagnum moss beneath your feet, listening to loons call out from the lazy depths of late afternoon... that ancient and vital need to be back where it all began. Wilderness. Innocence. Days of lazy dreams.

This is what it's all about, Harold Swain once told his children. The trees, the sky, the lake... this is what it's all about. You'll always have this, you'll always be able to come up here and get away from everything. Sound good?

The children said it did. It sounded good indeed.

5

"I don't know," said Hawkins, his voice more grizzled than usual as it took in beer and campfire smoke. He was a flickering black-yellow shape across the fire, though his face was well-lit. Behind him was a wall of night. He settled back in his little fold-up chair and sighed. "I often wonder when it was I stopped caring."

Jonah waited a moment or two, expecting the older man to continue, and when he couldn't take it any longer he said: "All right, that's a strange comment. When you stopped caring about what?"

"Anything. Everything."

Another pause. Jonah frowned. "Again: a few details here, to help me out, maybe?"

Hawkins laughed and leaned forward, poking at the fire with his by-now-shorter stick. "I was thinking in general terms, but like... see, this coming election. I don't know, but...." He looked across the fire. "Let me ask you this, as a young man, a reasonably intelligent young man. Do you think there's a difference between the two parties?"

Jonah poked at his side of the fire, sending up sparks like startled fireflies. A fresh tongue of flame swirled up at the new breath of air it had been given. Fire is born. Early man must have stared at those first few fires with fascination, in awe of the force pulsing and swelling and dying and rising. Fire is born, and with it this thing, civilization, this beast, this monster, looming at the edge of wilderness, poking and prodding at the borders of forests and deserts, biding its time, waiting to pounce. Fire was born, yes, and with it died the reason it was needed in the first place.

"I didn't know you wanted to get into a detailed political discussion."

Hawkins shrugged, poked at the fire some more. "What else is there to do...?"

Jonah sighed. "Well, I can think of better things to talk about than elections."

"Not a political junkie? A young, intelligent, culturally-aware man like yourself?"

"Politicians creep me out. But... well, always vote for the smarter man, I say. *Not* the one you'd want to have a beer with."

The night seemed heavy around them, a black presence, alive and breathing.

"This is such a beautiful place," Hawkins said. "These woods, the lake, everything. I really like it up here. This is the most fun I've had in a long time."

"Me too."

Hawkins fell silent again, then said, softly, his voice heavy and solemn: "I'd hate to think of someone building a fucking house here."

Jonah nodded. He thought of another lake not too far off, once surrounded only by trees but now helmed in, strangled, throttled, by a dozen or more grossly inappropriate ugly impudent inexcusable worthless no good vacation homes. The memories that lake held were less than ghosts now, they were the stuff of ancient myths and legends. The old lime-green cabin was gone, long since reduced to rubble.

Hawkins sighed. "But I suppose some asshole already has his eyes on it. It would be a tragedy. A goddamn tragedy."

Jonah nodded again. Out there in the darkness a barred owl called. The sound echoed flatly through the trees, and was not answered.

"A goddamn tragedy...."

6

Harold Swain showed his youngest son how to put a worm on a hook. The hook was a rusted old thing that looked like it had rested for years on the bottom of a lake, but it would serve. The worm wriggled and struggled vainly as it was punctured. The boy looked up at his father and asked if it was in pain.

No, said Harold Swain.

How do you know?

They don't feel things the way you and I do.

Oh. Why not?

Harold Swain gently tapped his son's head. They don't have the brain you do.

They were sitting on the dock by their cabin, the lake a blue-gray saucer two feet below them, completely still in the late afternoon. On its far shore the trees were already black with shadow. Fish jumped out by lily pads sixteen feet from the dock, and the boy looked there and smiled.

They're hungry, his father said.

Me too.

Maybe we'll eat some fish, if you catch them.

Yeah!

Shhh, now, you'll spook them. Here, I'll cast for you.

And he did, expertly, landing the hook and sinker where he wanted, two feet from those lilies. The bobber sat there in a fading ring of concentric circles, then went under once, twice, three times.

Give it a tug, Harold Swain said as he handed the pole to his son.

Jonah Swain jerked back on the pole roughly, pulling the bobber out of the water. It landed a foot or so closer to the dock.

106

Gently, his father said. But firmly, too. Like I showed you. Remember?

Yeah.

Just wait, don't move it... just wait.

The bobber trembled, then slipped below the surface.

Okay, gently, Harold Swain said.

Jonah tugged as gently as he could. The bobber floated back up and was still. Jonah frowned.

The bobber trembled again and went under.

You got him! said Harold Swain. Reel him in!

Jonah started reeling, just as his dad had showed him, slowly but steadily, watching the bobber come to the dock just slightly below the water, taking a zigzagging course as it did. He could feel an opposite force trying to pull the bobber back out to the lake, a strange muscular presence fighting him below the water. When the end of the line was closer he could see the dark shape of the fish struggling valiantly against him.

You got him! Harold Swain said, putting a big hand on his youngest son's shoulder. You got him! That's a bigger one than Tom caught.

It is! Jonah said joyfully. It is! It's bigger!

Okay, okay, easy, just pull him out.

Jonah lifted the end of his pole as he reeled and the bobber, the sinker, and the fish came out of the water, the latter flopping and spinning, its fins stretched out, searching for the water that was not there.

Bring it to the dock or you might lose him.

Jonah did as he was told, and his father reached out and took hold of the animal with one hand as he removed the hook from the mouth with the other.

Not bad, huh? Harold Swain held the fish so that Jonah could look at it. A fighter.

Jonah smiled. The fish stared at him with its wide eyes, looking into his own with something like acknowledgement. You caught me, I'm yours.

Or was it: Let me go please, I don't belong out here.

What should we do with him? Harold Swain asked. Keep him?

No, said Jonah. No, let him go, I want to see him swim.

You want to see him swim?

Yeah.

All right. And Harold Swain bent over the side of the dock and placed the animal back into the lake. Watch, he said to his son, who was bent over too, already watching. Ready?

He slowly let go of the fish. Jonah's eyes widened. The animal took off like an arrow, swimming quickly down to the bottom of the lake, where it rested for a moment, perhaps gathering its strength before darting off.

Should we cast out again, try for another? asked Harold Swain.

Yeah, Jonah said, amazed that such creatures were living out there, going about their strange lives under the water.

You cast this time, said his father. You can do it, just like I showed you.

Jonah lifted the pole, looked out to the still lake, tried to decide where he wanted the line to go.

Just like I showed you....

The boy smiled there next to his father, with evening settling down around them, with the far shore turning dark and wild, with the sky soon to blossom into stars. The smell of trees and water and clean air surrounded them. Tiny black shapes hovered above the surface of the lake, dipping every few feet to gently ripple the dark water. Crickets chirped. Green frogs belched. The forest around the lake was still, mostly dark, just the very tops of the tallest pines lit by the golden glow of the fading sun. Nothing out there but trees, deer, a bear or two, maybe a bobcat. Here, at this little cabin, the Swains felt the coming night settling down like a blanket, holding them close. They turned sleepy, peaceful. A pleasant exhaustion fell over them as the air began to sigh, the water to sleep, the sky to whisper its secrets to the trees. For the Swains there was nothing now but the woods, the lake, each other. The world beyond these trees and this water did not exist, there was only this family, only the Swains. The lake was theirs and theirs only. Not another living human soul could call it home.

The Nicolet National Forest breathed out its sweet soft breath, and slowly tucked them in.

7

"I could stay out here forever," Hawkins said. He'd been saying it every hour or so, like a mantra. Jonah sensed something in the words, a darkness, a glimpse of depression, of regret. Perhaps it was that old familiar beast, the subtle hatred of one's *other* life: the job, the home, the routine. He wanted to ask the older man about this but didn't think it was proper. Sometimes, maybe even *most* times, it was best to let silence reign, to allow personal thoughts to wander and ramble. Jonah looked over at his friend, still a dark shape flickering with orange and yellow, a sketch of Hemingway through smoke and flame, and knew that asking the older man to elaborate would have resulted in a sudden weight to the mood around the campfire, so he let him sit there in peace. Which this was, too, a pure peace of the sort only camping in the deep forest can provide. There was something calm about a campfire, a tranquility released by the flames. You can sit there thinking the darkest thoughts and still have the peace of mind to feel you are a thousand miles from your troubles.

He looked at Hawkins and tried to guess what might be on the man's mind. Death? Work? Life in general?

A long period of quiet went by, perhaps twenty minutes, each man stirring the fire every so often, sparking fresh flames, letting gusts of heat fly out into the night.

"Yep, I could stay out here forever," Hawkins said, sighing and turning his head to look off into the dark woods.

Jonah nodded and stared into the fire.

"You're young," Hawkins said suddenly. "You could do it, too. Here, or Canada, Alaska. Australia, maybe. Live off the land. Be your own man, free and loose."

"You must not know me that well. I'd starve within a week."

"That's right, that's right. Jonah Swain is not a practical man."

"To say the least. Me Canoes For Shit."

Hawkins smiled and poked the fire. "What you should do, then, is find yourself a woman who *is* practical. A woman skilled at hunting, trapping, sewing, cabin building, gardening...."

"So she'll do all the work and what will I do?"

"Love her till you die."

Jonah laughed. "Jesus Christ, you've lost your mind. What are you smoking over there, anyway?"

Hawkins smiled, poked the fire some more.

A cool breeze swelled up suddenly and Jonah wondered what time it was. It felt like midnight.

"So what do you think?" Hawkins asked. "Where do you see yourself down the road, if not living off the grid in the wilds of Canada?"

Jonah's turn to sigh. "God... sometimes I just see myself down the road, is all. Older, no wiser. Just down the road."

"Where would you *like* to see yourself?"

"I don't know. I'd like to see myself not feeling trapped. I'd like to feel less... transitory, you know, like I'm not waiting for something to happen, some future life to come. I'd like to realize that my life is going on right now, right this moment, that this is all I have, and make something of it. I feel like my work and apartment and whatever are just preparation for some other life. I've always felt that way. I've never really been in the moment, you know? I'm always thinking that this moment is just a step, just a step towards something else. That's really not a way to live."

Hawkins nodded but said nothing. There was a very tiny smile on his mouth as he stared into the fire. Jonah saw that smile and wondered if the man thought he was a fool.

Finally Hawkins said: "I was always that way, too. I don't know if you can shake it."

"The danger is growing to accept where you are, and I don't want to do that."

"Because you don't like where you are. Eventually you'll find where you want to be, what you want to do, and you'll be happy. It'll happen."

"You think?"

Hawkins looked at him. The smile broadened. "Yeah."

Jonah raised his eyebrows and looked deeply into the pulsing orange coals before him. He took in a deep breath and blew on the coals and they burned brighter for a second, with little bits of ash rising on their heat. He thought of who he was and where he was. Jonah Swain. The Nicolet National Forest. Alone here save for this man, his friend Hawkins. Alone in the world save for his mother, his sister, his brother. Jonah Swain, adrift at thirty, anchored to nothing yet tethered to much: work, family, memories. Can a man ever escape and be free? He doubted it. No matter where he went he was still haunted by thoughts, images, moments from the past. He was always able to sense some shape hovering nearby, some shadow over his head. *Jonah Swain*: he didn't think there was such a person.

110

There was a composite, an image, a two-dimensional character in a play saying the same lines over and over, but a person, a true flesh and blood human being with gravity and purpose? He wasn't sure. He sensed it might be so but had no way to know for certain, that knowledge was simply blocked to him, a secret. If a Jonah Swain existed who had depth and weight, who wasn't just fulfilling a prescribed role to the delight and fulfillment of other people's own private plans, this Jonah Swain here by the fire in the middle of the Nicolet Forest, this half-empty shell of a Jonah Swain, had no way of knowing it. He wished he didn't have the need to know, wished for blissful ignorance, but instead found himself contemplating the idea deeply. He stared into the flames and thought about this other Jonah, who he might be, what he might be like. A free Jonah, bound to nothing, with obligations to no one, responsible only for himself. As it stood, this Jonah here was too caught up in a web of connections, each step he took haunted by this Presence right behind him, this invisible Shape of obligation and concern. Whatever he did he had to look back and wonder what that Shape thought and felt. Everywhere he went he had to trail a long line of Swains along with him, second-guessing his every move, his every decision: What would his father have thought? What did his mother think? His brother? His sister? No matter what he did Jonah Swain was not alone, his family tagged along like chaperones. He was obliged to people he had very little in common with, people he only saw a few times a year. And yet he couldn't shake them, he heard their voices echoing in his head every time he made a move. Family is a curse passed from generation to generation.

He thought of his dead father. There was always an obligation to the man... or, more properly, to the memory of the man. His teachers in high-school had all been friends of Harold Swain, and they had expected certain things from his children. Tom and Tina had done their best to fulfill those expectations. They played sports, excelled academically, had gotten into little trouble, and now they had lives, families, careers. And here was Jonah Paul Swain, still looking for himself, still floating through his life, still without direction or purpose.

Harold Swain had been a father at my age, he thought as he stared into the fire. The thought hung there, meaningful in and of itself.

He wondered how Tina and Tom had managed this act of fulfilling their obligations when they too had been young when their father died, and young as well when their mother began her descent into depression and drink. It was a question he knew he'd never get the answer to, because he would never ask it. The Swain children did not talk about such things. Their conversations were shallow and uncomplicated. And yet, though he would never give it voice, it was a question he would have given anything to hear answered: Tom and Tina Swain had not been much older than him that day their father dropped dead in the kitchen of their house. Tom had been thirteen, Tina sixteen. Was it some flaw in his own character that made him so lost, so ambitionless and aimless? Had the death, and the subsequent falling apart of their mother, come at a time when Jonah had been particularly emotionally sensitive? Had it come at the right moment in time to retard him in a state of anxiety and uncertainty, a state he was still in now, at thirty? Had that trembling little moment at the age of ten been the exact wrong moment to lose a father and begin losing a mother? Jesus, here's a worse thought: maybe that had nothing to do with it, maybe he was just... fucked up.

He glanced across the fire at Hawkins, who was staring into the flames too, seemingly hypnotized by the heat and color. The man was his mother's age, and the age his father would have been if he were alive. And yet Jonah could sit here with this man and feel entirely comfortable, more relaxed than he could with his mother... more relaxed than he could with Tom or Tina, or anyone else he knew, for that matter. He supposed some might look on this friendship, separated by nearly thirty years, as an obvious father-son parallel, Hawkins a surrogate for the dead dad, Jonah still a little boy at thirty, searching for the father figure that had been taken from him.

Jonah tried hard to honestly see it this way and could not. He didn't see Hawkins as a father figure at all... almost the opposite, with Hawkins often displaying a playful immaturity that made him seem younger. Hawkins was a friend, that was all. They had much in common, not all of it good.

He wondered what his mother would have thought of this relationship. And Tom, or Tina....

That Jonah's a strange one, hanging out with that sixty-year old man. It just isn't natural.

112

They wouldn't realize that when he looked at Hawkins he felt like he was seeing himself in thirty years. Their relationship was like a *Twilight Zone* episode with the older man visiting his younger self, advising him, warning him, telling him of roadblocks and pitfalls in the years to come.

Jonah looked at the older man now. There was much to admire in Hawkins, much to emulate. And much to avoid and fear.

"When was the last time you talked to your son?" Jonah said.

Hawkins looked up quickly, as if he had forgotten Jonah was there.

"What? My son?"

"Yeah. I was just wondering… unless you don't want to talk about it…."

Hawkins appeared to think over whether he wanted to talk about it or not. Eventually he shrugged.

"Been a while, a phone call a year or so ago. Haven't seen him in person in more than a decade."

"What came between you?'

Hawkins shrugged again. "Who knows. Little things, an accumulation of little things. Maybe he didn't like the way I treated his mom. Maybe we're just different people."

Jonah nodded.

"I think that sort of thing is much more common than people think," Hawkins said. "I think more families are estranged than they are happy and together. Maybe it's too much to ask to be happy and together, I don't know. I *do* know that his mom talked bad about me when he was younger, so that probably had a lot of influence on him. She told him I was a worse man than I was. And I wasn't nice to her, I'll admit that, but I was never a bad father, I really wasn't. I was with his mom until he was thirteen or so, something like that, and I was a good dad to him. Still, though, I suppose the tension between me and her bled through. Hard for a kid to miss something like that. And I moved far away, too. That didn't help."

Jonah nodded again, not having anything to add to this. He looked at Hawkins and saw the distant look in the man's eyes. Hawkins stared into the fire for a while, then stood and fetched another log from the little woodpile they had gathered earlier. He set the log over the flames and stood there watching as it immediately started to burn.

"Stuff's dry," he said. "Burns quick."

113

"What time is it?" Jonah asked.

"Why? You tired?"

"No, just wondered."

"You can go to bed if you want, I'm gonna stay up."

"I'm gonna stay up, too. I have nothing better to do."

Hawkins smiled. "You're a sad young man. Nothing better to do than hang out with an old guy like me."

"Yeah, well… someone has to do it."

Hawkins laughed and sat back down in his chair. He was noticeably more inward-looking now, and Jonah regretted bringing up the topic of his son. He hadn't meant to send Hawkins into a depression, but he apparently had. The older man sat there staring into the fire, the flames painting tragic surreal colors on his beard and skin, the shadow behind him framing him heavily. Jonah tried to think of a topic that might lighten the man up but could think of nothing, and he knew it was sometimes worse to try. He himself poked at the fire, once more making sparks jump, and thought of the Hawkins he would never know, the younger man, the husband, the father. He thought of a man his own age living somewhere out there, never knowing his dad though that dad was alive and well. He knew what it was like to bury a father, but to have lost one in the labyrinth of the world was something he could not understand. Pick up the phone, for Christ's sake, give the old man a call. Give the kid a call, Hawkins. Life was too short.

But we all have our estrangements, Jonah knew. And sometimes we're estranged from people we see all the time. That was how life was.

Falling silent like this made Jonah feel more adrift in the world, more cut off from everything and everyone. He looked at the man on the other side of the fire and realized he might never truly know him, that there were mysteries in his heart that would never be revealed, codes that would never be cracked. Each man takes a puzzle to the grave. If life was anything it was an attempt to gather whatever clues you could before those you loved the most, but did not truly know, left the world forever.

And yet if this was so, thought Jonah, if it was truly so, then what about those secrets and mysteries we carry in our own hearts, and which we keep from ourselves? Was it ever possible to crack *them*?

There had to be a way, thought Jonah. Or what was the point of any of it? There had to be a way.

"I suppose," Hawkins said, his gruff sandpaper voice soft, low.

Jonah looked over silently. It was a moment or two before Hawkins continued:

"I suppose I should call him. Give him a ring one of these days and ask him how he is. That's the right thing to do. I let too much time go by and I'll be dead before I know it."

"Would he want to hear from you?"

"I don't know. Doesn't matter, he'll be civil, we were both civil the last time. I should do it, either way. We should talk...."

Jonah nodded.

Hawkins shifted in his chair and smiled an odd little smile at the fire. He was a master of such smiles, Jonah knew. They usually signified he was about to change the topic.

"You know," he said, "I don't think I could ever camp like this with him, no matter how well we get to know each other. He's not that sort of person. We're really not alike at all. I bet he's never been out in the woods like this."

Jonah poked at the fire. A minute or so later he said: "I'm sure he'd like a call, at least. You might never end up camping with him, but...."

Hawkins shrugged, any trace of the smile gone now. He too poked at the fire with his little stick so that both men were disturbing the logs and coals at opposite ends. There was a battle of thin flames and billowing smoke in the center.

"I suppose..." Hawkins said again, so low it was a whisper. He leaned forward as if to say more but before he opened his mouth he glanced off into the darkness. A frown creased his flickering orange forehead.

"What's wrong?" Jonah asked. He turned to look into the black forest.

"That," Hawkins said, gesturing with his chin. "What is that?"

Jonah looked beyond the trees and saw that the sky was glowing with faint light.

"Christ, it's not morning, is it?"

"No," said Hawkins, though he didn't sound certain. "Is there a town over that way?"

"None that would light up the sky like that. Not up here."

Hawkins's frown deepened and he stood and walked in the direction of the glow.

"What *is* that...?"

Jonah stood too and walked away from the fire with the older man, instantly feeling the cool night on his skin as they left the flames behind. The darkness engulfed them, covered them like a cold sheet. The fire popped and cracked at their backs, its smell omnipresent and soothing. In front of them the black forest was without sound save the sighing of a soft breeze through the upper branches. The sky beyond the trees was lit as if with a blue bulb.

"What direction is that?" Hawkins asked.

"West, I think...." Jonah stepped further away from the fire's unsteady glow. The tops of the farthest trees were sharp against the sky, pin-prick silhouettes touching that flickering glow.

"Hey," he said. "It's moving...."

Hawkins came up beside him. They stood side by side, barely thirty feet from the ring of their fire but lost now in the forest night, the campsite forgotten, each man silent, for a moment cast away from who and what they had been just moments before, the cool air like ancient kisses on their skin, the thick shadow of a wooded night lying over the world, the dancing blue light of a strange sky swallowing their eyes and minds.

4. After the death of the Ice Cream Man

1

I killed her years before she died.

Jonah Swain had this thought at his mother's funeral, right around the time Father Harvey signaled for some woman up in the balcony to start singing "Oh Heaven When Your Light is Near" in a powerful but off-key voice. Zoning out like he did to most such songs, he happened to look absently over to the casket up front and, just like that, realized it was his mother in there... his *mother*, not his *mom*. His mother had been dead for just a few days, but his mom had been murdered a long time ago. He had done this deed without ever really realizing he had done so... and without any guilt until this very moment.

Sorry about your mom, people kept saying to him over the past few days. Sorry about your mom.

I was her baby, and I abandoned her. Once upon a time we'd been so close, she was my best friend, I was her shadow, we went for walks late at night, swung on swings in the park, made up stories about the houses we passed, and then I just let it all go. I stopped looking her in the eye, afraid I'd see reflections of memories, those dark things I wanted to avoid, to ignore, to forget. I pulled away. I went distant. My idea of growing up was cutting her off. I was her baby and I abandoned her.

He thought about this during the whole song, staring at the casket five feet away like he'd never before seen such a thing.

Oh Heaven when your light is near, the woman up above sang, *I will reach for you and be free of sin*.

He wondered if he'd stopped loving his mom. Killing her was one thing, but no longer loving her....

117

I will walk into your light and know the darkness is no more.

He wondered if she knew he killed her. This thought made him feel violently ill, he felt his empty stomach flop like a dying fish. Enough of this, he told himself. Just sit here and do nothing. A funeral is no place for thinking. There is no logic in the casket, the priest, the gathered mourners, the nauseating flowers some people feel the need to send, and which throw a thick reek through funeral home and church that smells like Death himself, all primped and perfumed for his big show. Funerals are for base emotions... honest, raw emotions, yes, but not deep ones. Primitive emotions. The power-punch of sorrow, anger, even fear. And, of course, those even more primitive displays of forced humility and absolution, the fake smiles and stiff handshakes, the uncomfortable reunions of long lost friends and family. It starts at the house, when the family receives visitors expressing sympathy and offering help as they drop off baked goods and hot dishes. It carries over to the wake, that disturbing and sickening ritual where people can stare at the body and bow their heads and pray to whatever god they hold sacred, as if the whole scene does any good to the dead. It is doubtful that the scene does any good for the living, either, although perhaps some people truly do feel they need that sense of closure, to gaze upon the lifeless, cold, awkwardly posed and mutilated body of their loved one. Mutilated? Of course: there is a reason those lips and eyes don't open, they are glued shut. And if the person in the casket looks healthy and plump it is only because they have been filled with formalin, not because they ate well and took care of themselves. Religious folk call the body an empty shell, as if this offers hope and faith for the living. The thought of souls and eternity is a nice, pleasant image to gather one's thoughts around, but not so the cold realities of autopsies and embalming. Perhaps this is why none but the most morbid among us ever dwell on such topics. Easy to bow one's head and ponder the existence of the soul, not so easy to realize that everything the funeral directors do is designed simply to make a facsimile of a once vital and vigorous human being, to keep "alive" a false impression that the deceased is at peace, simply resting there with his or her hands clasped together nicely, a pleasant expression of sleepy-boredom on their face. It was a disgrace, really. More than a mutilation, a desecration. The Jews had it right, into the ground before sunset. In fact, do away with the

118

whole funeral thing. They were dead, the poor folks, and there was nothing that could be done about it.

No, the whole atmosphere of a funeral is actually rather hostile to complex thinking. Perhaps this is just as well. No need, after all, to stand before the gathered mourners and reflect upon the whole nature of the deceased, his faults and follies... much healthier, in the general scheme of things, to white-wash a life, to say he was a good man, a kind man, that he is at peace in heaven now. Forget for a moment the fact he was an asshole. A church is nothing if not a place for lies. We gain comfort from formal deceits.

No more thinking, he told himself. Just sit and listen and watch.

Through your light I will walk, into your open arms.

He watched his family, studying how they handled this particular death, trying to compare it to the other that haunted them, that of their dad twenty-three years earlier. He watched to see how his brother and sister responded to the religious trappings, watched how precise and practiced they made the sign of the cross, quick yet fluid movements of arm and wrist, as effortless and smooth as a Nazi salute. Their mother had been a Catholic but it wasn't believed she'd been to church in some time. As for his stepfather, Biff, well... Biff appeared to treat things like church and god the same way he treated the tattoo of the eagle on his left forearm: like something to display.

He watched Father Harvey, too. In the middle of the Our Father he thought of a priest joke told to him by Hawkins. How many priests does it take to screw in a light-bulb? Thousands, and then the arch diocese will cover it up.

He studied the casket itself. It looked like maple, so smoothly-polished it was like glass, the woodgrain beautiful, warm, exceedingly pleasing to the eye. And the church, too, of course, he took that in like a man who had found himself in an alien landscape, staring up to the peaked ceiling, studying the saints in the stained glass, admiring the statues of Mary and Jesus. He'd been a Catholic once, too, years ago. He'd gone to this same church, St. Michael's. He'd attended religious class until his sophomore year of high-school. He'd learned how to draw pictures of Jesus using only three colors of crayon (black, red, yellow). And he'd learned how to spot hypocrisy. His sophomore year, he couldn't even drive yet, and he had already left one religion and rejected all others. An atheist? Not yet,

119

that came later. He would consider himself an agnostic for the next few years, gradually disavowing even that label before coming to view himself as something altogether different: by the time of his mother's death he had come to believe it didn't matter, god or no god, either way he wouldn't change the way he lived, wouldn't act differently at all. It was a complex, yet entirely natural and nearly instinctual train of thought and logic that had led him to this view, this Apatheism. If given proof of the existence of a single all-mighty supreme being he would not have worshiped him or bowed down or said a single prayer. He didn't believe a true god would need such things.

St. Michael's was a beautiful church, though, if he was going to be objective. A classic church, gaudy and gigantic. The human voice carried on an angelic echo, a gothic reverb, right to the last row of pews and straight up to the steeple. The world is speckled with new churches these days, soulless modern architecture rising like tumors from what was once farmland or woods, cold, sterile-looking buildings that did not appear to offer peace or compassion but rather a business-like atmosphere where God was the CEO and righteousness the bottom line. St. Michael's was old, and everything about it suggested warmth, a place you could slip into to escape the rain or cold. You couldn't help but stand before its steeply rising spire and feel awed by the holiness that was at least *suggested* by that sharp needle-point poking into the sky, that cross defiant and proud as it strained to tickle the nose of God. If you were going to have a church, this is the sort to have: dominant, sturdy, suggesting jurisdiction over all it surveyed, a commanding presence calling all worshipers to its doors through the simple fact of its very existence. Those new churches, breaking the once beautiful green landscapes, those ugly artless economical boxes, have all the beauty and style of dental labs, brokerage firms, proctologist's offices. If there *is* a God, one God, certainly He lived in the fields and woods that had been torn down to make room for those new monstrosities. The destructive, terrible logic of humankind: killing their god to make a place for his worship.

When the woman finished singing and Father Harvey returned to the podium, Jonah studied the flowers and plants that had been placed around the altar. Each plant had a white card stuck into it, a note of sympathy from people he didn't know: *So sorry, our sympathies, with love and care*, etceteras. There might be pictures of flowers on the front of them, or blue

120

skies smeared with cumulous, or a white dove flying from a tree, or an etching of a cherub, but where, he wondered, is the truth, the reality? To truly suggest comfort to a mourner you need only show a photo of food or liquor. A bottle of wine or whiskey, a pan of lasagna, a plate of cookies.

If he was looking for truth here, though, he knew he was looking in the wrong place. Father Harvey was now talking about Linda Swain like she'd been one of the most perfect people in the world, a saint, a classic Rockwellian wife and mom, and if anyone else spoke they'd do the same thing, give some inane story they remembered from years ago, something designed to make people laugh and think oh gee, how sweet she was, how nice. No one would mention the drinking, the bulimia, the depression. And, though they would hint at it, no one would talk about *how* she had died. They would speak of her "untimely" passing, they would hint at the Lord's "mysterious plan," and all that assorted bullshit, but they wouldn't speak about the simple truth: the absurdity, the horror, the fucking pointlessness. If God had a plan it was a bad one. Back to the drawing board, Lord, you're fucking up royally.

There are many ways a person can die, of course, the human body is nothing if not fragile. Take your local paper, open it at random, the ways you can go are legion: cancer, car-crash, choking, drowning, falling from a building, being blown to pieces by a terrorist, blown away by a storm, hit by a truck when you're crossing the road, crushed by a meteor or a bit of space junk. You can fall down a well, slip inside a sink-hole, get mauled by a dog, eaten by a bear, get bit by a West Nile-infected skeeter, trip and hit your head just right on the corner of a desk. Old age might take you, too, sure, always possible if not statistically likely, or you can get poisoned by carbon monoxide, lay down your motorcycle in the rain, get dropped by a heart attack, felled by an aneurism, laid low by pneumonia, timbered by a widow-maker, eat something bad in a can of beans, suffocate in your crib, get stabbed and dumped in a dumpster, vaporized in a factory accident, freeze to death in a winter storm, get decapitated on a roller coaster, catch some disease so rare they have to name it after you. You can always get taken out by an unknown sniper on the side of a highway, just one of those lonely and mysterious psychopaths that haunt the mansion of modern America. Many ways. Death is everywhere. Any wonder people need to see a reason for it, to label it as worthwhile if only to a being whose logic could

121

never be understood by the finite mind? Harder to view it as insanely absurd, utterly without meaning or sense.

He listened to Father Harvey talk about eternity. Strange how the finite minds who invented religions threw into the mix all this talk of eternity. Every religion negates the present, renders this life here meaningless. Little wonder mankind feels it has the right to brutally violate not only the other creatures that live here but this very earth itself, to poison and rape it into an unrecognizable mess of steel and brick and plastic and glass. Why not shit where you eat when you believe the *real* purpose of your existence is to "live" as a noncorporeal being in some plain-less world of ether and sunshine for the rest of time immemorial. Such a belief enables you to give less credence and concern to the real issues at hand here, on this wonderful beautiful precious physical wonderland, enables you to focus on your little corner of the world, your small little petty day-to-day tribulations, and not on the matters of life and death (and everything greater than both) that exist every second of every day.

If there was a heaven, he thought that day in St. Michael's Church, and it was anything like these people said it was, then they could have it. Hopefully he'd be given the option: an eternity as a sensually numb spirit with nothing to do but gaze unendingly into the arrogant and vain glow of God, or only this lifetime here, now, seventy-five years on this chunk of rock and water where the songbirds sing, the frogs hop, the fish swim, and joy is felt as a physical presence on the mind and body. Obvious which option he'd choose, if allowed....

Yet still, how sweet to have that easy belief that there are answers, that there is indeed meaning and logic to the things that happen here on this earth. How wonderful to close one's eyes at night and rest believing that no matter what happens to you or the ones you loved there was a reason behind it all, even if you may never know what it is. How beautiful to believe there is a plan.

God works in mysterious ways, his wonders never cease.

It was a closed-casket affair. The funeral director had tried his best to make her "presentable" but had found it too hard. He failed, in other words. His job was to make the dead look like they are sleeping, and he could not do so this time. He failed, there should be some sort of discount. He would be the last person to see the woman, the last one to speak to her.

122

God works in mysterious ways.

Not technically, true, of course, the people who would do the cremating would be the last to see her. They would have to remove her from this casket here in order to place her in the wooden box she would be cremated in, that was how it was done, no way anyone would cremate this casket here, it was too pretty, worth too much money. Those two or three strangers would be the last to lay eyes on his mother. He wondered where they were at this moment, while everyone here bowed their heads for the Lord's Prayer. Our Father who art in heaven....

Probably young guys, he thought. Maybe in a bar, throwing back a few. They had to work in a few hours, might as well stop in for a tapper. Later that afternoon they would be sending some strange woman into a four-thousand-plus degree chamber. After that her grey brittle body would be crushed and rendered to powder. It was a job. It paid the bills. It was what allowed those young guys to buy those beers. After it was over they could go home to their wives or girlfriends, tell them what they saw, what she looked like, why there hadn't been an open casket, maybe have some more beer, make love while the baby slept, get up and do it again tomorrow. There was always someone to burn.

His wonders never cease.

Some time in the near or distant future the ashes would be given to Biff, the woman's husband. He would perhaps hold on to them until a location for their final resting place was determined. There was talk among the three children that she should go next to their father, her first husband. But was this fair to Biff, her husband of the last ten years?

Fuck Biff.

He'd nearly said as much in their hushed conversations.

Jonah, his sister Tina said calmly, in that sort of way-too-patient voice usually owned by kindergarten teachers. Jonah, we can't just do what we want, it's not up to us.

Right, he'd said, nodding, letting her think he agreed. But fuck Biff, he thought. It *should* be up to us. And that voice, that tone, that kindergarten teacher attitude of placation and pacification, talking to him like he was either an idiot or a madman who needed calming: he heard that voice and he wanted to slap its owner. Relax, that voice sometimes said. Calm down. Relax.

Fuck you.

123

He tried not to look at Biff much at the funeral, or even for the rest of the day. A quick glance, a small hug, a brief conversation about something mundane, but that was all. He felt sorry for the man, hard not to considering the situation, but feeling sorry for someone didn't mean much in the end, not at all. You can feel sorry for someone you hate.

What should happen was she should go next to her first husband, the love of her life. That man there, Biff Oldenberg, was secondary, a minor figure, someone who wouldn't be around if things had gone the way they were supposed to. If life had been perfect that son of a bitch wouldn't be known to any of them, their mother and father would have grown old together, watched their kids raise their own children, perhaps eventually passed on from this world hand in hand, satisfied and happy, at the end of a full life.

But things don't go perfectly. God works in mysterious ways, his wonders never cease. Harold Swain died and his widow married a coarse and stiff-brained jackass who treated her like she was the dumbest person in the world.

Fuck Biff. Fuck God. Fuck Father Harvey. Fuck that motherfucking trucker out on I-41. Was there some grand plan us mere mortals could never fully know? If so, it was being carried out through the growling roaring stinking engine of a semi, through the searing heat of steel on steel, the impact of asphalt on flesh, destroying the body of a woman who never wanted anything more than to not be a young widow, to not raise three children on her own, to not lose the love of her life, to have it all be just a dream.

Stop thinking, he told himself, stop thinking. But there was so much here to think about, so much here to fear.

How are you doing, Jonah? Father Harvey asked him after the funeral.

Fine, he said. I'm fine.

*

Imagine, Tina said at some point during that week they were all together. Imagine, when Dad sees her in heaven he'll still be so young and she'll have aged so much.

Jonah thought, to nothing and no one in particular: Please save me, somehow. From this, from everything.

What got him through was Jess. Sweet, warm Jess. It was she who suggested he go for a walk that afternoon before the wake, when he was looking particularly frazzled, worn-out, empty. Go, she said, get some air, no one needs you here. She was right, that little house where his mother once lived, where that sunken old widower Biff now wandered, was suffocating, full of fluttering unfocused thoughts that hovered and landed and took off again like invisible butterflies. Such a small house, and there were already too many people inside it, he and Jess and Tom and his wife and child and Tina and her family, and any number of well-wishers dropping in, and of course Biff, looking more than worn-out yet unwilling to acknowledge it, he being from that old school where men were strong and could get through anything. Yeah, Jonah said to Jess. Yeah, I'll go for a walk.

He didn't walk, though, he took the keys to his car and drove off through his old hometown, seeing what had changed, what had stayed the same. It was a strange little town, Oakton on the Bay. It seemed to have a chip on its shoulder and a bit of an identity-confusion: it had little to offer the outside world save the highway that ran through it, but rather than simply put up a gas-station and a McDonald's to service that transitory outside world and concentrate its efforts on cementing its own internal economic strength, dependent on no one, they had put up *three* stations and *four* fast-food restaurants and let the few factories go to waste, thereby solidifying Oakton's place in the world as nothing more than a way-side. Once a quaint town of historical import, Oakton was now dying under the crushing weight of a misguided American dream. There was no reason to stay there anymore, only a reason for passing through. The newest and largest building in town was the Super 8 hotel on the highway, an invite to linger for only a night, have a good sleep, a continental breakfast, and then move on.

Yet parts of the town reminded him of the one he used to know, the one he had explored by foot and Schwinn back in the wistful days of childhood. At least the town wasn't quite dead: the neighborhoods that were run-down now were the same ones that were run-down back then. If anything, Oakton was in a state of suspended decay. He drove to these blocks and pondered the houses where friends had once lived.

125

Everyone he knew back then had moved on, perhaps never to return. He hadn't stayed in contact with anyone from his graduating class, and this was probably for the best. Yet still, it was strange not to recognize any of the faces he saw, and it would have been nice to pop in on someone and go over those old days. He thought it would have been nice to play catch-up, to see those familiar faces again, to ask them what they were doing.

Eventually he drove out of town, down the highway that left Oakton via the east-side, right along the bay. He contemplated taking Harbor Road and going out to the breakwater but stayed on the highway, past the few bay-side homes, out through the marsh and swamp that bordered each side of the road. The highway was empty of cars, there was only him, cruising along at seventy, looking up at the occasional V of geese that passed over the gray sky. When he was a kid they would bike out to this highway and go swimming at the County Park, a good ten miles ahead. He had done so with his mother once, during one of those summers after his father died. The ride there wasn't so bad but the wind over the highway on the way back was terrible.

He pulled onto the old gravel drive of the County Park, happy to see that no one had bothered to rebuild the place. You still had to walk down through an expanse of knee-high grass before you hit the sloppy beach. From that beach it was a good hundred yard walk through alternating muck and sand and weeds before you came to anything even remotely resembling swimmable water, but it was that walk itself that gave the place its charm, at least to a child. That squish of stinky bay-muck between your toes, the feel of a fish bumping your calves, the sight of an occasional dead carp, belly-up and picked by birds... it was perfect. When he thought of swimming as a child these are the things he thought of, not the community swimming pool in town, full of chlorine and piss and the screams of bratty children.

He parked his car, killed the engine, climbed out into the cool afternoon. That gray October sky, muffled by a thin layer of clouds, made the day feel gloomier, and it was quiet, just the sound of a rising wind through the weeds and the steady rush of the bay's waves. There was that smell of beach, dead fish, ancient sand, and rotting vegetation, and he stood for a moment breathing it all in, letting it wash memories over him. After swimming here he would come back stinking this same

126

way, his hair strangely thick, conditioned by whatever lived in the brown-green water. He looked around, saw a house roughly two-hundred yards off, mostly hidden by twisted trees. No sign of life there. Back behind him a car flew down the highway, the first he'd seen. He turned and walked down to the beach, taking what was now a narrow path over-crowded by those weeds, sinking down into its mud, thinking that they must have gotten rain here in the past few days. By the time he came to the beach itself his shoes were covered and his legs were speckled with brown dots. He walked onto the beach, studying the sand, spotted just one dead fish six inches long, missing eyes and tailfin. The water level was low, the beach wider than he remembered. The waves lapped up onto it in a nearly pathetic display, poorly mimicking the grandeur they may have once had, just flopping weakly onto the beach like dying men. The sound they made was like a sigh.

A bird floated a hundred yards out, a black silhouette bobbing slowly up and down. With the brown water and gray sky he felt he was looking at an unfinished painting, a canvas awaiting color, with that bird as the subject, a symbol to be read from the otherwise prosaic setting. He watched it for a long time, then thought of his mother.

This would be the first time he'd truly cried since hearing the news. The tears came over him forcefully, violently, and he was overcome with the weight of the absurdity, the sheer physical *meaninglessness* of the whole thing. He felt like looking to the sky and crying out "Why? Why?" to whatever god might be listening, but he just stood there, crying, hoping this gray world might envelope him and make him disappear. When he'd biked out here with his mother she had sat on the shore reading while he waded out and splashed around like an idiot. Now there was no place to sit, those weeds were seven-feet tall, rising like softly bowing walls on either side of the dirty path. No place to sit and no mother anyway. No one to watch him.

Jess or no Jess, he felt more alone in that moment than he ever had before, lost in the world, absolutely without comfort or love. He had lost a connection with his past, he had lost a connection with himself. And of course it was more than this, too. There was guilt here, mixed with an utterly overwhelming sorrow in a single noxious, exhausting stew. He let it all overcome him and just stood there, taking it.

I killed her years ago. I was her baby and I abandoned her.

This was the sort of gray overcast day that would not have an evening: it would go seamlessly from the murkiness of afternoon to the blackness of night. He would stay there on the dirty beach until it did.

Then he would go to his mother's wake.

*

He was there for a week in that old ranch, his childhood home, monitoring the passage of time, studying the absurdity of memory, avoiding any but the most mundane of conversations with his siblings, nieces and nephews, Jess, his stepfather, generally haunting the house and the town that surrounded it like a worn-out ghost slowly fading into oblivion, inhabiting only his mind, contemplating the long liquid run of moments and the eternal melting of seconds into minutes into days. A life is nothing but such a slow melting of moments, but if it was possible to look at them all together, like a deck of cards laid out for inspection, would it drive you crazy or render you enlightened? Would you see trends, motifs, an essential logic previously hidden, a Plan for how things work out and how they fail, or would it seem even more illogical, and would its absurdity drive you to madness? They say that before the moment of death it is possible to see your life flash before your eyes, but for what purpose, to give us the chance to see successes and failures, maybe to look upon familiar faces one more time, or to give us the opportunity to make that final decision: to look and see if there was logic behind it all, to gain enlightenment or to go insane? If and when it comes to that, he hoped that at the moment of his death he would not see any flashing of his life, it would be too much to bear, like a slap in the face, a sort of teasing, like *Here's what you once had and maybe could have had and now you'll have nothing ever again.* He hoped that when that time came, if he was offered the chance to see all the seconds and moments he had passed through, he would be able to avert his eyes and take in nothing but the sweet blackness of the coming oblivion.

This, however, was not so different. Mourning is a kind of death, then: as he haunted that sad house he was indeed presented with all the moments that had come before, not like a deck of cards but like the pages of an endless book, torn from the spine, shuffled by the Idiot hands of a pointless intelligence, chapters missing, paragraphs blotted out, whole sections rendered meaningless in narrative terms but working in tandem with the others to create a mood, an atmosphere, this general feeling of mournful awareness. Sentences smudged. Pages ripped in half, the missing sections appearing later, either cued in through associations with similar sections or senselessly tagged on, pasted haphazardly over and under and onto the others, all of it making some sort of sense, though… the sense of God, he supposed: meaning that which he might never fully comprehend. God works in mysterious ways, His wonders never cease. Like memory. Like mourning. Like the criminally insane.

My life is flashing before my eyes, he said as a joke to Tina as they were doing dishes two days after the funeral. She was washing, he was drying, and he looked to her face to see if she knew what he meant. She had to. She had to be thinking about the same things, seeing her life suddenly in a new light, remembering odd and previously forgotten moments from the past.

What kind of life have you had? she asked, half-serious. You've had it easy.

What do you mean by easy?

You've just… you've never had to deal with certain things. That's all. She looked at him, gave him a bright smile meant to be friendly, playful. You're the baby….

He dried his dishes and said nothing more.

*

He cared about these people, but it was not about them. He felt sorry for Biff, wandering that house now, suddenly alone, shockingly alone, faced with his own run of days. He cared about Tom and his wife and their kid. He cared about Tina and Mark and their three little ones, suddenly thrust into a world without Gramma, but it was not about them. This wasn't even about himself. There was something greater than all of them at work here, something tenuous yet omnipresent, something brewing and living in their hearts and minds, at once good and bad, beautiful and ugly, violent and peaceful, hateful and loving. Something they might never see. And was it up to them to see it? He wasn't sure. They may or may not notice it coursing through and around them but it would help to actually look, right? He had always seen such things. He used to lie in the backyard and study the passing shapes of clouds, where he saw elephants and cows and castles and birds and crocodiles. This here might not be so different, the mind in mourning the same as the mind in cloud-born daydream: you had to be sensitive, alert. You had to care. You had to open your mind to the connection of things, to those lines that exist but are not visible. That cloud there would not be a crocodile if you didn't imagine a line connecting snout to body, body to tail.

Pareidolia, it was called, this finding of specific images amidst randomness. It was an ancient activity, the reason we have constellations, the reason mankind made gods, to explain the inexplicable. Humanity is cursed with this need to see things where nothing exists, to find reason in the meaningless. The human mind inherently despises happenstance and absurdity. The drawings of Escher frustrate our primal souls. Cubism was radical, shocking. Surrealism made people riot. You can stand before a Pollock and feel torn between attraction and repulsion: he abstracted from the abstract, made images that represent nothing, rendered it impossible to pull a figure or reflection or even the suggestion of a *thing* from those mesmerizing and beautiful swirls of black and red and blue and green and yellow. A Pollock is not a Rorschach. Rorschach sketches are cumulous.

And that is life, Jonah believed. Life is not a Jackson Pollock kaleidoscope of the nonrepresentational, it is more like the Rorschach. It is more like clouds.

One had to look, though, in order to see.

*

He was standing in the backyard of this little ranch, much as he had done as a child. A crisp autumn had dried out the grass, turned it a subtle shade of brown. From where he was standing he could see the entire property, from the little shed that held Biff's lawnmower and boat, to the trees that marked the end of the yard three acres away. It was a view he was familiar with. He knew it intimately, and yet of course it was not quite the same, was changing all the time, subtly, and not always for the better, not *usually* for the better. Biff was a mad man when it came to pruning and cutting bushes and trees: there had been a good deal more of each back before he had come along, the yard had been thick with them. He was a type

Jonah knew well, a prick for pruning, the sort of man who felt threatened by the tiniest display of wildness, who could not rest if the grass was higher than an inch and a half, who could not tolerate the impudence of dandelions, who could not handle the thought of one single shrub deciding on its own course of growth. There had been a beautiful array of lilac bushes along the lawn's southern side, popping out gorgeous displays of light purple flowers, attracting equally beautiful bees, sending that familiar heavy scent through the late-spring air. Now they were no longer. Biff had gone into them years ago, chopped them down completely, leaving nothing but a sad-looking little thing that was full of thorny vines and which was probably doomed to die of loneliness. Back when Harold Swain had owned the place the yard had been lush, so thickly green it felt like there was a private front of humidity hanging over the whole works. The very last acre and half had been a mysterious wildflower field, perhaps a virgin prairie remnant, one of the last of its kind. Jonah remembered seeing red-tail hawks circling over it, hunting the mice and snakes that lived there.

Alas, Biff had mowed it all down and then paid a neighbor to churn the ugly bare earth with a tractor. Why? Why not. For the hell of it. Because it was there. And the thing had never needed work, not one single bit of tending or weeding save the small path that Harold Swain used to mow so his family could walk through it and witness close up the life that teemed there.

Prick, thought Jonah, thinking of Biff. Was this fair, he wondered, to judge the man so harshly over such a thing? Yes. If you judge a man by the contents of his heart, what did such an action, the pointless destruction of a beautiful benign entity like that little prairie, say about the heart of the man who had done it? There had been no logic in the action, no motive save the action itself. Biff was man who pounded things down, beat them into submission, berated them into compliance. He was the same with people or plants.

The garden that Harold Swain had loved was gone, too, but that had been his widow's decision. Five years after his death she had finally allowed the garden to be seeded over and turned to lawn. Tom and then Jonah had mowed it mindlessly, at first glad it was gone, happy to be rid of all that weeding, but overtime the regret sat in. The last time Jonah had eaten a carrot freshly pulled from the ground he'd been fifteen. Now

131

his veggies were store-bought, laced with pesticides, shot through with poison.

He could see where that garden had once been, even now, standing here in the yard on what was a partly-cloudy afternoon. The grass there was different, a shade or two darker, and elevated above the rest. He stared at it a long time before he realized it resembled a grave, the gently rising mound of earth in front of a headstone. If there was a giant tombstone in front of this plot of ground what would it say? THE WAY IT HAD BEEN. Perhaps. Or just CHILDHOOD. Maybe INNOCENCE.

He contemplated the vestigial garden for a long time. Behind him he could hear voices in the house, the occasional burst of laughter, the clinking of dishes and silverware. How long had it been since the Swain family had been together like this? A lifetime, literally. Tina's son Micah had been the only kid then, a fresh-faced baby full of gurgles and spit, the center of attention. His Gramma Linda had devoted every moment to him, grinning into his face, making faces of her own, sticking her tongue out, making noises. That had been a Christmas weekend seven years ago, and it had been a rather coincidental reunion. Tom had not been meaning to come but had found a change in his plans at the last minute, and though he had not been able to bring Kathy to finally meet Tina he never stopped talking about her. And Jonah, what had he been thinking and doing? He could barely remember. He thought perhaps he had just started at the printing job, but he wasn't sure. All he really remembered about that weekend was the tension between his mother and her husband. They'd been married three years by then, but they talked like they'd been together all their lives. He remembered no single conversations, no pivotal moments, but he sensed that there was a prick-ish quality to the man, that he wasn't entirely respectful of his wife. Of course, she was not easy to live with, not even then. She could be quick to snap, even quicker at self-pity. She was still drinking, of course. And one night while the family tried to play *Trivial Pursuit* she broke into tears for no reason. No *known* reason, anyway, though she surely had her own private ones. Christ, what a memory. Such a quick change, as all of hers were, such a sudden move from jocularity to jaundice:

Tina, to Tom: So what's this wife of yours do?
She works in advertising.
Oh yeah? In what way?

132

She's the head of marketing for a local firm.

Oh, cool.

And then their mother had jumped in bitterly with: No one ever asks me what I do... I sacrificed my life for my kids. She spat the words out venomously, tears in her eyes, her mouth trembling, glistening with brandy and Coke.

No one said anything for a few moments, until Tina broke the ice and asked if anyone needed anything from the kitchen.

But there were many such memories, they were all too familiar. And still, despite all of that, what right did this man, this Biff, have to berate her, to make her feel stupid, to correct everything she did and said? What right did he have to treat her like a backyard bush in need of trimming or... cutting down.

You lose everything, Biff had said to her often. Keys, purse, shoes... doesn't your brain work?

That was a Biff staple: Doesn't your brain work?

Cocksucker.

Jonah didn't want to feel this bitter as he stood in the backyard. This was a meant to be a simple little alone time. The three siblings and their better halves were planning on going out to the bars that night, just to get out of the house, to forget their mourning, to shake off the doldrums, to get pleasantly buzzed. Perhaps to get to know each other again, these new versions, these new people they'd become. Jonah was looking forward to it, and yet he couldn't stop his thoughts. He stared at that giant grave where a garden had once been and felt something heavy on his shoulders. It was memory that did that, he knew. Memory had both weight and presence, each oppressive. He tried to will it away but could not. He felt like he'd gained fifty pounds, and could do nothing but just stand there. Memory, sweetened through the ages just like wine. Well no, that's not how it worked, he knew: even the sweetest memories turn rancid, if only because they can never again be reality. He thought of the happiest memories he had and how they were washed with bitterness, framed in regret, coated with sadness like a painting in sepia.

If only that wildflower field was still there, then he could do what he had done as a child, disappear inside of it and forget about everything else. It would mean more now, he knew, because there was so much more to run from. Back then it had been fights with mom and dad, a bad report card, a broken toy. Now it was all this, this funeral crap. And more:

133

the world at large, suicide bombers, rapes, wars, criminal politicians lying to a naïve (or worse, blasé) public, homeland security, pop culture, reality TV and the new realities of life in the 21st Century, the Great American Contradiction. A War on Terror in which no one was really at war because no one could ever win or lose and no one was sacrificing anything for the effort, a world after September Eleventh in which nothing was changed, no one was different, everything was as rotten and evil as before. Once he'd been a kid, a simple kid in a simple time. Now he had woken to a modern nightmare so complex it was downright Byzantine, a labyrinth of confusion and fear. And it was one thing to wake and look absently upon such a thing, quite another to have your own life intertwined with it. He knew he was within the nightmare when he Googled his mother and found her all over the place, the accident snatched off the AP like there was something to be learned from it. Welcome to our modern times, he thought. The Swains had come to our new century.

*

JD's Bar.

He could get drunk on three beers because he didn't drink much, but this evening it took five, the alcohol perhaps being absorbed by all that rich and fattening mourner's food everyone kept bringing over, all those hot-dishes and cinnamon rolls and cakes. Still, he went from feeling nothing to feeling happily buzzed right after his third sip of that fifth beer, actually not really feeling much of anything until he looked over at Jess and saw her mouth the words *You're drunk.* He gave her the finger, playfully, and received the wrath of his sister, who'd seen the whole exchange.

Don't treat her that way, she said in mock-anger. This might be a long-term thing here...

Yeah, Tom said, turning to him. What's going on with that? Are you guys gonna get married?

Why would we do something like that? Jonah asked, knowing the buttons to push to irritate his family. We've only been dating for, what, three years? We hardly know each other.

Three years? My god, man, get a ring on that woman's finger!

Tom's wife chimed in with: I can help plan the wedding...

Soon that was all they were discussing, the apparently imminent marriage of Jonah to Jess. They joked, but there was an undercurrent of seriousness. It was a source of family intrigue, this relationship, a topic of gossip.

Do you have a fear of commitment? Tom asked loudly, shouting over the country music blaring from the bar's juke.

No, Jonah said, smiling sassily. I have a fear of marriages.

Oh, man, marriage is wonderful, it's beautiful, if you find the right person it's an absolutely beautiful thing. The look in his eyes said he believed this.

Jonah nodded. The song on the radio was telling him the complete opposite, and he listened to it and his brother argue and tried not to laugh out loud.

Ain't never gonna settle down again, the music said in classic redneck double-negative.

It's a beautiful thing, Tom said drunkenly, pleasantly.

Won't get me to wear no ring.

It's like finding that person who makes you complete.

I'm gonna love you forever. At least until my wife gets home. Yeehaw.

Tom's end of the argument was eventually lost under the blare of the guitar-solo bridge, leaving the entire debate open for further exploration, later.

What kind of music do you guys like nowadays? Tom asked Jonah and Jess after a few sips of beer. Grunge? Death metal? What are kids into these days? You like country? He talked like he was more than two years older than them. He had inherited a presence from their father, a preternatural age, the aura of a man who had been fifty since he was twenty.

No, Jess answered. It's… what's the word…?

Great? Tom suggested.

No….

Real?

No… predictable and….

What? It's good old American music, it's…

Oh you'll listen to it when you're older, Tina chimed in, really only half-listening, more interested in making faces at her husband. They didn't get out much by themselves, they had both admitted. Their children occupied all their time, so this little outing, this break from all the funeral crap, was a nice little mini-vacation for them. Odd how that works, Jonah had

135

thought earlier, during his first beer. Come up to your mother's funeral and end up drinking in some divey little bar.

Good old all-American music, Tom said again, to Jess.

I'll pass, she said.

You gotta love country, it's pure music.

Wilco, Tom Waits, Radiohead, Jonah said, apparently to no one.

Hank Williams Junior, man, Tom shouted to Jess. Pure, simple, honest music.

Boring melodies, terrible lyrics, she countered.

Grandaddy, Jonah said. Beatles. Dylan. Townes van Zandt....

When you get older you'll listen to it, Tom said. He patted Jess condescendingly on the arm. You're just a kid. He winked at her.

I like *old* country, she said. Roots stuff. Bluegrass...

Steve Earle, Jonah said. Neil Young. Gram Parsons. John Cage.

Allison Krauss? Tom asked.

Del McCoury, Jess answered. She turned giggly and perky when she was drinking, became all smiles, all eyes and teeth.

Liszt, Mozart, Bach, Vivaldi, Jonah said, still to no one. He slowly sipped his beer and thought about the music he liked and why he liked it. He needed emotion, melody, experimentation, energy. Restlessness. Danger. Noise. Harmony. In his changer back home was Radiohead, Uncle Tupelo, *Abbey Road*, *Yankee Hotel Foxtrot*, *Rum, Sodomy, and the Lash*. From "The Sick Bed of Cuchulainn" to "How to Disappear Completely" to Bach's cello suites, he saw no difference, if it moved him he liked it. Fuck labels. Fuck these sorts of conversations. Elvis Costello. The Ramones. Loose Fur. Aaron Copland. Gershwin. Elgar. Jess when she sang in the shower. Jess when she moaned under his weight.

I want to glide through your brown eyes dreaming, take you from the inside, baby hold on tight.

Energy. Excitement. Oddness. Melody and dissonance. Three chords and a symphony to disappear in.

Phish, he said, moments later, as an afterthought. By then, of course, the conversation had drifted elsewhere and the song on the juke was fading and he was just a drunken idiot shouting out a band's name to a bar full of people that probably

136

thought he was calling out the names of animals, or the standard line to a kid's game of cards.

I have to piss, he announced, just as loudly, for all to hear before the next song kicked in, and wobbled over to the men's room, not feeling overly drunk, yet not feeling much of anything, either. Feeling, as they say, strangely fine. His mother had been ashes for only three days now and here he was, happily drunk, not thinking about her at all, thinking about music and peeing and beer and whether he knew the bartender or not. Thinking about *now*, away from the weight of memory, away from images of large graves and giant headstones and murdered prairies and chopped up lilac bushes. He peed in peace, read the jokes penciled on the walls.

Wonders never cease, he knew. The world works in mysterious ways. Our world. This world. Our only one.

He came out of the bathroom and caught a glimpse of familiar faces shooting pool across the room. He avoided looking over there, instead once more wobbled across the floor to where his family was sitting at a long table. There were three such tables in this bar, only this one fully occupied, one of the others bare save for some crumpled napkins and a few spilled kernels of popcorn, and the third keeping company with a fat middle-aged man who also looked familiar to Jonah.

Mr. Novak, Tom said to Jonah a few minutes later.

Mr. Novak had been the phy-ed teacher when they'd been in high-school. Something had apparently happened to him since then.

He was fired, Tom explained. The rumor was he molested a student.

Holy shit.

Right after that he got divorced.

Jesus. What's he do now?

Tom shrugged. Sits in here and gets drunk.

Jonah stared at the man for a long time, looking away only when the man looked back. In that time Jonah was able to conclude with certainty that he was looking at a man slowly killing himself. It was in the bloodshot eyes, the patchy cheeks, the hunched back bearing the burden of sin and sloth.

Think he recognizes us?

Tom shrugged. Tina's husband had come back with two more beers, which he set before Jonah and Tom. Both brothers looked up at their brother-in-law and smiled their thanks, then they emptied their old glasses and picked up these new ones.

You're not gonna get sick, are ya? Tom asked.

Naw....

They lifted their glasses, drank deeply.

The sound of the balls slamming together at the pool table was loud, like the laughter that accompanied it. Jonah risked a look over there and no longer believed he recognized anyone. He watched them play for a while then looked around this bar, for the hundredth time this evening. They had actually started out at another bar, this little party of Swain's and McDowells. They had had one beer each before walking across the street to JD's. Pub crawling in Oakton took absolutely no effort whatsoever, all the taverns were located within one block of each other.

Jonah liked this bar, liked the atmosphere... what little there was. Perhaps it was the simplicity he liked, that open and spare utilitarianism. Basically it was your typical northern redneck place, bare of any stylistic touches save the bikini calendar on the wall, the requisite neon beer signs (SCHLITZ! MILLER!), the bottles of strange-colored liquid behind the bar that no one ever ordered from and which might have been colored water or someone's stash of illegal absinthe and moonshine, decades old by now and liable to make a man blind. There was a small spike-horn set of antlers on another wall, a list of dumb-blonde jokes on yet another. A small television set up high on the wall to the bar's left was playing the Green Bay news. There was a crawler across the bottom of the screen and Jonah could only make out every fifth word or so. He saw IRAQ, WETLANDS, KIDNAPPED. He looked away when he thought he saw SNIPER. It was all too much.

You all right? Jess asked him, leaving her stool to sidle up to his side as Tom held a conversation with Tina's husband.

Yeah, you?

She gave him such an absolutely lovely smile he was suddenly rendered breathless. This was his girl. He was her man. She put her arm around him, leaned down to press her soft warm lips to his forehead and he was overcome with a strong feeling of lust and love, a desire to both place her on a pedestal and take her in a hot tent, or on cool sheets, or on the dew-spattered grass under a moon so fat and big he could feel it on his back, the sun's light filtered through lunar-dust, moving through the eternity of space, past worlds known and alien, through all the mysteries of the universe, out to the depths of blackness. He wanted to take her home now, strip her bare, revisit what it meant to be alive.

Though drunk, he was aware of how much he owed her, of how much he loved her. Look at her, he thought: that moon-face, those doe eyes, that fall of hair over her forehead and down along her cheeks. He reached up and brushed a strand from her eyes. In return she gave him another smile, once more put her arm around him and squeezed. He closed his eyes, rested his head on her shoulder, started to drift off through the blackness of his eyelids, thought of it as a portal to the rest of the universe, wondered what the scientists thought of such things, the mystical qualities that seem to lie at the center of their field of study, the daydreaming it both arose from and continued to inspire. What sort of mysticism had Newton possessed? Einstein? Einstein was an atheist, Jonah believed, but that was okay, he wasn't thinking in religious or even spiritual terms here, he was thinking of pure daydreaming, the act of lying on the ground and staring up to the heavens revolving and streaming overhead. Coming wholly natural from that act, which had surely been the mother of a million scientific theories, were the crazy ideas the human mind seems uniquely suited to give birth to, like this one here: if the Universe is everything and everything is in the Universe, why couldn't a man sitting in a small bar drinking piss-warm macro beers and resting his head on the arm of the woman he loved not close his eyes and slip away through the blackness he found there, through Time itself, emerging at last on the other side of Everything? If Everything is Nothing and the Universe is an eternity of Nothing, then....

Hey, Jess said in his ear. He felt her breath, hot and alive. Hey.

He opened his eyes, came out of the darkness into a strange pearl-colored light. He had done it. He was on the other side of the Universe. He was Nowhere and Everywhere. He himself was Nothing and Everything. There was no sound but a very quiet humming, like electrical wires, the music of the spheres. He could see no shapes, just that light. He felt numb. This part of the Universe was beautiful, opaque, radiant, and so, by extension, was he. He wanted nothing more than to sit here on this new plane, feeling nothing, thinking nothing, floating in space, noncorporeal, absolutely without concern. But....

I'm sorry, Jess said, her lips still close to his ear. He blinked and the pearly-Nothing was gone, he was back at JD's Bar, zapped across the Universe at the speed of light. Jess was looking at him with a painful expression of sympathy turning down her mouth, lifting her eyebrows. She said nothing more. No one at their table was speaking now, there was only the sound of the pool game and the dull thump of another shit-kicking song to rattle their ribs and massage the ache in their hearts.

On the television was the ruined car that had been his mother's. It was impossible to tell what was being said about her accident, but when the picture switched to the speaker Jonah saw what looked like an official of some sort, perhaps an investigator. He had a bushy mustache and a comb-over and a serious and seriously-exhausted look on his face, the result of much stress and many late nights. Perhaps they were talking about that year's tally of highway fatalities. Perhaps they were talking about truckers who were too tired to drive, who were hopped up on pills, who were getting handjobs from cheap hookers as they flew down the road.

Jonah closed his eyes again, but it was no use: he was stuck here now, on this side of the Universe, spinning and revolving through the only world he would ever know.

*

We're the only family in the world who would go out bar-hopping at such a time, he said to Jess later that night, after they had both fallen at last onto the bed in his mother's guest room.

She kissed his cheek. Shhh....

That's because everyone else is normal, he said. But this isn't normal.

Of course not. Nobody expects this kind of thing.

No, not that. *This*. This isn't normal.

What isn't?

This....

You're drunk. Go to sleep. You want some water?

This isn't normal. Other families lose people all the time but this is different.

I'll get you some water.

It's complicated.

Let me have my arm back and I'll get you some water....

It's complex.

Jonah....

It's just not normal.

This was a guest bedroom now but it had been *his* room once upon a time. He was intimate with the play of the streetlight on the ceiling, with the sound of the furnace thumping unhappily in the basement, the running and gurgling of the sump pump. He had lain there many times listening to the house... or to the hushed conversations down the hall. He had heard everything. Voices carried in this little ranch. A whisper was like a scream in the muted darkness of night. He had heard arguments about love, marriage, life. He had heard his mother crying. She tried to use Johnny Carson to cover the sound but it was no use, not in this house, not with every little sound sharp and clear, amplified down the little tunnel that was the hallway, those perfect acoustics for bitterness and drunken mumbling. He had heard too much. He used to listen as long as he could and then, when he could stand it no longer, he would turn to the wall and cover his head with his pillow, suffocating all sounds save the ringing in his ears, pressing the pillow down onto himself with all his strength, a mimicry of suicide or murder.

Tonight there were no sounds from down the hall. They had snuck in as quietly as possible, hearing only Biff's harsh breathing. Biff was an old man, old men breathe hard, like it takes all their effort to do so. Jonah and Jess brushed their teeth in the bathroom across the hall, then each stood for a time in front of the bedroom door, listening for any indication they had woken Biff, stirred him from whatever dreams a widower dreams. But his breathing remained, steady and loud, rattling like a baby toy.

I wish everyone else was still staying here, Jess said. Tom and Tina and their families had moved to the hotel on the highway after two nights in the ranch, ostensibly for more room but also, Jonah knew, to get away from this house. He didn't blame them, and would have done likewise, but it didn't seem right. A quite odd guilt had threatened to erupt in him at the very thought of leaving Biff alone here, and though he hated that guilt he acquiesced to it. It would have been better for his mental health to take a room at the hotel, but someone had to stay and keep Biff company. Goddamnit, someone had to.

141

My head is spinning, Jess said as soon as she was lying down.

Which direction?

She stared up to where the streetlight threw hazy designs across the tile. Counter-clockwise, she said.

Jonah smiled. Mine's spinning clockwise, maybe together we're—

Maybe together we're sober, she finished, hitting him playfully on the arm.

He started to laugh and, struggling to withhold it, began to giggle like a schoolgirl.

Do you want water? Jess asked, just minutes later. She was already half out of the bed.

Complicated, he said again, letting the word fade off, like dust blown by a breeze.

I'm gonna get some for myself, she said, but when she started to swing her legs down to the floor Jonah reached out and took hold of her.

Wait, he said. Shhh... listen.

She listened. A moment later came the sound of feet shuffling down the hallway to the bathroom. The door closed on squeaky hinges.

Do you think we woke him? she asked.

No....

They remained motionless until the toilet was flushed and Biff was once more shuffling back down the hall. Jonah listened to each protest given by the floor beneath his weight, each creak in the floorboards, each subtle muting of the man's step by a loose section of old carpet.

Each one of those sounds carried a memory, Jonah thought.

He fell back down to his pillow, and looked at the light on the ceiling, those hazy yellow swirls, the soft shadows of the bushes near the window, created by the sickly glow of the streetlight as it fell weakly against the house. He remembered when the city put that light in. He'd been ten. Up until then his nights had been set comfortably in solid darkness, but after that summer there was a constant battle between light and shadow on the ceiling above him, each vying for possession of the little room. He would lie there studying the way the shadows of those bushes would move just slightly in the breeze, then the way they would swing madly across the room and down the opposite wall when a car happened to fly down the road, returning to normal only after the car had passed. He had never liked that light, had never seen the point of it. More than once he had devised plans to be rid of it, but only once had he ever tried. He snuck out one night with his bb gun and tried to shoot the damn thing to death, but the gun hadn't been powerful enough, the bb's just bounced right off the glass. He had snuck back in feeling like a failure, only to run into his mother coming from the bathroom.

What are you doing? she asked him, her voice groggy, her words slurred, her eyes squinted to see him.

Nothing.

She gestured to the gun. And what about that?

He tried to think of something to say but could only shrug.

She nodded. You were trying to shoot out that light, weren't you?

Yeah, he answered sheepishly.

She thought a moment, looking down at him, then nodded again. You're just like I was at your age, she said. Then she continued on down the hall, back to bed.

Jonah smiled at this memory. Jess had decided not to get water and was now pressed back against him, one leg draped over his. He could feel her warmth, the heat of her skin. He lay motionless, waiting for her to sleep, which she finally did after rolling away from him and curling herself up fetally.

He listened to her exhausted, drunken breathing for a long time, until he was certain she was asleep, then he slowly climbed out of bed and opened the door to the hallway. He listened, heard Biff snoring.

Feeling less drunk than he had just minutes before, Jonah stepped out into the hall, closed the bedroom door behind him, and made his way out of the house, shutting the front door slowly, feeling like a burglar in reverse. The night that greeted him was cold, the stars above him clear and white, like tiny shards of ice. He saw his breath rising like a parting fog as he made his way down the driveway. He hesitated a moment before stepping onto the black lawn, where, forty-feet away, the streetlight sprouted like a pathetic facsimile of a tree, tall and sturdy but lacking a tree's character or spirit. He was wearing only socks on his feet and that grass looked wet with dew. Only a moment's hesitation, though, and then he walked out to the pole, coming up to it with his eyes focused on its top, where the light was ringed with a gauzy halo. He felt like a

143

worshipper coming to stand before a beloved totem, but only in the physical act of his slow approach: his mental state was something altogether different, altogether less reverent and more distrustful, the way a Jew might walk up to the image of Jesus on a barnyard fence.

He stood under the light for a long while, bathed in its pale, wide radiance, just staring up to the bulb and that halo of moist nighttime air. A month earlier and the halo would have been made of moths and beetles, with the swooping black figures of little brown bats entering and exiting the glow like satellites coming and going through a galaxy of insects. Instead of this loud wall of silence there would have been the electrical hum of crickets and amphibians. Those were always his favorite sounds, the purring drone of field crickets, the pulsing rhythm of toads. This ranch was always a good spot for such sounds, sitting out here near marshes and forest and that big backyard. He remembered spring peepers, and chorus frogs, and the calls of cardinals, cicadas, doves. This was the soundtrack of his childhood.

He thought about moths, drawn to lights like these for reasons perhaps they themselves didn't understand, pulled from the darkness of night to hover and rest in the blinding glare of sun-brilliant light, dazed by the enormity of the brightness, confused by the buzz of the bulb itself as well as the pattering and fluttering of a thousand other wings… to say nothing of the occasional ominous blur of a bat flying in from the outer edges of darkness to steal one, two, a hundred fellow loopers and underwings. He wondered what it was like to be drawn like that, illogically or otherwise, to some great blazing brilliance, to be blinded by an awesome whiteness, to enter a world within a world, a fiery beacon in the cold dark midnight. Of course, no need to wonder, it was what he was doing now, called from the warm body of his woman, drawn to this light, pulled by forces he could not understand to stare up to its halo and ponder the alien minds of insects and bats. He wondered what lurked out there now, what black shapes sat at the outer fringes of the light's reach, waiting to swoop in and grab *him*, carry him off, sink fangs into his neck, make a feast of his thoughts and flesh.

He looked up at the light and wondered if he had the strength now to hurl a rock up there and put it out for good. And would that solve anything. And how good would it feel.

Turning his head, he looked back at the little ranch home, obscured partly by a large pine tree and some fat evergreen bushes Biff had not gotten to yet. He wondered if the old man would let the yard go now, or whether he would take to the chain saw and lopper as an outlet for his mourning. Old men liked to stay busy, old widowers even more so. And was the man so old? Just past seventy, more than ten years older than his dead wife. Why had she picked a man so much older than she? Why had she picked *him*....

Easier to contemplate the mind of a moth, Jonah thought, looking back up to the light, than the mind of a mother. She had picked him because she loved him, he supposed. Twelve years ago they'd been married in a stuffy little office in the Oakton Court House. There had been hope implicit in the act, the idea that perhaps this was the moment when her old life was over, when she'd finally put her first husband behind her, when she might move on.

But you don't move on, thought Jonah. You can't move on from such a thing, losing the love of your life, the father of your children, any more than a moth might be able to move on from the light. You don't move on until dawn comes or a bat flies in to take you out with claws and teeth.

Life is strange, he thought. Stranger than death, even. Death is not so complicated, is rather simple, in fact: you are no longer of this earth, you are gone. For the dead, all problems are solved.

He felt the dew soaking his socks, felt the silence of early morning around him, felt the presence of that house at his back, looming there, waiting, felt the light's glow on his eyes and face. He looked around for a rock, saw nothing. He was fairly certain he could get the velocity necessary to take that light out, but wasn't so sure his aim was good enough. And again, would it solve anything? It was just a light that had haunted his childhood bedroom, his childhood nights, painting its surreal swirls and lines on his ceiling. Just a light. Signifying nothing. They put it up the summer before his Dad died, and now here he was, looking up to it just days after his mother had gone. We give reason and meaning to the meaningless, he knew. It was dangerous. This was just a light, no different from any of the others that lined this street. Except this one shone its unhealthy glow into that bedroom, that lonely little bedroom in the middle of a lonely little house. He stood there a long time, the whole town quiet, sleeping deeply, dreaming, not even a car or truck passing on the highway five miles away. His feet were cold and wet, his neck hurt from

145

staring up to the light. He felt like he might stand there until morning, like it might be the best thing to do, let the new sun warm him, wash over him like a golden baptism. But the house behind him was calling, just like this light had, drawing him back to its shadows, its familiar creaks and moans, the intimate claustrophobia of its walls and ceiling. He turned at last and made his way back there, slipping off his wet socks, finally crawling in bed next to his sleeping woman, careful not to touch her with his cold, damp feet. He fell into troubled dreams but remembered none come morning.

*

He tried to look at his mourning objectively, to step back from it all and see if he could learn something interesting from it. He thought he noticed at least two stages in himself, not the usual denial and acceptance, no, but bitterness and confusion. He lay in bed listening to Jess slowly waking and Biff already up, trouncing around in his old-man way. Through the curtains the light of morning was trickling in, so different from the dirty light of that streetlamp as to make the latter seem alien, something from a dream, a nightmare. This light here was clean and golden as it spilled down the wall and across his eyes. He lay there thinking about mourning and morning, feeling as if he was on the verge of finding some connection between the two, a symbiotic relationship perhaps, perhaps only a parasitic one. It seemed that mornings were when he thought most clearly about this death, and when he was most accepting of it. Towards afternoon he would get depressed and sad, and come nightfall he grew alternately bitter and melancholic. If he had to choose a time to contemplate the death of his mother he would pick morning. If he was a religious man he would think it was God in that new sunlight, warming and comforting him. As it stood he had no idea what it was, just that he believed morning was a time when his mind was fresh and open to the rambling of his thoughts.

After a time he rose to go to the bathroom, leaving the bedroom as quietly as he could. He slipped across the hall, into the bathroom, and emerged several minutes later. As he crossed back across the hall he happened to glance toward the kitchen and caught Biff's eye.

Biff smiled and gestured for him to come over. Shit, Jonah thought, but he went into the kitchen and offered his own

146

smile, hoping he looked decently pleasant. The old man, for his part, looked even older, more frail, and yet there was within his eyes some new form of strength, like a new determination, a new focus. Old people tend to deal with death and mourning by finding something to work on, something they could give all their energy to, in order to not think about the situation at hand. He supposed they'd soon hear him hammering something, or mowing the lawn, or fixing something in the basement which he'd long been neglecting.

"How was last night?" Biff asked.

"Good. Much needed."

Biff nodded. He was leaning against the counter by the sink, a cup of coffee in his hand. "Hard to believe, isn't it?" he asked.

Jonah knew he meant the death, and he nodded.

"She'd like having you all here, though. She would have loved it."

"Yeah."

Biff sipped his coffee and stared down to the floor. He was quiet for several moments and then he said: "She never was a good driver. I always told her to be careful, but she drove without thinking, she'd be looking all around, checking out houses, watching people."

"It wasn't her fault."

"I can't tell you how many times she came back with little scratches all over the car, a new little dent almost every other day. She'd go down to the store and somehow manage to scrape up the whole passenger side."

"It wasn't her fault," Jonah said again. He had no idea *how* he was saying it, if he was being forceful or if the old man even heard him at all. I should slap the dentures right out of the cocksucker's mouth, he thought. His fists tightened but of course he did nothing. He poured himself a cup of coffee, just to be doing something, and headed back to the bedroom. As he closed the door behind him Jess rolled over and smiled. He smiled back, set the coffee on the nightstand, and crawled back in bed with her.

"Hey," she said.

"Hey."

"What time is it?"

"I don't know. Seven?"

She rolled again to face the ceiling.

"You feel all right?" he asked her.

147

"Surprisingly fine. You?"

"All right. Not hung-over. Hungry."

"Me too." She brought one of her arms out to touch him, then turned her head to look at him again. "How long have you been up?"

"Half hour, maybe."

"What were you doing?"

"Watching you sleep," he lied.

She ran her fingers over his forehead and through his hair. "I like to watch you sleep, too."

"Yeah?"

"Yeah. You always look so peaceful."

That's what they say about the dead, he thought. He smiled at her.

"Is Biff up?" she asked.

"He just went outside. He's going to mow the lawn."

"How do you know that?"

"Because it doesn't need mowing, that's how."

He was right: within ten minutes there rose the distinct sound of a ragged, asthmatic two-stroke engine, breaking what had been a quiet and peaceful morning. The two young lovers took the opportunity to rise quickly and raid the kitchen, without the presence of a shuffling old man and all the baggage his mere presence trailed. They were both starving, having had nothing in their stomachs for the last twelve hours but beer and bar peanuts. Jess made scrambled eggs while he fried up some bacon. Feeling naughty, like little kids left alone to raid the cookie jar, they also had a slice apiece of a chocolate cake someone had dropped off two days earlier. Mourner's cake. Sickeningly sweet.

"We're gonna get fat," she said, licking crumbs from her lips. Through the window behind her Jonah could see Biff on his rider, going up and down the lawn, up and down, up and down, occasionally moving over the vestigial garden to cut the already-short grass growing there.

"It's not like we had *ice cream* with this, or anything..." he said.

Her eyes widened. "We never checked for ice cream...." She said the last two words like they contained magic one had to be careful with. An incantation of uncertain power.

"Don't," he said, holding up a hand to quiet her. "No more food talk... I'm going to explode."

"How about a beer?"

He flashed her his middle-finger and she gasped in shock.

"What would Tina say?" she said, feigning offense.

"She would say I'm a bad, bad boy."

"You are. You know you are. Stop smiling like that, sassy."

He made a face like a naughty little schoolboy and said: "Maybe I need a spanking…."

"Oh Jesus…."

They laughed, and in mid-laugh the phone rang. They looked at each other for the first three rings, and then Jonah gazed out at Biff, still riding up and down, headed now for what had once been the prairie.

"Shit," he said. He rose from the table and picked up the receiver. "Hello, Swain residence. I mean, Oldenberg residence." He listened, then sighed. "We're not answering questions, you piece of shit. You call back and I'll beat the fuck out of you." He slammed the phone down.

"What was *that* about?" Jess asked, her eyes wide, her mouth open in real shock.

"The press," he said. "Some prick from the Green Bay paper. We've told them already, we're not…." He shook his head and ran his hands through his hair.

"You all right?"

He looked at his hands, hooked into tense claws, the muscles and tendons sharp and taught, the veins like wires straining against the skin that held them. He could barely recognize the hands as his own.

"I guess not," he said, sighing and looking at her apologetically. "Sorry."

"Don't apologize to me. You have a right to be mad."

He nodded, felt his heart beating at his ribs. "I don't feel so good now."

"Sick?"

"Claustrophobic. I'm going to shower and then I want to get out of here."

"And go where?"

"Wherever. Somewhere. Anywhere. Maybe go sit by the bay. Drive around. Something."

Instantly, without further questions, as if any of these were things she wanted to do, she nodded and said: "All right."

149

That was why he loved her. She knew what he needed and did not judge.

*

His hometown. Oakton. Population 4500. (*Salute!*). He drove through it with Jess by his side, for a moment stepping outside this world he lived in, this life he led, this nightmare he'd woken to, and felt as if he were back in high-school, cruising the streets with his chick, feeling healthy, happy, arrogant as a peacock, leaning back in his seat with his left hand draped casually over the wheel (steering with his wrist) and the right settled comfortably on the warm thigh of his girl. It was a bright day, nearly spring-like despite the turning leaves and the crisp air. There was a feeling of promise in this day, despite the way it had started. He felt a rush of confidence and peace. He took a moment to try and live this illusion to its fullest, to daydream himself back to those days cruising Oakton's streets, looking for friends, a party, waiting until dark to find a place to drink beer or screw. He reached down and flicked on the radio, tuned it to the Green Bay channel, smiled when something suitably '80's came through the speakers. Dire Straits. Money for nothing and your chicks for free. He looked over at Jess, who was staring out her window, admiring the old houses in this neighborhood, the brick facades and cupolas and gardens. He could imagine her quite well at seventeen, fresh-faced and perky, with honey-colored hair and wide eyes looking to the future. Now, of course, there were faint wrinkles at the corners of those eyes, well-earned and beautiful, but he tried not to notice them, preferring for now this illusion of teenage wasteland he was enveloped in. He looked out at the town and wondered if he'd see Jeff, goofy old Jeff in his broken down Ranger. Where's the party tonight? Jackson's Hill. Manson's cornfield. The boat landing. See you there, fucker. Suck it, bitch. Later.

Electric guitar raged from the speakers, squalling out a ragged melody. That ain't working, that's the way you do it.

They followed up this song with one of Steve Winwood's sappy comebacks. Higher love, indeed. He wondered what the format of this station was. Back then it had played Top Forty, now it appeared to be the greatest hits of the '80's, which amounted to the same thing, of course. If a radio station sticks around long enough it doesn't need to change its

150

format at all, it just becomes a classics station. He knew if they listened to it long enough they'd hear Simple Minds. Depeche Mode. Pet Shop Boys. Fucking Duran Duran. Wang Chung. Cyndi Lauper. Old Madonna. The Bangles. Guns 'N Roses. If they were lucky, perhaps some Replacements, Springsteen. Mellancamp.

He stretched out the little finger of his right hand and softly tickled his girl between the legs.

"Hey!" she said playfully, swatting him away.

"What?" he said, all innocence.

She gave him a bad look and turned back to the houses. "These are nice, hey? Old."

"Lumber baron homes. All the big-wigs lived there. The Man."

"Some are pretty."

He said nothing to that. They all still looked to him like the gross display of wealth, at odds with the state of the rest of the town.

"We used to nigger knock over here," he said.

"Nigger knock?"

"Yeah. Ring the bell and run away."

She grimaced. "We called it Doorbell Ditch."

"You were more racially sensitive than we were."

"I'd say…."

"Actually, there *was* a black kid in my class. A girl. Nice. Popular chick. She was a good friend of mine when we were in sixth, seventh-grade. Then she fell in with the wrong crowd."

Jess nodded.

"And when I was a real little kid there was a black guy that lived on the North side of town. Someone burned a cross on his lawn one night."

"They did not…."

"They did too. Ask Tom or Tina. Lit up a cross one night. He left town the next week."

"That's terrible…."

He shrugged. "Well… the story goes he was a bad guy. Drugs or whatever. It wasn't like he was Martin Luther King."

"That's still terrible…."

"They had to get rid of him."

"They could have found a better way."

"Like?"

151

"I don't know. Wrote him a nice long letter?" She cocked her head at him, flashed a sassy smile.

"Yeah," he said. "Yeah, that might have worked too. But they had this big cross lying around, right? Nothing else to do with it, might as well light her up...."

They left this neighborhood and entered a newer one, relatively speaking: these homes here were still big but not Victorian, more the style popular in the twenties, bungalows and Cape Cods and other variations on the two-story theme. Quite a few had been remodeled over the years to resemble odd-shaped entities, as if the previous home had developed a thyroid problem or had sprouted tumors of garages and dens and decks. The yards were more open than those in the older neighborhood, with fewer gardens and more flat grass with a spattering of bushes. Here and there large trees loomed over everything, at once ominous and comforting, great canopies of green and black.

"This was my favorite neighborhood to trick or treat in," Jonah said. "Back then they had trick or treat at night, and it was always so dark and spooky here, under the trees. You'll notice there are few streetlights."

She nodded.

"I either went as a vampire or a zombie," he said.

"I was a princess, a pumpkin, a mermaid, or a witch. Once I was a vampire."

He turned a corner, drove for half a block, then suddenly slowed, put the car in reverse, and backed up.

"What's wrong?" Jess asked.

He stopped in front of a large, two-story white home, stared at the big garage it was connected to.

"What is it?"

"Nothing. Just...." He shook his head. "I forgot about that place." He said this softly, mostly to himself, letting it escape on a breath.

Jess looked at the house. "What about it?"

"The Ice Cream Man," he said.

"The who?"

"This guy... once a year, July or August, he'd throw open that garage and have this big table there with all sorts of buckets of ice cream, all the flavors you could think of, and invite all the kids to come. For five cents you'd get this huge cone."

152

"Wow. No one could do that now. No parents would trust the guy."

"He was old. Real old. But nice. God... I remember walking there with Tina and Tom, holding my five cents like it was a million dollars. You'd get this huge, *giant* cone, just *heaped* with ice cream, like four scoops. It was crazy."

"Why'd he do it?"

"I don't know. Just to do it, I guess. He liked kids. He used the money to buy next year's flavors. He just liked to see all the kids lining up, smiling, then walking off trying to balance these massive cones, faces all covered. He was a nice guy. If some kid dropped a cone he would call them back and give them a new one, free."

The house looked empty now, not vacant so much as lifeless. Quiet. The windows reflected back the outside world, their glass black and unfriendly.

"Then he died one year, and there was no more ice cream."

"Sad...."

"It was. I remember that summer. We were left with the Dairy Queen on the highway, but that wasn't the same. Jesus, that was fun, walking over here to get a cone...." He shook his head at the memory.

"And no one else ever took up the tradition?"

"No. Who else was there? He was the Ice Cream Man. Someone else bought this house and nothing was ever the same."

Jess reached over and rubbed the back of his neck with warm, soft hands. "We'll get some ice cream later. I'm feeling a craving coming on." She purred: "Chocolate-vanilla twist...."

He smiled at her. Then drove off.

*

They had a light lunch with Tom and Kathy and their kids at a small café called Beyer's. They had invited Tina and her family but they had some people they were going to visit, little reunions of their own to attend. They invited Biff, too, but he declined without any real explanation. Perhaps there were some bushes that needed punishing.

So how'd you guys feel this morning? Kathy asked, smiling at each of them as if she knew something they didn't.

153

Fine.

Headaches?

No.

You're the only ones....

Once the food was ordered and Jonah felt the kids weren't listening he told Tom about the phone call.

Assholes, Tom said.

Maybe someone should give them a statement just to stop them from calling, Kathy suggested.

It wouldn't stop them, Jonah said. They'd just want more.

They all agreed this was most likely the case, and fell silent for a few minutes. The thought of reporters calling to ask you how you felt about the death of your mother was so strange to them they could not think of words to describe it. Now and then you see people on television talking about such things, sometimes the very day their loved one died, and you wonder how they can do that, stand there and give a statement, answer questions. Certainly no one in the Swain family would have been able to answer questions that first day. Or the second. Or any day thereafter. You wonder, too, how the reporters can even ask their questions... but the first thing you learn in journalism school is how to lose your heart. You take Losing Your Humanity 101 and then you're Bob Novak.

Jonah thought of his mother's mangled car popping up on the television at JD's Bar the night before. It had never occurred to him before how much that might hurt. He had certainly seen enough photos of accidents on the news, the wrecks of cars and trains and planes, had even seen videos of the accidents themselves, but he had never thought of how it might hurt the survivors. This was a bit of empathy he had never wanted to experience, of course, but there it was, clear and bright. Of all the things he had never wanted to be (and the list was legion) the survivor of someone whose death was mentioned on TV was definitely one of them. It was absurd. Surreal. And yet entirely American.

He thought about this as he ate. The idea of a highway accident seemed so utterly American as to be cliché, up there with serial killers and toxic waste and actors turned politicians and people selling their babies and reality television and porn and the World's Largest Ball of Lint and –

You guys going to church tomorrow? Tom asked.

Tomorrow? Tomorrow's Sunday already?

154

Yes it is. We were gonna hit the eight o'clock mass. Wanna come?

Jess and Jonah exchanged brief glances. Part of Jonah felt obligated to say yes, but the other part, the one that knew better, winced at the idea.

That's all right, he said, and let his tone suggest an ellipse.

You sure? It's probably what you need.

What the fuck does that mean? Jonah thought. He said: What I need is a day to sleep in. Go with Biff.

I thought we might all go.

Jonah, tensing, heard himself say: I go with Cheeses, not Jesus.

Can we talk about something else? Kathy, the mediator, asked.

Are you confirmed? Tom asked Jonah.

No. Then: A confirmed what?

Catholic. Or Lutheran. Or whatever.

No. Why?

Gotta have God, Tom said.

I'm a confirmed non-confirmist. A confirmed nonconforming non-confirmist.

Gotta have God, Tom said again, as if by saying it more and more it might come true.

Since when did you become so religious?

I'm not that religious, I just believe what I believe and I believe you gotta have God.

I believe you gotta dance.

Your mother raised you to go to church.

My mother rarely went to church herself.

She believed in God.

She also believed in drinking heavily and throwing up after she ate. Should I take those up, too?

Come on, Kathy said. You two, shut up and eat.

Yes, Jess agreed. Maybe I *do* have a headache, and you're not helping it any.

Well, we're going to church, Tom said before turning his attention back to his sandwich.

This is the best croissant I've ever had, Jonah said softly. He stared at its flaking crust and took in a deep breath, tried to clear his mind. He felt as if he wanted to either disappear or rise up, fade into nothing or stand tall and speak out. Stay a wallflower or become a redwood.

He didn't like this trembling between options, though he'd been used to it all his life, it was part of who he was, hesitant and careful and unsure, and right there in Beyer's Café in Oakton, Wisconsin, he knew it was time to finally fall one way or the other. Wallflower or redwood.

His mother was in ash. The world was waiting for him. It was time.

*

I don't know who you are, I don't know the real you. *Is* there a real you? You're distant and defensive and... unknown. Who is this Jonah Swain? What does he love and hate and think and feel? I need to know, I need to know whether to like you or not. Let me into your world so I know whether it's one worth visiting.

This had been a girl from his senior year in high-school. Her melodramatic little speech had come out of the blue one winter evening after a basketball game. He had certainly never thought of himself as closed-off, distant, defensive, or any of the other pop-psychology crap she threw at him, and had thought she was nothing but a drama queen, a possibly disturbed young woman without control of her emotions. They had not been dating but he had long suspected she had a crush on him. When she said all this that evening in the high-school hallway he had laughed it off, but it came back to him in the days after his mother's death, when he was spending so much time with a family he rarely saw. Fifteen years later and the girl's words were still there, plain as day, fat with meaning.

Was that how he'd been for all these years, cautious and unknown and guarded? He realized it was probably true. It was not, however, how he wanted to be, not anymore. Perhaps such shielding of his true self behind smart-ass comments and a sometimes cold façade had served as protection, to keep that true self, his feelings, his thoughts, his beliefs, safe and secure from harm and abuse. But what good was it now, in a world where some fuck might send his truck into you as you drove down a highway? What good was protecting yourself from those closest to you when the real danger lay *out there*, in the mysterious and dangerous world of modern life? Why be hesitant when life itself was so quick and short? We are here, then we're gone. Just like that, in the turn of a wheel, the changing of a lane, the pull of a trigger, the bursting of an artery. Gone. We have no control over the beginning or the end, it's what lies between that we can shape as best as possible, it's what we do and how we do it that sets the basis for the sort of life we live. Reveal your heart and soul and be hated or loved. It was a fifty-fifty chance. The other option is to be unknown, untouchable, an enigma. Yet we are enigmas at birth and death, why be one during life itself?

Who is this Jonah Swain? What does he love and hate and think and feel?

He and Jess took a walk around Oakton that afternoon, holding hands like the young lovers they were, taking in the autumn sunshine, speaking very little, occasionally flashing smiles at each other. It was a beautiful day. Jess was a beautiful woman. He knew without doubt that he loved her.

It was the idea of some day losing her that he hated with all his heart, and yet it was inevitable, wasn't it?

As inevitable as this: the sun slipping below the horizon, and the world cooling into night.

2

The days before the Ice Cream Man died were a blur to the adult Jonah. A nice blur, though, like a pleasant painting of a rustic old farm slowly faded with age. He imagined them in sepia tones, soft at the edges like a TV movie flashback. In his mind they had all been happy days, those of his preadolescent youth, full of joy and laughter and wonderful lazy afternoons of sunshine and blue skies. What rain there was had been needed, what tears there were had been tears of happiness. He remembered long days of reverie and play, his every need met, his every wish fulfilled. He remembered playing with his brother and sister, games of tag and catch and hide and seek. He recalled watching them ride bikes and wishing he could too. He remembered scratches and cuts met with kisses and band-aids by a mom skillful in the application of each. He imagined piggy-back rides on a dad's shoulders, and grammas and grandpas who gave him anything he wanted. He remembered losing himself in the worlds he created with Matchbox cars and Weeble Wobbles and a Fisher-Price Farm set. He remembered wasting whole days with a box of crayons and some paper, and watching television with the whole family whenever something special was on, *Rudolph the Red-nosed Reindeer*, or *The*

157

Wizard of Oz, or *Santa Claus is Coming to Town*, or *Merry Christmas, Charlie Brown*, or cheap made-for-television horror flicks like *Salem's Lot*, *Gargoyles* and *Don't Be Afraid of the Dark*. He remembered TV shows like *Sigmund the Sea Monster*, *The Incredible Hulk*, *The Six-Million Dollar Man*, *Charlie's Angels*. He remembered Christmas and Easter and every birthday there had ever been.

As an adult he would know it couldn't have been this way all the time, there had to have been sadness and fear and anger, and yet even knowing this he would be unable to recall any such thing. Which was fortunate, of course, and yet it also made the fear and anger and sadness that was to come all the more awful. To compare the realities of adulthood with the reverie and idyll of being a child was to come face to face with harshness, bitterness, the very idea that life was a failure, for what adult life could not be considered a failure when compared with the dreams and fantasies of childhood?

Nevertheless, he recalled no disappointments, no collapse of plans, no great sadness in those days before the death of the Ice Cream Man. He had been a child, a small fragile boy. He had laughed and loved and played and dreamed. Everything he had wanted had been given to him, everything he had needed had been provided. A toy may have broken, a planned trip to the beach cancelled due to rain, a television show postponed for a Presidential address or, worse, a ballgame gone to sudden-death, and yet these were minor inconveniences met with the resourcefulness of an imaginative mind: instead of the beach, he would have headed to his room to draw or play, in lieu of a TV show he could have listened to records, and a broken toy could become just one more bit of scenery in an impromptu play starring Luke Skywalker, Darth Vader, Spiderman.

They were beautiful days. He'd had a Mom and a Dad. He'd had a big brother and a big sister. He'd been loved. The backdrop of childhood: soft green grass and a warm bed in the evening.

He was seven the summer the Ice Cream Man died, and he had no great understanding of the concept of death. The man was gone, his mom said. He was gone and there'd be no more ice cream from him.

He'll never be back? he'd asked.

No. He's gone and he'll never be back.

He still didn't quite get it, other than to know that the old man would never again give out giant scoops of vanilla and chocolate. There would, though, be ice cream from other places, they couldn't take ice cream away, not for good. There was still a Dairy Queen across town, still a gallon of chocolate-vanilla in the freezer. The boy didn't care all that much that the old man wouldn't sell any ever again, there would still be plenty around, it was a constant, a staple of childhood, a fact of life.

It was when he imagined all those gallons of ice cream going to waste in the old man's house that Jonah first began to really understand death.

Death was pointless. Sad. It was ten gallons of the best ice cream you'd ever had growing old and unused in an old man's quiet, dark house. It was a garage door that would never again be opened to sunshine and smiles.

It was something being gone for no reason.

And suddenly, it seemed to be everywhere.

*

He came home one hot day in August of that same year, 1977, to find his mother sitting on the floor in front of the livingroom stereo. Familiar music, moody, operatic, grand, was coming through the speakers. She was crying.

What's wrong? he asked. It was terrible seeing her that way. Frightening. He had a sense of her being out of control, and it was something she had never been before. Out of control, broken down.

He's dead, she said between sobs, taking in a great gasp of air to do so.

Who?

It was Elvis Presley, the man on the stereo. She sat there all afternoon crying and playing his records, one after the other, saying nothing, just listening and crying and staring at the photographs on his album covers. Jonah didn't know what to do, so he stayed in his room, drew pictures, played with his cars, looked at books. He felt something heavy in the air weighing him down, making him feel awful. He had been outside watching insects in the backyard, happily lost in his imagination, and now he was depressed, confused. From the partially open door of his bedroom he could hear the music, at times upbeat and energetic, at others moody and sad, all of it, however, united by that single singular voice he had known all his life: baritone, rich, fat with emotion. All of his short life he had known Elvis, had listened to the records on his own, had watched the concert films on TV, had even tried his hand at an Elvis impression, and now the man was dead. Which didn't mean much to the boy, really, other than the fact that the death had apparently taken its toll on his mother. Why? he wondered. Why would she be that broken up over it, she certainly hadn't known the man.

Horns and guitars and drums rose through the house, anchored by that voice. Jonah stayed in his room for nearly an hour before going back out to the livingroom, where his mom was still sitting on the floor, holding a record sleeve in her hands (*Elvis in Hawaii*). He came up behind her.

Are you all right? he asked.

She sniffled and looked at him. Her eyes were red and puffy, streaked with the distinct run of tears. The front of her shirt was damp. She smiled at her youngest son, her baby.

I grew up with him, she said. It's just a shame, a tragedy.

I'm sorry, Jonah offered. She reached out and patted his leg lovingly.

Sit here and listen with me, she said.

So he did.

*

A year later his father's mother died. His gramma, yes, but she had never been close to the children. This was because she had never approved of her son's choice of a wife. Linda Connor was not, she believed, worthy of dear sweet Harold. As a result, the old woman's love never fell too hard on Tommy and Tina and Jonah, was instead saved for the children of her other kids. Which was all right, too, as far as Jonah was concerned, because the woman was a crotchety old thing who lived in a big old scary two-story house at the grungiest end of Laona, a place so uncomfortable for him in its layout and atmosphere that he dreaded going there. Years later his siblings would tell him they felt the same way. It was a combination of the old woman's coldness to them, and the overall feeling of darkness and claustrophobia that permeated that slowly dilapidating house. The children would grow to think of the place as haunted, and when they had to spend the night there they would never get any sleep, they would lie in bed listening to the creaks and moans and rattlings that filled the place, Jonah and Tommy in one bedroom, their sister in another, their mother and father in the third. This was upstairs, the creepiest place in the house. If they ever ventured out of their rooms in the middle of the night (which they each did at least once, to fetch water or run to the bathroom) they would hear the equally scary sound of their grandmother snoring in her bedroom downstairs. The old woman had been a widow for more than fifteen years by then, and Jonah thought he knew why: after enough years of such raspy, ugly snoring, he figured her husband, the grampa he would never know, had killed himself. When he imagined the man's ghost forced to haunt the house, Jonah laughed. Poor man. He still had to hear that snoring after all.

Her funeral was the first one that Jonah would ever go to, but he would remember little about it. Only that it wasn't what he expected.

*

The body is behind glass, and you have to go up and look at it, a girl named Wendy Sanford told him the day before the funeral, in the few minutes before school started. She was telling him what to expect because, he believed, it made her feel better than him. *She* had been to a funeral, *she* knew what they were like. She would still have this egotism when she became the class's Valedictorian years later, of course, and then she would go the way of all such over-achievers and promptly burn out in college.

You go up and look at the body? Jonah asked, horrified at this thought.

Yeah, she said. They make you go up there and look at it.

She was kind of right: the only thing Jonah would really remember about that first funeral was that he had been led by his mom up to the front of the funeral home to gaze upon the body of Gramma Swain. He wouldn't remember what she had looked like, only that there had been no glass, just a wood coffin gleaming like marble. Why do I have to look at her? he asked. Because that's what you do.

But why?

Because.

161

But—

Shhhh!

After that, he remembered nothing.

*

Death is a presence in all families, of course, either in its actuality or its potential. Wherever a group of people has gathered to form a group, however big or small, death looms at the periphery... and sometimes at the center. Wherever there is love there is the fear of parting. For Jonah, this fear had not existed until that first funeral, and then it came in with a vengeance. He had dreams about his dead grandma... not nightmares, nothing raving or lunatic about them at all, just dreams, simple little scenes set in the kitchen of her old house, she at the sink washing dishes or cleaning freshly-peeled potatoes, Jonah at the table, watching her as she worked. He might never have liked Gramma Swain all that much but he knew she had been a good cook, her meals these great feasts that filled you up and put you in a coma afterwards. The sort of woman who still cooked with lard, who kept a tin of grease handy under the sink, who had never heard of hardened arteries and wouldn't have cared about them if she had. A large-boned woman over whose large bones lay a thick layer of fat and muscle. Add a tight, short, quasi-beehive hairdo and cat's eye glasses and you had a portrait of Harriet Swain. This was the woman Jonah dreamed about. Except....

Except he knew, upon waking, that the woman in the dream, the one doing dishes or washing potatoes, was dead. She never spoke to him as she worked, but now and then she would turn her head and smile, not at him but as if to someone unseen. He was able to see her profile, those glasses and her black eyes and her plump blushing cheeks, and then she would turn back to the sink. In the dreams she was always wearing a faded yellow dress with a very light blue flowered print. The dress was formless, hung like a dead thing over her big frame, but the effect was not unpleasant, it was in fact rather grandmotherly. In the dream Jonah was looking at the woman with affection, feeling as if she were a warm, kind woman that loved him, the way he felt about Gramma Connor.

When he woke he would lie there, looking at the dark ceiling above his bed, thinking about what it meant to not have that person around anymore, what it felt like to have someone be *gone*. Dead. It was a strange feeling, a little emotional tickle somewhere deep inside him. Odd. One day she was there, the next she was gone. One day he had two grammas, the next he had one. Strange.

The content of the dreams, and whatever meanings they might have had, were of no concern to the boy. They were just dreams about an old woman working at a giant white sink. She said nothing to him and he said nothing to her, she just kept working and he kept watching. When she turned her head to smile at whoever else was there, the boy just stared at her face. When he woke he knew the woman was dead, because those blushing-cheeks were just like the ones she'd had in her casket and not the way she normally looked. It was the make-up the mortician had put on her to give her a "life-like" appearance. In her living days she had been a white, washed-out woman, but in death she had looked nearly pink, like she'd been slapped repeatedly.

He never mentioned the dreams to anyone, not out of embarrassment or fear but simply because he knew there was nothing to tell, they were just dreams. He had seen his first dead person and it hadn't been what he expected and so he dreamt about her. As the years wore on he would come to forget he had had these dreams and start to believe they were a real memory, Gramma Swain working at the sink while he watched her from the table. Never mind that he had never been alone with her, or that she had never done any sort of cooking with children in the kitchen (she'd insisted they be ushered out to another room). By the time he was twenty Jonah would believe the dreams he'd had at eight were real.

None of which matters, none of which altered how he viewed the woman. In life she had been distant, guarded, cold, perhaps even mean. In death she became a symbol for him, his first dead person, his first experience with having someone and then losing them. Within months he would be able to say he had only one Gramma, and would rarely think about Gramma Swain at all. She was there once, then she was gone.

It was the rest of his family Jonah started thinking about. If Gramma Swain could be gone, what about everyone else? He tried imagining what it would be like to lose Mom or Dad or Tina or Tom, and could not. It seemed absurd, insane. They would always be there because they were *his*, they were part of his life. Gramma Swain had been someone they saw maybe three times a year. But Mom and Dad and Tina and

163

Tom? They were much too great a part of his everyday life to ever be gone.

Gradually this logic began to take hold in him, returning him to a secure and solid belief in the stability of his family, in the permanence of the things nearest him. He went through three months of thinking about losing someone else, of people being here one moment and then gone, of death (whatever it truly was) coming to take someone away. After three months the old comfort returned. Nothing bad could happen. Mom was Mom and Dad was Dad and they would always be there, just like Tina and Tom would always be there, just like this house, this yard, the cabin, the forests, the lake would always be there. School and summer took over his thoughts, occupied his time. He stopped dreaming and thinking about Gramma Swain and returned to living his simple little life. There were new *Star Wars* toys to play with, new books to read, shows to watch on TV, games to play. Death slipped into the deepest recesses of his thoughts, exactly where it belonged in an eight-year-old mind. There were clouds to watch, daydreams to follow, secret places to slip into and disappear. Whole afternoons lay waiting for him to waste. Life started to blossom around him.

He was a child again, safe and sheltered, comfortable and happy, joyfully lost in his own little world.

3

When they had left Tom and Kathy after lunch it was with a promise to meet at the House (as Biff's home was being called now) later that afternoon. Biff had mentioned that he wanted all three kids to get together and go through all the old photographs and take what they might want, or at least make notes on what they might want later. There were stacks of photos that he had no interest in, they being of Linda Swain's pre-Biff life: her former husband, her kids, even older ones of her childhood, her mother and father, various cousins. Everyone agreed that it was much too soon to do any such thing, yet they did not say this to the old man. The old keep busy in odd ways when they're mourning, let him have this, they decided. They each knew they would probably start to go through the pictures but not take any just yet. Much too soon. Barely a week had passed, no one wanted to commit to the finality of removing anything from the House. Biff might even agree that this was so, should one of them finally admit their reluctance. He wouldn't mind if they returned later, of course, it would give him a guarantee of company in what was certain to be, now, a much lonelier life. So, tonight would be dinner (probably delivered pizza), some beer, maybe a bottle of wine or two, old jokes, memories, that was all. Jonah wondered if he would even want to look at any of the pictures. It was far too early in the entire mourning process for him to know how something like that might affect him. He would hate to break down in tears in front of everyone. Perhaps he would just sit with his wine and watch the others.

After walking around Oakton until late afternoon, Jonah decided he did not want to go back to the House, not yet. He and Jess got in his car and drove out to the bay's harbor. They drove down the thin, ancient arm of compacted gravel and recycled asphalt that was the breakwater and parked at the very end. He killed the engine and rolled his window down so they could hear the roar of the waves, smell the bay water, see the blurred sliver of Door County on the blue-gray horizon. The waves were loud as they crashed dark and blue and white on the jagged spill of rocks that lined the breakwater, loud and ceaseless and angry. Deafening. Jonah stared down into the space one particular wave kept slamming into, mesmerized by the few moments when the wave rolled back and the rock was allowed to be alone, unbothered. There was relief in that moment, a sigh, a brief few seconds of peace before the wave came violently in again, throwing itself against the limestone and exploding into a frenzied white spray. He grew disturbed by the monotonous brutality of the whole thing, grew nearly sick with the constant slamming, then the pause, then the slamming again. The endlessness of it all made him feel terrible. He turned his head and looked at Jess, who was looking back at him.

"I love you," she said.

"I love you too," he answered.

"Do you want to talk about what you've been thinking?"

"I haven't been thinking anything."

She appeared to accept this for a moment, but then she bit her bottom lip, cocked her head, and gave him a look that meant she was not going to take any bullshit, not now.

"You shouldn't keep everything inside," she said.

165

"You're right." And she was: he shouldn't keep anything inside, not anymore. Things had changed. What was good for him and his little world one week ago was not good anymore. Those old rules no longer applied, they'd been rendered obsolete by the sudden presence of a roaring stinking oil-burning eighteen-wheeler.

Who is this Jonah Swain? What does he love and hate and think and feel?

"So...?" she pressed.

"I'm thinking..." he began. What to say? How to put into words what he was thinking when he was thinking so much? He said:

"I'm thinking that life is too short and too long to not be yourself. I'm thinking...."

God, there was no way to put this.

"I'm thinking that there's a change in the air. Maybe something big. Maybe something small."

Jess was looking at him with little diamond flakes glistening in her eyes. The stars perhaps, or tears.

"I'm thinking that since we're here, on this tiny little planet, we'd better be here for a reason. I'm thinking... I'm thinking no more foolishness, no more masks, no more fears, no more...."

He realized he must sound stupid. There was no way to give words and voice to the things he was thinking and feeling. He looked into his girl's eyes and smiled.

"I'm thinking...."

"Yeah?"

"I'm thinking...."

She smiled, not in expectation but because she knew that was it.

He leaned forward and they kissed until darkness fell around them, hiding the waves, which crashed on and on endlessly into the night.

*

"You're late!" Tom said jokingly when they finally made it to the House. Everyone was sitting or standing around the kitchen table, where a pile of loose photos and three stacks of large albums were resting on display. Museum artifacts. Relics.

166

"The pizza will be here any minute," Kathy said, smiling.

"You owe thirty bucks," Tom said. But he winked at them. "Have a beer."

Jonah had a moment to reflect on the familiarity of the scene: everyone focused on the kitchen table, with that strange faux-gothic chandelier overhead, a few beer cans sitting here and there, the pleasant clutter of the ranch house around them. He'd seen it all far too often this week. There was an intimacy in these mourning rituals, a closeness, but one that was mixed with a deliberate, even necessary distance, as if the mutual feelings between them all had to be kept at arm's length for safety, and he was growing weary of it. He was growing weary of everything. He wanted to be back in his other life, alone, just he and Jess, with these people miles and miles away. He loved them all, yes, but he wanted to be gone. Everyone was so absorbed in this act of mourning, of going about the rituals of sadness and sympathy, that the whole thing was growing tiresome. He'd seen far too much of these people already, it was time to be away from them... and he was sure everyone felt the same way.

A beer was in his hand within seconds and he sipped at it, relished the taste. He thought: I usually see these people for one, maybe two weekends a year, and now it's been a week that we've all been together, every day, every night....

He stood behind his sister, looking at the pictures over her shoulder. She didn't know he was standing there at first and when she finally saw him she jumped as if he'd scared her.

She was looking at photos of herself as a young child. It took him a moment to realize the album she had opened in front of herself was one their mother had put together of just Tina-pictures, from the earliest baby photos to one taken just last year. As Tina flipped the pages it was possible to see her aging, five years every other page, a toddler to a five year-old to her first day of school to her braces in fifth-grade to high-school, right up to the day her own first-born had come into the world. Circular order. The uniquely human desire to organize things cyclically, to have a beginning and an end. Not every culture was like that, though, Jonah knew: some Native American tribes did not believe Time ran that way, from past to present to future. To them, all Time was present, whatever happened or will happen was occurring right now, somewhere.

167

There was something both beautiful and pointless to that, Jonah believed. Perhaps beautifully pointless.

"Yours is right there," Tina said, pointing out a gray photo-album that was lying on the table.

Of course it was. He hesitated, took a few sips of beer, then reached for the album. He'd seen it before, of course, but it had been a while. He held it for a moment, until it grew too heavy for just one hand, and he quickly swung it around and set it on the closest bare counter space he could find. He took a large drink of beer and glanced at the faces around the table. They were all absorbed in the photos, even Jess, who was laughing at the huge glasses Tina had worn in high-school. Jonah turned back to the counter, leaned down, opened his photo album, watched his life unfold through the magic of Kodak.

Actually, the first thing he saw was his birth announcement: it was a folded card-board cut-out in the shape of a football, which, when opened, said this:

An END Has Been Added To The Swain Team. Arrived: August 24 at 4:47 am. Height: 20 ½ inches. Weight: 6 lbs 10 oz. Helmet size: 13 inches. Team Physician: Dr. Haug. Proud Coach: Harold. Proud General Manager: Linda. Note: This player is too valuable and will not be for trade.

Next to this was a very old, washed-out picture of the young Jonah Swain in his crib, lying there on a baby-blue blanket, his mouth open in either a yawn or a cry, one hand at his face, the other making what resembled the OK sign, with one fat little leg bent and the other extended fully, as if he were kicking something away. A cute baby, chubby and pink, fragile and yet full of vigor.

Jonah took a deep breath and turned the page.

There he was in the arms of his happy young mom. In fact, Linda Swain looked more than happy, she looked positively radiant. And confident, too, sitting proud and upright on a brown couch. She looked like she had no doubts about anything, as if she knew, absolutely *knew*, that having this child was what she had been put on Earth to do. By then, of course, she'd already had two children, she was an old pro. She looked happy and healthy, alive with youth and promise.

He would have stopped looking at the photos right there but the next one was hilarious: it was a very shocked looking Tina, five years old and standing next to her new baby

168

brother, who was in the arms of their mother. She looked as if she had no idea what was going on, as if her world had been flipped upside down. And of course it had, she was one of three now. Being the oldest would mean something from then on.

The next two pictures showed Jonah's maternal gramma and grampa each holding the new baby. Loretta Connor in particular looked uneasy with the child, as if she too, like Tina, was not quite sure what to make of this new addition. He knew, though, that she had in reality been elated: Jonah had been born on Gramma Loretta's birthday, just as she had insisted... or so family legend would have it.

Tom was the next to be pictured with the baby. He was lying on the floor alongside Jonah, looking bored. Everyone had always remarked upon seeing this photo that the two brothers did not look anything alike, and it was true, mostly, but if you looked closely you could see the familiar Swain chipmunk cheeks on both children.

The next page was filled entirely with pictures of Tom and Tina posed next to Jonah, who was held by his mother. He could imagine the situation behind the scenes, their mother insisting they come closer, smile, one more picture and then they could go play, just smile at your brother, smile at the camera. It was possible to see a progression in the two older children's annoyance: Tom in particular was starting to look like he would have rather been anywhere else in the world... he was just three then, of course, and had other concerns.

A question was forming in Jonah's mind and with a turn of the page it was answered: Where was Dad...?

Four pages into the book Harold Swain made his first appearance: he was sitting casually on an ugly red-and-yellow checkered chair, his fat little baby cradled back against one arm. The happy father's other arm was resting at his side, as if awaiting a cigarette or a beer. The arm that was cradling Jonah was doing so loosely, yet the baby was safe and secure there, staring at the camera with wide eyes. Harold Swain, in turn, was looking at Jonah proudly, curiously. At the time his youngest had been born Harold Swain had been just twenty-six, and perhaps he was thinking, as he gazed at this new bundle of trouble and energy, of how much he had obtained in his short life. Three children. A good wife. A good job. Perhaps there was a touch of regret there, too: how much did a parent have to give up for their kids? How much needed to be sacrificed?

169

Jonah looked long and hard at his father. Though just twenty-six, the man looked at least ten years older. This was due largely to his own physical make-up, he being a well-structured man with broad shoulders and large arms, as well as a prematurely receding hairline and a face chiseled and square. And yet, too, this had partially to do with the nature of his life, all those demands on his time, the work and the wife and the kids. Johan thought of himself at twenty-six and could not imagine having been the father of three children. It was a frightening idea. He thought of what a different life he had from his parents, but an odd feeling of guilt threatened to surge in him. Guilt, why? He had no clue. We all have paths we take, we all make decisions, choose courses.

The photo under this one was again of Jonah and his mom, she sitting in an old wooden rocker, cradling her son gently. The baby Jonah had a binkie in his mouth and was staring up to his mother with a look that suggested he knew how safe and comfortable he was there... a look that also suggested he believed he would always be this safe, that those arms would always be there to hold him.

Jonah stared at this picture for a long time. It was mesmerizing. He thought about how the people in old pictures had no idea how their lives will turn out. This was good, of course, since it kept them sane, safe, free from knowledge about the bad things that were bound to happen. And yet it was haunting, too, all those people believing that only good things will come, that the future was bright and clear and open to any possibility. There was something sad in their blissful ignorance. They could maintain a belief that everyone they knew would live happily ever after, that everything would turn out as it should. It was sad because the opposite was true.

That woman there, Jonah wondered, looking at his twenty-five year old Mom. That woman there, what hopes did she hold for herself, her children, her husband? Anything was possible back then, the future was theirs to grasp. This newborn child, he could do anything, he could be anything he wanted. By the time he was his mom's age the world would be a better, more beautiful place, the great and wonderful Future everyone had been promised. He would be twenty-five in 1995, a year that must have seemed so outrageous back then, that must have sounded like the distant future, with hover-craft and teleportation and space travel and moon colonies and fifteen-hour work weeks and world peace and everyone living in harmony with nature and each other. How could it not have sounded promising? In 1970 the country was torn by Vietnam and the end of the era of Peace and Love. The Sixties were over, the Revolution was about to fail. Four student protestors would be killed by National Guardsmen at Kent State, two more in Mississippi ten days later. Nixon would start his Enemies List before Jonah was one, and within a few years he would be toppled by the Watergate scandal and slip away into the American shadows. OPEC would hold the world hostage. Madmen would come out of the Middle East. Terrorists would strike all over the world. An energy crisis would swell. A century of pollution would give rise to an urgent environmental movement. America would enter dark years….

Most of which was not known or suspected in 1970, of course, but there was perhaps a feeling in the air, a sense that there was a yawning abyss in the center of the American path, a great danger in the road ahead. The country was divided, involved in a war it could never win, its military killing its own civilians, its President a liar and a cheat, its corporations and industries continuing a tradition of raping and polluting the natural world. Death and violence seemed to be everywhere. Paranoia and injustice were rampant. There was a feeling that those in charge did not know what they were doing.

It couldn't possibly stay that way, the future had to be better. Every generation had been promised that it would be so, that everything would be bright and beautiful when they grew up. How could Harold and Linda Swain look down at their new smiling little baby and not believe that the world would be a far better place when he was older? How could they not forget the world that lay around them, the madness and the nightmare that seemed to be hovering at the outskirts of their American dream?

The purpose of a family is to create an insular world of safety and comfort, Jonah believed. And that was what he saw when he looked at all those old pictures.

But pictures lie, of course. That was just their nature.

He closed the album before he got to any photos where he was older than two years. He finished his beer and looked at everyone else.

Perhaps everything lies, he thought. Not just the pictures but the times they come from. Not just the subjects but the people behind the cameras.

"Anyone need anything?" he asked.

171

"Beer," Tom said.

"Same," said Mark.

Biff said he was good.

"Sure," answered Kathy and Tina, in unison. They were drinking wine.

Jonah turned to fetch the drinks.

He was thirty two. Everything he'd just thought about 1970 could still be applied now, to this futuristic year of 2003.

He wondered if that meant anything. If it did, it wasn't anything good. In fact, it was goddamn terrible. Pathetic. A man wants to see progress in his lifetime, not degeneration, not deterioration, not collapse. You want to feel that the world has become a better place since the day you were born. You want to believe it. You want to know it.

1970. 2003. What was the goddamn difference? And what was he doing to make it any better?

Jonah handed out the drinks and tried his hardest to stop thinking.

*

Twenty minutes later, in the bathroom, he looked around at the shelves and counter over-stuffed with tubes of lotion and bottles of hair-gel and cans of hairspray and vials of make-up and he realized how lost this stuff was now, how vestigial. What would Biff do with any of it? Toss it out, most likely, but the place would be bare then, no trace of the woman who once lived here. The old man might have a razor or two, a tooth-brush, maybe a comb… but that was all, the rest would be gone. Strange how the loss of a human life can render such material things so sad. Just a week ago and all of this product belonged to someone, now it was lost, adrift like the family itself, cut loose from significance, rendered unnecessary.

Well, we can't let that happen to ourselves, Jonah thought. We had to find meaning in this meaninglessness. And not spiritual meaning, not a meaning about the after-life or how the spirit of the dead will enter all of our hearts and watch over us… no, none of that, but *real* meaning, something important to the here and now, a significance to *this* life, not to an unknowable, and therefore ultimately insignificant, life beyond death. This life here needs to have meaning. Right here, right this moment, is all we ever have. Now is all we are given.

172

If the dead die for any reason, perhaps it is to make us understand this. The only life we can ever truly *know* is this one, the Present. Here on Earth, 93 million miles from our sun, our star. Here on the hazy outskirts of the Milky-way.

It all seemed obvious to Jonah, and yet it struck him there in his dead mother's bathroom with all the force of an epiphany. Hadn't he always known this? Maybe. Maybe he'd known it but had never fully *felt* it.

He stood there staring at all of her useless beauty products and realized that she would never be back. Of course he'd known this before, but was struck again by the truthfulness of it, that truth presented here so harshly to him. She would never be back. She was gone.

But he and his family had to move on. *Everything* had to move on, there was really nothing else to do. It was transcend or waste away.

Was this the meaning he'd been looking for? Maybe, but there were other meanings, too. Other truths.

He flushed the toilet and went back out to his family. By then the pizza was there and everyone was eating.

*

Jonah? Jess's voice in the darkness, muted, soft, barely a whisper. Her hand reaching over to his side of the bed, finding it empty.

Gone to the bathroom, she thought absently, and fell back into dreams of waves and dogs. It was just before midnight. The witching hour. The house of the dead woman was silent as a grave.

*

The streetlight gazed down at Jonah much the way he was gazing up at *it*: expectantly, as if something was to happen here, as if either one of them was about to propose a suggestion or offer up a philosophy... or perform a jig, perhaps, there in the streetlight's own glow, which was of the same force and hue as that from the half-moon in the otherwise black sky. Jonah had been standing like that for some time, perhaps nearly twenty minutes, looking up at the light that had haunted his childhood darkness. The town was absolutely quiet, like a *Twilight Zone* town in suspended animation, with him as the lone hero

173

confused and frightened about this stalling of time, this hiccup in the continuum. The house behind him was black, the street that ran to his right and left a gray strip, a scar. The other houses on the street, and the large elms and maples that towered over them, were barely sketches of themselves, an artist's doodles in a black-paper notebook, thinly outlined by this light's weak and dusty golden glow.

Jonah was thinking about what he'd thought in the bathroom, that everything had to move on, that it was either transcend or waste away. He had slept for only a few hours before being stirred awake by forgotten dreams, and then, as he recalled it, the nonsense of that statement had kept him awake. He sat there on the edge of the bed, in the ugly glow of this light, and remembered the Cosmic Evolution class he'd taken in college. He'd taken a number of science classes, but mostly biology. This had been his first real exposure to anything outside the realm of the living.

Everything had to move on. Bullshit, of course. He thought of comets. Comets come along, go away, and come back again, over and over endlessly, or at least as long as they kept getting attracted and repelled by the gravity of heavenly bodies and swung back along their routes. They orbit the sun on elliptical lines, ice and rock and dust with a shell of gas. It was possible to see something symbolic here, at least for the religious: the comet as a metaphor for the human soul, perhaps, or even the human body itself, a soul surrounded by bone and muscle the way the ice and dust of a comet are surrounded by a gaseous cloud. And if one looked at it this way, one could make a comparison, however tenuous, between the comet's existence and that of the soul of a departed human: perhaps the dead do not go away, perhaps they continue to exist, on another plane, coming around and around again, endlessly. If the comets do not really move on, then maybe likewise the deceased.

But Jonah was not a religious man, it all struck him as absurd. However, this said, it did not strike him as absurd that the *idea* of the dead might go on existing. It had nothing to do with the soul, as most consider it, but everything to do with the memories, the emotions, the space that the dead had once occupied in the hearts and minds of the living. Did Jonah remember his father, what he'd been like, what he'd felt like, what the man's *presence* had meant in the little house behind him? No. But he remembered what it had been like to have a

174

dad, to have someone there who was his protector and his teacher. Perhaps the details fade away, like the comet's glow fades from our view, but the *idea* of the person remains, like the memory of the comet. Was this what Jonah believed, was it what he *needed* to believe?

He had no clue, and the streetlight's dull glow gave no answers. He looked up to the sky above the light but could see only a crestfallen blackness through a jaundice-yellow haze. He wondered if it would be possible to see a comet there now, or a meteor, or even a star. Probably not, not with that light, however weak it was, competing with the much fainter lights of the sky.

Again, Jonah thought of how he'd always wanted to get rid of that streetlight. It wasn't needed, certainly wasn't wanted. The darkness would have been better, would have made sleep easier in that little bedroom, would have allowed the stars and moon to shine alone.

He supposed he could find his old BB gun in the attic or the basement, take it out here one night, do the deed once and for all. Perhaps his aim with a rock would be better now than it was when he was thirteen. Perhaps....

He walked down to the street, followed the curb for a while searching for a rock of suitable size and weight, but found nothing. He returned to his place under the light and looked up at it again.

It was a cold night, full of an early-winter chill. October's thin air was like the coldness of a skeleton, like one skeleton calling to your own, reaching through your skin and flesh to touch the bones beneath. Jonah shivered.

So, he thought, if not everything moved on, if some things in fact come back around again, where did that leave him, in terms of his philosophy of life? If it wasn't truly "transcend or waste away," what then was it?

That he didn't know bothered him. Yes, he was young, yes he had his whole life ahead of him to figure it out... but this was bullshit, too, of course, because you never knew when it all might end. His whole life might lay ahead of him, yes, but that might only be until tomorrow, or next week, or next year. If losing both his parents had taught him anything it was that life was short, it could all end at any time. He was maybe more aware of mortality than others who had not yet known the loss of a loved one, so not knowing the answers to the questions he was asking bothered him, made him aware of an invisible clock ticking out the seconds that remained. We are not long for this world, any of us. Even some of the comets don't come back around for tens of thousands of years; they are dead to every life they leave behind.

So, then, either way he looked at it life was short, and one had to do something with the time given.

Why didn't this satisfy him as an answer?

He stared up to the cursed light, waiting for it to blink. Instead, it was his eyes that closed and opened. The light was endless, endless, and there was always a city worker to come around and replace the bulb should it ever burn out.

He thought of all the nights he had spent tossing and turning, unable to ignore the glow through his bedroom window, unable to fall into the deep blackness behind his eyelids. He hated the light. It symbolized something, but just what he could not say. He would toss and turn and end up just lying there thinking about first the light... and then his father. It was the summer after his dad died that they put that thing up, and so on those sleepless nights he would lay there long past midnight thinking about the life he had once known, the uncertain future where the comforting darkness of childhood naivety, childhood's vestigial womb of shelter and security, had been invaded by the ugly glare of bitterness and loss.

"Fuck you," he said to the light, and his voice was not strange at all in the night's silence, it seemed to fit. He supposed he would look like a crazy man should someone see him out here, talking to a streetlight, but he didn't care. He said it again.

"Fuck you."

The light was steady, unblinking.

Fuck you....

5. Morning

...the morning after the phone call, a chilly gray dawn with the trembling smell of coffee and the overwhelming feeling of possibilities killed, doors shut, wonders revealed as facades, truths as myths, beautiful mysteries as mundane lies, like thinking all your life that the moon was following you and finding out it follows everyone, like dreaming as a child of the mysteries of space, the alien secret blue depths the sea keeps to itself, like believing in Sasquatch, the Loch Ness Monster, vampires, ghouls in the midnight, only to grow older and not be so certain, to know biological answers, botanical revelations, the truth of ecology: porcupines don't shoot their quills, less than ten percent of snakes are venomous, bumblebees sting, toads don't cause warts, like believing when you were seven that some things would always be there, mountains and forests and deserts and fields and houses and buildings and skylines and parents and friends and love and safety and comfort and home, like thinking that there would always be a place you could return to, and people who would welcome you back, and places once and always familiar where you could disappear and think and daydream and be safe. On a morning like this you look at the steady stream of the familiar, the old sheets you haven't changed in more than a week, the windows across the room in need of cleaning, the trees outside them in need of pruning, the sunlight veiled in its morning cloak, the birds crying out their laments, the impatient barking of a dog two streets over, the rush of traffic growing on a Thursday morning, the blood-red glow of the alarm clock next to the bed, the smell of that coffee brewing out in the kitchen, all so familiar you could for a moment be tempted to close your eyes again and feel it was just another day, same as the one before and the one to come next, that nothing had changed anywhere and there was

177

a pause, the world holding its breath again until you finally got out of bed to greet it. Was it possible this was just another morning? If you didn't move maybe it would be so, nothing changed anywhere, everything the same. Maybe if you never turned on the television or talked to the one you loved you could stay in this waking dream, lost there in that pause, in that held breath, that this moment of birdsong and curtained sun and barking dog might last forever... and why not, why must things move on, why can't there be stasis, atrophy, pause? Why can't we pick a moment to live in forever, just find a single moment when we felt maybe not our best but maybe safest, happiest, or even just most satisfied, and live there for the rest of our lives? Was that too much to ask of Time, that it pause for each of us in our chosen moment of rest so that nothing further could happen, that nothing bad would occur with the next ticking of the next second, with the next rising of a veiled sun, the next waxing of a bone-yellow moon, that Time simply wait there, with everyone we knew paused, safe, alive, held away from danger for an eternal moment? That all around the world no one was dying, that wars could not be started, that planes were stuck fast in the safety of pure blue sky, that any gun or knife raised in anger was stilled until the sun died out... or that the sun itself would never die out, it too held in a moment, veiled for some behind clouds or fog, brightly blazing for others, hidden on the far side of the world for still more, never to be a supernova, never to flare violently and go black. Was this too much to ask? Who says Time had to be continual, why can't the whole works, the Universe and everything in it, just stop, take a rest, hold itself in a moment of its choosing? No one would judge it, no one would protest. Everyone would simply stay where they were, unharmed, motionless, lost in a dream or embrace. No one could die. The dying would be held peacefully between final breaths. Bullets would pause in midair. Semis would stop just inches from cars going through stop-signs. Love-making would be endless. Goodbyes would be eternal. Hellos would be infinite. Planes would hesitate just feet from the ground, the passengers inside frozen in a half-second, caught in their last few thoughts, their final prayers, the final memories of the ones they loved.

And yet it all had to go on, of course, the Universe had to turn and march forward. Bullets had to find their targets, planes had to crash, love-making had to end, hellos must slide into goodbyes, semis must crash into cars. There was no other way.

He finally rose slowly into what he knew was a changed world. From now on, everything would be new, everything would be different. A steady stream of the familiar would never be known again.

Like crisp cool sheets, barking dogs, the trembling of an early morning, the secrets held in overgrown trees outside unwashed windows, the whole vast and smooth monotony of the way things had been before....

6. Beautifully mortified

"My name is—"

"I know what your name is. It's Jonah."

He smiled. "Are you psychic?"

"That... and I asked around." Her turn to smile, a quite pretty, somewhat shy smile with a light hint of sass just under the surface. It was a smile that lit up her face, as if her cheeks were sweetly dimpled solar panels that took in the most minimal light, changed it, altered its makeup, and sent it out through her eyes like Millennium Falcon lasers.

Good god, he was regressing here, getting nervous, turning into the shy clumsy nerve-wracked little stick of a kid he'd been when he was eight, nine, ten. The Millennium Falcon? She was just a girl, just a young woman, he'd been seeing her around for a long time now, they'd exchanged brief words in the halls in her section of Jetco, Incorporated whenever he stole a moment from *his* work in printing. But this was different, this was the lunchroom, they were alone except for the woman who worked the front desk and who was slowly getting herself coffee so she could eavesdrop on them. Jonah had gone into the lunchroom intending to do nothing but retrieve a particularly plump and gorgeous Gala apple he'd placed in the fridge that morning and what do you know, there she was, the equally gorgeous, deliciously plump girl of his daydreams herself, the lovely Jessie Fina. This was his chance to actually talk to her, he knew, and he likewise knew he had to take it. Good god, he was dying.

I asked around, she had said. He swallowed, felt blood rush to his face, turning him as red and warm as... a bruised Gala. She asked around? Christ, why? Because she liked him or because he gave her the creeps? Shit.

180

"You asked around?" he asked. "You mean like, the FBI or something?"

"No."

"CIA."

She cocked her head. "Mhhmmm... maybe."

"Interpol?"

She frowned. "Interpol? You sure go a long way for a joke."

"You should hear me do a knock-knock." They fell into silence. He thought quickly for conversational points but could think of none that didn't make him sound like a stalker or some other brand of psycho... or worse, a fumbling bumbling idiot with a crush. A knock-knock joke?

"I asked around because I always saw you in the halls. And," she shrugged, a heart-breaking shrug that suggested she was either bored with the topic or did not want to give the appearance that she was *not* bored. "And you didn't look like you *belonged* there, up in the human resources slash payroll pit."

"I look like crap, is what you mean?"

"No, you're just not in..." She looked him quickly up and down, appraising him. "You're not in proper dress code."

"Neither are you." He gestured to her thick-soled, scuffed, dirt-smeared half-boots.

"Most of me is."

"Right." He felt the blood pounding in his temples. "Right. I work in printing." He glanced nervously down at his own scuffed brown boots, faded jeans, black t-shirt.

"That's what Janice said."

"Janice?"

"My boss."

"Oh."

"She said you were in printing and she didn't know why you kept coming down to our end. She assumed you were always either lost or on some sort of errand. Maybe both."

"Oh...." He didn't know what to say.

She sighed. "Speaking of my boss, I should get back to work." She smiled again, an absolutely meaningless smile, and turned to walk off. He watched her go, carrying her can of diet soda, hips moving beautifully but self-consciously, because of course she knew he was watching her. Another image from elementary school: swatting flies. Jesus.

Crestfallen, feeling like an idiot, Jonah shook his head and took a deep breath, released it, tried to relax, wished his face wasn't always so quick to blush, and glanced over to the front-desk woman, whose name he couldn't recall.

She was looking back at him, shaking her head, giving him a sympathetic raising of the eyebrows as her new cup of coffee formed a steam halo around her face.

"Better luck next time," she said, and was gone. He was alone there with his Gala in hand and his tail between his legs.

Shit. Shit and goddamn. Hell fuck. Shit.

*

"We have to talk, Jonah," his boss said when he finally returned to his desk in the little room off the main printing area. The sound of machinery was a constant here, as was the smell of chemicals.

The boss was standing in the doorway, leaning there like an ass. Every boss Jonah had ever known had been an ass, that was at least one constant in his life.

"We do?"

"Yeah. About you leaving like that all the time."

"I have a bladder problem, you know that, I told you that before."

"A bladder problem, right."

"More like a urinary problem. A problem with my... urination. My urethra. My urethra Franklin. Something...." He tried to smile charmingly.

"Cute. Well...."

"Sorry, but I need to go when I need to go, and I need to go at least ten times during a regular work day."

"Well...."

"If I don't I could have an accident or, worse... I don't know, start bleeding internally, maybe my bladder will rupture. The doctors were vague, they said never let it get that far. Never let it get that far Jonah, they said, or it could be bad."

His boss frowned down at him. "Jonah...."

"Yes?"

"Jonah...."

"Yes, Dan?"

182

"Jonah, I...." Dan shook his head and let out a nice boss-like (and entirely ass-ish) sigh. "Forget it. Keep working."

Jonah nodded, then smiled at his boss' retreating back.

Oh Jess, he thought. I would tell a million lies for you. I'd kill for you, run a gauntlet for you, stay at this goddamn job for the rest of my life for you.

He looked down at the assortment of manuals and pamphlets before him, studied them for only five minutes before starting once again to daydream about her. Her, his future girl, his reason for tolerating Jetco, his only chance at happiness, his one and only ray of hope and sunshine. His Jess....

Of course, all solitary odes of faithfulness and love were rendered moot simply through the very fact of their solitude, as well as by the fact that when she was around he was someone entirely different from the person of his mind, imagination, and daydreams. In his mind he was Fonzie, in her company more like Potsie.

Good grief, another Seventies reference. He really *was* regressing.

He didn't see her at all the rest of the day following the lunchroom meeting, and he was frustrated and disappointed, as well as a little disturbed. She had not taken her lunch in the lunchroom that day, and he of course had to wonder if it had been because of *him*. Perhaps he had frightened her, made her feel awkward, the way most girls do when they're aware that someone they don't know or don't particularly like has a crush on them. Perhaps he really had creeped her out.

The next time they met, things were both better and worse, perfectly balanced and yet as messy as things can only get when in the grip of such an enchantment. They happened to meet again midmorning a few days later, this time in the hall leading to the restrooms, a place he had never seen her before. He rounded a corner and she was standing there talking to a woman he did not know. He swallowed and tried not to look nervous as he approached them. The strange woman said something he couldn't catch and then turned and walked away, leaving him alone as he came up to his Jessie Fina.

When he was close enough to do so he started to say hi to her but caught his foot on something (just what he would never know, perhaps his tongue) and fell flat on his face. A very graceless sound came from his mouth, a bark, a grunt, a groan. Some sort of zoo noise.

"You all right?" she asked, her face a mix of worry and withheld laughter.

"Yeah," he said, trying to muster dignity as he stood.

"Nice trip," she said, and then she turned to walk away, flashing him an enticing smile of teeth, lips, and dimples. "See you in the Fall."

"Cute," he said.

Cute, he thought.

Good grief indeed. And yet, as bad as that could have been (and it felt terrible to watch her walk away) there was also hope there, nestled in that final little joke and that final coquettish smile. It was the way she had looked at him as he stood brushing away embarrassment and dirt. There had been a friendliness, a new familiarity with him, the very distinct sense of ice broken, doors opened. He watched her walk away and felt like an earlier, much more awkward phase had ended. So she knew he was a klutz, big deal. They now had a shared memory, even if it was one he'd rather forget. They had something between them. A funny story. An experience. The next step would be an easy one.

If only he knew what it was.

*

He had started e-mailing his mother during this period, cautiously telling her about this new girl that might possibly be entering his life. Her responses were hopeful and, he knew, prodding. She'd been wishing for him to get serious with someone ever since he had broken up with his college steady, Becky.

Tell me more about this new "friend" she wrote.

He responded:

She's not yet a friend, just an acquaintance. I don't know what to do to get her to be a "friend." There ought to be a manual. A How-To book.

She answered: *Just talk to her. Be yourself.*

Be yourself. Right.

An eternity passed. Out of a desire not to appear too eager to talk to her, which was starting to feel nigh-impossible, he made a conscious, and difficult, decision not to go down to her end of the building for a few days. And he no longer looked for her after work, which is when he used to try and catch one final glimpse of her face to guide him home. Instead of looking around for her, he simply strode out to his car and left. And yet even as he did this he knew it might be a mistake. What if she was interested in *him* and thought he was avoiding her because of the fall? Didn't that make him look insecure, like a little boy unable to recover after a minor setback?

He figured it was a greater risk to look desperate. So he stayed at his desk and proofread copies of catalogs and technical manuals, making a good dent in what was proving to be a backlog of work. His boss thought something was wrong.

"No bathroom breaks anymore, Swain?"

"Doesn't appear so, Dan."

"On some new medication?"

"Nope."

Dan frowned. "You sure. Let me see your eyes."

Jonah opened his eyes wide at the man. "See any drugs, Dan?"

"No." Thoughtful pause. "Do you take anything for that... urinal trouble?"

Jonah smiled. He liked that. Urinal trouble. "No Dan. But if you have any, I'd be willing to pay. I'll meet you in the parking lot after work."

Dan frowned. "You're a smart ass, Jonah, you know that?"

Jonah nodded.

Hey Ma: How are things going there with you and Biff? Hope all is well. Everything's good here, nothing new. I was hoping to buy a new futon for the apartment this weekend so I can make my place look like some place people might want to visit (was thinking maybe you if you wanted, and I was going to invite Tina and Tom some day) but can't find anything cheap. I should have been a business major, huh? Or gone into politics.

*I don't think I should have to pay off school loans if I can't get
a job using my major.... wonder if the loan people would go for
this logic? Anyway, hope all is well and I'll try to get up there
by you guys one of these weekends. Take care. Jonah.*

*

*Hi: why don't you go to St. Vinnies for a futon or
whatever? Things are cheap there. Let us know when you
want to come up, we'll be gone two weekends from now,
headed up north to see some cousins and friends of Biff. Next
month Biff has a high-school reunion, his forty-fifth! Can you
believe that? Should be fun. Call sometime. Love you!*

PS: Have you asked that girl out yet?

*

He just didn't know how, so he plotted and planned.
The first step, he figured, was deciding exactly what sort of
young woman she was, and that seemed easy enough:

Cute. Smart. Earthy. Sassy. Cute. Smart....

Well, perhaps he didn't know her that deeply, but
certainly she didn't come across as the type who would have
been impressed by any sort of oily and urbane smoothness, nor
any ultra-hip, super-cool, free and loose attitude. Had he tried
the latter he would have come across like world's whitest black
man:

"Wassup? You wanna go hang somewhere sometime,
maybe chill with some mini-golf?"

Terrible.

Was it possible she was just out of his league? Always
a possibility, but it was best not to contemplate such a thing.
And if it turned out that she was, if it turned out that she was
the sort of girl who was impressed by crap like flashy cars or
clothes or jewelry or simply the pure unholy pleasure of money,
money, money, then he wouldn't want her anyway.

Ah, but that was bullshit: he would still want her, she
was his Jess! She had cast a spell on him and he could not
shake it. She had enchanted him like a witchy princess,
drugged him with a touch of owl breath in the water cooler, a
few words whispered over the PA, a magical kiss blown his
way across the lunchroom. He could not shake his desire for
her, his need to hold her hand, kiss her lips, pull her close to

186

him, feel her warmth. And worse, it was pure pleasure to feel this way, this evil anticipation of that moment when he might get to do such things. When he thought about her he grew giddy, when he saw her he shivered with joyous anxiety. When he spoke to her he felt light-headed, as if caught in a dream.

Some might call it an obsession. Jonah simply called it his life.

*

Once, not long after the fall in the hallway, he caught her eye in the lunchroom. She was seated three tables away, laughing and chatting with her fellow HR co-workers, the khaki-pants crowd. He himself was sitting silently with two guys who ran the presses, each of them stained with ink and stinking of chemicals and grease. They would speak to each other now and then, grunting simple words about cars and what-not, a conversation to which Jonah had nothing to add. He sat there eating his meager little lunch (peanut-butter sandwich, Oreo cookies, a baggie of potato chips, an apple, a root beer) and tried not to look over to where Jess was sitting. He'd watched her come in with her friends, watched her fetch her lunch from the fridge, watched her take a seat while she smiled at some other girl across from her. Then he looked away, not wishing to be caught staring at her, although he could have stared at her all day, although he believed he could spend the rest of his life staring at her. He absorbed himself in his little bachelor lunch, this pathetic meal he was starting to get sick of because it was all he brought lately. He ate slowly, only half-listening to snippets of talk from his own co-workers as they discussed the merits of Chevies versus Fords and all sorts of other shit he had no interest in. Some people can talk about anything.

At certain times of his life he felt disconnected from everything, adrift in a nether-world slightly above this one here, separate from the day-to-day activities around him, floating in a zone a half-second behind this one. It was a feeling of drunkenness without the abandon. Such was the feeling he had that day in the lunchroom, thinking about the girl and suddenly hating the anticipation he'd been enjoying, hating the games people must play, the give and take of courtship, the testing of relationship waters. He wanted it to be later, next week, next month, a year from now, when he *had* her, when they were together, when he could look into her eyes and know that she was his. He wanted this moment, this brief little world of the Present, to be over. Wherever you go there you are, they say, but fuck that, he hated this place, this moment, this very second. He wanted to be elsewhere, wanted to move on. The suspense that was his life, the feeling that everything he was thinking and feeling and doing was transitory, preparatory, was wearing him out, possibly even killing him, possibly leading him downward to that vicious and vile land of acceptance and entropy. Good god, imagine spending a lifetime here, in this godforsaken place, proofreading instruction manuals for heavy machinery, power tools, kitchen appliances, checking and re-checking manuscripts of department store catalogs, the odd book of regulations and specifications for industries you'd never even heard of before. Imagine starting to *enjoy* it, to look forward to coming to a place where you knew everything and everyone and nothing was ever new or exciting, where everything was safe... imagine actually learning to like paying attention to the minutia of catalogs and manuals, to gain pleasure from sitting at your desk and comparing final copies to originals, to getting lost in the idea of doing your job well. It was horrifying to contemplate. He felt the thick concrete walls of Jetco closing in, practically heard them scraping together as they pushed toward him, not to crush but to constrict, slowly. He knew older people at this place, men and women who'd spent all of their lives here, doing their jobs well and never getting anywhere, never growing, never challenged or appreciated. It was like prison. The smell of acceptance, of atrophied hope, was strong and rank in these hallways. This is what he had gone to school for, to find his degree useless, to end up here, in this building of lost souls, this penitentiary for broken optimism, this no man's land of forgotten dreams. It is sad when the best part of your day is a soggy peanut butter and jelly sandwich. He imagined looking forward to that, relishing at last the oozing viscera of grape jelly and the four Oreos he'd packed himself for dessert. He imagined that being the highlight of his day.

He sat back, suddenly sick, everything he'd just eaten sitting sour and rancid in his stomach, and looked across the room. It was just a random look, absolutely without thought or intention, but his eyes fell on the beautiful and fresh face of the lovely Jess, the single image of earth and sunshine and blue sky

188

in this place, the single living soul in this world of glass and steel and plastic.

She was looking back at him.

Smiling.

*

From an e-mail to his mother:
How do you know when someone likes you?
Her response:
You just do.

*

But it was an old joke with those who'd known him for any amount of time: he'd be saying his wedding vows before he knew the woman actually liked him. It had been that way with Becky back in college, she practically molesting him one night after what seemed like months of serious flirtation on her part, none of which he'd noticed. You didn't notice any of the signs? she'd asked after that first bout of heavy kissing. Not really, he said, feeling stupid. You're lucky I kept after you, she answered. And he was, even though that relationship was doomed to end and he would gain nothing from the experience save a few warm memories from the early days, a good deal of practical on-the-job experience with the female body, and a hard-earned wisdom on trust.

Dude, that chick likes you, friends of his were always saying.

She wants your dick, man.

She wants a piece of Swain!

And on and on, the same old story. He just didn't see any of it, was as oblivious as could be. And so, even though he caught the lovely Jessie Fina throwing glances his way, he had no clue if it was out of morbid curiosity on her part, or perhaps fear, maybe even amusement. At a certain point he grew certain that she knew he liked her, but he could not tell how she was taking the revelation. There was no one around to tell him, it wasn't like this was high-school and all he had to do was ask a friend of hers to give him the scoop... which was for the best, of course, because rumors and gossip spread violently through office buildings and he didn't want the whole company to know what was going on. So he waited. Bided his time.

Obsessed.

*

The reason he was so hooked on her, he decided (and again, he was regressing here, going back to childhood references because, apparently, they were the only ones that had gravity with him), was because she reminded him of Lindsay Wagner when Lindsay Wagner played the Bionic Woman. Earthy blond hair, a face fresh as sea breezes, eyes as clear as a pool of desert rain, skin soft and covered with faint little hairs, a mouth quick to laugh, a warmth radiating from her whole being as if she had risen from some pagan landscape to rain sun and wind and clouds on his soul. A young woman of athleticism and energy, a pony-woman, twitching with nerve and excitement, muscles quivering with anticipation beneath the surface of her being, a mind and body ready to go to forest and lake and field at a moment's notice. He thought of words from cheap romance novels: unbridled, fiery, wild. She was the kind of woman he believed he could be with forever, the sort to challenge him, tease him, push him to do better than he himself believed he could.

He was unsure what it meant, this Lindsay Wagner fetish, to say nothing of all the other damn Seventies references, but he figured it had to do with comfort issues, this Jessie Fina giving the impression that she would make him feel safe, secure, the way he'd felt when he'd been a child, when the whole world had been his neighborhood, when life was all comic books and TV.

A psychologist might have a field day with such things, but to Jonah Swain the idea was soothing, and he didn't dwell too deeply on it. If she made him feel as warm and safe as he'd felt as a child, then all the better. He wouldn't fight it, wouldn't analyze it, wouldn't do anything but lie awake at night and wonder what it would be like to hold her, to kiss her, to walk with her, to love her.

He spent one restless night staring into the darkness, trying to remember what the Bionic Woman's name had been. After three hours of fitful sleep he suddenly woke and said to the silent morning:

"Jaime Sommers."

And felt instantly warm and comforted.

190

"She's out of your league, man," a co-worker of his said one day at lunch, having caught Jonah staring at her across the rows of tables. It was hard not to stare at her, she practically glowed, a beacon of freshness in these dour surroundings. Eating her microwaved spaghetti, sipping her Diet Coke, laughing at the people around her, placing a single grape into the dark recesses of her mouth, where she swirled it with her tongue, crushed it with her teeth.

Jonah tried to play it cool. "She's not my type."

"Not your type, right."

"She's alive," said the other guy he worked with. Ricky.

"She's a girl."

The two of them had a laugh at this while Jonah shook his head. When they finally quieted down he thought the topic might move on, but the first guy, this fellow everyone called Tanner, said:

"She's hot, hey?"

Rick turned his head to look. "Primo."

"Pasta primavera," said Tanner.

Jonah frowned. "Pasta primavera? What the fuck does that mean?"

"I don't know... finger licking good?"

"You need help."

Tanner kept staring at her and Jonah began to grow uncomfortable. What if she were to glance over and see him? Or all of them, a lusty trio of drooling monkeys? He had to change the topic.

"What was Dan yelling about earlier?"

"Tanner spilled some ink," Rick said.

"Dan can bite me," Tanner answered, his eyes still on the girl.

"Stop staring at her, you're gonna creep her out," Jonah said, not able to take it any more.

Tanner stuck out his tongue and wagged it in her direction.

"Fucker," said Jonah.

"Yeah, man," Rick said. "Don't ruin it for the horn dog here." He winked at Jonah.

"She's out of his league," Tanner said softly. "Way, way out of his league."

A full two and a half weeks went by, during which Jonah had not one single interaction with her. He returned to wandering her area of the building but did not see her there. He began to grow certain she was avoiding him. He, not Tanner, had creeped her out, and she was doing her damndest to avoid facing that awkward moment when he would inevitably ask her to a movie. Easier to avoid him than to have to go through the pathetic ritual of turning him down, which he began to see as the only possible outcome. Either she was out of his league or creeped out or had a boyfriend, or a combination of all three, but there was no way he could get that girl, he knew that now. Look at her: a portrait of confidence and charm and beauty, the very epitome of the word *attractive*. She had to have hundreds of friends, most likely a boyfriend as well, and everyone she worked with seemed to like her. She just *looked* like the sort of person people wanted to be around, quick with a smile and a flash of warm eyes. God, what was he thinking here? What the hell was he in comparison? Depressed, dark, irreverent, absolutely without ambition, a man of baggage and bad hair. A natural sloucher, a wall flower, content to sit on the edge of things, to think his odd thoughts, to question everything, to form strange philosophies and ponder bizarre daydreams.

You, Jonah Paul Swain, are not the sort of guy a girl like that wants on her arm. That fair-haired young lady desires in a man the following attributes: ambition, personal charm, a warm, gregarious handshake, all features sharp and defined. Muscles, too, not lots but enough to suggest a dabbling in some sort of athletic pursuit, tennis or swimming. Sensitivity, but not of the poetic sort. The sort of skin that tans bronze, like a nicely toasted marshmallow. Broad shoulders. Large hands. A practical mind, adept at assorted power tools and gadgets, able to fix leaky faucets and roofs, put up shelves, and look under the hood of a car with some degree of authority. A lover of refined and mindless hobbies like toy trains, model airplanes, golf on Saturdays. The sort of man who was going places, as they say, not only ambitious career-wise but also personally, meaning he had a talent in cultivating friends and acquaintances in bulk. Not a rich man, yet able to give the impression of wealth... a man who would not be uncomfortable with sudden affluence. A frat boy. Everyone's buddy. Everyone's pal. A back-slapping kind of guy, a giver of nicknames, a lover of a good loud joke. An eater of red meat. A reader of La Carre, Ludlum, Clancy. A smoker of the occasional cigar. Drinker of burgundy. A Republican. Catholic.

Good goddamn what was he making her into?

If this was indeed the sort of man she wanted on her arm, then she was not the sort of woman Jonah wanted on his.

He began to think deeply about her as he lay in his bed at night. She fit in with the khaki-crowd there at Jetco, and she always looked neat and clean, and there was indeed a sort of too-friendly smile that was always present with her, but there was an edge, too, he could sense it. A depth, a grit, a coarseness lurking just under the surface. A feeling that she would not be uncomfortable in a Coleman tent somewhere in the middle of the Nicolet Forest. And requisite khaki-pants or no, what about those thick-soled brown boots of hers? It was like her own little rebellion against this cold and soulless place.

So, Jessie Fina with a back-slapping-golf-playing-model-airplane-loving-Clancy-reading-fuck? He didn't believe it. And yet certainly part of his assessment might be true, that the man she desired needed to possess ambition, charm, charisma. Healthy good looks. Probably a tall man, broad-shouldered, with a smile to melt ice. She was a beautiful girl, you just didn't see her type running around with unkempt awkward ragamuffins like him.

What was Jonah Swain offering her? He was what, a drinker of beer, an aficionado of camping, an eater of sloppy burgers, a lover of wildlife, a dreamer of dreams, a philosopher of cumulous? A pagan. A man of few friends who had never slapped a single back in his life or expressed a desire to do so. A reader of Abbey, Vonnegut, Robbins, Thompson. An underachiever. A man with a constant inner dialogue. The sort of guy other men were unsure of and women struggled to read. Jonah. Simply Jonah. Jonah Swain, daydreamer. Wallflower. A man who wasn't going places, who was, indeed, for the moment, going nowhere, stuck in the tar pit that was Jetco, Incorporated. If he let himself think deeply along these lines he began to see that there was no way he was going to end up with her, he just could not picture the two of them walking down the street, could not imagine going to visit her folks at Christmas. What sort of home did she come from? The image he kept having was one of affluence, upward mobility. A family that maybe said grace before eating, or dressed up for holiday meals.

A family that tried very hard to keep traditions alive. A family that drank lightly, if at all. A family outwardly perfect, that kept its secrets deep, held its darkness deeper. If there were skeletons in its closet they'd been nicely polished and dusted. Jonah tried to imagine himself walking into this world in all his klutzy gruffness and could not. He pictured himself looking nervous and uncomfortable during grace... good fucking Christ, pictured himself actually being asked to *say* the damn thing before some distant Thanksgiving meal! He imagined all the conversations: So, Jonah, what do you do? So, Jonah, tell us about yourself. They would be unbearable, their questions at once cliché and predictable and yet impossible to answer... honestly, anyway.

So, Jonah, what do you do?

As little as possible.

So, Jonah, tell us about yourself.

I'm considered a fuck-up by my family. But that's okay, because that's what I am.

So, Jonah, would you care to say Grace?

Grace.

How did you two meet?

I stalked her for about six months until she finally gave in.

What are your plans tonight?

Find a dead end somewhere and see how comfortable two people can get in the backseat of a Corolla.

Would you like something to drink?

A beer or three would be nice.

And so on. He absolutely could not imagine himself in any such world. And yet was that truly the world she came from? And if so, did that mean she was still part of it?

He thought of the coarseness she radiated, that feeling of raw humor, the glint in her eyes that suggested she knew a few ribald jokes, that she understood a little more of the world at large than her parents would ever have believed, and that said, maybe most of all, that she had a desire to see more of that world, its secret alleys and mysterious corners.

Khaki-crowd or no, he absolutely believed there was something raw and passionate in the woman, something more like flannel than satin. She had the wind and sky in her eyes, forest and field in her skin. Red-tail hawk in her hair. Wild raspberries in the deep red of her lips.

God but he wanted her! And that was the easy part, was it not? It was getting her to want *him* that was difficult.

The bedroom in his apartment was pitch-black save for a silvery line of light around the closed curtains. He stared at this for a long time, thinking of her, every night thinking of Jessie Fina. And every night he dreamt of clouds and silver linings and himself floating through them. He would not fall asleep until close to midnight, only to wake wanting her there beside him some crisp cool morning in the not too-distant future. It had been so long since he had held anyone, and he absolutely knew he had never held anyone quite like her. His Jess.

*

Hey Ma, got your note on Tom. A promotion, huh? Well, us Swains are on the way up in life, it seems. How's Tina? I haven't heard from her in a while. How are things by you? If Biff needs help with those gutters I can come up some time, give me a call. Love ya, talk to you later.

*

We're all fine here. Have you asked that girl out? You wait too long and someone else might snatch her up.

*

Two weeks went by and he decided to do it, he would ask her out. He would head down to her side of the building, find her wherever she might be hiding, and just come out and ask. What did he have to lose? Nothing but his self-respect, his dignity, his pride. Small things, simple things, the sorts of things a man can do without. Pride, dignity, self respect... these are not necessary ingredients for a full and satisfying life, but balls, cajones, the ability to say fuck it and do what you must, now *those* are required. You can't succeed unless you risk failure. A life not lived is a living death, a functional coma. He decided one nondescript morning that this was the day, he would ask her out in the plainest language possible. Hi, would you like to go out sometime, say Friday night? Dinner and a movie? Something else? Your pick.

195

He knew she would say no... but he only half knew this, the other half not being so certain. At least he would be able to look back some day and remember the beautiful girl of his dreams and how he had mustered the courage to talk to her, how for one moment, the moment it took the words to leave his mouth (*would you like to go out sometime?*), there had been the possibility that she would say yes and she would be his forever. The sweet, sweet possibility. He would be able to relive that moment for the rest of his life, forgetting the inevitable *no thank you*, or *I have a boyfriend*, forgetting the terrible and emasculating walk back down the hallway to his sad little place in printing, forgetting the steel heart and numbed mind he'd been left with. It was that one moment, the brief and beautiful chance there had been for happiness, that he would take with him to his grave.

He woke, showered, shaved, fixed his hair (a rare thing), ate a decent breakfast of fried egg on toast with cheese, and went easy on the coffee, wishing to remain calm and even-keeled this day. No good going into this venture shaking with nerves and caffeine. Like all good ventures, all mad wonderful and certain-to-fail endeavors, this had to be approached with confidence and ease. The looser he was, the more casual, then the easier it would be to face the inevitable end.

He thought he looked good this day, very well put-together: newer jeans without holes or stains, a dark blue t-shirt he normally only wore under a cream-colored shirt but which he had discovered, late last night, was the only truly decent t-shirt he owned, the others having holes or stains or just not fitting right. He tucked this t-shirt in, then added a belt to the jeans for accent. Stepping before the mirror in his hallway he examined himself critically, objectively. He thought he looked all right, the tucked-in look giving his body a decent line from shoulders to waist. If he were to pull the shirt out and let it hang he would look over-thin, in need of a good meal, but with the shirt tucked he looked almost athletic. Almost. Now, for shoes, he had a choice of three: tennies, hikers, or a brown pair of low-cut ankle-high boots. He decided against the tennies right away, although they would have been the most comfortable. And the hikers were out of the question because they *looked* like hikers, scuffed and torn and still smeared with dirt from his last outing. The brown boots were scuffed too, but the more he pondered them the more he realized it was in a grungy, fashionable way... if grungy was still fashionable.

196

They certainly didn't *shine*, but he didn't believe he would feel comfortable in shoes that shone, and comfort was what this day was all about. He slipped the brown boots on and then stood before the mirror again. There. He looked young and healthy and cool, casual enough for his crap job and yet clean enough to look like someone a girl might actually want to go out with.

He examined his hair, decided it was too neat, and mussed it up a bit with his palm. He had the sort of head and face that threatened to look nerdy if his hair was too neatly cut and styled. He needed a bit of messiness up top to give himself edge.

Now. He smiled, looked at both this smile and the teeth it revealed. He'd been told once long ago that he had a nice smile, that it gave him a kind face, the sort of face a person trusted. In fact, he'd been told he "radiated trust." So perhaps that smile might work in his favor here, if used deliberately and judiciously. He assumed a casual stance, the sort he might be able to take in the hallway of Jetco, Incorporated, and imagined what Jess would think when she saw him. What sort of smile should he give her? Anything too small might not do the trick, anything too big would look goofy. He decided he would try to match her own, would in fact try to mirror whatever stance she was taking. If he leaned up against the wall while she was standing stiff and business-like he would look like he was trying too hard to appear relaxed. If, conversely, she was casual and he was standing with his arms folded over his chest he would obviously come across stiff and awkward. And yet if he really mirrored what she was doing he might *look* like he was mirroring what she was doing, and that was both mocking and creepy.

All right. Deep breath. Inhale. Exhale.

He decided to do what felt right at the moment, to trust his own instincts, even if he had never had reason to trust them in the past. He was normal, he was not strange, he knew how to behave in social situations. All he was doing here was asking another person out for a night of fun.

Good god, Jonah, he thought. Don't, for the love of Christ, word it *that* way: So, wanna go out for a night of fun?

That sounded at once childish and vulgar, something both an eight-year old and a pornographer would say.

All right, once again, another deep breath.

He looked into the mirror. With his hair mussed, his shirt tucked, his boots on, he looked young and fit, a nice guy.

Attractive? Who knows. Certainly he didn't look like a serial killer or a rapist or, the other extreme, a geek. He looked like a normal average guy, someone a girl would be able to take home to Mom. Hopefully this was the sort of guy Jess wouldn't have minded going out with, but who knows. Maybe she was attracted to guys with tattoos and dyed black hair and tongue piercings, the old shock value to rock Mom's little world back in subdivision land.

You're over-thinking this, Jonah.

Indeed.

He looked in the mirror again and then went to begin his day.

*

He let hours go by, until mid-morning rolled around and he decided it was time. He wasn't getting any work done anyway, might as well take a walk... *the* walk. Dead man walking.

He left the printing area slowly, not wishing to give any indication that he had something planned. He looked for Dan but did not see him, which was good on a whole host of levels. Jonah couldn't tolerate another inane conversation about his "urinal troubles." Bosses are assholes. This is a maxim. The word "boss" has no positive connotations.

Once out in the quieter halls of Jetco, Jonah took a moment to take a deep breath and slip a piece of gum into his mouth. Double Mint. He thought briefly of how his father would pull out his gum when he took a call, leaving little dimpled balls on the counter by the phone... thought, too, of that old joke about ABC gum. Already been chewed. These were pleasing memories and he smiled, thinking too of the regression he was undergoing. All those Seventies references. He felt at once refreshed and ancient, wise and innocent. The image of Jaime Sommers running in slow motion across a California field came to him and made him shiver.

Feeling calm, or as calm as he was going to get, he started down the hall. The quiet swallowed him, made him aware of the whish-whish of his feet on the carpet. Passing one open door he heard the hum of electrical wires and the soft whistling of the company electrician. From another he heard the equally soft whisper of paper being printed. He tried not to look into these rooms, preferring the slow but steady march

198

down the beige halls to *her* end of the building. Through a variety of open doors he heard snippets of conversation flittering like moths, little half-sentences rendered absurd via his ignorance of their subjects and contexts. Someone in a corner office may have been having phone sex. Someone else was crying.

He was rounding a corner when there came a brittle, dry voice behind him. Nothing warm or comforting in that voice at all. It was the sound of snapping branches:

"Excuse me."

Shit. He continued to walk, hoping it had not been directed at him... though he knew it had.

"Excuse me," the voice cracked again, louder, full of authority's asinine coldness.

He stopped and looked back.

He'd seen the woman before, but he had no clue who she was. She was thin as a maple sapling, with a long face punctuated by a narrow but long nose, and her lipless mouth had been painted a bright red. He looked at her, raised his eyebrows, tried to appear friendly, non-threatening, everything he really was.

She walked up to him. "Are you lost?"

Shit. "Umm... no, I was just... I needed to ...."

The lunchroom, you idiot!

"I was headed to the lunchroom to get something from the fridge."

The woman nodded. She stood there with her hands folded over what should have been her breasts and stared at him. He didn't like the look in her eyes: it was judgmental, predatory. She was sizing him up. Quite possibly she was trying to decide if he even worked at the company or had just wandered in to do a little stealing. And he supposed he *did* look like a thief, nice clean clothes or no: nothing about him said *office worker*. If he was an office worker he would have looked beaten down, with the darting eyes of a nervous mouse.

He stared back at her, lifting his eyebrows again in a prodding manner, hoping she would get to whatever point she might have had. She hade nice eyes, he thought. They were a soft amber with traces of what might have been human warmth set deep inside of them. The place hadn't gotten to her yet, then. There was still hope.

She said nothing. He said nothing. The overhead lighting began to buzz.

199

After what felt like forever she suddenly reached out and took him by the arm. He didn't know what to make of this and had no choice but to let her lead him down the hall, the same direction he'd been headed himself. He figured this was some sort of arrest, that she was leading him to Security. Which was all right, he would be able to prove he worked for the company, but he wondered what Jess might think should she spot him being led off this way. What the hell kind of guy would she think he was?

This sapling-thin woman marched him quickly down the halls, rounding corners as if not caring that someone might be approaching from the other side. She said nothing, and Jonah did likewise. What could he say? Her fingers were firm on his arm but not painful, not uncomfortable at all. She led him with determination and strength, he one step behind and struggling to keep up. A few people looked up from their desks as the couple passed their offices, and Jonah noticed that, for whatever reason, no one looked surprised to see him being led this way. They all looked rather bored, in fact. Office workers, he believed, are mind-numbed by computer screens and air-conditioning and the endless monotony of pencils pushed.

"Hey Janice," a shorter, heavier woman said as Jonah and the thin woman passed her.

"Hey Mary."

The shorter woman gave Jonah a pleasant smile and continued on her way.

So this is what this day has become, Jonah thought. I've been arrested by corporate cops. He felt stupid and helpless and wondered if this would make an interesting story some day down the road, something to crack Hawkins up. Canoes For Shit gets busted for trespassing in his own workplace. Goddamn.

"Here," the thin woman said finally as she came to a small office. Through the open door came the familiar sound of books being shelved: that hollow thump on a plastered wall.

The woman led Jonah right into this room (the interrogation room, he thought) and stopped abruptly, causing him to nearly run into her back.

In that brief little second of contact he had detected the lovely odor of strawberry body wash, mixed with a very faint fragrance of delicate sweet perfume. One would not have looked at this woman, with her off-putting aquiline nose and too-red lips, and expected her to smell so fruity-fresh.

"Finally, for the love of God," the woman said, "one of you just please ask the other one out."

"Oh God!" said the lovely Jessie Fina, standing before a tall bookshelf with a thick manual on corporate ethics in one hand and a thinner volume of inter-office policies in the other (both of which Jonah had proofread). She looked radiant, surprised, beautifully mortified.

Jonah stared at her. Blinked.

That was how it happened.

7. The breaking of an American heart

1

This is how it happened.

He stayed home from school that day, feeling too sick to do little but lie there in bed as the morning grew brighter and brighter. Eventually he fell asleep for a few hours, oblivious to any sound his mother might have been making out in the rest of the house.

When he woke it was to simply move achingly from the bed out to the livingroom, where he flopped on the couch and wrapped himself in an afghan his gramma had made years ago. He didn't know where his mother was, she might have been in the basement doing laundry, she could have been in the bathroom. He reached for the remote, brought the TV to life, and rested back to flip mindlessly through the channels. He didn't get far before he saw it:

The shuttle Challenger exploding into a thick ball of cloud and fire.

It was January 28th, 1986.

Jonah was fifteen.

*

Isn't that terrible? his mother asked when she came in the room.

Jonah just nodded.

Seeing the shuttle blow up in that burst of violent beauty was the first time he had ever seen lives snuffed out. In that one terrible instant all those astronauts were gone. It made him feel sicker than he already did, as if his nausea was compounded by the sudden weight of all those souls. He thought of their lives for a moment as if *life* was a tangible entity and not a mysterious quality, thought of all those wasted

202

lives up there floating slowly down to Earth. All those *lives*…
it was a strange image for him, and stuck with him for days. In
a thick white blast of gas and rubber and metal all that life had
been sent into the atmosphere to rain down on the living.
Somewhere someone would inhale that life, or simply have it
fall down to rest like dust on their skin. It was the *life* he was
thinking of, not the flesh, the cindered bone and vaporized
sinew, the microscopic remnants of clothing, eyeglasses, dental
work. The *life*, settling over the whole planet, spread out more
or less equally among the countries and seas, perhaps
shimmering for a moment in sunrises and sunsets, tiny little
dust flames, minute meteors flaring like glitter in blue-red skies.
Life. You could look at that exploding shuttle and know there
were no survivors. The whole thing roared into an angry
mockery of cumulous, pure white with brilliant centers of
flaming orange and red. The image would be shown over and
over on television for weeks, months. Jonah would think of the
lives ended, would obsess on them late into the night. One
moment you are here, the next you are not. He would wonder
if the astronauts had seen it coming, if they'd been aware that
their end was near.

Just terrible, his mother said every time they showed
the film. Why do they have to keep playing it over and over?

I don't know, he said.

But he knew why: they had to make it monotonous in
order to render it safe. They had to take away its power.

On January 28th, 1986, Jonah Swain saw the face of
pointless death. By January 29th it would be imprinted forever
on the American mind, one more icon of tragedy, one more
classic photo of disaster printed on the front pages of
newspapers and the covers of magazines.

A terribly beautiful burst of white smoke and sun-
yellow fire, and a rain of silvery souls.

*

When he was ten someone rolled a television set into
his classroom and quietly set about plugging it in while the
teacher, Mr. Clifford, exchanged whispers with another teacher
in the doorway. Jonah and his fellow students took advantage
of whatever odd sort of interruption this was to toss spit-balls,
tell stupid jokes, pull pony-tails. They figured they were going
to watch one of those inane but entirely welcome short movies

203

Mr. Clifford liked to lay on them once in a while: documentaries about the postal system, how milk is processed, what can happen if you ignore NO TRESPASSING signs at construction sites. When you are ten you welcome any sort of digression from the typical routine of school. Someone throwing up in the back row was seen as a chance to take a breather, a mini-vacation while the janitor poured saw-dust on the puke and the teacher escorted the sick kid down to the nurse's office.

This day, when the TV was plugged in and turned on, the children all instinctively turned their heads, as if towards Mecca, feeling that involuntary pull toward their surrogate parent, feeling its soothing glow, sensing the familiar caress of its electrical current. Mr. Clifford said nothing, nor did the other teacher; they too turned their heads to stare at the screen.

It wasn't *The Electric Company*. It wasn't a documentary on milk. It was certainly not a scary reminder to stay away from abandoned buildings or heavy machinery.

It was President Reagan getting shot.

They showed the footage over and over.

*

In March of 1981 his father had been dead only four months, but the boy was already moving on. You had no choice, you move on. Years later he would look back on that time and not remember thinking about the loss of his dad at all, not remember feeling any sort of residual sadness, any feeling of mourning or melancholy. And yet, of course, the death had been a turning point for him, how could it not? But to the older Jonah looking back on the younger there would not seem a definite line separating the Before from the After. In November his dad had died. By March 30th of the following year the boy would be once again mired in the daily muck of elementary school, absorbed, as much as was possible, in math and science and social studies, in avoiding embarrassment in phys ed and staying under the radar of older kids, bullies who knew and hated his brother Tom and took out their hatred on the slighter Jonah. By the time March was drawing to a close Jonah had started noticing girls, the slow and subtle changes in the way they looked and acted. The first girl in his class to develop breasts was named Kelly. Jonah was stealing glances

204

at her strange, and strangely intriguing, chest when the image of the waving President getting shot drew his attention.

Is he dead? some kid asked Mr. Clifford.

Mr. Clifford said he didn't know. And shhh, please, just watch.

*

The older Jonah, decades later, would remember nothing else about that time, just the television being wheeled in and turned on and the whole class watching the coverage. He would not recall going home. He would not remember anything his mom might have said about the incident. He would not remember the following few days. All he would know was that Reagan recovered and continued on as President and the Eighties flew into a blur, a mosaic of half-remembered summers and Christmases and secrets and magic. Life was going on, as it always had. He was growing up, slowly, steadily. And all around him, waiting, hovering like a shadow, was a ragged world. A world of tears. A monster. He grew aware of a dark presence, a black shape tailing him, staying both one step behind and one step ahead, an ominous force patiently biding its time. But waiting for what? To drop a tendril down, to break through the fragile bright world of childhood, to scratch at the surface of all that was, or should be, true and good.

*

Are you all right? he asked his mom.
I'm fine.
Did you throw up?
I'm a little sick, leave me alone.
I was just—
For crying out loud, leave me alone!
And that was what he did.

*

The shape haunted everything, the country, the world, the planet, perhaps even the Universe itself, a ghost on the edge of all that was alive or wanted to be alive. The boy, Jonah, grew sensitive to its presence. It reared its head whenever it

205

wanted to break a placid surface, shake up a pretty scene, render ragged and beaten a face of innocence.

It had been there, he came to see, when his dad died. It was there, too, when Reagan was shot. And it was there that winter day when the shuttle Challenger exploded into fiery brilliance and rained life into a crystal clear sky. Jonah couldn't imagine a more terrible scene, such innocence destroyed in one otherwise insignificant instant. It was absurd, pointless. And, he would come to see, totally in keeping with how the Shape worked.

Sucks to be them, Tom would say, all cool and insensitive, when he saw the footage later that night.

Yeah, Jonah would think. Like it sucks to be all of us....

*

Ma?

Yeah?

She was sitting on the couch, her legs pulled to her chest so that she looked small and curled, a fragile shape there in the jaundiced glow of the end-table lamp. That lamp was the only light on in the house save a night-light that had been plugged into the bathroom wall for as long as Jonah could remember and which sent out a pinkish spectral glow down the hall at knee-level. He had not been able to sleep and so had gotten out of bed to look cautiously out his door and down to the livingroom, where the shape of his mother was sitting in a halo of lamplight and cigarette smoke. A can of Diet Coke rested on the end-table near her, silver and red. It was a scene Jonah was more than familiar with, it was omnipresent, so well known to him that he would be able to recall it vividly decades later. It was part of his childhood, his mother's tan legs curled there on the couch, her head and neck obscured by that lamp, the cigarette smoke rising up through the lampshade to pour from the top like smoke from a winter chimney. The glow of the television. That can of Diet Coke.

He hesitated before going down to her, as if trying to gauge how awake he really was. Perhaps if he just turned around and climbed in bed he would fall asleep.

He glanced back into his bedroom, where the darkness was in perpetual battle with the streetlight streaking in through the window. The shades were drawn but the darkness was

206

losing, was always losing, would *always* lose. He looked back out to his mother.

A moment later he was walking down the hall.

Ma?

Yeah? Her body rocked forward and her head peered from behind the lampshade.

I can't sleep.

So stay up. Watch TV.

He fetched himself a glass of water first and then entered the livingroom and sat on the recliner where his father had always sat, pulling his own legs up to his chest the way his mother's were.

The news was still on. They had found footage of the exploding shuttle that was from a different angle than the ones he had watched all day.

Just terrible, his mom said.

Jonah nodded. Such a clear sky, he thought. It was likely the last thing those astronauts had seen.

Do you think they'll ever send another shuttle up? he said. A man on the TV was saying the incident might be fatal to the program.

His mother shrugged, reached for her cigarette, tapped ashes into the tray and then placed the cigarette between her lips.

I don't know, she said.

How many shuttles do they have?

Well... I don't know. She placed the cigarette back in the ashtray and looked over at him.

Don't you know that? she asked. What are they teaching you in school?

Nothing.

Well... I should get a refund on my taxes.

He half-smiled as he stared at the screen. From a distance the exploding shuttle looked more graceful than the close-up, trailing its thick white plume of smoke before parting like a giant snake being ripped in two, one massive orb of fire headed left, another going right, each arcing across that clear sky, smearing it with thick trails of smoke that looked like they'd never fade, like they'd scar that sky forever.

Didn't you have a shuttle? she asked. A little toy?

Yeah.

Wasn't it the Challenger?

No, Enterprise.

207

They stole that name from *Star Wars*.

Star Trek.

Do you think they *should* send another one up? she asked after a few minutes of silence, during which they listened to some talking head going on about possible reasons for the accident.

I don't know, Jonah said. Probably. There's so much they could learn.

What do they learn up there? What do they *do*?

I don't know. Experiments and stuff. See how people move in weightlessness... I don't know.

Why would they need to know that? Are they planning on living on the moon some day? A moon colony?

Sure. Why not?

She took another drag on her cigarette, then a drink of the Coke. I don't get it.

That's what learning's about, Jonah said. You just do stuff just to see what happens, just to see what you can learn. Experimenting, or whatever....

But all those *people*, she said, and by the sudden ragged lifting of her voice he knew she was crying. He didn't want to look over but he did. Her face was red, her eyes were glistening, the cigarette was back in her hand, resting between her fingers. She was staring at the television sadly, a broken-down look to her face.

They didn't *experiment*, she said, not taking her eyes from the screen's blue glow. They didn't *learn* anything. They just... died....

She barely got that last word out, it came as more of a sigh. Jonah stared at her until he grew certain she would look back at him, but she never did. She stared at the TV like she couldn't look away.

He looked there too and said nothing.

Well, I'm not gonna watch this all night, she said, her voice up now, as if dismissing her previous sadness. She put her feet on the floor and crushed out the cigarette. She smiled over at him.

You can do what you want, she said. You can't sleep? Do you want to take something?

No.

Sure?

Yeah.

She stood and left the room. He heard her mucking about in the kitchen, a few glasses clinking together, the remains of whatever had been in the Diet Coke can poured down the drain, where it bubbled and foamed. Jonah watched the television, thought about what the woman there had just said, that NASA didn't believe any of the astronauts had lived past the initial explosion. There had been some discussion that they had, that perhaps one or more had continued on, alive, inside one of those flaming segments hurtling out to the sky and down to the earth. But no, the woman said, that wasn't believed anymore.

Do we have any word on the astronaut's final transmission? she was asked.

No.

Jonah looked up when his mother came back in the room. She stood for a second and then sat down on the couch again, at first leaning forward with her arms folded over her legs, then leaning back and bringing those legs up to herself, the way she'd been when he first entered the livingroom.

I don't know if I can watch anymore, she said, though she did not look away.

Anything else on? Jonah asked.

She sighed. Probably not.

Is it supposed to snow tonight?

She sighed again. I don't know....

Jonah looked to the bay window, saw nothing but muddied blackness smeared with the glow of the streetlight, and then back at the TV. They were showing the far-away view of the accident again, that now-familiar trail of smoke bursting into a thick storm-cloud of violence and then those twin flaming arcs streaking across the sky, the whole thing strangely beautiful, framed so nicely by the camera, and with that perfect sky behind it all, that it looked staged, a terrible bit of performance art.

Why do they keep showing it? his mom asked for the hundredth time. Jonah shook his head.

Which shuttle is this? she asked.

Challenger.

That's what you had, right?

Jonah sighed. No.

What was that?

Enterprise.

Enterprise, she repeated softly, almost to herself.

She sounded odd to Jonah, but he was so used to that oddness by now that he paid it little attention. The mood of the house was one of hesitating anxiety, something brewing, something bubbling just under the surface, but it was one he'd known for years. There was always a storm front coming to the Swain house, always a heavy cloud hovering.

Terrible, she said, still softly, a whisper.

I think I'll go to bed, he said, starting to stand.

I thought you said you couldn't sleep.

I'll try.

Do you feel all right? Think you can go to school tomorrow?

Yeah. Maybe it was food-poisoning, that crap they feed us.

She laughed a forced laugh. It wasn't food poisoning. You don't think it was food poisoning....

I don't know.

He stood fully and glanced at the TV. The image was different now, it was of the crowd down in Florida, watching the Challenger take off earlier that day. The voice-over was saying how some of the family members thought the explosion was something that was supposed to happen, and how some had even applauded when that ball of white had first mushroomed. It reminded him of how when he was first told his father had died he thought it was a joke.

Oh god, Jonah's mother said. He could tell she was crying again, really crying, if he were to look over there he'd see tears streaming down her cheeks.

The TV showed two quick shots, first some of the people clapping, then a cut to a few minutes later, when the truth was starting to settle on them that something terrible had happened. Those people looked suddenly older, worn-out, beaten down. Something had been taken from them, it was obvious from their eyes. They looked like they couldn't believe it, though they'd all seen it happen.

Jonah's mother took a deep breath, the sound wet and heavy, a breath taken through heavy tears.

And the lives of all of us, not just those folks there but indeed all of America, have been changed forever, said a somber male voice.

Jonah and his mother sat quietly, she crying and he trying not to feel anything at all.

2

It was quiet, an intense quiet of the sort found only in midnight graveyards and off-hour churches. Some Novembers slip in with this sort of stillness, as if sneaking up on true Winter, as if not wishing to spook the coming Holidays. Linda Connor stood at her bedroom window, studying the tentative snow-covered world outside but not really thinking anything at all, though there was a host of things she could be thinking and perhaps even more things she *should* be thinking. Somewhere out in that cold white and gray world was Harold, her *man*, not lost, no, not traveling the far reaches of the globe, not pursued by dark and nameless forces, but simply *away*, not with her, not in her arms. She was in love. *They* were in love. She knew he was planning their future, as much as such a thing can be planned. He had said the other day that he wanted her to be part of his life. He said that he was not playing here, which meant, of course, that he was *serious*.

People had asked her if they were "serious," and she had shrugged off the question, considering it a) personal and b) unanswerable. Serious, what was that? Is anything ever serious? Is anything *not* serious? She knew she was in love and she knew he was too but *serious* was something else, something without shape, without definition, perhaps even an unnecessary label, an extraneous weight given to something that was true and fun and beautiful.

The more she looked at the world outside her window the more she realized it was *not* just white and gray, but shaded with a multitude of subtle colors, blues and greens and faint reds, not just the snow-covered trees but the sky, too, and the shadows spreading over the white and off-white ground like spilled blue-gray ink. There was an eternity of depth in a snow-covered yard, she realized, a run of never-ending shades melting into an abstract smear of muted colors. This world here was all she had ever known... the North woods, both Summer-fat and Winter-frosted. She wondered what the world of her future would be. She wondered where Harold Swain would take her, how far from Crandon, Wisconsin she would end up.

This was November 1963. Linda Connor was seventeen.

211

She was also in love. It was a feeling like none she had ever known before. A woman given to superstitious beliefs, she sensed deep in her heart that what she was experiencing was fate, that she and Harold Swain were meant to be together. No amount of doubt was allowed to enter her mind.

Not that any ever threatened to do so: the love she had for him, the care and concern she felt, were powerful things, so strong they sometimes frightened her. Like standing at the window that November day, gazing out at the white world the way she imagined young women once gazed longingly at the ocean as they awaited the return of their sailor husbands. She wondered where Harold was and how he was doing. He'd be all right, she knew, because that was the way things were meant to go. He was meant to be all right, he was meant to call her later that day, they were meant to be married. They were destined to be gone from this corner of the world.

She thought of the city, looming always on the horizon of their future like a distant fairy tale land. For a young woman from Crandon even a place like Green Bay was the center of the world. She wondered what kind of person she would become there, what sort of adventures she might have. Correction: what sort of adventures *they* would have. She and him. Harold and Linda.

"Harold and Linda Swain," she whispered to the cold glass, and smiled.

The world outside that window was more than what she could see here, in this little yard with its tall trees and small garage, each dusted with snow. The world was open, waiting, spreading its arms, inviting her to come and see the wonders and magic that lay beyond that furthest line of treetops, beyond that dark horizon of white pine and hemlock and spruce. She felt like Dorothy, trembling on the edge of the Emerald City.

"We're off to see the Wizard..." she sang softly, quietly, so no one could hear her. "The wonderful Wizard of Oz...."

3

The night the first Gulf War started Jonah was almost killed by a train. He was driving with Becky along a lonely and dark stretch of rugged country highway, coming back from a movie in Green Bay, when the radio was interrupted with reports that the first sounds of war had been heard in Kuwait. Gunfire, mortars, the boom of explosions and the hiss of tracers.

"Shit," said Becky sadly, then they both fell silent, listening to the news, the old road unwinding in front of them endlessly, leading them through a pitch-black stretch of night. Jonah, driving, was in a daze, hypnotized by both the news and the green glow of his dashboard. He drove mindlessly, staring straight ahead but seeing nothing. Thinking nothing, too, his mind filled with a droning buzz. All over the world, at any given moment, people are dying, but rarely do you hear it as it happens, rarely are you even aware of it. Liberation, the politicians will call this action, but in the midst of the battles, among the explosions, blood, screams, and fires, there is no such thing at all, no way to tell the liberation from the horror. All war is a nightmare. To be gung ho for battle is to be without a soul. Yes, it must happen sometimes, a terrible means to a better end, perhaps, but to go to it with any sort of glee or thrill is—

"Jonah, Christ!"

They were coming to a sharp curve in the road, and right at the apex of that curve was a set of tracks. Jonah snapped out of his thoughts and at first saw nothing to cause alarm, just the same wall of night he'd been seeing all along. But then...

"Shit!" he shouted. As he started to round that corner his headlights touched on the speeding wheels of a train. Black metal flashed back at him as the boxcars raced past.

He slammed on the brakes, careful not to lock them up and send the car into a tailspin. Becky put a hand out against the dash as the car came to an abrupt stop, which it did within feet of the train.

"Son of a bitch," Jonah said.

Becky sighed. The thunderous clattering of the passing boxcars went by with its rhythmic violence, one black hulk after another banging their way along the tracks and over the road, until the last one flew by and faded into the night and there was only the excited voice on the radio.

"You all right?" Jonah asked.

Becky looked at him and nodded. "Sure. You?"

"Yeah. I'm awake now."

"Well good. What were you doing?"

"Thinking."

"Thinking?"

213

"Yeah."

She sighed. "Goddamn Jonah, always *thinking*."

That was January of 1991. War time.

*

Two nights later Jonah and Becky faced a pregnancy scare.

I'll be with you no matter what, he told her as she cried in his arms. They were sitting in her car, parked on a dead end road while snow fell like sad confetti to cover their windows. I'll love you no matter what, we'll figure everything out, it'll be all right, it'll be all right.

He had never been so afraid in all his life.

*

She got her period three days later. Anxiety from school had made her late, she said, plus all the war stuff, and the stress of missing the damn period itself. But everything was fine now, everything was okay. I love you, she said, thank you for being there with me, thank you for caring.

Of course.

*

His mother told him her only story from the Vietnam era a few weeks later, reminded of it by the weak murmurings of Draft reinstatement that were circulating like a breeze those days. It was a simply story: she remembered seeing the son of a neighbor arriving at the funeral home in a plain wood box. The box came on a bright and clear summer day, altering the mood of the street immediately, like a smear of blackness over a placid suburban scene, like the obvious and bold face of Death itself rearing up for all in that sheltered little corner of the world to see. Linda Swain remembered thinking about her own children and what that must feel like, to have them die so young for so little.

If they have a draft again, she said to the older Jonah, run to Canada.

What if it's a noble war for a noble cause? he asked.

Go anyway.

214

They never had a draft, of course, which was in the end just as well, for a variety of reasons, chief among them Jonah Swain's inability to decide if he would flee or not. He was not a pacifist, never would be, but nor was he big on war. Most likely he would have taken Gram Parsons' advice and headed for the nearest foreign border, but at the time he just wasn't sure. Some things were worth fighting for, after all, but was another country's freedom among them? He wasn't sure. His first instinct was to say fuck it, if they can't fight for themselves then to hell with them. And, of course, fighting because your country tells you to is different than fighting *for* your country. An invasion of American soil was a reason to fight, but the liberation of some sad-sack piece of shit country? No thanks. And yet, did he want to spend the rest of his life on the run, living in exile until some future President might find the balls to pardon all the deserters? Was that how he wanted his life to go? Perhaps. There was at least a sense of adventure in such an existence.

Well, it was a moot point. The Gulf War ended, America liberated Kuwait. Oil kept flowing, Saddam Hussein's people were sanctioned, America had its new heroes. And by the end of the next year George Herbert Walker Bush was kicked out of office, a failed one-term president sent into retirement by the American people. Poor George, didn't have the balls to get the job done in Iraq, choosing instead to neglect the economy here at home. That economy was close to finding itself in its own wooden box, and the American people wanted change.

It was a new time.

*

Ma? he asked, cautiously, always cautiously.

She didn't look at him as she set about making coffee. This was early morning, some Saturday in the middle of some summer. It had rained the night before and it was still dreary outside, a Poe haze over a fractured Rockwell world, the sky hanging low and heavy and gray, the colors of everything faded and flat, a mist over the far ends of the lawn.

She stood there at the sink, filling the pot with water, wearing her bathrobe. Her feet were bare, her hair pulled up

215

but spilling a few straggles like weeds over her forehead. Her skin looked yellowish, her eyes dark.

Hey, he said, going to the kitchen table and sitting there to look at her.

She offered him a weak smile, those black eyes showing not one single glint of light as she stepped back to the coffee maker. Jonah watched her.

What's up? she asked once she hit START and the coffee started brewing.

Nothing.

What did you want?

Nothing.

Well, she said, laughing a little pointless laugh and fetching a mug from the cupboard. She set the mug next to the Mr. Coffee and then went to the fridge.

You hungry? she asked.

No.

Oh yes you are. Pancakes?

No, I'm really not.

Well, there's cereal there, then, do what you want.

He watched as she turned and pulled two pill bottles from the shelf above the sink, aspirin and something else. She poured a few into her palm, filled a small glass with water, tossed the pills into her mouth, and washed them down.

She looked beaten, ragged, like a doll tossed and forgotten.

How are you feeling? he asked.

Fine. Another pointless smile. Fine. Why?

Just wondered. You look....

Yeah?

You look tired.

I *am* tired. Can't I be tired?

No, I didn't mean anything—

Can't I be tired? Isn't it okay for your mother to be tired?

Yeah, I just—

Can't I ever be tired without someone asking me why? She was nearly yelling now, slamming her glass of water down into the sink.

I didn't mean anything by it, he said, standing and going back to his bedroom. He expected her to follow, to stand in the doorway and say she was sorry, she knew he hadn't meant anything by it, she was just tired, she didn't sleep well, she was sorry. But she never appeared.

He heard her out in the kitchen, pouring herself coffee, mumbling one half of some secret conversation. They didn't talk much the rest of the day. Jonah pretended he hadn't seen what he had seen in the bathroom. Again. Pretended again.

*

He had a conversation with Tom around the time of the First Gulf War, nothing overly deep or dramatic, just a few sentences spoken as if to the air and not to each other, no trade-off of ideas involved whatsoever, no give and take to speak of, just words given to the sky. It went, in part:

Jonah: I couldn't imagine getting invaded like that, just wake up one day and someone else is running your country....

Tom: Fucking Arabs.

*

The Presidential election of 1992 was Jonah's first. He was walking through the Birnbaum University student union one late September day when he saw a display listing both major party candidates and their positions. He stopped and absently perused each of them, reading first about George H.W. Bush and then about William Jefferson Clinton. He hadn't even been thinking about the election at that time, in fact knew very little about either man except that Bush had been Reagan's Vice President, was now President, and was considered so out-of-touch he'd been amazed at the space-age technology of a grocery store scanner, whereas Clinton was a Rhodes scholar, a supposed womanizer, and a rumored draft dodger. He read about their positions on the death penalty, abortion, crime, foreign affairs, the environment, and made his decision.

*

Clinton was elected the 41st President of the United States in November of 1992. Jonah voted in the student union and then walked across campus, headed for an empty classroom where he could read in peace. He had a paper on Rousseau to start before his next class in two hours, an analysis of a single

217

thought of his choice from *On the Social Contract*, and after that a biology paper comparing life in an aquatic environment to life terrestrial. For the Rousseau paper he had chosen the following: "If I were to consider only force and the effect it produces, I would say that as long as a people is constrained to obey and does so, it does well; as soon as it can shake off the yoke and does so, it does even better." For the bio paper he had no argument to make, only a few select details with which to compare the respective needs of life spent on land or in sea. His world, so newly Becky-less, was a blur, fast-paced and yet allowing so much contemplation... too much contemplation. He often thought he should have been a poet, he liked to sit and daydream so much. An old thought, and yet wishful thinking, of course. Jonah Swain was a terrible writer, fairly decent with an essay but lacking any skill for lyricism. Besides, the things he sat and daydreamed were not meant to be set to paper, they were meant to exist in his mind and his mind only. And he didn't always dream good things, either: often what filled his mind was dark and rank and depressing, soaked in menace and gloom, dust clouds on the horizon signaling the coming of an army or a monster, some sort of holocaust there might be no escape from, the sun blackening, the sky filling with soot and ash, every last star slowly dying under the weight of an asphyxiating darkness, a Nothing, a great and shambling Nothing smashing hope and happiness, a thundering approach of something evil and omnipresent, God's evil twin, Godzilla on the warpath, or... or a more quiet menace, graying a formerly clear-blue horizon, slowly fading a sun previously bright and warm, something hovering like a Satanic guardian angel, a presence in the sky, in the shadows, in the corners, coming. But it wasn't always such things, it was just as often giddiness that filled his daydreams, large sprawling visions of things that might happen and *should*, beautiful dreams of happiness and peace. These dreams swirled and danced in his mind like crazy horses chasing their own shadows in the far corners of golden pastures.

He had neither type of daydream that day in November, just a slow-motion drone like the sound of ventilation humming in his brain, drowning all thought. He sat at the back of a quiet and empty classroom, the Rousseau open before him (the book's previous owner had highlighted the well-known "Man is born free, and everywhere he is in chains") but his eyes staring straight ahead, into the dusty expanse of the blackboard, where someone had written the following:

REMEMBER TO VOTE.

After a while he fell asleep.

*

A bomb exploded in the underground parking area of the World Trade Center in early 1993, a rare act of foreign terrorism on American soil. Jonah Swain barely noticed this bit of news. He was at this time growing increasingly infatuated with a young woman in his Philosophy of Religion class, and so was therefore otherwise preoccupied.

This was also his final semester at Birnbaum. Jonah Swain was graduating.

*

She was the sort of young woman who could and would say something like the following even when you had two fingers in her and your mouth at her neck:

"I don't think a watch necessarily implies a watchmaker… if enough watch parts happened to be dropped into the play of things, statistical probability alone would allow for at least *one* fully functioning timepiece…."

They saw each other only until the end of school, when Jonah, freshly liberated from the confines of academia (as tenuous as those confines may really have been for him), headed north, to his hometown, to Oakton….

4

"Linda Connor, are you there? Hello…?"

Linda Connor turned her head and smiled.

"Staring at that thing won't make it ring, you know," her mother said.

"I know…." Still, she couldn't take her eyes from the phone. Harold had promised he'd call.

Loretta Connor sighed. "Maybe it would be best for everyone if you two just never left each other's sights."

"Mother…."

219

"I mean it, just stay shoulder to shoulder, no more than three feet apart at any given moment. It would make living a lot easier for all of us."

Linda Connor laughed. "You make me sound like a little schoolgirl."

"You are a schoolgirl. Is your homework done, by the way?"

"Yes, Mother."

Loretta came up and played with her daughter's hair, took her chin in her soft plump fingers, looked down into her eyes.

"You're not a *little* schoolgirl, though, are you? A woman already. Where did the time go?"

"It went slow...."

"Not to me it didn't." Loretta Connor looked suddenly sad, her own eyes misty now, thoughtful.

"You all right?" Linda asked.

"I'm fine. It's just... you're so grown now...." She pulled her daughter to herself and gave her a quick hug.

"You knew it was going to happen."

"I suppose I did." Loretta Connor sighed again. "Doesn't mean I have to like it, though, does it?" She smoothed out her daughter's hair and stood tall. "Go back to looking at that phone, now, I guess. If your homework's done, what else is there for you to do?"

"Mother...."

Loretta laughed and left the room. The phone rang precisely one and half minutes later. It was Harold Swain.

*

She found it hard to concentrate on schoolwork that November. This was her last year of school, and with that, of course, there loomed the whole rest of her life. Harold would be off for Birnbaum after summer, headed into the future. Suddenly everything seemed so important, so *adult*, all the choices that were being laid out for her unlike anything she'd had to think about before. She'd been contemplating moving to Milwaukee before she'd met Harold Swain, and now that just didn't seem possible. She loved him, he loved her, it made no sense for them to separate like that. As the winter of 1963 got under way she was seriously considering applying for Birnbaum herself, the thought of which would have been alien

220

to the Linda Connor she'd been that last July, and yet which was so appealing to the Linda Conner she was now. She'd never before considered college, figuring it was easier to get a job down in the city, live her life a little... but why not? With Harold around to encourage and help her she knew she could do anything, he wouldn't let her fail. She could find something to major in and be the first person in her family to get a degree, make them all proud, show them what she could do... what *they* could do. Harold and Linda. Linda and Harold. The future Mr. and Mrs. Swain.

She smiled as she thought this, and the sky opened to a light fall of snow.

5

Then there was the great cloud of soot and ash that covered America the year Harold Swain died, a blanket of grayness, Mount Saint Helens exploding like it couldn't take the pressure of modern life or the ominous future looming on the horizon, spewing a vicious dark cloud over everything, perhaps wishing to cover those things it could not bare to witness. Those were the days of Reagan and his cronies, the start of pop-culture on a grand scale. Vacuous times. Surfaces and solitude. Egos and greed. St. Helens was our American Vesuvius, perhaps wishing to kill the society that had sprung up below her. But she failed. As always, life went on.

*

She would be mumbling to herself late at night, arguing with her dead husband. Why did you leave me? What kind of bastard are you....

Jonah would look over to see if Tom was awake, but saw only a steady rise and fall of his brother's chest, heard only the soft slow intake and exhale of deep breaths. He was alone there in that sickly yellow glow. Alone and listening.

His mother crying, quietly hysterical. No strength radiated from that woman, not anymore, not then, not late at night. And how could a boy be strong?

He never cried himself, though. It was enough to lie there, quiet and alone, listening.

Why did you leave me?

221

That house took every sound and made it solid, set it in place like a statue that would last for years.

It was a house of monuments.

*

And in mornings, under fresh piercing clear sunlight, she would look anything but fresh, as if she had gone through the world's darkest night, had swept across the bottom of her soul's abyss and seen things she thought she'd never see, and as she stood there by the sink or fridge and her youngest son ate his cereal at the table she would look beaten and wasted... until she noticed him watching, and then she would flash a smile under dark sunken eyes and ask him what he was thinking. Nothing, he would say. And she would ask him what he was going to do after breakfast and he would shrug. Beautiful day out there, she would say, and then start to sing:

"Oh what a beautiful morning...."

She was like some lost and ragged creature tossed out of the night to stand thin and weak in the sunshine, hope and despair still battling within her. You could see that battle in her eyes and the way her frail body met each day. She trembled under the weight of that war. You wanted to reach out and hold her, guide her through it all, but you never knew which one would reach back to greet you: hope or despair. One would hug back, the other would push you away.

So you did nothing. After a time you got very good at doing nothing. You did it all the time.

*

You did nothing the day they blew up the Murrow Federal Building in Oklahoma City. You were embarking on what you hoped was a life in Milwaukee, and when you heard the news you thought: of course. Because that is what people did, they blew things up. It seemed to make sense, the absurd horrors of *that* life out there, while here, in your own private orbit, life was less certain. There might not be a future, apocalypse might be just around the corner, but it would have nothing to do with terrorists either homegrown or international, it would have to do with whatever choices were presented to you and how, and if, you chose to take them. Life was lying open in those first few years after graduation, but there was

222

horror in that idea as much as there was hope. The economy would start to grow strong, all the analysts said, but you knew you'd most likely be too slow to grab on when it did.

You looked at your double-degree in philosophy and biology and wondered what the fuck you'd been thinking.

*

Work, decent work, was hard to find… and of course there was the fact that the idea of "decent work" was becoming meaningless for him. Jonah stepped out into the world with his useless degree and found (surprise) that no one wanted him for the skills he possessed: vivid daydreaming, a pliable imagination. No, what people *did* want him for was his ability to do what he was told, to follow directions when needed or be independent when it was called for. He was able to function in an environment where a boss was omnipresent, as well as in one where he was required to work on his own. More than any of this, however, he became certain that what employers liked about him was that he was smart enough not to fuck up too much, unlike some of the people he ended up working side by side with, unimaginative and intellectually lazy folks who couldn't tell a good time to mess around from a bad one. Jonah was never himself an ambitious worker, and certainly not a self-motivated one, so he was never above stealing a moment halfway through the work day to take a nap or tinker with some bit of equipment he wasn't meant to touch. He was also particularly adept at making new games with company supplies, passing many hours with various versions of basketball (tossing balled clumps of duct-tape into open boxes at the back of quiet warehouses) or bowling (same clump of duct-tape, with cardboard tubes for pins) whenever the "boss" was in a meeting or on vacation. These other people, though, always seemed to fuck around at the wrong moment, and as a result many ended up being fired. You're a good worker, Jonah was told during yearly reviews, you're responsible and you know what it takes to get the work done.

He would just nod.

He went through many jobs in his first few years in Milwaukee. The economy was sizzling around him but the only job of decent pay he could find was doing quality control for an asphalt company. He did this for a year and a half before finally getting the proofreading gig at Jetco. He was glad to leave asphalt: it was a smelly, loud, and vapid environment full of rough men and women of stagnant intellect. He took the Jetco job immediately and gave his asphalt boss a two-hour notice.

I'm leaving, he said over the phone.

When?

Now.

Now? Christ, you can't leave now.

No? Then… I'll give you two hours. I'll finish what I'm doing and then I'm leaving.

For fuck's sake, Swain, who's gonna work for me tomorrow?

You'll have to do it yourself.

I can't do it myself, I have a meeting.

Tough.

Jonah, listen—

Later.

Jetco, though in no way perfect, was like freedom after years of prison. The asphalt job had required him to be up at four-thirty, six days a week, but as proofreader at Jetco he wandered in at eight, sat at his desk, and examined, to whatever degree he felt necessary, the latest catalog or document or manual. In other words, it offered him ideal daydreaming time.

He would, of course, come to dislike the place as much as he'd disliked any other, but he knew it would serve. For now.

And of course, it led him to Jess.

*

It was Jess who woke him up one morning and said President Clinton was accused of having an affair with a White House intern.

That's all? he mumbled beneath the sheets. Christ, there are worse things a President could do….

He rolled over and went back to sleep, figuring whatever was going on would blow over like everything else. Presidential affairs were as old as the Union itself, were probably beneficial to democracy. If he's screwing some chick then he didn't have time to screw us.

The Republicans saw it a different way, spending the next year and a half pursuing the issue, shutting down the

224

government and any productive work it might have done to push an Impeachment they knew was ultimately destined to fail.

What real work could they have been doing? Jonah would wonder. What great and useful things could have been accomplished with all that money and time and energy....

6

Principal Kalinsky was a normally stone-faced man, not given to displaying any emotions save the thin smile he sometimes gave students in the hallways. Not that he was a cold man, one of those overly efficient administrative types who watched the bottom line and viewed the students less as future members of society than as widgets on the academic assembly-line. He was, after all, principal of the small Crandon High School, and knew every kid there by name... knew their parents as well. Indeed, he had been to more than a few of their homes, visiting those parents. And still, he did maintain a respectful distance from the students, as he expected them to do for him. He would offer them his thin smiles and go on about his business. It was hard work, being a principal in any day and age, and there was always some important matter to consider.

On this Monday Principal Kalinsky was more than stone-faced, he was downright pale as limestone. He stepped into Mrs. Lowe's room and gave her an expressionless look, which she returned with a wide-eyed one of trepidation. They did not speak, Mrs. Lowe simply stepped aside as Mr. Kalinsky strode to the front of the room and looked out at the students, who were looking back like they expected him to announce an early end to the school day.

"I have some news," he began, then hesitated. With the tone of his voice there came a feeling in the room like a breath held. Through the windows could be seen a gray Wisconsin sky, smeared with wispy clouds slowly, imperceptibly, moving east. It was November, 1963.

President Kennedy had been shot.

*

By the time Linda Connor made it home Kennedy had been pronounced dead and a very light snow had begun to fall, sparse flakes like cottonwood seeds floating through the air at

225

the mercy of faint currents. Linda entered her home and found her mother in the kitchen, a comforting image she would keep with her all her life, the small woman looking strong and steady in a white apron.

"It's terrible, isn't it?" Loretta Connor said.

"Yeah," Linda answered. She felt sick, anxious. She had never been one to keep up with current events but she knew the President, of course, he was the President of the United States. And now he was dead.

"I can't believe that would happen," she said.

Loretta Connor was fetching milk from the fridge, and when she placed the bottle on the counter she looked at her daughter and shrugged.

"Lots of terrible things out there," she said, meaning the world.

"I feel sick."

"You should drink something."

"No, I want to lie down." She didn't believe she would be able to lie down, however, there was something new in the air, a million times heavier than that snow, like a fog of lead pressing on all of them. It was crazy, she thought. Some things you just don't expect to happen. She went down the hallway, gave the picture of her father a quick look, like there might be comfort to be found in those sepia-toned eyes. Ray Connor had been one of those heavy-necked men, thick in the face and shoulders, who radiated comfort and security. She remembered what it had been like to be held by his arms, to sit in his lap while he told her stories. He had smelled like woodsmoke and beer and the feel of his heavy flannel shirt was soft on her cheeks. How many terrible things can happen in a lifetime? Linda wondered. She'd been five when her dad had died, and for the first time she truly realized, with all the terrible gravity it entailed, that some day her Mom would go, and her stepfather, and everyone else she knew. Some day she herself would go, an old woman slipping off in her sleep, passing from this world here to whatever world lay beyond. Who would she leave behind? A husband, children, grandchildren?

There was a knock on the door. It was Harold Swain, dusted with snow.

"Hey," he said. "Let's go for a ride."

226

*

"I heard Johnson took the oath on Air Force One while they brought the body back," he said to her. The afternoon was darkening quickly and he had his headlights on. She was not sitting in her customary spot at his side but leaning against the passenger door, staring out the window to the graying evening. The radio was off.

"How awful," she said, "to lose your husband like that. To be sitting right there while he was shot dead. I just couldn't imagine it."

"Yeah. It's one thing to lose someone, but...." He let the obviousness of the thought trail away.

They were just driving around, down old forest roads, taking their time, the snow so light they didn't even need the wipers on, it just blew off the windshield and floated away. They passed a few cars but were mostly alone, the surrounding forest holding them close, like a secret.

"I wonder who did it?" he asked after a time.

She shrugged and kept staring out the window. Why, she wondered, would this world here seem so different now, why should isolated little Crandon, Wisconsin be altered by what happened in Dallas? She hadn't thought that was possible, that the outside world could ever affect this little place here, some place so distant and alien as Texas changing this peaceful and private forest... which is why she wanted to leave, to go out there into the world, to see what it had to offer, to see how it differed from where she had grown up. But now, looking out at what had been a familiar landscape, she barely recognized any of it. It was as if something had been painted over it, grayer than gray, darker than dark. There was an undeniable new hue to everything. She didn't recall ever seeing a November like this, the trees bone-like and powdered with a snow absolutely lacking festivity or joy. There was no feeling of Christmas in this snow, it was lifeless as ash. Thanksgiving was a few days away and what did anyone have to be thankful for anymore? It suddenly seemed Winter was coming to kill everything, to smother the world in a colorless blanket.

"You all right?" Harold asked her.

"Yeah." She was crying.

"Everything will be all right," he said, reaching over to touch her shoulder. "Everything will work out."

227

She watched the gray world unfold, then slid over next to him, pressed her face into his arm as he drove her onward.

*

Everything was unraveling. They had a suspect and within two days he too was killed, right there on live television, the day before Thanksgiving. Linda Connor saw it happen. She had taken a little break from helping her mother prepare for the next day's dinner (there was bread to make, pies to cook, cleaning to be done) and had slipped into the livingroom to flick on the television. The suspect, Lee Harvey Oswald, was being moved from one jail to another when some guy stepped up and shot him in the stomach.

"Oh my god," Linda said. It was unreal. She felt she had slipped into a dream. She wondered when she'd wake.

*

Within a year Linda Connor and Harold Swain were married at the St. John's Catholic Church in Crandon. The bride and groom both wore white, the ceremony was flawless, the reception joyful. The groom's family got too drunk and someone passed out in the backseat of the couple's car. JUST MARRIED, the banner on the back of the Ford read. HAROLD AND LINDA SWAIN!

Life went on.

7

Jonah Swain's life was full of assassinations and accidents and riots and natural disasters, as is everyone's, but there were periods where nothing seemed to happen, he was living his life and nothing came to interrupt its monotonous and insular flow.

In the summer of 2001 he and Jess were fully involved, and were living together by the end of August. This happened less as a willful act than as a matter of circumstance, her roommate having moved out upon her own engagement and Jess needing someone *now* to help with the rent. Since their relationship seemed healthy and strong, she asked Jonah to move in. He said sure, what the hell. They'd been dating

228

roughly four months by then, and they both knew it was a risky move but... what the hell, life was short. He found a sub-letter for his own little place and moved into her larger, nicer, one. They consummated the new adventure with a bout of lovemaking on her couch and, later, an order of Thai food that made him sick.

Everyone at Jetco was, by then, fully aware of their relationship, though they were keeping the matter of their living together a secret from everyone. Jess had certainly not told her parents (they would not have approved) though Jonah had told his mother.

I moved in with Jess, he said via e-mail one night.

Her response came the next day: *Hope she keeps her place cleaner than you kept yours.*

Jonah's friend Hawkins was more to the point: "Finally," he said, "you've got someone who can crack the whip on you."

Life was good.

*

Jess liked Hawkins. Hard not to, he being the sort of man everyone likes, warm and gracious and intelligent, a wonderful raconteur. When they first met it was like a colliding of Jonah's worlds, his old selfish one and this new, more open one, and for Jonah there was more than a little symbolism in it: he saw two disparate (and desperate, perhaps) parts of himself finally reconciling, a private Jonah that was closed off to everyone, and a new Jonah that was warmer, more loving, happier. It meant more to him to introduce Jess to Hawkins than it did when he introduced her to his mother. Not that he was looking for Hawkins's approval... more like he was looking for approval from that old Jonah. He was looking for a sign that what he was embarking on was the right thing for him, that this new person he was could indeed overcome the ragged and distant creature he had been.

"You guys seem good together," Hawkins told him later. "She brings out something different in you. It's nice." Pause. "Don't fuck it up."

Jonah wondered what exactly this *something different* was. He could feel that there was something new about him but he couldn't give it a name. Certainly he was happier, more confident, quicker to see joy in small moments, but he believed there had to be something else beyond these obvious things. The way he felt was a way he had never felt before, not with Becky or anyone else. With Becky there had been a sense of adventure, of something new and strange in his previously mundane life, but with Jess there was still adventure but also something altogether more steady, like he had stumbled upon a constant state of happiness or... no, he couldn't place it. There was just, quite simply, the feeling of a Fate fulfilled to his life now, as if he was entering a place where he'd been destined to be all along. He and Jess even joked that they had known each other as kids, seeing that as the only logical explanation as to why they had gotten along so well so quickly. Perhaps they had met camping once, or on a playground somewhere. Perhaps they were just cosmically linked by the stars. Perhaps they were just that most clichéd of things: soul mates.

"I haven't seen you smile this much in..." Hawkins paused to consider. "I haven't seen you smile this much, ever."

"What was he really like before he met me?" Jess asked. They were at Hawkins', enjoying one of the old man's classic stuffed-pepper dinners.

He flashed a Hemingway smile at her, all crinkly eyes and gray beard.

"It was a sad sight," he said, voice low. "Poor man was the saddest thing I've ever seen, could barely drag himself through the day."

"That's about right," Jonah agreed, wiping sauce from his chin.

Hawkins laughed and leaned towards Jess. "I'll tell you what, when he first told me about you, last October—"

"October?" Jess said, frowning. "We didn't know each other then."

Hawkins touched her arm, as if giving her comfort. "Listen, dear girl, you didn't know him but he knew you. He may very well have been stalking you, but that might be a matter of perspective. It was last October, on a particularly enjoyable camping trip up North, that your Jonah there first mentioned the name of Jesse Fina."

"Really?" She looked at Jonah, who felt stupid.

Hawkins continued: "And I could tell, just from the tone of his voice, that he was smitten."

She laughed. "Smitten?"

"Well Jesus, I don't know what they call it these days. He just sounded... there was something in his voice that made me think oh boy, the kid's got it bad. And compared to the way he'd sounded all the rest of the weekend it was a welcome change."

"You sounded pretty bad there for a while, too," Jonah said.

"That may be true. We were both... thoughtful, let's say."

Jess was smiling at Jonah, giving him a wide-eyed look of the sort she usually reserved for puppy dogs or kittens. "Smitten," she said. "That is *so* sweet...."

Jonah frowned. "Yeah. Sweet. Thanks, Hawkins."

Hawkins leaned back, clasped his hands over his belly, and smiled, satisfied. "No problem."

Jess kicked Jonah playfully under the table. She couldn't stop smiling at him, her eyes sparkling like water touched by the sun. She was smitten, too.

*

When the Twin Towers of the World Trade Center crumbled into dust Jonah felt something leave his body. He heard the whole thing on the radio at Jetco, sitting there behind his desk like a zombie. The reporter said that when you look out at the New York skyline the buildings are gone, they're just not there anymore.

The image this birthed in his head made Jonah feel sick and lost. It was how everyone would feel that September 11th, sick, lost, reduced... like there had been a massive amputation, something taken from the nation's collective body. He dreaded going home and seeing it all on the television, though he knew he would have to. Like everyone else, he wouldn't be able to stop watching. He would see the second plane hitting the building over and over, a new tragic icon, a new version of the nightmare, presented to everyone in living color. Another rearing of the Shape.

The plane hit the building and for a moment there was nothing, a fragile little pause, like the plane had disappeared, disintegrated into a harmless vapor. Then came the explosion, thick and black and yellow and vicious, smearing that beautiful September sky, ruining its pure blue, its infinite innocence.

I cannot find the words to convey what this means, a talking head on CNN said. Words do not do this tragedy justice. Anything that could be said would be meaningless.

231

Jonah cried. Of course he cried. The destruction of innocence was just too much.

*

The phone rang around five-thirty.
Hey, said his mother.
Hey.
Just terrible, isn't it? she said. Just terrible.
Yeah.
You two are doing all right?
Yeah. We're fine. You?
She took in a deep breath. Just sitting here watching TV. But I'll have to turn it off soon, I can't take it anymore, it's just too much. It's killing me. I'll have to put on some records.
That sounds like a good idea.
I love you, she said.
I love you too.

*

Late at night when he was home from college he'd hear his mother arguing with Biff, their voices low but tight in tone, consonants clipped off by tense lips, vowels spat on venomous tongues. Sometimes they said his name, whispered but clear through the thin walls of the little ranch home, Biff's voice accusatory, his mother's defensive. Biff thought Jonah was a slacker, utterly without ambition or direction, all he ever did was go to work at that factory and come home and lay around. And what was with that degree? Leave him alone, Jonah's mother said. He'll figure everything out. He's a smart kid, he's very, very smart, I have smart children, I raised very smart children....

He has no direction, Biff would say. If he thinks he's going to live here when he graduates he's got another thing coming.

Fuck you, Jonah would think, lying there in his old bed, covered in the jaundice-yellow glow of the streetlight. You are not my father. This is not your home.

On the evening of September 11th, 2001, Jonah heard the voice of his mother calling from that little ranch back in Oakton and he thought of that word, *home*. What the hell was

232

home anymore? The familiar walls of the apartment seemed as strange to him as a Martian cliff, the sidewalk outside where Jess was talking with the neighbors as odd and foreign as a moonscape, an African savannah, even as a gorgeous clear sky lay over it all like a cliché water color of a late summer afternoon. Certainly there was *home* in his mother's voice, coarsened with age and time but still, for all it had borne witness to, sweet and soft and soothing. He thought of the past, when that house there in Oakton had been everything, the center of his Universe, the Universe itself, the only place he had ever thought of as Home. Back then he would not have believed he would live anywhere else, or have any other sort of life. Back then his world had been steady, safe. There had been his yard, his bedroom, his brother, his sister, his dad, his mom. What kind of God would allow any of it to change?

He thought of Biff back in the ranch house, sitting in his recliner, watching the television, surrounded by his own life, artifacts from travel and other marriages, strange objects the Jonah of all those years ago would not have recognized, objects he would have flinched from, seeing them there where his dad's things had been, the old familiar heirlooms of Harold Swain which the young Jonah would stare at, covet, play with. And Jonah thought of his mother sitting there also, knees pulled to her chest, a can of Diet Coke on the end table, her eyes dark and sunken, her arms thin, the phone to her ear, the hesitant and fragile voice of her youngest child searching for comfort from miles away. Who were these people? What life was this, what world? What happened to everything known and familiar, what happened to Home?

Jonah watched those Towers crumble over and over until he could take it no longer, then he and Jess went off to restless sleep.

*

This is how it happened.

233

8. Autumnal

1

It was a black night, featureless and flat. His reflection in the window was a ghost without depth or weight, the eyes soulless pits, the mouth tight and still. It was barely eleven o'clock but the town was lifeless. Somewhere in other towns just like this sat his brother and sister, lost in shock and confusion, that dreamland in which sadness dwells. It had been an hour since the phone call and Jonah Swain was feeling terrible. No, more than terrible: he himself had been killed. He was after all a ghost looking back from a black world. It was a long time coming.

Jess was downstairs making coffee, setting the maker to go off at six the next morning. When that was done she was going to call work, both hers and his, and tell them they weren't coming in. She would leave messages on their bosses' phones. I can't come in tomorrow, Jonah's mom died. Jonah can't come in tomorrow, his mom died. The less said the better. He didn't want to hear what she actually said, didn't think he could bear to hear it put in real words, given weight and texture. It was a dream right now, he wanted it to stay that way as long as possible. It was a dream and he was dead. He looked his ghost in the eyes and dared it to blink.

He could hear Jess running water. He looked through his ghost and studied the oceanic night. He would always remember this night, it was the night his mother died. But he would not cry, it was all a dream and it meant….

Nothing. Nothing had meaning anymore. Meaning was extinct. His mother was dead and he would not cry.

He sat on the edge of his bed and stared out the window, thinking very little. The window was cracked and a chill slipped through to tickle his skin. A beautiful October night, capping a beautiful October day. The leaves were blazing in color at noon and now, approaching midnight, rustling in that breeze, a perfect Halloween sound, clicking softly like dry dead skin. This little town was still, sleeping deeply. He couldn't see one single light in one single window. It was a world under waves, a sunken suburbia lost to the ages. Atlantis. He would always remember this night, it would follow him into the future.

He wondered if there was cloud cover this evening, or whether or not he might see the stars should he go outside. He supposed there were clouds. Such Autumn nights, skeletal and secret, are not meant for Pegasus, Aquarius, Sagittarius, Sculptor. Even the moon, itself a yellow skull, was not meant for such nights. There had to be blackness, total and impenetrable, a wall of clouds hanging low like a shroud.

He could feel that blackness on his face, and with it something else without name or form, a Presence reaching out to caress him, a familiar Presence returned after many years, something he'd known all his life. There was something familiar about this night, the feelings in his heart, even the darkness. He'd seen this before. He'd looked out windows just like this, seen starless moonless nights just like this, sensed the same heavy drooping of the clouds. It was all more than a long time coming, it was in some way overdue.

There was the sound of Jess downstairs, and the smell of coffee grounds, he could smell them like he was down there with her... and he was, he was down there and up here and out there. He was everywhere. He was inside and outside of himself. He was transitory, empty, incorporeal. He was the ghost in the window, he was the undead looking out. He was nowhere. He was nothing.

An hour since the phone call. Tina on the other end, when he had always thought it would be Tom. But she was the oldest, it was her duty. Perhaps she too had been prepared for such a night, perhaps she too felt within it something familiar. Perhaps she herself had been expecting whatever phone call she had gotten, seeing it in dreams, feeling its approach in her heart. The Swain children had always known this day would come, but not in this way, with this particular news. The alcoholism, maybe. The bulimia. A gunshot. Pills. Not *this*....

Jonah's own phone calls were done. He'd immediately called Tom, who seemed calm but shaken, then tried Biff, but he had been unable to get him. He figured he was at the

235

hospital or wherever it is people go at such times. So Jonah
had called Tom back. I couldn't get Biff, he said. Tom told
him to try the hospital, he said Tina had the number. When he
called Tina she said no, Biff was at the funeral home. She gave
him the number and Jonah dialed it. The voice that picked up
was young and female and all business. She told him to wait a
moment, please, and then there was silence. When Biff came
on he too was all business. Jonah said he and Jess would be up
in Oakton by mid-morning and Biff said good, good. All
business. Jonah wondered if that was how you were supposed
to be.

I could not be all business, Jonah thought after hanging
up. Not while living in such a dream. I hope I never have to sit
and make arrangements at a funeral home at eleven o'clock on
a Wednesday night.

He heard Jess downstairs. He closed his eyes and his
ghost did too, then they each faded away from the black glass,
Jonah to the bed behind him, the ghost to the darkness where it
lived. Out there things shivered and clicked and rustled.

It was the night his mother died, and it would follow
him into the future.

*

You wake from the fog of dreams to the fog of reality,
a lead emotion keeping you down, a heaviness in your chest
and lungs. Everything has changed and you know this
immediately. Nothing was the same.

Jonah got up and waded through the smell of brewing
coffee, now unmistakably filling the whole house. He
showered for a long time, and when he finally came out of the
bathroom Jess was lying on the bed, fully dressed, flipping
through the television across the room.

There was a little thing about it on the news, she said.
But they didn't mention your mom. Just that there was an
accident up north of Green Bay.

Turn it off, he said, and when she did he lied down
next to her, naked, and curled one leg over her like in Annie
Leibovitz's photo of the doomed John Lennon cuddling next to
Yoko. He closed his eyes and wished for life to be different.
Anxiety filled his mind, raced his heart. It was unreal,
everything: from the total blackness of a haunted night to the
bright sunshine falling through the windows this morning.

236

I've been expecting this, he thought, but I am so unprepared.

Jess held him and they lay like that for some time, in silence, feeling each other breathe, feeling the hollowness of the day, feeling the change lying fat and awful over everything, the sunshine, the windows it poured through like dust, the room, the ceiling, the smell of Folger's French Roast, the sound of traffic outside, the honking of horns, the humming of tires on asphalt. Everything was different.

Are you hungry? she asked after a time.

Yeah, he said.

Eggs?

Sure.

She kissed his forehead and got up to make breakfast. Jonah lay there for a while in a wash of sun, naked as the day he was born.

*

Are you angry? she asked on the drive up to Oakton.

Jonah nodded. Yes he was. Angry at the trucker, yes, but angrier still at the cold logic that seems to infuse everything, and the even colder ironies that logic pals around with:

It had taken a redneck idiot with a semi one second to do what Linda Swain-Oldenberg had been trying to do for more than twenty years.

There wasn't much talk about the trucker in those first few days, and Jonah hardly thought about him at all. He had just been the catalyst for something the Swain children had been expecting. He'd just been the means to an end.

Jonah and Jess arrived in Oakton at ten in the morning, wired on anxiety and shock. You going to be all right? she asked.

He said he didn't know. Entering his hometown this morning was like entering an icy cold lake. His breathing grew difficult, his heart raced. We're going backwards through time and forward through the future and spinning madly all the while. Years of childhood came forth, shimmered like heat waves on a highway, then became intimations of the future. These buildings, these roads, this whole town… there it was, laid out before him for his inspection, awaiting judgment and sentencing. On this morning Oakton was too open for his comfort, too patient, like it had been expecting him, opening its

237

maw so he might step inside and be swallowed. Deceitful, that was how it felt to him. It was at once meek and threatening. He didn't trust it, this town, didn't feel comfortable with what it had to offer. The past and the future lay shivering and incestuous within its limits, and he had no idea what he was looking at, twenty years ago or twenty years ahead. He felt nauseous. Tense. This was a homecoming of a sort he'd been dreading. Hell opens up and the angels come home. These streets he'd walked, the sidewalks he'd run down, that bay where he swam as a child, the Dairy Queen on the south side of town where he'd hung out in high-school, the trees he'd climbed, the doors he'd nigger-knocked, bushes he'd hid inside, old buildings he'd snuck into on dares, windows he'd smashed, places he would hide, side streets they'd gone racing down on quiet summer nights, laying rubber on the blacktop behind them, engines whining, sometimes the headlights off to make it more fun, the alleys they'd pull through to escape the cops. Here it all was, waiting. And waiting, too, was this present, vicious and cold, his family coming home and somewhere across town his mother lying in a cold basement room without windows, submitting without complaint to the mortician's skills, that ghastly makeover, more alone than she'd ever been, lonelier even than those nights after her first husband had died, when drunk and full of sadness she'd sit in darkened rooms and mumble secret words to her secret self. Lonelier than when her children had left her and she'd been alone in that house, that house fat with memories and melancholia, crying for the love she'd lost and the life she'd never known. Lonelier than on lost and empty winter nights, the snow outside the window lit by the porch light, clear and white just beyond the glass, falling silently to Earth while she sat listening to old records scratch and pop and hiss their way back through time. She was lonelier now, there in her cold room, eyes glued shut, hands at her sides, while the mortician performed his art. The radio might be on while he worked and she might have liked the music, but there was no window to stare out, to dream through, and no one around to love.

And waiting, as well, was the future, but when Jonah looked there he could see nothing, only vague impressions of he and Tom and Tina on the phone, older, closer, chatting like they'd never been distant. The rest of the future was a blur to him, as if there wasn't just one future but a multitude, each overlapping the others, bleeding through here and there like a ghost in a photo, one picture presented phantom-like behind another, the heron in the tree over Gramma's right shoulder.

I love you, Jess said as they turned onto the street he'd grown up on, the street where his mother had lived.

I love you, he answered. He reached over and touched her leg. She was not a ghost. She was truth and weight and depth.

Oakton narrowed down to a sad little ranch house pressed back onto an expanse of lawn. There were cars in the driveway with out-of-state plates, and the halo of mourning hung over them all. They parked against the curb, the engine was killed, the day was silent and ominous.

You okay? Jess asked him.

He nodded. Yeah. What the fuck.

They went inside to greet what remained of his family.

*

The eyes of the mourning are black holes: they are looking for light. This is why there is such a focus on inanities among the gathered loved ones, on discussing the finer points of weather, sports, the crust on a certain pie brought over by a neighbor, the shirt a younger brother happens to be wearing, the sudden growth-spurt in a niece or nephew. The mourners look for something, anything, not related to why they have gathered. Their eyes gaze out hungrily for softness, fluff, trivia. So how's work? That a new car? What the hell happened to the Packers last week? No one wants to think about the dead, or their own feelings toward them. They may as well have gathered for a game of cards. And yet despite all the surface talk of weather and cars there is, in the posture of those gathered, an unease, a tension, that is impossible to mask or break. Muscles have tightened, skin has shrunk. The eyes long for joy while the body takes the weight of sadness.

Except.

Except Tom pulled Jonah aside after the greetings and pleasantries and hugs and led him down the hall of their mother's home. Jess stayed behind, talking with Biff. Biff was a master at small talk. He had spoken of the surface of things his whole life.

People have been calling, Tom said once they were in the back bedroom, which had once upon a time been Tina's room. The bed was piled high with suitcases and jackets.

239

People?

News people. They want us to make a statement.

Why? It was just an accident, they happen all the time.

That stretch of highway takes a lot of people, I guess. Supposedly there's a story there. Anyway, Tina and I thought it would be best if we didn't. What do you say about it, anyway?

Right. Say nothing.

And listen, Jonah....

Tom bit his bottom lip and looked momentarily at the floor. Jonah sensed something coming on here, something definitely not shallow or trivial, and he felt himself quiver with nervousness, a swelling of sudden grief threatening to burst through his whole body and out his eyes and mouth.

Tom sighed and looked at Jonah. It's going to be a closed coffin. They said we could see her if we wanted but didn't recommend it.

His voice as he said this was so soft it was as if it had been spoken without a breath behind it, the words flat and without weight. There was a world of meaning in that final statement, suggesting things too awful to contemplate.

Jonah bit the inside of his mouth to keep from crying, though tears were right there behind his eyes and a debilitating grief was trembling in his bones. He felt he might collapse into a quivering mess.

Biff saw her, Tom said. But me and Tina didn't want to. They didn't recommend it.

He said this as if he was sure the words were going to send Jonah into hysterics, but Jonah just nodded and kept his emotions to himself, refusing to let anything raw slip through the cracks and choosing instead to present a steady sadness of the sort everyone was showing. This house was good for withholding emotions. The ghosts that lived here let nothing show through.

So what exactly happened? Jonah asked. His own voice was soft, too, mirroring Tom's.

She was driving down Gravel Pit Road, out there off of 41, coming back from seeing that friend of hers. Debra?

He looked past Jonah at the doorway, where Tina was now standing.

Debra, she said, nodding.

And it just happened. They think she went through the stop sign, and the truck... well, the truck was there.

240

Are they still investigating it?

Yeah. They're doing toxicology and all that. Still measuring distances. They don't really know for sure what happened. She might have gone through the sign. The trucker might have been speeding. They're not sure. This was around five or five-thirty in the evening.

Jonah sighed and shook his head. Crazy....

It is, it is, Tina said.

Yeah, insane, Tom added. You don't expect something like this.

Do you think there was alcohol involved?

I don't know, said Tom.

Who knows, said Tina.

Jonah felt like he was floating, everything here was unreal. This was his brother and his sister, he had not thought he would be seeing them for another month or so, at Thanksgiving or Christmas, had certainly not been thinking of them the day before. But plans change, something comes along to alter everything. A truck speeding in the early evening. Cancer. A heart attack. Something.

Tom reached out and touched Jonah's shoulder. Well, anyway, that's what I know. The news keeps calling.

The AP, Tina said.

Yeah. So I've been answering the phone and just saying we have no comment.

Tell them not to call.

We did. Someone else calls. They want something to print. Apparently this is a slow news period.

I'll give them something to print.

Listen, Tina said. There's food all over the kitchen if you're hungry. Grab something. There's so much it'll go to waste if you don't.

Okay, Jonah said, though he didn't feel like eating. He felt like closing his eyes and disappearing.

Tom clapped him on the shoulder again all brotherly-like and walked out of the room, following Tina.

Jonah turned to watch them go. He wondered what Tina had been thinking as she looked into this room. This had been her world not long ago, the center of her universe, where she listened to her music and wrote in her journal and talked on the phone. This was where she had gone when she was mad at her parents, or when they were mad at her. Her prison. Her sanctuary. Yet she hadn't appeared to be considering any of

241

that at all. Maybe she'd let it all go. Maybe she'd put it all behind her. Maybe now simply wasn't the time for her to revisit such things. Perhaps later she'd wander down here alone and stare out the window at the familiar view and think about then and now and everything that lay between. It wasn't long ago that this had been her place, not long at all, only eons.

Jonah looked at how his mother had decorated the room. A flower-themed bedspread, yellow curtains, rather tasteful paint job. Next to the bed a little table with a reading lamp and an alarm clock, against the opposite wall a dresser on which sat candles and a magazine. *Good Housekeeping*. The room smelled fresh, pleasant, like the flowers on that bedspread. Like Spring, dew-speckled grass and clear skies. Life returned, reinvigorated, blossoming. Renewal and hope and energy.

The opposite of everything he was feeling.

He left the room and went out to the kitchen. There was food out there, so much it might go to waste.

*

The things left behind by the dead are themselves haunted, weighted with new meanings, bloated with significance. This house was full of magazines and crossword puzzles and records and CDs and makeup and combs and clothes and knick-knacks and photographs and the various flotsam of an everyday life. You could look at it and think how useless it was now, or you could not think of it at all. It was your choice, you were living, you were here. Slip into the bathroom and see the hair in the brush, golden-brown and frosted with gray. Smell the perfume on a recently worn shirt. See the crossword puzzle paused on 17 down. A seven-letter word for a family get-together.

*

Funeral. A polished-wood casket on display, flowers stinking by the altar, a priest trying his hardest to be warm but not too warm. Tear-filled eyes, the rustle of rarely-worn clothing, meaningless smiles. Babies rocked gently in the arms of aunts and in-laws. Taking of communion, reading of scripture. The crinkle of cheap thin paper. Eyes wandering skyward, blocked by the ceiling. Spill of Autumn sun through glass stained red and green and blue and yellow, the unnatural

242

colors of an unnatural rainbow. Stations of the Cross presented as statues along one wall, the familiar agonies of a familiar death. Dad's funeral was here too, once upon a time. The Swains had sat in the exact same spot, heads down, praying, crying, Jesus open-palmed to the right, Mary to the left. Absolution. Tenderness. Sweet beckoning. Most of the people believing in the god they prayed to, but why, when they believe as well that it was He that took the dead away? Never question the motives of god, he has a plan we can never know. Yet why accept such a statement so blindly, when the authority of a god, of *any* god, is not without doubt? The priest looks smug in his belief, hidden there behind robes and incense and candles and voodoo. A play is what this looks like, the Theatre of the Macabre. Magic is magic whether black or white: unreal, without logic. If something needs questioning goddamnit I will question it. What is the great and wonderful fucking point, dear God, dear Father, dear sweet and loving and kind Holy Ghost? The priest smiles warmly through thin lips, hangs his head, the organ swells, a woman with a reedy off-key voice sings a song of heaven. And the smell of the flowers was the smell of life rotting.

*

Eulogy. Tina rose and stood behind the podium, took a moment to gather herself, spoke nicely of ancient times and half-true memories. There were holes in what she was saying, things unsaid, pauses in which sadness and regret hid. She finished crying, and her brothers put their arms around her when she sat back down. They cried too, there in the front row. Another song or two and they were on their way.

*

Prayer. Father, dear Father, who art thou in heaven. Hallowed be thy name. Mother dear Mother, your casket was so heavy my arm still hurts. We placed you in the hearse and watched it drive away.

It was a beautiful autumn morning. I wished I was off alone, moving by myself through that clear lucid sunlight, away from churches and flowers, away from all memory, walking above the pain, sheltered by the lonely sighing of aspen and pine. But there was a luncheon to attend in the basement of the

243

church, hands to shake, people long forgotten to meet once again, a priest to thank for his kind words. And after that?

Afterwards was a great and black secret, looming like a valley stretching from one mystery to another, this meaningless present and that unknown future, an expanse of shadow and fear.

You wanna take any of the flowers home? someone asked.

I left the church sighing, and was born anew.

*

The week after the funeral was a dream, an absurd reunion, everyone back in Oakton as if things hadn't changed at all, going to breakfast, lunch, hanging out, hitting the bars, driving around. It was as if the Swains were still children brought suddenly into this future to fit into their adult skins, yet still stuck here in their hometown, wandering the same old streets and reliving the same old lives. Each of the Swain kids ended up over by the high-school at various times, either alone or with each other. The school loomed like a totem, thick with memories and moments that meant everything, incidents that shaped them or ones that had been missed, the cool cream-brick façade a symbol for private holiness. Their father had taught there and then one day their father was gone, no longer seen in the halls by Tina, who was the only child to have him as her teacher. Perhaps the school meant emptiness and sadness to her, but to Jonah it meant a place separate from home. Life had been lived beyond those walls and through those doors, yes, but life had been avoided as well. This was where they had gone to escape the darkness of home. Each Swain sibling gazed at that building like there was still something to be learned there, some part of them either forgotten or torn away. They said nothing as they looked, and the Oakton High School gazed back indifferent and cold. Had they become adults there, or had they simply lost their childhood in those halls and classrooms?

Hey, Tom said on one of these drives past the school. Did you ever think you'd be this old driving past this place?

No.

Tom sighed. It's strange....

This old and motherless, fatherless, adult orphans, driving lost through a town that no longer meant anything to them and yet which meant everything just the same.

244

Jonah thought: I went out to find myself and found myself lost. I stumbled through a world I couldn't understand and dragged myself at last kicking and sighing to this place here, searching for acceptance or peace or maybe simply a smooth and breeze-filled calmness like in an open patch inside a copse of pine where the ground is all soft needles and you can lie down and rest your head and stare forever into the eternity of blue above you while owls watch from the darkness of shadowed branches and the vultures slowly soar a million miles up, black Vs silhouetted against what passes for God. I went out to find myself and came lost to this sweet forest of luminous sun and deep shade, arms out Jesus-style to the wild eyes and breath of pagan gods in earth and sky, life trembling on the underside of leaves, hesitating in the high branches, whispering in the clear ruminations of streams. Judge me, I said. I am here now. I am me. And I took the decision of the earth that made me and moved forward to spread the word of my idolatry. If there is a totem, a ghost, a Presence, a monument, a sacredness, a shrine, a temple, it lies in and under each of us. Everything plastic and steel and concrete is a golden calf. I am blood and flesh and bone. I am me.

*

You know, I've known about the bulimia since I was eleven, Jonah said.

Tina looked at her youngest brother.

You must have thought I was naïve. Or blind.

No, Jonah, it's just….

Or sheltered. But I've known. And the drinking, of course… but more, so much more, stuff I'm not even sure you know about. She talked about killing herself all the time back then, those few years after Dad died. She'd lock herself in the bedroom and say she was going to blow her brains out.

Jonah….

I just wanted you to know that. I've seen things. I've seen everything. I saw my mother like a ragged scarecrow walking down this hall at night.

Jonah, it's not that we thought you didn't know, it's just….

245

We've all seen everything. And we shouldn't have had to.

Right. Everyone heard and saw things. Tom heard her at night, he said you were always sleeping.

No, I was awake. I heard everything too. So it's fucked us all up. You think we'll ever be able to admit that?

Jonah, none of it was our fault.

I know that. But we're not entirely innocent. What did you do to stop it? What did I do?

I confronted her once.

Me too. I confronted her once. Once.

It got better when Biff came along, right?

It didn't get better. It got different. She still drank, she was probably still throwing up, she wasn't healthy. It just got different.

So what are you saying to me, now? What do you want to tell me?

He shrugged. I don't know....

They were in her old bedroom, whispering like these were secrets. Out in the kitchen Biff was telling Jess a story. Tom and his family were off somewhere, enjoying the day.

Jonah shrugged again. I don't know. I guess I just wanted to say something.

I do too.

He looked at her, and waited. She wanted to say something. Everyone wanted to say something. If there was telepathy in a family, meanings passed between minds like leaves tossed from branch to ground when the days turn autumnal and the wind cold and fragile against a thin sky, it was perhaps strongest at moments like this, secret little meetings stolen from reunions and parties, two people slipping off for a brief conversation or maybe only leaning in to whisper a few simple words over a dish-filled sink or brat-loaded grill. Brother and sister looked into each other's eyes and maybe he was wrong, maybe the truth was something else entirely, but what Jonah sensed at that moment was that Tina wanted to tell him she loved him, that she had always loved him and always would, that it didn't matter that their father's death and their mother's bad response to it had shattered the Swains emotionally, that her problems had scattered them across the expanse of their own hearts and minds. It didn't matter. They'd been dealt a hand and it sucked but it was the hand they'd been given. It didn't matter. They were a family. Some kind of family. And every kind of family had some kind of love.

Just... come see us sometime, she said, punching him playfully on the shoulder. We have room for you two. You know, I like Jess a lot. She seems real good for you. Don't be strangers.

Right. Sure. That'd be cool.

Another look into each other's eyes, and then they left the room.

*

Every night flowed from days of emptiness, afternoons spent thinking about nothing and everything: lonely little acres of forest, apathetic curves of rivers, a certain café on Michigan Avenue where he and Jess liked to go whenever they could get to Chicago, little bookstores they liked to browse, bars down by the college where they would go on New Year's Eve, dark little places that served micro-beers and strange wines. Thinking, too, of even darker and lonelier corners of childhood, events lost to memory but wavering up from a haze of time here in the aftermath of the funeral, conjured by the closeness of this house and yard and these people. He thought of himself at seven, ten, fifteen, twenty, thirty, was able to see no similarity between those Jonahs but at the same time no difference. Little Jonah Swain. Jonah Swain. Mr. Swain. He spent his nights lying awake listening to Jess breathing and searching for something that might connect who he was now with who he'd been then, some sort of emotional sinew that might make the two people closer, that might bond them and make the run of their lives more clear. But there was nothing, and maybe that was how it was for everyone. Still, he lay there thinking, one moment picturing himself daydreaming in the back field, surrounded by wildflowers and bees and the slow march of clouds, and then seeing himself at work two weeks ago, or getting pleasantly drunk with Jess on her birthday. In the glow of the streetlight on the ceiling he saw himself with bowl-cut hair, bringing garter snakes home to show his mom, and in the next second saw himself living the life he lived now, getting up at god-awful hours, heading to work with Jess, coming home to eat dinner and maybe make love before bedtime. He could see no connection. Once he'd been a daydreamer in the fields, now he was lost in his life. Once he'd played ball with Tom in the

247

backyard, or gone swimming with Tina in the bay, and now he rarely saw them. Once he'd known how his future would play out, once he'd known he'd work in a zoo and tend to lions and elephants and apes and seals and giraffes. Now he had no idea what tomorrow held, if it held anything at all. Now he was living each day like any other, unsure of where he was going, unsure if there was anywhere he *wanted* to go, unsure if he was even really truly lost. One moment he felt exactly like that little kid, as if he was still little Jonah Swain, and the next he felt absolutely no connection with him at all. A person isn't set in place as an adult, everything had to lead to this, all the roads and paths and choices and mistakes, but when Jonah looked at his life he saw only that boy and then this man. There was a missing link.

Every night flowed from these days of emptiness and disconnection, and gave him this miserable streetlight to stare at. With Jess breathing deeply beside him he stared at the same ceiling he'd stared at all those years ago, hoping some day to see through and beyond it, to whatever might wait there, be it the shape of a cloud or the humming of bees or simply another ceiling covered by another ghostly streetlight. Maybe it would be me there, he thought, revealed like a comet passing close to the earth, seen for the first time ever by human eyes, shown to be what I truly am, whatever that may be. Jonah Swain. Flesh and blood. The real Jonah Swain, without masks or pretension. A Jonah Swain naked and open to the universe that surrounded him, a Jonah Swain unafraid to be what he'd been all along. Which was? Which was Jonah Swain, plain and simple.

Jess lay breathing, sleeping fetal, while he thought and dreamt and hoped for revelation. It had to come, he knew. There was nothing to stop it anymore.

*

Fuck you, he said to the light, and his voice was not strange at all in the night's silence, it seemed to fit. He supposed he would look like a crazy man should someone see him out here, talking to a streetlight, but he didn't care. He said it again.

Fuck you.

The light was steady, unblinking.

Fuck you....

He felt the skeleton beneath his skin trembling, touched as it was by the bone-cold air around him.

Fuck you. I'm Jonah Swain and I was here first.

He stared up to the sick yellow halo around the bulb and frowned. This thing had haunted him since he was eleven, and he couldn't have it haunt him any more. He looked to where the first rusted steel rung was set in the pole, roughly six feet from the ground, then glanced back at the house. Exactly how crazy would he look if someone were to glance out and see him, or if a car were to pass by? Not as crazy as he felt. He took a step back, then jumped for that rung, catching it easily but struggling to pull himself up, his feet searching for purchase on the cold wood of the pole. Jonah Swain was no athlete and this was slow going, taxing him physically to the point where he felt he'd have to let go and fall back to the grass, and yet he managed to reach higher rungs with his hands and finally set his feet on the first. Steadied now, breathing deeply, he stood there, taking in the familiar street from this new perspective. The street where he'd grown up, played hide and seek, learned to ride a bike. The street where his dad died. The street that had been his whole world once upon a time. He knew this place and it knew him. When he talked of coming home he was talking about coming here. And nothing had changed, the yards and houses looked the same, the trees as familiar as old friends. They had resurfaced the road a few years back but it hardly mattered, it was the same too. This was home, this little neighborhood nestled in the middle of Oakton, Wisconsin. This was where he came from. And yet it wasn't the same, was it? It only looked unchanged, but everything was different. The eight-year old Jonah Swain would not have recognized it at all, and it had nothing to do with the presence of this light. It had to do with all these ghosts. There simply hadn't been any back then, but now they were everywhere, comforted by the streetlight, thriving in its glow.

He caught his breath and then craned his neck to see the light at the top of the pole. This was a challenge now, he couldn't stop. He began the slow and careful climb upwards, his shadow spilled below him on the lawn, the image of something at once ancient and new, some creature from a mythology not yet written, rising and rising to face a private battle.

*

I want to call her, Jonah said to Jess. I want to call my mom and talk about her death. I feel this overwhelming need to call her up and see what she has to say.

But if he wanted her she was here, sitting next to him. Hers was a ghost for the ages. She'd haunt every square inch of the rest of his life, all he had to do was reach out and hope she'd reach back.

*

When Jonah saw a photograph of his mother looking happy or sad in some forgotten year he bit his bottom lip and tried not to think too much about the things that pulled at his heart. Ghosts caressed him, cold fingers swept across his cheeks. Such a long yet short life she'd had. In every photograph her eyes were haunted by fate and mortality, as if she knew how it would end.

I'm sorry, he thought. I love you.

Some words hang like dead leaves on dying branches, or a butterfly pondering a fake flower, trembling in meaninglessness.

Some words are too little too late. Some words are like cloud-break at sunset. Some words could not be said, can never be said. Some words sprout guilt like black wings. Some words hover like thick skies, tornadoes on the horizon, the thundering of giants approaching from the west, unknown diseases festering in the brain, a loaded gun in bed with a child, a shadow over the earth, the approach of a meteor, the birth of apocalypse and the end of everything.

There was so much he wanted to say. He had treated her badly, took her for granted, ignored her, turned his head when he should have helped, hurt her more than he could ever know. He had spoken to her like a stranger. He had not loved her as he should have. He had avoided eye contact through guilt and shame. He had killed her years before she died. And what could he do about any of it now? The guilt would stain him forever, would lie over his life like the dried corpse of a guardian angel, mocking him, terrorizing him, hanging just above his head, a vestigial scarecrow, to remind him of how he had treated the woman who'd given him life, taken care of him in sickness, sat up late with him to watch old movies. He was helpless in the face of it. Come quiet midnights he would tremble and cry to see it before him, awe-inspiring and evil, a part of himself he hated. Come lonely and quiet midnights he would wonder where everything good had gone, the things he'd been promised as a child, the dreams he dreamt, the love and hope he had once been swaddled in. On these nights he was adrift. Separated. Estranged, from both those dreams and everything around him. Midnight was not his friend. He had nothing and no one.

And this is where we go when we know we're alone:

*

Jonah, Jonah... there's nothing you could have done....

Each day a cold sheet of hovering glass, threatening decapitation. Each memory a page from history, a blank sheet in a neglected log. Each regret bearing his signature. The weight of everything a reminder, a haunting, a caul over every history, both private and public. A funeral shroud. A shadow.

A ghost.

*

He knew Christmas would come like Christmas has always come, following hollow-eyed Octobers and shadow-stained Novembers. Just like Christmas came in 1963, that season of mourning, a President laid to rest and a future suddenly more uncertain. History trembled, it seemed, like the whole rush of things was suddenly not sure how to go on. Hadn't there had been a route, a course, a definite Plan? In the blast of a sniper's gun the whole thing was rewritten... or not written at all, but smudged, smeared. The chalkboard had been vandalized and it was seat of the pants from then on. Let none of them fool you: no one knows what they're doing, not priest or politician or pundit.

A blind man drives a canoe down a river, hoping the roar he hears is the madness of his own head and not the terrible moaning laughter of the rapids. If there is another blind man in the boat with him he tells him all is fine, he knows where they are, he knows what to do. Trust me, he says. You need to relax and trust me.

251

They drank Kool-Aid in Guyana. They killed Sharon Tate and carved swastikas on their foreheads. They flew planes into the World Trade Center. They killed Matthew Shepard. They killed Emmit Till. They took a gun to the Beltway. They trust their leaders. They believe in a god they cannot question.

We are blind and this is where it leads us.

A man who needs a leader is no kind of man.

I will follow you down like all the others, into the great black depths of madness and ruin. I will stand transfixed when you tell me what I think.

I have seen my world shattered into madness, disintegrating to ash, decomposed and delayed. Show me transcendence and I will gladly destroy it.

Show me my mind and I will wash it with tears.

*

I'd like to give you the truth, he said.
They waited.

*

And where would he go from here? From lying sleepless on the guest bed of his dead mother's home, her spirit and all it trailed ragged and worn around him, the weight of a thousand worlds borne upon his head, from here to where? From here on out life would be what, a river like time? A lake sometimes placid, sometimes chopped with waves? A filmstrip unfolding layer after layer, one moment sad or bitter, the next happy and joyful, each frame a shaky scene from a life not yet lived?

What now? Could a balance be found between the bitter and the sweet, between the joy and anger that swirled within him? Would there be no balance but a fading of one or the other, the future filled with either love or hate in extreme, without equilibrium? Life would be what, decrepit or beautiful, decayed or wonderful?

From here on his mother would be a shape always above and beyond him, always present but never tangible, never again tangible, hovering there each and every moment, hidden in the landscape, buried in the scenery like a private symbol or joke laid into the background of a play or movie, omnipresent, a design etched in the fabric. Like everything else

252

in his life, of course, she would form the backdrop for his personal odyssey, though her shape would be heavier, weighted with a significance he could not name. She would be a symbol he might never decipher, a peculiar shape he would see in the eyes of passing strangers, a tone heard in a laugh, a sparkle of light on a shirt spotted with beads, a glimmer from a hanging necklace, a dangle of leather on a moccasin, a certain tone to a tanned shoulder or calf, a piece of music heard in a mall or restaurant, a fragrance of perfume, the unreal color of a painted fingernail, a shy wrinkle at the corner of an eye, the click-clack of dentures, the curl of permed hair, the embarrassment of age, the look of one hunched under a life unfulfilled, burdened by regret. A misplaced burst of raw joy. She would be there, set into the patchwork of the Universe, blended into a crowd, faded into the hearts of her children.

Listen to this, she once said, setting him down for *Rhapsody in Blue*.

He would have to listen now: her ghost would forever sing to him.

*

Seeing into the insane brilliance of that light was like looking into the eyes of a childhood nightmare, the bogeyman that had haunted your dark closet since you were five, the scraping bloody thing that had lived under your bed, the gnarled reptilian demon that peered in through your window when midnight crept around. He was aware of the irony, of course, of the light haunting his childhood darkness, but he was equally aware of the symbolism: this light had illuminated more than he ever wanted to see. He gazed into its cyclopean eye and felt its power tugging him forward, threatening to pull him into its white heat so that he might live there beyond the scraggly thin strands of ancient spider webs, the dangling moth corpses, the thick layers of decades of dust, the white shroud-like cocoons stuck quick behind the bulb, a world of illumination beyond thought and feeling where he could look out with indifference to this one of wars and death and lies. And yet it was a lie itself, the light offered no comfort, it was cold and harsh and full of nothing.

There was a symbol waiting to be born here. The night was pregnant.

253

He felt like a flower about to bloom, a galaxy trembling on the edge of existence, a constellation seeking shape. Somewhere out and beyond him was the world and all its ghosts, somewhere above the deep formlessness of space. Somewhere within him was a struggle about to end, a choice to be made.

He was in a halo of dusty light, feeling psychic and transcendent, both aware and beyond. He was the history being written, the fate being challenged, the life above death. He was the Nothing seeking form.

The light shone into and through his eyes. It was luminous and dying.

*

Who are you? Who is the real Jonah Swain? What does he love and hate and think and feel? Who does he want to be?

I want to be what I am. It occurs to me that I am America. I assassin down the avenue. I'm not here, this isn't happening. I came in from the wilderness, a creature void of form. I loaf and invite my soul. I skip the light fandango. I scream, you scream, we all scream for ice cream. I am a soldier. I am nature. I am a ghost. I am oblivion. I am luminous and dying. I am Jonah Swain. I am wallflower and redwood. I am blood and flesh and bone. I am Jonah Swain.

I am here.

2

The forest was green and alive and breathing. They were making their way up into it, as deep as possible, via an old logging road that curved insanely every fifty feet or so, as if the people who'd originally cleared the land for it had been drunk. This particular logging road had stopped being used by loggers upwards of two decades ago, and was now traveled mostly by deer, bear, and the occasional hunter. It was in the process of being retaken by the forest around it, and at some points was nearly impassable. Jonah and Jess were moving through and around the thickening saplings and deadfall trees that covered it, and trying not to trip into one of the many potholes that dipped here and there, while the increasingly agitated early summer sun fell on them and sapped their energies. Around them was quiet, strangely enough: they'd noticed that the further they got from their campsite the less and less birdsong they heard. They're holding their breath, waiting for us to get out of here, he told her. They don't like our kind.

Look at that, though, she said, and stopped to point to a red squirrel perched on a nearby stump. What about him?

He considered the animal before pronouncing: He's not right in the head.

He's not the only one, was her answer, and then they continued.

They'd been walking for two hours and it was close to noon now. They kept going until the woods around the old road changed from deciduous to conifer, a thick growth of pines laying ahead of them, promising greater shade, larger mysteries. Before the pines, though, was a tangle of bushes, and right at the start of these bushes a series of giant boulders that had been pushed out of the way when the road had been made. Jonah made for these boulders, and when he'd reached them he turned back to Jess.

"Lunchtime," he said.

She came up and they each took a seat on a boulder, relishing the coolness of the stone on their bare legs. Jonah removed his backpack and took out the peanut-butter sandwiches, apples, and water bottles they'd packed earlier.

"Did you and Hawkins come in here?" Jess asked.

"No. We stayed around the lake."

She looked off for a while before turning back to him. "He said you guys were depressed that week."

"Hmmm…."

"What were you depressed about?"

"I don't remember. That was before you. I'm not depressed now. Why don't you eat?"

They ate in silence for a while, looking out at the forest around them. After a while he sighed. "I remember feeling cut off from everything, that's one thing. Cut off but not free. The opposite of free. The only bright point was you."

She laughed. "That's right, you were working up the nerve to ask me out."

He groaned. "Let's not go over that again…."

She laughed again and the sound seemed entirely natural and at home in the woods.

"I think I was trying to find something then. Maybe not *myself*, really, but… something. Trying to find the nerve to ask you out was part of it. I think I was trying to find a way to…." He shrugged and made a cutting motion to the left with his hand. "Turn a corner, maybe."

They fell silent again. The longer they sat the more that forest started to come alive again. Back the way they'd come more squirrels began to chatter and scamper across the ground, and ahead in the darkness of the pines small birds called out defensively.

"Thanks for bringing me up here," Jess said after a time. She was looking at him sweetly, a smear of peanut butter at the corner of her mouth.

"Of course." Pause. "Did I have a choice? You've been bugging me about it for a year."

"I was pestering you, not bugging you."

"Is there a difference?"

"Of course. It's a matter of style."

"Pestering sounds like something a wife does."

"I'm not your wife. I'm not even wife material, according to my mother…."

He frowned. "Nonsense." The frown became a smile. "On second thought, maybe you're *not*…."

She looked comically hurt. "Why…?"

He gestured to his own mouth, and laughed when she reached up and wiped the peanut butter away. She licked her finger clean and moaned in fake delight. He noticed that there was now a line of dirt where the peanut butter had been, matching others just like it across her cheek and forehead. Her bangs were stuck to that forehead with sweat, and both of her knees were scraped and bloody. She was beautiful.

"I'll tell you something, Mr. Jonah Swain, I—"

"Shhh."

She was sitting on a boulder closest to the pines, and as he was looking in her direction he noticed movement back there, a heavy shape loping down where the road faded into the shadows.

As she turned to look where he was he said, quietly but sharply: "Don't move."

She was already half-facing that direction when the bear came into view, its brown snout sniffing the air, the whole neck and head swaying slowly back and forth. He was certain the animal didn't see them yet, but was less concerned with that

256

then with Jess' reaction. He wanted to say something to her, *keep quiet* or *stay calm*, but didn't need to: she turned her head slowly in his direction while still keeping her eyes on the bear, and whispered:

"He's gorgeous."

Jonah watched the bear closely, trying to decide if it was actually coming up the road or was planning on staying where it was. When he realized it was indeed coming their way, however slowly, he quietly placed the backpack by Jess' feet.

"Put this on," he said, thinking of something he'd read (if you're attacked a pack can serve as protection) and she did it as slowly as she could. The whispery sound of the nylon against her arms made the animal stop and listen for a moment, though it continued on almost immediately.

"Let's stand," he said, louder. He and Jess stood at the same time, and the bear noticed them immediately.

"He's so black," Jess said.

Standing now, realizing they were seen, Jonah decided to speak in a much louder voice: "He's a beautiful bear, and he wants to just turn and go back the way he came."

The bear had stopped and was watching them, its neck still swaying back and forth though much slower now.

Jonah placed a hand on Jess' shoulder and guided her backwards as he himself stepped out front. "Turn and slowly walk back down the road," he told her, and she began to do this at once. He never took his eyes from the animal until it seemed that several minutes had gone by, then he turned and looked to see that Jess was perhaps a hundred yards back. She had stopped walking and was looking his way.

"Come on!" she called out softly when he looked at her.

He gestured for her to keep going and then turned back to the bear, which hadn't moved. They stared at each other for a long time, and for his part Jonah wasn't thinking about anything as he did so. Impossible to say what the bear had on its mind, but Jonah would remember having no thoughts, only a deep *feeling*, a physical sensation coursing through his body. It wasn't fear and it wasn't awe, nor was it fascination or curiosity. It was more a magnetic hold, like he simply could not take his eyes off the animal even if he'd wanted to, that they were bonded there in those few moments by something neither of them could understand. Jonah was certain the bear felt this same sensation: there was intelligence in its eyes, he could see that even from so far away. There was certainly intelligence in its posture. It was looking at him and it was seeing him and it wasn't threatened or scared. What does it want? he wondered. And for that matter what do *I* want?

"Jonah...." He knew this was Jess behind him, but it didn't sound like her voice, and it seemed to come from somewhere else. Inside, maybe. Or *out there*, wherever that may be. He stayed where he was, motionless but alert, looking at the beast as it looked at him. When he finally began to think again it was to realize how alive he felt, how much a part of *now*, this moment, this world. Jonah Swain might be floating through his life but he was here, now, stuck in this reality, facing this animal while the woman he loved stood behind him, refusing to walk on, a tableau of human and beast so perfectly arranged it looked like it could mean something. And did it? Was there anything to be learned or gained from this moment? He had no idea. Perhaps he would know later. Maybe it would come to him when he needed it to.

"I'm Jonah," he said at last, not quite knowing why, and when the bear broke its gaze and bolted back into the darkness of the pines he smiled. Of course, I'm Jonah Swain and why should you care? I'm just Jonah Swain, plain and simple, and you are... you are the god of these woods.

He turned to look at Jess but waited a few moments before going to her. Behind him the bear could be heard bullying its way ever deeper into the forest... and then it was gone.

3

The light hummed and buzzed madly, inches from his face, like the souls of crazed insects trapped insane behind the glare. He thought of all the darkness that had been killed by this light, pushed back to the periphery where worthless shadows dwelled. He thought of the peaceful nights he'd never known, the dreams he might have had, the darkness where his eyes were useless, where his mind might have traveled the distance of its imagination, envisioning worlds and ideas not yet dreamt by any man. How much different things might have been if it were not for this harsh yellow glare, how different his mind, his soul, his heart.

This is where we go when we are luminous and dying, to a place haunted by the souls of insects, where there is nowhere to go but onward, where we have no choice.

He looked into the light, and it looked into him. He didn't know what it saw, but he saw the darkness behind the glare, hidden, waiting. It was time. It had been years. What did he have to lose?

*

The trapped souls found liberation, floated away from the earth to the star-spattered sky, and came at last to haunt some dark eternity far from this one here.

9. Aurora

1

"What is that?"

Jonah stared over to the horizon beyond the forest, feeling the night breeze on his cheeks, smelling the smoke from the fire. Shadows surrounded him, held him close, teased him with their secrets. He felt both vulnerable and safe.

Hawkins continued to stare with fascination at the glowing sky. Jonah looked there as well and saw a wave of light ripple through it, like a distant airport beacon making circles in the clouds. The glow was blue with a faint pinkish hue, so subtle you had to stare at the center of the thing to notice.

"You know what that is," Jonah said. "It's the Northern Lights."

"Son of a bitch, you're right," Hawkins said. He took a step further into the woods, cracking twigs underfoot, and continued to stare at that part of the sky.

Jonah watched the pulsing glow, thought of heartbeats, the flow of blood through vessels. He thought he could actually hear the phenomenon, as if the glow was making music as it pulsated, some melody it was possible to hear only if you believed in it. Moving over the horizon like that, sending out its pulse every few seconds, the *borealis* seemed to possess the forest, to render it smaller than it was and yet somehow more wild, perhaps even prehistoric, to give the two men an awareness of eternity they never had before. They were silent, watching the show. Each throb of ghostly light seemed to touch them directly, set itself on their faces, caress their skin. The world gives its wonders freely if you are open to them. There was beauty everywhere.

They stood there watching for a long time, the night cool and quiet around them, the sky lit like the spirits of fallen stars. But it was alive, that sky, and giving itself only to these two souls.

"There's this girl," Jonah said after a while, keeping his voice quiet, as if it were possible to disturb the Northern Lights, to spook them.

"Where?" Hawkins whispered, as if she might be nearby.

"At work."

Hawkins thought a moment. "Yeah? And?"

"And I like her."

"Oh yeah? And does she know this?"

"No."

Hawkins was quiet again for a few moments, watching the sky. "So what are you gonna do?"

Jonah sighed. Shook his head. "I don't know."

The sky continued to ooze color, soft blues and pinks, a touch of silvery gray, pulsing and pulsing across the horizon, a flickering ripple like a cosmic exhalation, a celestial sigh, moving over the treetops like luminous magma forming a new world of radiant mountains far above the heads of whatever walked in the deep and dark forest below.

"So... why'd you bring her up now?" Hawkins asked.

Another sigh in the darkness. "No time like the present, I guess," said Jonah Swain.

2

Jess stirred when he came back to the room. She moaned and rolled over to look at him. "Where were you?" she asked. "Is it darker in here?"

"Go back to sleep." He slipped into bed beside her, felt her warmth like that of a fire.

"Seriously," she said, sitting up on her elbows and squinting into the dark room. "It was lighter before, wasn't it?"

"You're dreaming. Go back to sleep." He snuggled against her, and when she rested back down on the bed he pulled closer to steal her heat.

"Where were you?" she whispered. "You're so cold...."

"Nowhere. Go to sleep."

"You were gone for a long time. Are you all right?"

"I'm fine. Sleep."

"You went outside. What did you do?"

He kissed the top of her head. "Just be quiet...."

"Don't tell me to be quiet, Jonah Swain..." she half-murmured weakly, already slipping away. "I'll talk if I damn well feel like it...."

"Shhh...."

"I'll...."

"Shhh...."

He waited, listened to her breathing deepen. Soon she was asleep, and he continued to hold her for the rest of the night, the slow intake and exhale of her breath the only sound he could hear, the only sound he wanted to hear. The house was hushed around them, silent as... a tomb? No, silent as the sky, the stars, strange and distant dreamlands, the black dusty emptiness between it all. And as he held her there in that silence so the darkness held them both... like a mother, like a mom.

ABOUT THE AUTHOR

Todd Michael Cox was born and raised in northern Wisconsin, and still makes his home in the Dairy State. He has a great love for wild places and wild creatures, particularly reptiles and amphibians, and is the founder of the Snake Anti-Defamation League, a group designed to promote the conservation (and good reputation) of the noble serpent. He plays several instruments, and his spoken-word project Ripe For Shaking has been included on *ATTOHO (After They Tore Our Heads Off)*, a CD compilation put out by the Journal of Experimental Fiction. All of these passions were inherited from his mother, whose death inspired *After the Death of the Ice Cream Man*. He is also the author of the comic novel *Dizzlemuck: Love in the Time of Wee Folk*.